Elizabeth Moon joined the US Marine Corps in 1968, reaching the rank of 1st Lieutenant during active duty. She has also earned degrees in history and biology, run for public office and been a columnist on her local newspaper. She lives near Austin, Texas, with her husband and their son.

Find out more about Elizabeth Moon and other Orbit authors by registering for the free monthly newsletter at www.orbitbooks.net

D1362730

By Elizabeth Moon

The Serrano Legacy
Hunting Party
Sporting Chance
Winning Colours
Once a Hero
Rules of Engagement
Change of Command
Against the Odds

The Serrano Legacy Omnibus One

The Deed of Paksenarrion
Sheepfarmer's Daughter
Divided Allegiance
Oath of Gold

The Legacy of Gird
Surrender None
Liar's Oath

Remnant Population

Speed of Dark

The Vatta's War Series
Trading in Danger
Moving Target
Engaging the Enemy
Command Decision

with Anne McCaffrey
Sassinak (The Planet Pirates Volume 2)
Generation Warriors (The Planet Pirates Volume 3)

COMMAND DECISION

ELIZABETH MOON

orbit

www.orbitbooks.net

ORBIT

First published in the United States in 2007 by Del Rey,
Random House, Inc.
First published in Great Britain in 2007 by Orbit
Reprinted 2007 (twice)

A CIP catalogue record for this book is available
from the British Library.

ISBN 978-1-84149-379-4

Papers used by Orbit are natural, recyclable products made from wood
grown in sustainable forests and certified in accordance with the rules of
the Forest Stewardship Council.

Typeset in Berkeley Medium by Palimpsest Book Production Limited,
Grangemouth, Stirlingshire

Printed and bound in Great Britain by
Mackays of Chatham plc, Chatham, Kent
Paper supplied by Hellefoss AS, Norway

Orbit
An imprint of
Little, Brown Book Group
Brettenham House
Lancaster Place
London WC2E 7EN

A Member of the Hachette Livre Group of Companies

www.orbitbooks.net

Dedication

To John and Ellen McLean, good friends, experts in cattle and computers, our son's godparents . . . you couldn't ask for better people to have around in good weather and bad.

Acknowledgments

Sometimes the contributions people make to a writing career—or an individual book—aren't noticed or recognized at the time.

Sometimes people die before they can be thanked . . . so in the attempt to thank the right people while they can still blush and dig a toe in the dirt and pretend it was nothing, here are some of those whose words and deeds added a lot to this (and other) books. It's not chronological. And some have died, but I can't ignore them.

The Thursday fencing group patiently listened to chunks read aloud and asked good questions. David Watson, Beth Sikes, Allen Sikes, and Richard Moon even more patiently answered my questions about relevant technical bits. Friends in choir (yes, you)—thanks for your input and your patience. Way back, a long-overdue thanks to Marguerite Robinson, my senior-year English teacher in high school, whom we called Grendel (she wouldn't let us refer to her as Grendel's Mother, saying it insulted her daughter, but we could consider her Grendel). And another, almost as far back, to Katherine Fischer Drew, extraordinary medieval historian at Rice University, now retired, the first to suggest that I try writing novels. My wonderful hosts in Norway last year, and especially Heidi Lyshol, who recommended exactly the right overnight tour . . . she will recognize its contribution. My wonderful hosts in Barcelona probably won't, if I filed off enough serial numbers, but the visit gave me something I needed.

So did Debbie Harris and her husband. John McLean and James Summers performed a rescue at the last minute when my computer died less than a week before the book was due.

Finally, thanks are always due to my agent Joshua Bilmes and my editors—this book was begun under the guidance of one, Shelly Shapiro, and completed under another, Jim Minz. All three were invaluable, and the book would not be what it is had any of them slacked off.

COMMAND
DECISION

ONE

Rafael Dunbarger landed at Nexus Center Port as Genson Ratanvi, a staid, slightly paunchy middle-aged business-man in food service with a Cascadian identity. His tidy gray beard and gray-streaked hair, his padded cheeks and aged skin, his sober business suit with a few lines of Cascadian green through its subtle gray plaid all fit this image. Customs and Immigration passed him through, as his bioassays all matched his identity—as well they should, Rafe thought. Short-acting DNA subs programmed with his alter's bio-assays might give him a temporary headache, but that was a price he could pay. He had obtained this first false ID at Cascadia more than a decade before, and he'd used it here several times, on visits his family hadn't known about.

The trip from Cascadia had been no worse than usual; he had spent the twenty-nine days chatting with other business travelers, exercising in the business-class gym, reading in the business-class lounge, avoiding the gawking tourists and the family groups as his persona required, and carefully not thinking about Ky or Stella Vatta. Ky was beyond his reach, probably dead; he could not tease Stella now, not until she reached some equilibrium with her new identity.

Instead, he toyed with ISC's problems. How had so many ansibles gone bad all at once? Surely not chance . . . who had done it? Why was repair so slow? If he himself could restore function in a few hours, why weren't ISC's repair teams making more headway? How deeply had the pirates infiltrated ISC?

Landing on Nexus II—he carefully did not let himself call it home—Rafe pushed that puzzle aside. Genson Ratanvi needed to find a way to contact Rafe's family, discreetly.

First he headed for the Ambisor, a commercial hotel frequented by business travelers where he had stayed before; his minimal luggage trailed him on a rented hoverpad. Once installed in his room, he first dealt with the hotel's surveillance system and then installed his own unique gear. The hotel's system would now inform the hotel that Genson Ratanvi came in, bathed, slept, and went out, on a reasonable but not too rigid schedule; it would believe anything he sent it, including remotely from his implant. Pseudo-calls would be noted; pseudo-messages would be sent. Then Rafe called up the business directory on the room display, marking the sorts of businesses he should, in this persona, mark, then tapping the key to collapse the rest of the directory.

What he really wanted to know, he had noted in passing: ISC headquarters still had the same public access number. Not that Genson Ratanvi had any reason to call there.

After a mediocre meal at the hotel's café, Rafe headed out into the city. It was autumn in this location, just after midday, local time. He drew a deep breath, anticipating and then enjoying the familiar fragrance, childhood-deep in his memory. His favorite time of year, with apples ripe on the trees and the autumn mushrooms mingling their scent with that of fallen leaves, even here in the city's commercial district. Probably every world had its characteristic scents, but he spent nearly all his time on ships and stations. He felt a strange mix of nostalgia and fear: this was home, and home could be deadly.

The Number 161 tram still ran from the spaceport hotel district out to the northern suburbs; Rafe rode it to the last stop, seeing little change from the last time he'd been here except that the long-delayed northern extension of the freight monorail was finally in place. He got off in the bustling little market, now full of schoolchildren buying treats after school, and women—mostly employees, he knew—buying fresh produce and meat for dinner.

He headed for Luce's, sat down at an outside table, and ordered a slice of honeycake and tea with lime. The lime came partly pared, a curl of peel holding it to the rim of the glass. He stared at it a moment. Where was Ky by now? Off on that idiot attempt to build a fleet out of a bunch of untrained privateers? His shoulders twitched. Dead. She must be dead by now; he was not going to think about her.

Except that she had shipboard ansibles and intended to use them. That, he had to think about, and carefully, before he told his father. ISC must not decide she was an enemy. He owed her that much, just in case she was still alive.

His portable security system informed him that—aside from the general surveillance designed to notice and focus on suspicious activity—he was not observed. Humans were inattentive witnesses anyway, and no one really cared about a middle-aged, slightly paunchy man quietly eating honeycake and drinking tea. Nor would they care if he appeared to be talking to himself; almost everyone had an implant, and most of those had skullphones.

He activated his own skullphone and called his father's private number. His father might be in a meeting, might not answer at once, but—

"This number is no longer available. Please check the number you are calling and try again."

Rafe sat very still, then made himself breathe normally. It had been years; the number was in his implant files, but perhaps he had flicked the wrong one. That could happen. He entered it again.

"This number is no longer . . ."

He closed the connection and took a bite of honeycake. His father's number was no longer available? Had he changed it for some reason? That could be awkward; Rafe's business persona had no reason and no influence to get access to ISC's chief executive. Surely his father hadn't . . . died. Someone would have told him. His mother would have, surely . . .

He activated the table's local information file. His family's home number would not be listed in such a public place, but he remembered a lot of local numbers and he could see if there had been an overall change. No. He did not have his mother's private skullphone number, nor his sister's, and he had not wanted to call the house . . . all calls were recorded, and why would Genson Ratanvi be calling that number? Call ISC headquarters? Use one of his other names? One of the names known to ISC's internal security? Very dangerous if someone there was crooked.

He found a useful number only two digits off his home—Flasic's Bakery Supplies—and marked it on the table's list. Then he entered his own home's number—a simple mistake, if anyone asked.

"Please state your name and reason for calling." That was not a voice he knew, none of the household he recognized, though his parents could have hired new servants since his last visit home. But the hair rose on his arms. The link was hardbound, so that he could not simply cut off the call.

"This is Genson Ratanvi, just arrived from Cascadia," he said in Genson's voice, a prissy, plummy version of a Cascadian accent. "I'm trying to reach Flasic's Bakery Supplies . . . you are a purveyor of custom-designed commercial bakery equipment and specialized mixes, are you not?"

"You have the wrong number," the voice informed him. "Where are you calling from?"

It had to be official. Something was very wrong indeed. "From a place . . . er . . . Luce's? . . . they have honeycakes and lime tea."

"And when did you say you arrived?"

"A few hours ago; my ship from Cascadia docked at Nexus Station yesterday."

"Do not attempt to end this call. Just a moment." The connection hummed and hissed. Rafe finished his honeycake and sipped tea while he waited.

The voice came back, a little less strained. "You entered the wrong number, a seven instead of a five. We have confirmed your arrival today. You may end this call now."

"What is this about?" Rafe asked. "Is something wrong?" Genson would ask that.

"It is no affair of yours," the voice said; the connection broke.

"Would you like something else?" Luce's proprietor, whom Rafe had known since childhood, stood by the table, looking at him with suspicion but no recognition.

"It's very good," Rafe said, waving his hand at the crumbs on his plate. "But this is confusing. I need to contact Flasic's Bakery Supplies, and I entered the wrong number and someone was very rude to me."

"We aren't as formal as you Cascadians," Luce said, picking up the plate. "Don't assume we're rude if we're not all flowery."

"No offense intended," Rafe said. So Luce knew he was Cascadian? Who had told him? "I was just surprised. Do you know where Flasic's Bakery Supplies is? Perhaps I should walk there instead of trying to call. I don't want to make more mistakes."

Luce smiled. "I can take you there myself; I was going over to get the estimate on a new oven."

Rafe doubted that, but he was willing to let Luce walk with him the several blocks to Flasic's. Anything to convince the ants' nest he'd kicked that he was harmless and forgettable. On the way, he was able to convince Luce that he knew something about bakeries; Luce didn't seem to realize that it was mostly Luce's own knowledge that Rafe had picked up as a boy, being fed back to him in handy snippets.

Once in the store, he invented a problem with oven manufacturers on Cascadia, and inquired soberly about the possibility of importing high-volume, precise-temperature-control ovens from Nexus. He had shipping costs at his fingertips; he ran over the figures with the enthusiasm and thoroughness of any businessman, and finally shook his head. "I'm afraid not," he said to the sales representative who was talking with him. Luce, he noticed, was still hovering across the room, trying to pretend a serious conversation with another man. "It's simply too expensive, even if we went straight to your manufacturers. Perhaps we can hire some of your experts as consultants instead. I know ovens are supposed to be simple, mature technology, but every time we try to scale up bakery output, we end up with inferior product and unhappy customers." He smiled at his sales representative.

"Thank you for your time; you were very helpful, and I'm terribly sorry I can't promise a sale. You will forgive me?"

The man blinked at him. "No need to apologize, sir; it's my job—oh . . . you're from Cascadia, right?"

"Yes. I suppose we do seem overly formal to you—but that's not intended as an insult." Rafe had always enjoyed his Cascadian persona; overblown courtesy could be every bit as deadly as biting sarcasm, an art form with its lethal edges well concealed rather than exposed.

"Not at all," the man said. "We're a bit too direct sometimes, probably. It was a pleasure, sir."

"And to me, as well." Rafe stood up to leave, and was not surprised that Luce was also through, and coming toward him, smiling.

"Success?" he asked.

"Alas not," Rafe said. "Transportation is still too high. But don't let me detain you; you have a business to run."

Luce seemed willing enough, once outside, to turn back toward his own place. Rafe went to an information kiosk and looked up the manufacturers whose names he'd just learned, then called each one to inquire about offworld consultancy contracts. Since he could use the same spiel with each one, the rest of his mind was free to wonder how long it would take to bore the man watching him from the café across the street, and how soon he could evade his watchers.

By now it was late afternoon, time for workers to be coming home. Most people would be thinking of food or entertainment or both, and so might a businessman from offworld. He bustled across the street and interrupted a waiter at the café. "Where can a visitor get some . . . you know . . . ?"

The waiter glared at him. "Food, drink, or sex?"

"I was thinking, dinner and a show—music, dance, something like that. Anything but my hotel room."

"The Zedaiyah Dinner Theater's about six blocks that way—" The waiter pointed with his elbow. "Please excuse me; I have customers . . ."

Rafe's watcher was easily close enough to overhear, even if he didn't have a spike-mike. Rafe turned away and headed "that way," stopping several times to ask passersby if he was going in the right direction. He'd been to the dinner theater once as a child, when they'd had a special children's holiday program: something with fairies and unicorns and a wicked witch flying through the air. They'd been given all the candy they could eat, and he had been heartily sick on the way home. The next year, he'd refused to go. He hoped dinner would be better this time.

On the way, he called his hotel on the skullphone and asked the concierge to arrange a ticket for him; it was waiting when he came to the ticket office. He went in, while his follower had to stop and buy a ticket, and looked around. Tables arranged in steeply pitched rows around the playing space, which looked much smaller now. Emergency exits there and there . . . restrooms male and female . . . a stairway to the balcony level. The bar to one side, where the early arrivals were gathered at small tables or standing by the polished bar. He headed that way, showed his ticket to the usher, and chose a tiny table in an alcove.

Two hours later, replete with a surprisingly good meal, he was eeling out the emergency exit without tripping its automatic alarm. The business suit and certain other elements of his disguise were stowed in the men's room, behind a ceiling tile over one of the stalls. Handy that Nexus society, founded on communication, still believed in privacy to the extent of having some completely enclosed stalls in every public restroom. He wore a camouflage skin-suit, and in the soft autumn mist that always came up after dark he had no trouble passing unseen through the town streets, then along the private road to his family's home.

He knew every centimeter of the road, every bush, every tree, every place someone could hide, every surveillance device and its range and sensitivity. He was prepared to confuse, to fox the scans, to disable some completely if he must.

He was not prepared to find the place uninhabited and unprotected except by its fence and hedge . . . and one very obvious police guard at the gate. He got in unnoticed, which he expected, and into the house—the empty house, with only a few dim lights on and all surveillance gear disconnected. The furniture was still there, the gleaming tiles of the kitchen, the long polished floor of the grand salon, though the leaves of the ornamental tigis drooped and the soil beneath it was dry. Tall bookcases in the library still held their books, both modern and antique. The music room still held the priceless grand piano, the concert harp, the cabinets full of music scores and recordings. A pale irregular area perhaps one by two meters marked the floor, visible even in the dim light.

He could not resist going upstairs to his old room, telling himself he might find some useful clue on the second floor. He had suspected his parents would clear it, turn it into a guest room, but instead it seemed unchanged, a wrenching time capsule. A crude model of an ansible platform, a school project for which he had won an award when he was nine, still stood on a shelf, the faded ribbon beside it. Textbooks still jammed the low bookcase. Even his clothes—including the uniform of the hated boarding school—were still in the closet, carefully sealed in preservative packs.

For a moment, he leaned his head on the closet door

frame, his breath coming fast and uneven. He could not have said, in that instant, if it was rage or pain that wrenched so powerfully. He had been prepared to have his life erased, removed utterly from his respectable family's awareness, but they had kept . . . someone had kept . . . so much. Even—and tears burned his eyes—the fateful display sword that had saved his life and caused him so much grief.

He eased back downstairs and out of the house with his usual skill, while his emotions swirled . . . he had not known, he had not understood. What he had not understood, he could not say; he wanted desperately to see his father, talk to him. He forced that aside as he moved back across the property toward the road. Whatever had gone wrong, he must not be suspected or captured now.

Reentering the theater at the climax of the second act, he slipped unobtrusively into the men's room, into the stall he had used, retrieved his costume and put it on over the skinsuit, and then—sticking a finger down his throat—vomited into the toilet, noisily. It was easier than he'd thought it would be, and his face was suitably pale when he looked in the mirror. He returned to his table at the intermission; a passing waitress asked him if he felt all right.

"Too much travel," he said, smiling at her. "My stomach—it is delicate, I'm afraid."

"Should I call someone?"

"No . . . I should be all right now. But tell me—is it possible to get a private car to the port area? I don't know if I feel like riding the tram."

"Of course, sir. Would you like me to arrange that now, or do you want to see the rest of the play? It's quite good—"

"I will try to stay, but—"

"Just press this button, if you need me," she said, reminding him of the call button on his table.

"Thank you," he said.

Through the third act of the romantic comedy, he tried to think rather than feel. He had expected a chilly reconciliation or an angry rejection . . . not this blank nothingness of absence. Were they dead? Surely he would have heard . . . but he had not been at his last reported address; he had been in space, much of the time in FTL flight, utterly unreachable, for . . . more than half a standard year now. Perhaps they had died, and no one could find him. Yet . . . why then the odd response to his call? And if they weren't dead, where were they?

He clapped with the rest when the show was over, and the waitress came over to check on him and tell him she had arranged a car. He thanked her; he had already left a generous tip. His watcher was outside on the steps, feigning interest in a poster advertising the show. Rafe leaned on one of the pillars until a car drew up and the driver asked for "Gen-son Ra-tan-vi?" with the accent on the wrong syllable in both names.

The watcher stared fixedly at the poster—better than whirling around, but not much, Rafe thought as he got into the car and gave the hotel name and address to the driver. He made no effort to lower his voice, and besides, the watcher could always check with the car hire company. The paunchy foreigner had indeed gone straight back to his hotel after being sick in the men's room.

He lay a long time on the bed, wondering what to do next. The newsfeed in his room, its sound automatically muted this late at night, had nothing about his family, and only the blandest announcement that ISC was making good progress restoring ansible service. The talking head for that announcement was Lew Parmina, his father's closest associate and expected successor. Rafe remembered the man—intelligent, sophisticated, affable—who had been his father's messenger in the most difficult years when his father had virtually disowned him. Parmina had counseled patience, had promised to do what he could to mend the breach; he had sent friendly notes now and then with the remittance payments. He looked much the same, with the well-groomed gloss of the successful man of business.

Rafe turned off the newsfeed. He didn't care about Parmina unless the man had something to do with his family's disappearance. Which surely he did not: he was well up the ladder to the highest position in the most powerful monopoly in human space; what more could he want?

Where was his father—his mother—his family? He felt as if a crevasse had opened up beside him and half his universe had disappeared into it, as if he teetered on the brink of some bottomless pit. He shivered and dragged the bedcovers over himself. It was like something Ky had said— tried to say—about her family's death. He had been so sure he knew how she felt, what it was she had to cope with. An adult, someone who'd been out on her own . . . how bad could it be?

He had known nothing. As the shiver built into shudders, as he felt himself engulfed in a sorrow colder than death itself, he knew that she had felt this: the last of her family, as he might well be the last of his. Bereft, alone . . . and so much younger than he was, so much less experienced.

And she had gone on. He let himself hold to that, for the moment. That crazy idiot, that stiffly, stubbornly upright prig of a girl, who shared with him a guilty secret delight in killing: she had not collapsed under this sorrow. She had fought back. She had saved him—humiliating as that was—and Stella and Toby and her ship and her crew, and gone on being who she was.

He was warm again, and able to breathe. She was probably dead by now, or soon would be, and because of that it was safe to admit what he felt. To himself, anyway. And what would she do, in his situation? He almost chuckled, imagining that dark, vivid face, those intense eyes. What he himself would do—would find a way to do—when he'd had some rest.

What a team they could make, if they didn't kill each other. If they didn't each die before they met again. And on that thought, he fell asleep.

The smell woke him. A chemical knife, it stabbed deep into his awareness; he was sitting bolt upright before he realized he was awake.

That miserable implant. Ky. It must be Ky trying to use the cranial implant. He staggered into the bathroom—the only logical excuse for waking so suddenly if someone had breached his security.

Only the alarm functioned without an external power source. He did not want to link himself into the room's power outlets, and yet—he came out of the bathroom, checked his security devices, and burrowed into his luggage for the special cables. He had checked the quality of the line signal and was about to hook himself up when he had another thought.

What if it wasn't Ky?

Here, of all places, someone knew that he had a cranial ansible. His father knew. The technicians who had built and installed it knew. They were supposed to have been told that it had failed, that it was both useless and dangerous, and all their notes and so on were supposed to have been destroyed, but what if not?

What if whatever had happened to his family had let the enemies know not only that he had a cranial ansible, but also how to contact him?

He would be immobilized, nearly helpless, as long as he was hooked in.

But if he didn't hook in . . .

The hotel room had not been designed to be impenetrable, but he did the best he could, as silently as possible, with the chair and the ottoman. Then he arranged the cables, took a deep breath, and activated the ansible.

It was not quite like using an ordinary skullphone. Ordinary skullphones didn't smell like gas leaks, skunks, rancid butter, wet dog. The smell associated with being called changed to the one associated with a connection being made. Then a faint sound he associated with an open line, nothing more.

Somewhere, someone's telltales should have gone from standby to connected. Someone had placed the call . . . someone should be speaking. Rafe said nothing. Ansible-to-ansible was not the same as implant-to-implant; he could not strip data from someone's implant this way even if they had the same setup he did. Which he hoped no one but Ky Vatta did.

His only safety lay in patience—waiting out whomever had called.

Seconds passed. Minutes. A trickle of sweat ran down his back. If it had been someone friendly on the other end, they'd have spoken by now. Ky, certainly. His father, if nothing was wrong with him. Anyone else—would be trying to trace the signal? Would be planning to send some devastating blast right into his brain? At least he knew— hoped he knew—that wouldn't work. The safety interlocks prevented any excessive power surges. Nor should they have been able to trace his location from the ansible's response. But no one who wouldn't speak to him should have been able to initiate the call.

Finally he heard, dimly, voices talking. Not talking to him, but talking somewhere in the pickup range of whatever unit they were using. He boosted the sensitivity, shunting the input to storage for later analysis.

". . . the light's green. It has to be connected."

". . . not in the index. A private ansible? Would he have had a private off-list ansible?"

". . . knows? S'posed to be the son's private number, but nobody's there—"

"It's connected."

"Could be in automatic mode. If it's designed for relays or something."

Three voices, Rafe decided. Too far from the pickup to tell much about them, at least without signal analysis.

Then, loudly, "Hey! Answer me!" Male voice, not above middle age, used to having its orders followed.

Rafe said nothing.

"Got to be on auto," the same voice said, this time in a normal tone. "I don't hear a thing."

"So he lied to us. Not his son's number—"

"Or his son has it on auto but with no pickup message."

"We should leave him a message," a more distant voice said.

"Not until we know where he is," the closest voice said.

The connection closed with a snap; Rafe sat a long moment without moving before he unplugged the cable and re-coiled it into its place in his bag.

Two and two in this case made a very unsavory four. The most likely *he* to have told them the number was his father. He would not have given that number except at great need, probably under duress. That and the trap on the house number, the immediate tail put on what should have passed as an innocent businessman, the empty house . . . all that suggested an organization with enormous resources, if not the government itself, operating with the government's consent if not approval. Remembering what Ky and Stella had told him about the attacks on Vatta on Slotter Key, he wondered if the pirates had somehow intimidated the Nexus government into letting them kidnap the head of ISC. Or if they had infiltrated some group within ISC.

Not likely, he decided. The men had not sounded like expert ISC communications technicians; they'd used none of the jargon peculiar to the trade. That meant they might not be able to trace the ansible relay beyond Nexus and thus could not find him. On the other hand, they might have a skilled technician in their organization, or even captive.

Either way, Genson Ratanvi and his food processing needed to disappear in a way that would not alert anyone to anything. He would have to leave the planet, or appear to, on his way back to Cascadia. It was almost dawn . . . an energetic businessman with a digestive upset might well be up and making calls, hoping to find a place on a ship home. Then again—he'd been here only a day. Would he give up so easily? No. Nexus had other cities, other suppliers. Surely the man would travel around, unhappy stomach and all.

Rafe logged on to the hotel's travel information site and soon had an itinerary that gave him a reason to be in every major city over the next four weeks. He declined the hotel's booking agency and made the reservations himself, choosing to change carriers here and there. With excellent communications links, Nexus travelers were spontaneous in their schedules; no one would notice particularly if someone on a scheduled ferry or flight didn't show up, especially if the passenger called in.

By the time Rafe came down to breakfast in his business persona, he had determined that the contact attempt had originated here on Nexus; his illicit and—he hoped—undetectable probes of the Nexus ansible had gotten him that far. The origination code for the call was not his father's, and he didn't recognize it. He would have to hack into the main database to find a name, and it might not be the right one. The call had relayed through a communications satellite then covering an area two time zones away; beyond that, he had been able to find one relay, a surface installation near a town named, with no originality at all, Pittville, presumably for the nearby pit mine.

He ate a moderate breakfast, explaining to his waiter, in his persona's stuffy way, that something he'd eaten the day before had disagreed with him. After checking out, he went directly to the regional airport. Someone, he was sure, would be checking on Genson Ratanvi's movements. Let them. Genson would be boringly predictable for a day or so at least.

While waiting for his flight, he used the databoards as any other business traveler might do. All bore the ISC logo and—here on ISC's home planet—came with ads extolling ISC's technological and marketing genius. Rafe spent a moment downloading the public information to his implant, then went on searching for food processing specialists' current contact numbers at his next stop, and began calling them as he thought about the ISC listing.

Interesting . . . his father was listed as an ex officio member of the board, and Lew Parmina was now listed as CEO. Not surprising that he was the new CEO if something had happened to Rafe's father, but that didn't explain the empty house, the traps on communications, that call on his cranial ansible.

TWO

"Cousin Stella?" Toby's voice and the skitter of his dog's claws on the floor brought Stella Vatta out of another dismal reverie.

She glanced at the security escort, annoyed with herself for having missed the warning tone of the entry, and nodded to him. He nodded back and sketched a salute before leaving the apartment; she checked to make sure the exit warning came on. Then she forced a smile and turned to greet him. "Yes, Toby?"

"They moved me up another class," he said as he came in. "The test results are in . . . and can I have a snack?"

"Of course," Stella said, waving a hand toward the kitchen. "Go right ahead. But then I want you to clean up this mess—" Spread across the apartment's living room were boxes of what Stella dismissed as "tech stuff," whatever didn't fit in Toby's own small room. Stella had quit looking in there; the visual chaos gave her a headache.

"It's not just a mess," Toby said through a mouthful of sandwich. "It's all organized—ouch!" He had stepped on something. Stella hoped it was as sharp as the little knob with a sharp prong that she had stepped on earlier.

"I'm tired of walking on it," Stella said. "At least stack it all by the wall, can't you?"

"It takes longer to find things," he said.

Stella looked at him. If he had ever been impressed by her beauty—a weapon she'd wielded skillfully since childhood—he was over it now, and she recognized the tone as one she herself had used on her parents. But Toby was more malleable than she had been; after a moment, he flushed and mumbled "Sorry, Cousin Stella," and—the other half of the sandwich in his mouth—began moving the boxes.

In the several tendays since Ky had gone off on her insane quest, as Stella thought of it, and Rafe had left for Nexus, she had had more than enough time to examine her life in light of the revelation about her parentage. Her real parentage. Biometric data proved she was Osman Vatta's daughter, some stranger-mother's daughter, not the daughter of Stavros and Helen Stamarkos Vatta, as she'd always believed. Her blonde hair, her violet eyes, her beauty came not from the Stamarkos family, but from . . . someone else. Someone she'd never known, probably would never know. Ky had said it didn't make any difference, but she knew better.

She had tried to shake off the waves of anger, grief, and depression that washed over her several times a day, but except for Toby she was alone, absolutely alone, as she had never been before. How could she concentrate on trade, on finding cargo for the ship that had been Furman's, when she felt so empty? She had forced herself to do the obvious things—hire security for herself and Toby and the Vatta dockspace, talk to Captain Orem of *Gary Tobai* about what security clearances new crew should have, but it was so hard to focus on all that. If only she'd had one other adult Vatta to talk to . . . Aunt Grace, for instance.

"You know," Toby said, breaking into her reverie, "I really think I can make another one."

"Another one what?" Stella asked.

"Ansible," Toby said. "Like the one Captain—Cousin Ky left with you. Small enough to fit on a ship, I mean."

"That's—" She started to say "impossible," then stopped. Toby had already modified the appliances that had come with the apartment—giving them more sophisticated control systems—and upgraded the apartment's security system. She remembered Quincy and Rafe both mentioning the boy's knack for technical subjects and tasks. An idea tickled her, the first positive one she'd had in a long time. "If you could make another one . . . a few of them . . . we could put them on Vatta ships—"

"That's what I thought," Toby said, grinning. He stopped where he was, a box of components in either hand. "If you could get reports from our ships right away, even in systems where the ansibles didn't work, that would give us an edge—"

"Do you really think you can?" She could not imagine anyone cobbling together something that intricate in an apartment bedroom. "Don't you need a special lab or something?"

"Not really," Toby said, answering her second question first. "I'd love to have a lab of my own, but it's mature tech, really; it's not as finicky as it used to be." That sounded like a quote from Quincy. "I'm really close now," Toby went on. "Just another few days, I think. There's this part I don't understand . . . it seems like a backwards way of designing it, but there has to be a reason . . ."

"What made you think of copying one?" Stella asked. "Where did you learn—?"

"We need them," Toby said. "Captain—Cousin Ky could use more. Every ship, really, could use one, except it's not our design so we can't sell it. Anyway, Rafe talked to me a lot, you know. He's nice, even if he did scare me at first."

Stella blinked at the notion of Rafe, with his many aliases and his unquestionably shady past, being labeled "nice" by anyone.

"I kept asking him, when he was fixing those broken ansibles, and finally he said he'd explain if I promised not to tell anyone else about the ansible repair stuff he taught me, because it was an ISC secret. I understood some of it on my own," Toby went on. "I always thought it must be like FTL drives, but it's not, really. Well, sort of, in the basic theory of n-dimensions, but not in the practical application, or space travel would be instantaneous, too." He paused; he seemed to stare into the distance, and then he shook his head. "No . . . I haven't figured that part out yet."

"No rush," Stella said, her head whirling. Her own abilities—assuming she had any—lay very far from the things Toby talked about. "You can stick to ansibles for a while, can't you?"

"Oh, sure. I just need to figure out why there's a lockout circuit, what it's protecting the rest of it from."

"Or what it's protecting," Stella said.

Toby looked thoughtful again. "I hadn't thought of it that way. I thought it must be something to protect the ansible . . . but that's not necessarily—thanks, Cousin Stella." He wandered off to his room, followed by Rascal, without picking up any more of the mess.

Stella sighed and went back to her work. Standard Vatta trade routes made interconnecting rings rather than emanating from a few hubs; a Vatta ship from the

Orleans–Vishwa–Darien–Moscoe route should arrive insystem in the next few days. Ordinarily, *Katrine Lamont*'s captain—now Balthazar Orem, transferred from *Gary Tobai* because Stella knew him better—would have offloaded cargo consigned here, sequestered cargo that would be transferred directly to the incoming ship, acquired more cargo to take on from here, and left room for any cargo the incoming ship needed to transfer. But now, with trade down and Vatta's reputation almost as ruined as its head-quarters and coffers, nothing was that simple.

Still, there was always someone who wanted to ship something somewhere. Stella had put off hiring new crew for *Gary Tobai*, and *Katrine Lamont* was still undercrewed, but at least the ship was in perfect shape. Stella had sold off all the cargo that wasn't consigned elsewhere—about 30 percent was, and of that, a little less than half would need to be shifted to *Marcus Selene*, the ship due in. The sale of cargo, plus the company share of profits from Toby's dog's breeding fees, had kept her balance on the right side of the ledger, and in another thirty-five days she would have access to the late Captain Furman's accounts. And if Toby could actually build shipboard ansibles . . . maybe it was Osman's genes, and not Stavros', that presented her with an inkling of how profitable that could be, but maybe that didn't matter. In her imagination, a new cor-poration rose from the ashes of the old: Vatta once more, trade and profit; for the first time it seemed real, herself in a proper office, giving orders. In the meantime, her business office was the dining room table in the apart-ment.

"Cousin Stella! I found it!" Toby burst out of his room a few days later, Rascal scampering around in him in frantic circles.

"What, Toby?" Stella had just been running the figures again. *Marcus Selene* had arrived insystem and was making its way in from the jump point. She might afford a real office within the next week.

"What it was protecting . . . that thing I told you about. Not the ansible—or not this ansible—it's what keeps these from interfacing with system ansibles." He grinned, eyes sparkling. For an instant, Stella saw a ghost of the depressed, scared boy she had found in protective custody at Allray. Whatever else she had done wrong in her life, however vicious her biological father had been, she had changed Toby's life for the better. Then her brain caught up with his words.

"You mean they could interface—?"

"Yes. It's quite simple, really. Rafe said they couldn't, they were built so they couldn't, but he didn't tell me what they'd done. Maybe he didn't know; he said he didn't understand it all. Anyway, it's this circuit here—" He pushed a printout of a circuit diagram at her; to Stella, it was all lines and symbols, as meaningless as straws in the wind. "If I leave that part out, and change this bit here"— he pointed at something on the diagram—"then it could."

"That would be . . . very useful indeed," Stella said. Her mind filled instantly with the possibilities for profit—a lot of profit—but surely ISC had all the relevant patents. How could they come up with something on their own, something ISC couldn't interfere with, using Toby's ideas? "Brilliant, Toby. And do you think you can build a working model?"

"I could do it faster if I didn't have to go to school," he said, eyeing her sidelong.

Stella laughed. "Not that, my boy. You're going to school, and that's final. Besides, you've been enjoying the company; you said so."

"Well, yes. Some of the other kids are all right, especially since they moved me up a level. But I want to get this done. It would help us so much . . . and if ships went out with these, they could relay information from systems where the ansibles aren't working, until ISC had time to fix them."

"I can see that," Stella said. "But you have to go to school anyway. You can work on this in your spare time."

"Can I bring some friends over to help me?" Toby asked. "Some of them are really smart."

"No," Stella said; it came out harsher than she intended, and his expression changed. She tried to soften her tone. "Toby, right now this has to be a secret. You know the original technology belonged to ISC. We have to be sure it's legal for us to do this, or—"

"It can't be illegal to build one for ourselves—if we don't sell it—"

"Yes, it could be illegal," Stella said. "I have to find that out, and in the meantime don't talk about it. Not to your friends, not to your teachers—"

"But I don't see why," Toby said, with all the persistence of enthusiasm. "If it's just for us, why would they care?"

"Profit," Stella said. "If they own the rights and we make one instead of buying theirs—"

"But they're *not* selling them," Toby pointed out. "It's not costing them anything because they're not selling them."

"Just let me talk to someone who knows more about the law than either of us before you talk to anyone else," Stella said. He frowned, but finally nodded. "And Toby— thanks for all your work. If you've really solved that problem, ISC may be paying *us*. In any event, you're a real contributor to Vatta's recovery." A recovery that she now believed could happen, with or without the input of the Slotter Key Vattas.

Thirteen days later, Stella looked around Vatta Transport's new offices, redecorated in Vatta colors and fully furnished. Crown & Spears had been willing to advance the money on the expectation of her receiving Furman's accounts within fifteen days and the arrival of *Marcus Selene*. The offices were in an unfashionable quarter of Cascadia Station, toward the tip of one branch, but the rent per square meter was only 65 percent of that near the trunk. Besides, their business was shipping, and dockside was across the way.

"This is where you'll be," she said to the receptionist she'd hired for the front office. "We're just moving in— it's a little rough, but I assure you the security measures are first-rate."

"It looks lovely," the girl—young woman—said. Gillian Astin, Stella reminded herself. Native of Cascadia, just out of business school, up on the station for the first time. She looked too young, but her voice was brisk and she seemed to have confidence. "I look forward to serving you . . . I'm sorry, but I don't know what terms of address are correct for someone from Slotter Key."

"I'm living here now," Stella said. "Whatever's appropriate here—*Sera,* isn't it?"

"Yes, Sera Vatta." Gillian grinned. "This is so exciting. Mum and Dad never thought I'd get a job offplanet; they kidded me when I signed with the agency."

"Well, here's your desk. Let me know if there's anything else you need," Stella said. "I'll be in back—I've got a ship on approach and I need to talk with the captain."

"Thank you, Sera," Gillian said. The comunit on her desk buzzed. Stella paused in the door to see how she handled it. Gillian slipped the earbug in and said, "Good morning, Vatta Transport, Ltd. How may I help you?" She didn't sound like a child then. Stella slipped through into her own office.

Her father's office had been huge in comparison, furnished with antiques and artwork. Hers barely had room for a simple desk, a chair for a visitor, a credenza holding her comunit, cube reader, and—hidden inside—some supplies. The other door led to a narrow corridor, off which were the supply room and the toilets. Across that, a larger room where Toby could work. It had been the workshop of the small electronics repair firm and still had workbenches and shelving.

"Sera Vatta?" Gillian was at the door. "General Sales' local supervisor, Ser Sagata, would like to speak with you regarding the cargo coming in on *Marcus Selene*. May I tell him you will take his call?"

"Yes, thank you, Gillian," Stella said. Her stomach tightened. Now it began. Silly of her—it had begun long before—but now, in a real office, she felt a difference.

"Ser Sagata," she said, flicking on her comunit. "How may I help you?"

They exchanged the elaborate courtesies Cascadian custom dictated, and Stella assured him that the ship on its way in did indeed carry cargo consigned to General Sales. She gave him the invoice numbers as well.

"And our next departure will be three days after *Marcus Selene* arrives—the route is up on our site. If you have outbound cargo—"

"You will keep the same schedule?" He sounded surprised, and almost immediately apologized. "I'm sorry, Sera Vatta; that sounds as if I did not trust you, and I intended no insult . . ."

"No offense taken," Stella said. "I quite understand.

But yes, I intend to keep the same schedule, and in fact expand it as other Vatta ships come in. Cascadia has ample resources of trained ship crews; it will make a fine hub."

"I see." A long pause, then, "Yes, I believe we will have cargo ready for shipping by then. I'll get back with you shortly. Thank you for your service, Sera."

"Thank you for your custom, Ser Sagata." That had gone well. Stella let out a breath then went back to the front office. "Gillian, we're going to have an order for outgoing cargo. I may not be here when it comes in; please route it to my deskcomp, sorted by destination."

"Yes, Sera Vatta," Gillian said. "I was just thinking . . . do you want me to contact the other recipients of inbound cargo that their shipments are onboard?"

"Good idea," Stella said. "I'll send that file to your deskcomp, with the invoice numbers. Don't tell them the cargo contents, though. Just the numbers. And let them know that the departure schedule and route are up on our site, for their convenience. Maybe we'll get some more orders."

By the time Toby arrived that afternoon with a float pallet of his supplies, Vatta Transport had contracts pending with five different shippers for *Katrine Lamont*'s departure. Stella called Captain Orem.

"We have shippers," she said. "Do you think we should put up the available cubage on our site?"

"Absolutely," Orem said. "The Captains' Guild will display it for us, as well as the Shipping Combine. I can do that for you, with an automatic update as new cargo comes in." He paused. "Uh . . . I haven't thanked you, really, for the chance you've given me . . . you know, after I lost my own ship, I never thought I'd have a command again. And here I am on one of Vatta's top ships—better than anything I ever had before—"

"Please," Stella said. "Don't. I needed a captain; you needed a ship. It worked for both of us. I'm sure you can handle the *Kat* and the trade responsibilities."

"I had to say it," he said. He looked ten years younger now. "But for the moment—trade and profit."

"Trade and profit," Stella agreed.

From across the corridor, she heard thumps and bangs as Toby settled his things into the shelves. She went to look. "I brought it here, Cousin Stella," he said. "Under all the other boxes, so no one would see." In one corner, the plain gray box that Ky had given her, the portable ansible. Next to it, something roughly the same size and shape, but without the gray skin.

"That's the . . . "

"Yeah. What I'm working on. Not finished yet, though. It's still going to draw a fair bit of power—can we afford it?"

"Yes," Stella said, hoping "a fair bit of power" would fit into the budget. They had to try; this project was too important to fail because of a few credits.

"Can I sleep here?" Toby asked. "It'd save time going back and forth. And I wouldn't need a security escort as many hours."

"There's no food here," Stella pointed out. "And I want you in bed at a decent hour. For school. Don't worry about the escort charges."

"Excuse me, Sera, but there's an urgent message for you," Gillian said. Her gaze slid past Stella to linger on Toby.

That could be a complication. "From whom?" Stella asked.

"Sorry, Sera. From Crown & Spears."

"Your account has been credited with the sums formerly credited to the late Captain Furman," the Crown & Spears manager said when Stella picked up the call.

"Would you prefer to have these funds in hand or pay off the advance at this time? Crown & Spears has no problem with continuing the advance on the same terms." Exorbitant terms, to Stella.

"I think not," she said. "It was an unsecured loan before; now I could secure it, if I chose."

"Well, I'm sure something could be arranged," the manager said. "For a valued customer such as Vatta Transport . . ."

After the first few hectic weeks, as she dealt with *Marcus Selene*'s arrival, the departure of *Katrine Lamont,* the departure of *Marcus Selene,* customer inquiries, the sale of unconsigned cargo, and all the other minutiae of running a transport and trade company, Stella realized she had not thought about her own parentage, or Ky's adventures, for days. Whether Ky was alive or not, she herself was finding her identity as Vatta CEO more comfortable with every passing day. Vatta ships carried full loads of cargo, even *Gary Tobai,* for which she'd won a contract to carry cargo between Moscoe Confederation orbital stations. Vatta customers stopped by the office to chat and inquire when she would have more frequent departures. Another Vatta ship had reported in via ansible; its captain accepted her authority. Income still lagged behind expenses—not counting the contributions of Toby's dog Rascal, whose breeding fees kept them solvent—but it trended upward.

She had found an intellectual property lawyer who agreed to take up a patent search to see how much of the portable ansible technology was already controlled by ISC. Toby's school had called once, to congratulate her on his behavior ("We usually have much more trouble with students not from our system; he is an exceptionally polite boy, and we are delighted that you chose to have him attend classes instead of home tutoring"), and his marks in the first reporting period had been superb.

Startling, amusing even, that her family identity as "that idiot Stella" had concealed such abilities, even from her. Nobody here knew about the gardener's son or the family codes. Nobody here knew that Jo was—had been—the brains of the family, and her brothers had been brilliant in their way, while she was only a pretty face, "that idiot Stella." Nobody here seemed to care about her parentage, though as the result of a court case, it was in the public records. All that mattered to the Cascadians was her demeanor and her competence. Courtesy had always come easily for her; she found their social rules easy to follow. She'd never fully believed in that competence, but now she saw the proof of it every day, in the respect others gave her, in the contracts and the income. Trade and profit indeed.

She wished she could tell Aunt Grace, but the Slotter Key ansible remained stubbornly out of order, like so many others. Someday Vatta ships would carry Vatta ansibles, and she could send one back to Slotter Key—she surprised herself again by thinking of the name, and not "home."

"Sera Vatta?" Gillian tapped on her door.

"Yes?" Stella pushed all other thoughts aside. Business first, reveries later. Or never. She felt ready for whatever came through the door.

THREE

Once, a routine transition into FTL space had meant safety to Ky Vatta. That mysterious and undefined continuum in which the ship now existed had meant time to think, time to plan, time to interact with her crew in an untouchable capsule. She could not be interrupted from outside; she did not have to cope with outside.

What she'd known of earlier civilizations—pre-space and early-expansion—and their obsession with the vastness of space, the smallness of planets, had always amused her. She had grown up in a spacefaring civilization, embedded in a family whose fortunes came from traveling the spaceways; she had been in deep space herself at thirteen. Space was no bigger than the ship you were in. So many days in FTL from here to there, so many days or weeks from a jump point to a station . . . the rest of it didn't matter, really.

Now, for the first time, she felt it, that old awe at the size of the universe. Not days from system to system, but years of light burrowing through endless darkness. Though the ship's systems held the temperature at a steady setting, varying it slightly, intentionally, as the shifts changed, she herself felt cold, chilled by unwelcome knowledge.

Out there somewhere, beyond her knowledge as beyond her reach, were the pirates—the more-than-pirates now—who wanted to destroy all the comfortable assumptions of her life. Her life and the lives of everyone she'd known. The lives of billions of men and women and children who went to work, ate meals, went to school, played games, made plans based on the certainty that tomorrow would be like today.

She felt glued to the certainty—this unwelcome certainty—that they were wrong, pinned to that knowledge of imminent disruption, unable to think or move. She knew—she told herself repeatedly—that this FTL flight gave her respite in which to think, in which to prove that the bold boast she'd made a few days before came from some hidden core of ability, of moral strength. Her crew kept looking at her, giving her little grins and nods.

But for now she was paralyzed, mentally and almost physically, going through the motions of being the bold brave captain she knew they needed.

She had come on the bridge as usual, to take the first-shift report, and now she frowned at the data scrolling past on the screen as if she could do more than stare at the words and numbers. What did it all mean, anyway? This ship, the two others, even the pirates in their hordes, were just grains of dust in a vast universe that didn't care . . .

She glanced up as someone moved suddenly and saw Lee, her senior pilot, turn to Hugh Pritang, her executive officer. Lee's voice was strained, completely unlike his usual casual drawl. "Please—I have to go now—"

"What's the problem?" Hugh asked. He was facing away from Lee, entering something in the log. Ky glanced at Lee, whose face was a strange shade of gray-green.

Lee doubled over and spewed onto the deck, noisily. Hugh looked over, stiffened, and then caught sight of Ky. "Captain—" Then, "Mr. Quidlen—what's wrong?"

"He's sick," Ky said. She realized how unnecessary that was. She pulled a towel out of the dispenser by the hatch and stepped forward. "Lee? Can you talk?"

He shook his head and heaved again; the sour stench almost turned Ky's stomach. Hugh took the towel from her and bent down.

"I—I feel sick, too," her weapons officer, Theo Dannon, said.

"Leave the bridge," Ky said. It was probably just the smell, she thought, but Dannon also had an unhealthy greenish look around the mouth. She bent down to look more closely at Lee; his eyes were closed and his breathing was harsh. "We've been isolated on this ship too long for it to be any communicable illness," she said over her shoulder. "It's got to be food poisoning or something." She felt a stab of guilt; she hadn't inspected the galley the day before.

"I—feel really bad," Lee muttered, eyes still closed.

"Help me get him to a medbox," Ky said. Did medboxes deal with food poisoning? She had no idea. She felt stupid suddenly; she was planning to fight a war and she hadn't hired any medical personnel . . . it would take more than medboxes. She remembered the vast medical bay on the Mackensee ship that had treated her. Her mind seemed to wake suddenly from the daze of the past shifts. Later she could think how to increase their medical capability. Now . . .

"I can do that," Hugh said. He looked around the bridge. "One of us needs to be here."

Ky nodded. In FTL flight, nothing ever happened, but still a senior officer should be on the bridge. Especially if this was more than some random virus.

"And I'll send one of the techs up to clean up, in case it's infectious. Don't get contaminated. Captain." Ky nodded as Hugh hauled Lee up and got a shoulder under his arm. Lee was just able to shamble along as Hugh moved aft.

Ky turned up the bridge ventilation and queried the food storage units. All the readouts were in range—coolers and freezers all at the correct temperature. She had come through the galley already, without formally inspecting it; it had looked clean and tidy, as usual. Surely no one had cooked for the others without washing hands; everyone had that much sense. In minutes one of the environmental techs—not Twigg, but Bannin—showed up in protective gear with a wet vac. "There's another two sick, Captain," he said to Ky. "That's four so far. We don't know what it is yet, but we'll run it through the analyzers and see."

Four down within a half hour . . . not just some isolated bug Lee'd been harboring since their last time on a station. Possibilities sprang up like weeds: something they'd missed when clearing the ship of Osman's traps, something planted by the agent who'd joined the ship as a cargo handler and then died, sabotage by someone now in the crew. "Anything odd in the environmental cultures?"

"No, ma'am. At least, all the readouts are nominal, though we'll run a check of them. And we're not consuming anything ship-made anyway."

She'd known that. She'd spent the money to purchase high-quality rations, and they still had some of Osman's left as well. Osman's. Had he sabotaged random packs of his own rations for some reason? "Take samples of all the surfaces in the galley, any opened ration containers, everything in the cooler—"

"Yes, Captain. Mr. Pritang's told us that; Mr. Gulandar has people on it, and Mr. Pritang is asking everyone what they ate or drank in the last two days."

Bannin finished sucking up the mess, then sprayed with cleanser and vacuumed again, finally applying a decontaminating spray. "Just let that dry, Captain. It'll stay there twelve hours or more, and then we'll come give it another spray and vacuum. After that, it'll be safe for normal cleaning."

"Thanks," Ky said. "You will let me know what it is . . ."

"Of course, ma'am. As soon as we know."

Four so far. If it was something in the food, was it something in Osman's food supply? In what she'd bought? And was it intentional or accidental? And why weren't they all sick? They were all eating out of the same food supply; they rotated cooking duties, but—she called up the roster for galley work. If it was unclean pots or dishes, she would have someone's guts for garters.

Within a few hours, as Ky paced the bridge deck and thought of more and more items to test—from shampoo to cough lozenges—another five had come down with whatever it was: vomiting, abdominal pain, diarrhea, weakness that might be from the symptoms or from the cause. The cooking utensils and dishes showed nothing; there was nothing harmful in the water supply.

"Nothing shows up on the chem scan," Environmental Tech Twigg told her. "It's not any contact or residual poison in our database. It's got to be contaminated food—if it were the water, everyone would be down with it."

Ky went herself, when Hugh took over the bridge again, to inspect the latrines, the showers, the galley, the cutlery and dishes. She remembered that she had brought aboard dishes touched—if only briefly—by someone who wanted to send a coded message, a microdot, to someone on her ship. Both men had died . . . had they also left a persistent toxin on the dishes? She and her crew had eaten dozens of meals off those dishes since, with no harmful effects, and the dishes had been washed repeatedly. Why now?

Nine sick . . . but as hours passed and no one else came down with the mysterious disease, Ky concentrated on finding out what those nine had eaten or drunk that no one else had consumed. She had no qualified epidemiologist in the crew, not even a medic, but the environmental department, none of whom had gotten sick, dug through the trash that hadn't yet gone to the recycler, testing everything.

Meanwhile, Hugh and Gordon went through the crew list asking questions: who ate what at which meal, between meals, who had seen someone else eating, and so on. Even though no more crew came down with the mysterious illness, Ky pressed them to keep asking, keep searching for a cause.

Finally, Lee came out of a medbox able to answer questions. Ky went down immediately to find out what he knew.

"We had a little celebration the other night," Lee said. "Nothing big . . . just a box of sweet-snacks from stores, and some—" He paused.

"What?" Ky said.

"I'm trying to remember. Oh, yes . . . there was this jar somebody had in his personals. Stuff his grandmother made, he said. It had gotten knocked around somehow, and leaked a bit, so he offered it to the party; he didn't want to let it sit around unsealed in case it spoiled—" He frowned. "You don't suppose that could have been what did it? How could it spoil in just a few days?"

"What was it?" Ky asked, trying for patience. "Animal, vegetable, mineral? Liquid, solid?"

"I don't really know," Lee said. "I guess it did . . . sort of have a kind of . . . well . . . it smelled a bit alcoholic, but it also had a strong smell of fruit, and then kind of a fishy smell, too. But it was really good spread on those crackers. I can't believe that's what made us sick, though. He said they stored it in crocks back home."

"Who?" Ky said, suppressing an urge to shake the answer out of him.

"Uh . . . Jemison, starboard aft battery."

Jemison was still in a medbox; the readout said he would be out in another four hours.

"Not everyone in starboard aft is sick," Ky said. "Who else was at this party? Did everybody eat some?"

The party, it turned out, had involved much of the crew, who dropped in and out as they had time. Lee wasn't sure who had been there, or not, before he came and after he left. Jemison's contribution was only that single small jar of the stuff—whatever it had been—and only a few of the crew had had a chance at it.

Unfortunately, the jar and any remnants of its contents had gone into the recycler, and Environmental had no way to tell which of the stomach contents vacuumed up were responsible.

"The only bacterial and viral signatures we have on file relate to our own cultures," Bannin told Ky. "I'm sorry, Captain . . ."

"Not your fault," Ky said. "We need to get a medical database that goes beyond the medboxes." Whatever its cause and despite the guilt she felt over having insufficient medical resources aboard, her earlier lassitude had vanished. She put those needs on her list for the next station. How much did it cost to maintain a medical team? No matter—they needed one, and she'd have to fund it somehow.

At the start of the next shift, most of the sick were out of the medboxes and clearly recovering. Her spirits rose further; when Hugh came up to her on the bridge, she felt capable of dealing with whatever was coming next.

"Captain, could I speak to you privately?" Hugh looked more serious than usual.

"Of course," Ky said. She led the way off the bridge to her quarters.

"I'm concerned about some of the crew," Hugh said. "I know they've been with you a long time . . ."

"You're talking about the crew from my old ship?"

"Yes. Although there's also a potential problem with some of the crew you hired later. I don't know if you're aware of it, but you've created a situation in which the ship crew is entirely civilian in background and attitude—except for me as your exec—and the fighting crew is entirely military."

Ky scowled. "I'm not sure I follow—why is this a problem?"

"Attitude, mostly. This latest incident is an example of what can go wrong."

"The probable cause came in with one of the fighting crew," Ky said. "And he wasn't immune to it."

"True. The problem spreads . . . look, just let me explain." Ky nodded, and he went on. "Take your pilots, for instance. Lee, your senior pilot, is a highly skilled technician in his field, and you have used him as one of your personal guards at times. I know he has adequate weapons skills, and he takes pride in that assignment."

"So? He and the others performed well in that fight with Osman—"

"Yes. But in fact it required nothing of him but acting the part of a traitor, if I understood you rightly. He has never had military training. He is an amateur, at both security functions and at combat. He follows your orders—you are the captain and he's known you for some time—but I sense a certain resentment to orders I've given. Not disobedience—he's too good a man for that—but he always wants an explanation, or even just to discuss what should get simple obedience."

Ky thought back to her experiences aboard Spaceforce training ships. Of course everyone had been military, and military discipline had prevailed. Only the cadets asked questions, for the most part, and they were expected to obey orders without such questions at the time. But was that necessary here, for people without military training?

"My concern," Hugh went on, "is that when we're in combat again, your civilian crewmembers may be slow to respond to orders they don't understand, or—for those with more initiative—may do something unexpected, and either of these could put themselves or the ship in peril."

"You're really worried about this?" Ky said. "After we've been in combat and nothing like that has happened?"

"Captain, the last post-battle analysis, from the most recent engagement, shows that twenty percent of the crew with civilian background either questioned orders, delayed response, or engaged in unordered activity. Now, as it happens, none of those things was critical in the event—but that's not something we can depend on. And this latest incident—bringing aboard uninspected food items, failing to enter them on the ship's stores list, distributing them at a party neither you nor I knew about—shows that a casual attitude toward standard rules has spread even to some of the military crew. You're going to have to decide what to do about it."

Ky frowned. She had not made any connection between the crew's performance during combat and the food poisoning incident, and for that matter she hadn't thought of the crew's behavior as below standard. If Hugh was right . . . "You have a recommendation?"

"You're not going to like it." Hugh rubbed his nose. "We would be better off with an all-military crew. Retraining this one is going to be difficult, partly because the original crewmembers are in some way associated with your family—with your civilian identity—and partly because you have two distinct groups: the old crew, who have one kind of loyalty to you and your family, and the new crew, who haven't."

"Um." Ky steepled her hands to give herself time to think. "I hadn't realized there was this problem—"

"You haven't really had time," Hugh said. "You've been dealing with other crises. But it's something you need to consider."

"I don't want to get rid of people who've served with me through the whole thing," Ky said. "Loyalty cuts both ways."

"I thought you'd say that," Hugh said. "That's fine: that's laudable. But you're going to have to explain the reality of a warship to them. That's what we are, now. I know you were thinking privateer at one time, but it's clear your entire focus now is on fighting a hostile force. We cannot afford to have any gaps in discipline."

"I see that," Ky said. "I suppose—the ones who can't make the transition would still be useful to Stella, as civilian crew on other Vatta ships, if they're willing."

"Quite so," Hugh said, nodding. "You don't have to throw anyone out in the cold; you can transfer them to jobs for which they're more suited. I'd recommend acting on this as quickly as possible."

"But that means hiring new crew," Ky said. "I'm not sure how easily we can find what you're looking for. Or how quickly they'll bond into a crew—"

"The sooner we look, the sooner we can find," Hugh said. "And if I may, I'm not at all sure Ciudad's the best place to look, not with you—any woman, I mean—in command."

"I've been thinking about that," Ky said. "There's no reason they'd join up with us just to avenge the loss of their ship; they're more likely to blame us. But I can't tell the other captains that until we come out of FTL."

"In the meantime," Hugh said, "you could consider retraining those of your civilian crew who are willing. We have enough experienced veterans aboard to do that."

"I'll talk to my—the old crew," Ky said.

The remaining crew from *Gary Tobai* filed into Ky's office. She could not help but notice how casual they were compared to the ex-military personnel she'd hired. Respectful, but in their own individual ways.

"We have a problem to solve," she said, aware that this was not how she'd have started out with the Gannetts, or even Hugh or Martin. "You all know that *Vanguard* is now acting as a military ship—"

"Yes, I just want to know why we can't at least carry some personal cargo for trading," said Mehar. "Privateers still carry cargo, don't they?"

"Privateers do," Ky said. "And yes, when you signed on, that's what this ship was. But as things are now, operating as independent privateers will just get us killed when we run into a superior force of pirates. That's why we're teamed up with *Sharra's Gift* and *Bassoon*. We're forming as an interstellar defense force, a real space navy." From their expressions, some of them found this very bad news.

"I know some of you won't like this," Ky said. "And you're not being shanghaied—you'll be able to leave the ship at the next port, with pay due in your accounts, and a bonus for hazardous duty." She paused a moment; some of them shifted their weight but no one said anything. "Or if you'd rather, I can transfer you to Vatta Transport—the real Vatta Transport—and send you to work on the civilian traders Vatta is once again operating."

"I'll take that," someone said from the back; others turned to look, and Ky saw the number two engineer, Foxeham. "I'm really—I'm not—"

"That's all right," Ky said. "No need to explain. It's not what you signed up for. My cousin Stella, who's running Vatta Transport now, can always use more crewmembers as she acquires more ships. We'll pay your passage to Cascadia, where she is now."

Foxeham nodded, looking shamefaced but relieved. Well, not everyone was cut out for the military life, and she could run the ship with a short crew of engineers if she had to.

"The rest of you," Ky said. "If you want out of your contracts, or to have them transferred to Vatta Transport, let me or the exec know. We're due to drop out of FTL in another two days; I'll want a list by then. Those who know you want to stay, please remain behind; the rest of you are excused."

Those leaving began to mutter among themselves even before they cleared the cabin; to Ky's relief, the tone was more satisfied than worried. Facing her still were a half dozen, all who had been on the *Gary*, including Lee.

"I gather you want to be in this," she said.

"We've been with you from the beginning," Lee said. "And some of it's been the best time of my life. You bet I want to stay."

"Me, too," muttered the others.

"It's not going to be easy," Ky said. "And here's why." Quickly, she outlined the differences in discipline that Hugh had named most critical. "The thing is, if you continue to act like civilians, that could get you killed—or, at worse, the whole ship lost. Yes, even just one of you," she said to the disbelief in their faces. "Let me outline just one scenario. Say we're boarded. You'll say, Been there, done that, right? But I'm talking about actual penetration of the crew compartments, which didn't happen last time. If you don't do exactly what you've been told—what you're supposed to—without thinking up any heroic bits that backfire—"

"Why would they backfire?" Lee interrupted.

"And there's another problem," Ky said. She sighed and shook her head. "Lee, you and the others are used to talking to me as the captain, yes, but also as Gerry Vatta's little girl who needs taking care of." His eyes widened, and she nodded. "Yes, you are. That's understandable. But it has to stop. This is now a military ship; we will be maintaining military discipline. For some of you—including some of the best of you—that's going to be a considerable strain. You weren't trained for it; you're not used to it; you still have that history with me when we had a nonmilitary relationship."

Lee opened his mouth and shut it; Mehar raised her hand. Ky nodded at her.

"I don't understand why it all has to be military, Captain. I mean, why does it have to be that way for us as well as them?"

"Because a ship's crew has to be all one piece, bonded," Ky said. "You have to trust the military—the *present* military—and they have to trust you. Everyone has to know that everyone else will follow orders quickly, precisely, without questioning, in any crisis. And the newer crew have to know that they are equal with you, that you're all on the same footing." She paused again; they were listening intently—not rejecting it, but not yet completely convinced.

"Look," she said. "You are my oldest crew; we've been through a lot. I can never forget that, I trust you and respect you at a level the others still have to earn. But I can't treat you differently and be fair to them."

Lee nodded, as did Mehar. Lee raised his hand this time before blurting out anything; Ky nodded.

"I understand that," he said. "And—I guess—I understand the need to change. But . . . I'm not sure I can change, and I sure don't know how fast."

"Good points," Ky said. "Here's what I want to do. I've spoken to some of the military side about what might help you transition with as little difficulty as possible. You'll all need to do some physical training and some cross-training in other specialties. You'll all need to start learning, if you haven't, the correct procedures, in the military sense. The parameters have narrowed; I'll be pickier about precision; I'll be pickier about discipline. I want you to get to know the fighting crew, not stay aloof from them. Lee, I know you've partied with them—" Chuckles broke out, relaxing some of the tension. "You don't have to like them all, but you need to know them."

"Er . . . what if they . . . ," Mehar started. Ky looked at her. "Sorry," Mehar said. "Captain, if I may?" Ky nodded. "Some of them . . . they've made remarks . . . personal . . ."

"That will stop. I've told them. No hazing, none of that. It happens in basic training, but this isn't standard basic training and we don't have time for it. I've made up a cube with some of the procedural stuff for you—for instance, if someone makes an unwanted sexual advance, there's a procedure for reporting it. There will be consequences." Mehar had stood beside her in that corridor when she and Mehar together had killed the mutineer leaders; when Gary Tobai died. She was not about to tolerate anyone hassling Mehar.

"Another thing. No questioning orders, at least not without first asking permission, and never in action. That's going to be hard for some of you in particular." She gave Lee a grin; he smiled back, sheepishly. "But there are reasons, among them gaining the trust of the military bridge crew. They have to know that you do what you're told first, and ask questions later. And yes, before you ask, there's room for initiative and all that—but not now. Clear?"

Nods, murmured combination of "Yes, ma'am," and "Yes, Captain."

"Here's the cube," Ky said, handing them out. "Take it and look at it, first thing. If any of you change your mind and want out, either after looking at it or after trying the training, just let me know. I will always respect you and the service you've already given me—and Vatta—no matter what you decide."

More nods.

"Dismissed," Ky said. They all looked startled, but began moving out. "Lee, just wait a moment, would you?" Lee, Hugh had pointed out, was a critical person; he had been operating in a semi-military role for a long time now, and his cooperation and leadership would help with the crew transition—if he could stand the discipline.

"Sure, Captain," Lee said. Then he pulled himself into an exaggerated version of "attention" and said, "Am I supposed to stand like this when I talk to you?"

Part willing, part resenting. Ky shook her head. "No, certainly not all the time. Lee, when my father sent you out as second pilot under Riel, you were starting to get bored, weren't you?" He had told her that once.

"Yes, Captain," he said, relaxing slightly but still more formal than usual for him. His hand twitched; she knew he wanted to run it through his hair, as he often did while they talked.

"And you told me you actually enjoyed the excitement, that being with a privateer didn't bother you at all, right?"

"Right, Captain."

"Lee, you have a lot of potential. I think so, and Hugh thinks so. You already know how to use small arms; you've already shown yourself to be brave and resourceful. But I can't tell how much the tighter discipline will bother you. Some very brave and resourceful people just don't handle it well. Give me a clue."

Lee's stiff posture relaxed still more. "Honestly—I don't know, Captain. I always kind of hankered after the hero-stuff I saw in entertainment vids, imagined myself as a space ranger type, but I knew it wasn't realistic. And the villains were usually the ones hyped on discipline, all that standing in stiff rows and saluting and barking *yes sir, no sir, immediately sir* like trained animals."

"Um. And if you keep thinking of military discipline in those terms, it will be harder for you and you will resent it. Tell me, do you think my Exec is competent?"

"Hugh? He's brilliant!"

"So, if he tells you to do something, how likely is he to be right?"

"Hasn't been wrong yet," Lee said. Then he blinked. "Oh. But I always ask, don't I? Or nearly always?"

"Yes," Ky said, grinning. "You do. And I know, and he knows, that it's not really insubordination, that desire to understand his reasoning . . . I suspect you're picking his brain, actually, storing away how he thinks so you can use it if you ever need it. But what do you think it looks like to the military crew? Like, for instance, my weapons officer?"

Lee grimaced. "Like I'm a snotty civilian who won't take orders without a lengthy explanation, I'm guessing."

"Something like that, yes," Ky said. She said nothing more, waiting. If he could reason it out on his own . . .

"So . . . what you want me to do is just . . . follow orders, and if I want to know why and wherefore . . . ask him later, if he's not busy?"

"That would be perfect," Ky said.

Lee thought that over; she could practically see the gears meshing. "And you think," he said finally, "that if I adapt without an argument, the others will fall in line?"

"I think it would be easier for them," Ky said. "You've got a lot of influence, and rightly so. If you had gone in the military, they'd have recognized your leadership potential."

"Do pilots have a rank, in the military?"

"Why? Is there someone you want to pull rank on?"

"No," Lee said. This time he did run his hand through his hair. "I just . . . if I'm going to have to learn all that military stuff, procedures and whatnot, I don't want to be just that civvie pilot who's finally gotten some sense."

"Lee, you could never be that, not in my eyes," Ky said firmly. "But yes, military pilots have rank, and I'll tell you what—you get through a training period, and I'll pin those—" Her mind raced. They still didn't have uniforms, or rank insignia. "—those whatever we decide on, when we buy them, on your shoulders myself, at a formal ceremony. You and all the rest. Deal?"

He grinned. "Captain, I don't think military commanders make deals. I thought only traders made deals."

"As Vatta and as your captain, I make deals if I want to," Ky said. "And that's a promise."

"Deal," Lee said, nodding. "Er . . . yes, ma'am, Captain."

After some thought and discussion with Hugh, Ky assigned Gordon Martin as the civilian crew's trainer. "You did a good job with Jim," she told him.

"I've barely got Jim up to decent civ," Martin grumbled. "And now I'm supposed to get him to actual soldiering?"

"You've done better than that, and you know it. Thing is, the civilian crew know you from way back; they trust you. They'll take things from you that they might not from, say, Jon Gannett. At least it'll be an easier beginning."

"This has the potential to be a rolling doughnut," Martin said.

"I know. But it's worth a try."

"So am I working with all of them, or just the ones who want to stay?"

"All of them for now. Just in case we run into something when we drop out of FTL."

"Right. Makes sense. How many hours a day? You know, in real training—"

"You'd have them clock-round. Yes. But they're still ship crew, with real duties. Let's start with four hours and see where that gets us."

Nothing more was said for a few days, and Ky got no hints from the crew as she made her rounds through the ship. On the bridge, Lee seemed to be working well with Hugh, giving crisp "Yes, sir" and "No, sir" to orders. Gordon's first five-day report, a brief one-page summary, indicated no significant problems.

The very next day, Ky was walking the ship as she did every first-shift, just passing the portside aft battery, when she heard a comment from someone in the aft environmental chamber, inboard. "—didn't sign up for this," the voice was saying. "If I'd known I was getting shanghaied—"

"They told you it was a privateer, didn't they? They told me—"

"Yeah, but a privateer's like a pirate—no rules, no

saluting, none of this military stuff—just, you know, adventure and a share of the loot—"

"You've never been on a privateer before, have you?"

"Uh—no, but I thought—"

"You thought! You should've asked somebody who had—"

Ky decided to let them work it out for themselves, but she made a note to herself that Environmental Technician Twigg should be herded into Stella's end of things as soon as possible.

FOUR

When *Vanguard* dropped out of FTL in the empty system that had been their next programmed jump point, Ky immediately contacted the other two ships and explained the change of plans.

"So—we're not going to Ciudad?" Captain Argelos of *Sharra's Gift* asked. He looked confused, and Ky didn't blame him. She had been so certain that's where they should go, before that jump.

Ky shook her head. "No. Not at first, anyway. We need allies; telling them that one of their ships has been destroyed and we couldn't save any of the crew is not the way to get help."

Argelos nodded. "That makes sense. But what are we going to do, just the three of us . . . do you really think we can accomplish anything?"

"I should try to find others from Bissonet," Pettygrew said. *Bassoon*'s captain looked hollow-eyed, as if he'd lost kilos of weight while they were in FTL flight. "I can't just ignore what happened . . ."

"Turek didn't start with the resources he had now," Ky said. "We can do a lot with three good ships, and we'll have more once we have something to show others. Dan"— she used Pettygrew's given name for the first time—"I can't stop you if you want to leave, but consider—it's a big universe, and you have no idea where other Bissonet ships might be. Please consider staying with us for now—we can help you, and you can certainly help us."

"I don't know what's happening," Pettygrew said. "Back home—I don't want to think about it, but—"

"I don't know what's happening back at Slotter Key, either," Ky said. "And I know my family's mostly dead."

Pettygrew looked down, then nodded slowly. "All right. If you think we can do anything—"

"We did. We blew away some of their ships. We damaged others. Now—" Now, before anyone had too long to think, she had to get them busy about something they could do. "—I need to know your munitions status."

Pettygrew grimaced. "I threw everything I had, short of the galley sink. That's another thing; I can't fight without replacements—"

"And you?" Ky turned to Argelos.

He shrugged. "The same. No, I think I ended up with five missiles in reserve. And what I had in trade goods might buy another ten, at a cut-rate weapons shop. If the ansibles were up—"

"If the ansibles were up, we'd all have less trouble," Ky said. "We're low, too. So the first thing to do is resupply. I have funds—for now. We need to find a place, come in looking strong but not threatening—"

"That's a neat trick," Pettygrew said.

"—and see what we can pick up," Ky said, without answering that. "I've been searching the catalogs—Vatta catalogs—and there's a system near here that's listed as having a major outlet for munitions at good prices; they have manufacturers in the system. Even bigger than MilMart at Lastway, it looks like. Vatta picked up cargo there before—in the old days."

"Exactly the sort of place the pirates would be hanging out, I'd think," Argelos said.

"Quite possibly, and if so, we're in trouble. I'm sure they'll have agents there, at least. I'll admit that the Vatta database has warnings posted about it. Some fraud in the repair shops, for instance, selling old parts for new, that kind of thing. But it's likely to have what we need, and it's only one jump away. We've got experienced weapons crew who can detect substandard munitions."

They both nodded. "So where is this gun shop?" Argelos asked.

"One jump, five days." Ky hesitated. "Another thing—these shipboard ansibles are making communications much easier, but we know the pirates have them—we need to find a way to protect our messages."

"Scramble 'em?" Pettygrew said. "That's easy enough."

"But it lets the pirates know someone else is using the tech," Ky said. "I'd rather they didn't know that . . . though the ones who got away back there may have noticed. Do you have any technical wizards who might be able to add a channel or whatever, something the pirates won't know exists?"

"Dozi," Pettygrew said, before Argelos could say anything. "Dozi Lattin. She might be able to—she's been tinkering around with ours, very carefully."

"Nobody on my ship," Argelos said.

"That's good news, Dan," Ky said to Pettygrew. "If we can detect their transmissions, but they can't detect ours, we'll have a communications advantage even if we can't understand anything they're saying. It's definitely worthwhile hanging about here for a few days while your tech works on the problem. She should be able to give us a yea-or-nay in two days, right?"

"I'll ask her," Pettygrew said.

"Full scans, power up, and ready to jump out if trouble arrives," Ky said. "We can risk spacing at a half light-second, so we can use conventional tight-beam until we get the new channels on the ansibles." She wondered whether to talk to the other captains about Hugh's recommendation that they train all the crew in military skills, but decided to wait for more secure communications, if they could get them.

She considered contacting Stella to let her know the ship was still intact, but decided it was too risky. So far, no one but she herself knew that Stella had one of the small ansible units; if the pirates realized that one unit was on a planet or station, they might attack it—and she would not be there to protect Stella and Toby. Best to wait until she could use a system ansible, where her signal would be drowned in a million others. She didn't analyze the surge of relief that decision gave her.

Dozi Lattin's solution, as she explained the next day to Ky over the reconfigured system, was "not elegant at all, but it works." Between Lattin's Bissonet accent, much thicker than Pettygrew's, her rapid delivery, and the technical complexity of the explanation, Ky soon felt drowned in detail.

"So—the short of it is, you've modified the system so the pirates won't detect it? And it still works?"

"Yah," Lattin said. Onscreen she was a thin, unkempt woman whose jacket pockets bulged with data wands. She pulled one out. "It's all on here; your communications staff can have a copy when we get somewhere we can pass information hard. They don't want to be just following directions forever. And I'll be working on a better—"

"That's great, Dozi," Pettygrew said. He winked at Ky,

the first humor she'd seen from him. "But I need to talk to Captain Vatta. Later, eh?"

Lattin smiled and ducked away from the screen; Ky was not surprised to see that she almost ran into someone coming onto Pettygrew's bridge. Typical tech, that, striding along with head down, concentrating on anything but her surroundings.

"Now what?" Pettygrew asked.

"Now we can make our final plans, how we want to come in. I'll send your nav computer the coordinates of our next stop," Ky said. "On the new channel—" She pointed to her com officer, and the data went out. Argelos' face appeared on the screen, now split to show both the other captains.

"Got it," Argelos said, a split second before Pettygrew.

"Gretna . . . ," Pettygrew said, frowning slightly. "It doesn't have the best reputation with Bissonet traders."

"Dodgy repairs? That's all my company notes say."

"They never did sign off on the full Commercial Code," Pettygrew said. "They pad their station bills, too, according to my database."

"A lot of places do that," Argelos said. "My implant does have a yellow flag, but it's limited to several repair facilities and a caution about certain subsections of contracts related to the Commercial Code. But three armed ships like ours—unless we find a whole pirate fleet there, we should be able to handle anything we find."

"So how do we announce ourselves?" Ky asked. "We have three different flags, and we are all armed. Suppose they take us for pirates?"

"You want us to decide on an organizational name now?" Pettygrew asked.

"It might be wise," Ky said.

"I think we should wait until we have a chance to acquire

some insignia," Pettygrew said. "Like this, with our ships bearing different flags on their IDs, our crews in different uniforms, no way to prove we do belong together, other than circumstance, I don't think we'd have much credibility."

Argelos nodded. "He's right, Captain Vatta. I think we'd do better to come in as a group hanging together for security, which is really what we are at this point. We can certainly talk about what we want to call ourselves, and maybe pick up uniforms or patches or whatever at Gretna, but I don't see that we can afford to look ridiculous right from the start."

"I see your point," Ky said. "But let's take a few hours to talk over what we are, so we can gather the materials we need with the least waste of time."

"We need an organization with a name. We're not going to get anywhere as an association of privateers. Something solid, respectable. Something-something Defense, Force or Fleet or—"

"Spaceforce," Argelos said.

"United Planets Spaceforce? Needs to be something that makes a good acronym."

"Or very dull, and we let any nicknames take care of themselves."

"Space Service?"

"Combined . . . united . . . space service?"

"There's always Space Patrol . . ." Everyone groaned. In all the years, however calculated, of human presence in space, no one had ever called a military organization "Space Patrol," which was inextricably associated with bad children's programming. "Space Rangers?"

"Special ops name, Rangers," Hugh said. "We need a name that implies a solid military force authorized by a legitimate government."

"Which we don't have."

"Details." Hugh grinned. "It doesn't matter, really. Who's to know?"

"So we just do it," Ky said. "Space Defense Force, how's that?"

"Sounds good to me," Argelos said. Pettygrew nodded.

"So . . . we become the first flight, or squadron, or something, of the SDF?"

"Not first anything," Hugh said. "We want the opposition to think there's more of us, including some they don't know about. Pick another number, not too high."

"Third?" Ky said.

"Third Fleet . . ." Hugh said slowly. "About right. When we have four fleets, we can always shift ourselves to first, if that matters."

She could see the others trying it out mentally. Finally they all nodded.

"We need a design, a logo," Argelos said. "I've got a junior engineer who's talented that way."

"How about a spiral galaxy with a formation of ships shooting a bad guy?" Pettygrew asked.

"Too complicated, but I like the galaxy. Implies more than one system." Argelos squinted, thinking. "Galaxy and maybe the small formation of ships across it?"

"Fine," Ky said. "Now: we need to get our ships marked with the joint-force logo. I'm not talking about re-registration—the original flags are fine—just an indication of our organization. Unit patches as well as ship patches."

"Uniforms?"

"Not worth the expense right now, and to some extent the different uniforms reinforce the idea of a multisystem force."

"If Gretna's got munitions, they're bound to have

someone used to turning out military insignia," Hugh said. "Even a rough sketch should be enough."

Greater Gretna's advertising started at the jump point: WELCOME TO GRETNA, GUNS FOR THE GALAXY! blared from the welcoming beacon as soon as they had cleared down-jump scan turbulence. ALWAYS A FAIR DEAL! A SAFE PORT IN ANY POLITICAL STORM! HONEST TRADERS WELCOME; TRAMPS AND LAYABOUTS STAY AWAY! YOU KNOW WHO YOU ARE!

"That's an interesting combination," Hugh said. "Safe port in a political storm, but only for those we already know and like?"

"Did your company ever trade here?" Ky asked.

"Not that I know of. We bought our munitions from a dealer in our headquarters system. They might have bought here, for all I know, though. I wasn't in that end of things."

For such a supposedly busy marketplace of a system, there was little traffic showing up on longscan. Shuttles between the planet and space station, four small insystem cargo haulers on logical routes to the other planets, all with Gretna ID beacons, and a single inbound cargo ship whose beacon identified her as *Dryas,* from Polson. Ky queried her implant and found no information on Polson. The ship was barely crawling along, an approach that would give her plenty of time to gather information about system defense. Was this a shipload of pirates disguised as traders? Ky checked the course and alerted her weapons crews, though she didn't think a single pirate ship would attack three armed ones traveling much faster.

Shortly after that, Greater Gretna's insystem militia hailed them. Ky answered, as they had agreed.

"*Vanguard,* eh?" the uniformed man on the screen said. He was one of the palest humans Ky had ever seen, with ice-blue eyes and hair of an unattractive pale yellow. "We don't have you in the database . . . Cascadian registry? Don't see many Cascadians out here. You're the ones all touchy about manners, aren't you?"

"Cascadian registry, yes," Ky said. "Ship was salvage; I had to repaper her."

"Ah. And those with you—don't they have functioning coms?"

"Yes, but since we're traveling together it would save your time to talk to just one of us—that's *Sharra's Gift,* Slotter Key registry, and *Bassoon,* out of Bissonet."

"And you're traveling together because—"

"The universe has gotten dangerous," Ky said. "We were attacked by pirates; we got away but we need to resupply. If we'd been solo . . ."

"Ah. Well, you've come to the right place. We've got the best prices—and the best quality—you'll find anywhere. Now, the rules are, we don't tolerate troublemakers or people who can't pay their bills. We have a nice place here and we intend to keep it that way. You'll all need local ID, whether you're staying on the ship or out on the station: Port Security will take care of that for you. Fifty credits a head, and don't try hiding anyone or it'll be a stiff fine. No transients downplanet . . . and don't think you can sneak past our security." He grinned, a very unpleasant grin. "*You're* not going to fit in."

"What was that about?" Ky said to nobody in particular when she closed the connection.

"I think they're Fishbellies," Lee said.

"Fishbellies?" Ky said. Then she remembered. Some systems had been settled not by the usual mix of human types, but very deliberately by those of one phenotype or one religion. A few of these had populations with minimal melanin, and the rude term for these, among more . . . she tried not to think *normal* . . . societies was "Fishbellies." "My family didn't use that term," she said to Lee. "Though—if he is one—I can see where the name came from. Seems an odd choice . . . but then phenotypy always does, if there's not a good environmental reason for it. Maybe there's something on their planet to explain it."

"Fishbellies are strange," Lee said. "I met two of them once in a bar on Allray, years back. Sat there the whole time complaining about mixing—finally got a fight started, and then told the station police that it was everyone else's fault."

"Oh, any inbred group will do that," Hugh said. "There are some strains of genetic humods who go out of their way to be pushy and then complain. I don't suppose Fishies are any worse than anyone else."

"I hope not," Ky said. "If these are . . . er . . . Fishbellies, we have to deal with them."

"I wouldn't trust them a centimeter," Lee said. "They give people like me a bad name." He gestured at his shock of yellow hair.

"They're merchants," Ky said. "At least the ones we'll be dealing with. As long as we make sure the merchandise meets specs and they know our money's good, we shouldn't have a problem. Though I will be alert, of course."

Gretna Main Station had ample docking spaces—trade was down here, too—but the stationmaster refused to assign the three ships adjoining berths, on the grounds of station rotational balance. It made sense, but Ky felt a twinge of uneasiness. From the aft external monitors of *Vanguard,* she could not see even the aftmost tip of *Sharra's Gift* or *Bassoon,* though there were no ships between *Vanguard* and them.

Port Security waited at dockside, ready to issue local

IDs to the entire crew and collect the fee. All of them were as pale as the face Ky had seen onscreen before; though some had more pink color than others, all had pale eyes and hair. They were efficient about taking information and issuing IDs; tags with name, ship's name, and a local code number spat out the end of a machine in just a few seconds.

"You're now free to move about the station," the one with the most glitter on his uniform said. "You must wear the ID tag clearly visible at all times."

Ky nodded; his assistants pulled a cover over the tag-making machine, and they all left dockside.

"That was odd," Hugh said. "No welcoming speech, nothing."

"I'm going to call the others," Ky said.

"Ansible?"

"No. I know that's the most secure method we've got, but I want to know how the station's own system works. We'll need to meet. There's bound to be some central location . . . Captains' Guild, if nothing else. Let's get our security monitors mounted dockside—"

"Right away," Hugh said, nodding. "Munitions draw thieves on the most law-abiding ports." From his tone, he'd already decided that Gretna wasn't one of those.

Law-abiding port or not, Gretna Station had a Crown & Spears branch office just two doors away from the Captains' Guild. Ky found that Vatta Transport had a sizable balance there, drawing minimal interest, and the manager accepted her identity without question. He ushered her into his private office and set an obvious privacy device on his desk, flicking it on. "Trading in munitions?" he asked then.

Ky wondered why he didn't trust the privacy devices no doubt built into the entire branch, but that was not something to ask. She shrugged. "Trade goes where the profit goes. In these unsettled times—"

"Of course," he said. "If you want advice, I'd go with General Munitions instead of Gretna Munitions Outlet—"

"Thank you," Ky said. "That's the recommendation in Vatta's records as well; the notation is that quality control is better. I'm glad to have recent confirmation. I need to pick up medical supplies as well—any recommendations there?"

"Supplies alone or medically trained personnel? You might be able to pick up some of the latter at the local indenture auction house."

"Indenture auction house?"

He looked down, running his finger along the side of his desktop display. "You haven't been to Gretna before . . . there's a long-standing tradition of indentured labor here."

"You mean . . . slaves?"

"They prefer not to call them slaves. Criminals working off their court costs and fines, is the way Gretnans look at it. Recently, with less trade coming through, it's become more obvious. At any rate, if someone buys out a contract, they can get contracted labor fairly cheaply. I happen to know there's a surplus of medically trained personnel right now. The listing's available." He cleared his throat. "And you probably noticed . . . the native Gretnans are pretty much all of one phenotype, and they distrust those of other phenotypes. With your . . . uh . . . I'd be careful, if I were you."

With her darker skin, he meant. Ky scowled. "So why does Crown & Spears deal with them?" But the answer was obvious and she said it along with him as he shrugged. "Trade and profit, I know. All right—but I thought there was a prohibition in the Commercial Code about slavery."

"There is. Gretna isn't a signatory to the full Code and as I said, they don't call it slavery. Under their legal system, working out a debt or a sentence is quite legal. We asked about that before opening a branch office here; our legal staff have reviewed it regularly, and they say it's within the law as it now stands."

"Do they make up charges against transients—ship personnel, for instance?"

"They say not, but I would say it's happened. Recently, with ansibles down and trade in decline, I suspect it's become more common. More often, a ship runs out of funds, can't pay the docking or air charges, and they seize the ship and crew. Under their law, anyone on such a ship is equally guilty."

"I don't have any notations about that in the Vatta database," Ky said.

"No—well, Vatta's always maintained a healthy balance, as you see, and usually unloaded, loaded, and was out of here in just a few days. They don't prey on the prosperous who can always pay a few extra charges. We've tried to tell the Gretnans they're damaging their own economy— fifty years ago, they had much more trade coming through and even some outside investment—but they don't want advice from outsiders, they say."

"I'll be careful," Ky said. "I have no intention of overdrawing our account. Do you know if they're trading with this current crop of pirates?"

"I couldn't say, really. We have a very small staff here, and there are security concerns . . . I've been told not to pry." His expression said more. Ky could easily imagine the pirates dealing with Gretna for those confiscated ships. Or their crew.

"There's another ship in the inbound lanes," she said instead. "I didn't see anything about its arrival time on the notice boards. We looked at the beacon as we passed them, and it said Polson. I wondered if it was pirates."

"I doubt it." He grimaced. "Polson's a very small colony—we don't have a branch there yet—mostly genetic humods, like a lot of start-ups. Humods aren't popular here. There's been trade in the past, but the current situation has made everyone more jumpy. Word is they're not being allowed to dock without special inspections and restrictions, and so far they've refused."

That sounded more like pirates than legitimate traders to Ky; she wondered why the manager didn't think so. She had just opened her mouth to ask when his comunit beeped. He took the call then turned to her. "I'm sorry, Captain Vatta, but there is another matter I must attend to. Please don't hesitate to contact me again if we can assist you with your trading."

Within four hours, she had compared her balance with the daily dock charges and the prices listed at General Munitions, determined how much she could afford, and settled in for a meal at the Captains' Guild to discuss with Argelos and Pettygrew how the purchases should be allocated among ships. The Captains' Guild was almost empty; three pale-skinned officers, obviously local, sat at the far end of the dining room, well out of earshot. Even so, despite the telltales glowing on their table to indicate that its security block was on full, Ky felt uneasy enough to put her own privacy device on the table.

"We're going to need medical as well as munitions," she said. "How are you fixed for that?"

"I have eight medboxes and a small operating theater," Pettygrew said. "We have two surgeons and nine other medical personnel, mostly direct patient care but one specialist in medical imaging. I think that's all my ship needs, really."

"That's more than I have," Ky said. "I'm impressed."

"More than I have, too," Argelos said. "I have five med-boxes and two Spaceforce-trained medics. You've been on that merc ship—what did they have?"

"It looked like a military hospital," Ky said. "Operating suites, trauma sets, lots of medboxes, lots of personnel. I'm assuming also lots of equipment, though I didn't see all of it, by any means."

"Was it a specialized hospital ship?"

"No. One of their larger warships, somewhat larger than *Vanguard*."

"Hmmm. I can see if we get in more battles, we may really need additional medical capacity, but I don't know where I'm going to put it. I guess we could move some functions outboard to one of the cargo holds . . ."

"If we become the force we've talked about, the only cargo we'll be carrying is our own necessary supplies," Ky said.

"You're right," Argelos said, scrubbing his head with both hands. "I guess I'm still thinking like a trader-privateer."

"I had the same problem," Ky said. "It took a round of food poisoning to make me realize what was missing."

"So—do you think this place has anything in the way of medical supplies?" Argelos asked.

Ky told them what the Crown & Spears manager had told her about the Gretnan labor market. "I looked," she said, "and they list forty-six medical personnel, including two trauma surgeons, three surgical nurses, a medical imaging tech, a neuropsych specialist, and others. I hate the thought of buying people, but—"

"Well, we wouldn't keep them as indentured," Argelos said. "What's this likely to cost?"

"I don't know. I have the feeling that if they know we

want them, the price will go up. According to Crown &
Spears, we can bid through an agent, and the manager's
willing to act as our agent. He says he often does, and
they won't know that we're the ones bidding. He and I
both hope. The munitions are listed already; we know
what they cost. Same with medical supplies. But we need
to maintain a reserve—" She explained about the Gretnans'
habit of seizing ships and crews that defaulted on any payments. "I'll just have to set a limit for what we can spend
at the auction, and hope that yields something. Meantime,
I've looked at your supply requests, and this is what I can
afford." She handed over the hardcopies; Argelos and
Pettygrew looked them over.

"I can add some credits to that," Pettygrew said. "It's
not much, but it would cover my ship's docking fees, air
fees, and crew rations."

"That's a big help," Ky said. "I'm sure Crown & Spears
would set up an account for you, if you don't want to
merge with the Vatta accounts."

"Merging's fine," Pettygrew said, with a crooked smile.
"We're already sharing risks; we might as well share
resources."

"And I still have a little cargo to sell off," Argelos said.
"That may help, and it clears out a hold for military
supplies."

"Excellent," Ky said. "Now, since neither of you has
beam weapons and I have two, I thought I'd assign each
of you more than a third of the missiles we can afford.
That still won't fill your racks—well, not unless your cargo
sells very high—but it should give you something to work
with."

"That's very generous," Pettygrew said. "Thank you."

"Yes, thanks," Argelos said. "But don't leave yourself
too short."

Ky went back to Crown & Spears after lunch to give the manager her limits for the indentured auction and explain what she was looking for.

"I'll do my best," he said. "Most bidders are agents for someone; in fact, you aren't my only client this time. With any luck, they won't figure it out. I think the prices won't be too high at this auction; the hospitals and clinics here and down on the planet are fully staffed, so medical personnel have been selling as general labor. Especially if they're . . . um . . . more like you."

"Yes. Well, I appreciate your service," Ky said. Back at the ship, she told Hugh how she had allocated the munitions purchases.

"We could fight an engagement," Hugh said, shaking his head at the total. "I'd have to hope we weren't outnumbered."

"We have to have docking fees, and we need more supplies than just munitions," Ky said. "And I'm hoping to get some medical personnel. At . . . er . . . auction." She explained about the indenture policy.

Hugh grimaced. "That's disgusting. I hadn't heard that about them before. What about that ship we passed? Hear anything more about it?"

"The Crown & Spears manager knew about Polson," Ky said. "Legitimate small colony, he said. Apparently the Gretnans want to run them through some additional—and no doubt expensive—inspection procedure because they're genetic humods. So they're keeping them at a distance."

"They don't like us; they don't like humods . . . I'm coming to agree with Lee about these people. Fairly nasty lot, aren't they? Are you going to try selling these Fishies anything?"

"Nothing . . . interesting," Ky said. "If you find anything innocuous on inventory, I'd be glad to make a little more.

We're going to be tight, and we don't want to be caught short."

"Quite so. I'll see what I can find and check with you before listing it."

By the middle of the next shift, deliveries started arriving at dockside.

Ky could not help noticing that the Gretna workers— all as pale as the Port Security personnel—avoided looking at her and her crew when she faced them and spoke only when spoken to . . . but behind her back, as the security monitors proved, they stared and muttered to one another. The mutters, amplified and recorded by the monitors, did nothing to improve the crew's attitude toward the locals.

"I told you they were Fishbellies," Lee said. "All right: I have blue eyes and light hair, too, but I'm not like they are. I don't care what color someone's skin and eyes are, as long as they're decent; these idiots seem to think color's what makes 'em decent."

"You call them Fishbellies," Ky pointed out. "That's as bad as their calling some of us Mudders."

"It's not," Lee said, "because I'm not calling them that because of their color. It's their attitude that makes 'em Fishies."

"Well, stay in the ship, then," Ky said. "It's hard enough dealing with them without having to keep a lid on you, too." She did not mention that his recent training in military etiquette seemed to have vanished under the first real stressor. That would come later.

She had left Hugh supervising the unloading dockside; now she took a call from him.

"Better get out here, Captain; we've got a complaint from Port Security. They don't like our monitors."

"There's nothing wrong with our monitors," Ky said. "We aren't spying on anyone else."

"They want to see the captain," Hugh said, without answering her comment. Ky sighed and headed for dockside, glancing at the bridge display from those monitors as she went. A man in Port Security uniform stood next to Hugh; the Gretna workers who should have been moving pallets into *Vanguard*'s cargo holds were clustered, heads together, near the dock entrance. She reached out and increased magnification on one image. Yes, they were smirking. Ky introduced herself to the Port Security officer in a neutral voice.

"Private security monitors are illegal," the man said, not quite meeting her eyes. "Only law enforcement is authorized to place monitoring devices. Such devices must be removed at once."

"I'm sorry," Ky said. "Everywhere else I've been, dockside security is the responsibility of the shipowner."

"This isn't everywhere else," the man said. "This is Gretna, a place for *honest* people. People who don't need to steal."

Ky managed not to raise her eyebrows. No one proclaims honesty as much as the liar.

"If you don't trust our honesty," he went on, "how can we trust yours? Only the dishonest are suspicious."

"We'll remove the monitors," Ky said. And replace them with less detectable ones or human eyes . . . She had the weapons crews free to stand watches outside the ship, if that's what it was going to take.

"Very well," the man said. "No more cargo will be loaded until you do."

"Hugh," Ky said, struggling to keep all traces of anger out of her voice. "See that our equipment is removed from dockside. I will wait here while you arrange it." Very shortly, the Gannetts came out and detached the monitors from the dockside bulkheads. Ky followed them back into the ship without another word to the officer, leaving Hugh to supervise loading once more.

"They're up to something, Captain," Jon Gannett said as soon as they were well inside the ship.

"I could just figure that out," Ky said tartly. She was suddenly angry, so angry that she felt the back of her neck burning.

"Yes, ma'am," he said. "Reckon you'll want some special surveillance?"

"Yes," Ky said, struggling to hold down the anger enough to think clearly. "Inspect every missile and its control system—make sure they're not sabotaged in some way, and that they are what the invoice says. Check the other supplies, too: I wouldn't put it past these people to sell us contaminated food. Internal surveillance, in case they get the notion to wander out of the cargo holds or stick their own little devices somewhere . . . and I'd better go talk with the other captains." She called them and suggested meeting at the Captains' Guild again.

The others, she found, had had the same annoying experience. "It's our dock space," Pettygrew said. "They charge enough and they don't even provide surveillance; I don't see why they object to us having it. It's an insult."

"They've got to be up to something," Argelos said.

"I know," Ky said. "But we need the munitions and other supplies. I'm sure you've already thought of this, but have your people check—"

"—everything," Pettygrew said. "I am, believe me. Do you have external video monitors on your ship?

"Like nearscan?"

"No—actual video. We have external monitors that retract in flight, but in dock we can bring them up to see most of the hull. I've got mine out now, just in case."

Ky, remembering the near-attack at Lastway, felt a cold chill down her back. She had not thought of that. If the Gretnans were up to something like that—but surely, if they attacked ships in dock, it would be in her father's files. "All we have are the docking cams fore and aft," she said. "They don't begin to cover the whole hull." Though they could be useful, she thought; the Gretnans couldn't keep her from using equipment on the ship itself.

"I don't think they'll attack us," Argelos said. "I think they're more likely to cheat us some way, or try to. I've put two of my crew on watch at the cargo bay, just keeping an eye out."

"Pilferage we can handle," Ky said. "But I've been on a ship attacked from the outside near a station—so everyone keep an eye on the traffic around us. We can do that with nearscan, even though we don't have true video. I have to say I'm surprised at Osman on this one—I'd have thought he'd be more careful."

Second-shift the next day, the Crown & Spears manager called her. "I've got your personnel," he said. "Do you want them all to report to your ship? They're all right here in the office, with the guards."

"I'm on my way," Ky said.

"They're . . . um . . . listed as general labor," he said. "You said you needed more cargo handlers, right?" The warning in that was clear: he didn't want the Gretnans to know that she had specifically asked for medical personnel.

"That's right," she said. "We have a lot of stuff to shift; so does *Sharra's Gift*. We'll share them back and forth for a while. I'll be there shortly, with Captain Argelos."

She called Argelos and told him that they now had "enough cargo handlers."

"But—" he said.

"Cargo handlers," Ky said. "That's what we needed."

Even over a com line she could hear the gears clicking in his head.

"Right," he said. "I'm just hoping you got strong ones. We have some heavy loads over here."

"Meet me at Crown & Spears," Ky said. "We'll divide them up—better bring some guards along; I'm sure the Gretnans won't want these people wandering around unguarded."

"Right," Argelos said.

At Crown & Spears, she found the manager's office and the corridor outside crowded with men and women in skimpy gray tunics and short pants, their feet in what looked like cardboard sandals. They all looked undernourished and hopeless; they were all darker than the typical Gretnan. The Gretnan guards, pink and fleshy, smirked over them; they held weapons.

"You may go," Ky said to them. "I have my own guards."

"But—"

"Under your law, the indenture owner is responsible for security; I checked on that. These people are mine now; I will use my own guards."

They looked at each other; then the one with a couple of stripes on his sleeve shrugged, and the Gretnan guards shuffled out.

"Well, let's see what we have here," Ky said to the manager, who handed her a list; a stack of ID folders was on his desk. Her eyes widened. He had bought eighteen people for the amount she'd stated. Everyone she'd marked as especially interesting, plus an assortment of others.

"Please—" said one of the women. "I'm really not general labor; I'm a trained—"

Ky held up her hand; the woman stopped, almost flinching. "I am aware of your listed qualifications," she said. "At the moment, it is in everyone's best interests to concentrate on our immediate need for cargo handlers." She glanced from corner to corner of the office, hoping they'd understand. She saw dawning awareness. "Now, Captain Argelos, from this list I'm prepared to *lend* you numbers five, seven, nine, and eleven, along with fifteen, sixteen, and seventeen." She handed him the list. "Those numbers, stand forward."

Those numbers included one of the trauma surgeons, two surgical nurses, and four general nurses, two of them certified for advanced practice. Argelos nodded, handing the list back. "That's fine—they look capable enough. Stenson, take these workers back to our ship; make sure they don't stray."

"Sergeant Gannett, take the rest back to *Vanguard* while I settle up with the manager here. Captain Argelos, you'll want their ID packets."

A half hour later, she was back aboard *Vanguard*. As she came aboard, she felt the tension in her crew. "Where are they?" she asked Hugh.

"In the mess, eating the first decent meal they've had since they were taken," he said. "These people—!" She knew he didn't mean the new ones.

"I'm going down to explain to them," Ky said. "Here are their ID packets. Look them over when you get a chance, just in case there's a problem we need to know about." The ten were already changed, wearing a variety of clothes her crew had donated, mostly civilian but a few military knit shirts. The feet she could see had warm ship socks instead of the flimsy sandals. They were eating as if they were half starved. She didn't doubt they were.

"Captain on deck," one of the Gannetts said. They looked up, spoons and forks halfway to their mouths, apprehensive.

"Take it easy," Ky said. "First, I want to welcome you aboard *Vanguard*. I'm Captain Vatta. *Vanguard* is, as you probably figured out, a military ship, and you were chosen specifically for your medical backgrounds." No one said anything; Ky went on after waiting a moment. "Though it was necessary to purchase your indentures at auction, pretending we wanted general labor, in fact I wanted to hire— not buy—medical personnel. I apologize for continuing that pretense in the Crown & Spears office, but I deemed it necessary. From the moment you crossed into our ship space, I consider you free persons. If any of you do not want to ship with us, you are free to leave, though I cannot guarantee what the Gretnans will do."

"I can," said the same woman who had spoken up in the manager's office. "They'll put us back in the rack again. I'd do anything to get out of here."

"Then here's what I propose," Ky said. She hitched a hip on one corner of a table. "We'll take you with us; you'll do whatever medical duties come up. Right now I don't have enough resources to pay you a salary, but if we aren't blown up in some battle, I will when we get to a system with a working financial ansible. In the meantime, you'll have clothes, decent food, and good treatment. How does that suit?"

"You have medical work for us?" That was a man . . . the neuropsych specialist, her implant informed her.

"We have had, and we may well have more. We just purchased additional medical supplies. I'm afraid you'll have to make do with what we have, but I'll certainly take advice on how they should be employed. I suggest you finish your meal, sort yourselves into your assigned quarters, and then let me know what your other needs are. If you take a survey of the medical supplies and equipment we have aboard, and tell me of anything particularly urgent,

I might be able to fit it in—or not. Our accounts are low right now."

"Thank you," the woman said; the others nodded. She sounded near tears. "I can't—we can't thank you enough. You don't know—"

"Glad to help," Ky said. "I wish I could have freed everyone. By the way, I don't think any of you should leave the ship, for any reason, just in case." They all nodded. She glanced at Jon Gannett. "Assign someone to help them find their places; I'm heading back to the bridge."

"Wait, please!" It was the woman again. "You have to be careful—you don't know what they do. You said low on funds—they'll claim your ship didn't pay some bills, and seize her—"

"I have a reserve," Ky said. "Please don't worry—" Then it occurred to her that these people might know more details about how the Gretnans seized ships. "But tell me—what exactly happened? Did they seize you while you were off the ship, or did they board with some excuse, or damage the ship, or what?"

This produced a barrage of answers; Ky held up her hand and they quieted. "One at a time," Ky said. "You first." She nodded at the woman.

"I don't know anything specific," the woman said. "I was in my stateroom—it was a chartered passenger ship—washing my hair, when suddenly there were all these men in there, and they grabbed me and dragged me away. They said I was a criminal; they took my identification and shoved me out in the corridor—I still had shampoo in my hair; they wouldn't let me rinse it or anything—and shackled us all together."

"I was on the station concourse, eating with some friends," a man offered. "Suddenly Station Security came in, a whole squad, and grabbed us and everyone else in the restaurant just stared. They threw us down on the floor, put cuffs on us, wouldn't listen to anything we said."

"I haven't seen any of the ship's crew or officers since we were taken," another man said. "What I heard from people from another ship, taken quite a while before ours, was that they separate ships' crews from any passengers. One steward from that ship was mistaken for a passenger, and that's how they knew."

"So the attack came while you were docked," Ky said.

"Yes. We'd been here only two days, scheduled to depart third-shift, ship time. Some of us had planned dinner on the station, just for something to do. Others stayed in—it didn't matter."

"Have you heard about other forms of attack?"

"From other prisoners, you mean?" That was the neurosurgeon. "Nothing recent. Stories passed down through the cells . . . armed ships attacking out where ships come in, forcing them to dock here so they can ransack them. The people I met had all been attacked while docked at the station, like our ship."

"A woman in my cage said they'd used gas on her ship," said a woman at the back. "They piped it through the service umbilicals and put everyone to sleep—when they woke up, they were all caged."

"Any idea how long this has been going on?"

"Just since the ansibles went down, is what I heard." The first woman again. "I don't think they could've gotten away with it before—people would have known."

"Thank you," Ky said. "You've been most helpful. Let me assure you again that you are welcome, you are safe, and I consider you free men and women. And now I must return to the bridge." To ensure that they were protected from chemical attacks through the umbilicals, among other things. She called down to Sam Gulandar and told him to take protective measures.

"Put us on internal air supply only?" he asked. "That'll cut our safe transit time when we leave."

"Better than letting them capture us," Ky said. "I think we're safe until they think we've spent all we can—but be alert." Then she called the other captains, this time using the onboard ansible, and warned them.

A few hours later, a port official insisted on talking to Ky; she sighed and made her way out to the dock. "You bought indentured workers and I don't see them working!" he said. "What kind of scam are you running?"

Ky raised her eyebrows. She had anticipated something like this. "They are handling cargo aboard, not the dockside transfers," she said. "You didn't want me to deprive your citizen-workers of their pay, did you?"

His mouth opened and closed. "Oh. Well, yes, of course, you would still have to pay for dockside transfers . . . I suppose it makes sense."

"Believe me," Ky said, "I intend to get my money's worth out of those workers. We have a lot of load balancing to do, and my regular crew have their own duties."

"I see," he said. "Well." His pale eyes shifted back and forth, looking for anything he could complain about, but finding nothing. "All right, then," he said. "As long as you pay all your fees on time."

"I fully intend to," Ky said.

Over the next three shifts, almost all the munitions and other supplies were delivered, and Ky watched the Vatta account at Crown & Spears carefully. Already they'd been hit with unexpected "special delivery" charges, and she didn't want to hock one of the few remaining diamonds if she could help it.

Finally, she thumbprinted the last charge slip; there

were still a few credits in the account. Each ship still had
a pallet or two of mixed goods to load, but the three captains had agreed to dismiss the local dockside workers as
soon as the last order had arrived, not wanting to incur
any more charges.

"Can we be ready to leave in six hours?" Ky asked the
other captains. "The sooner we're out, the happier I'll be.
I'm switching to internal air supply immediately."

"We'll be loaded in four," Pettygrew said.

"Three for me," Argelos said.

"Three to four for us," Ky said. "I'll contact the stationmaster about the departure queue. There's been no traffic
for days, and we're already balanced—shouldn't be a spin
problem."

The stationmaster thought differently, no surprise there.
"It is impossible. You must not jump the queue."

"What queue?" Ky asked. "There's nothing on the
boards."

"Not all flights are listed," he said, his pale eyes narrowed. "It is none of your business what other flights are
in the queue; you outlanders are always prying into the
affairs of others. The earliest departure I can give you is . . .
forty-seven hours. You are required to remain in your ship
for the final twenty-five hours prior to departure, to allow
us to verify that all debts have been paid and no crimes
committed have yet to be discovered."

"I just paid the last bill," Ky said, feeling her anger rise
again. "And no one's been committing crimes."

"Regulations," the man said, sneering. "We've had
experience with your kind. Sneaking around off the ships,
crew buying personal items the captain claims not to know
about. Do you want that departure time or not?"

"Yes, thank you," Ky said, through her teeth, and cut
the connection as soon as he'd confirmed it.

"These have to be the most paranoid people in the universe," Hugh said when Ky had shut down the comlink and notified the other captains of their departure slot.

"Or greedy," Lee said. "This way, they get another two days' docking fees and air tax out of us."

FIVE

For the next forty-seven hours, Ky watched the dwindling credits in the Vatta account. If she had to sell that diamond, she would have to do it before the final twenty-five-hour restriction. With five hours to go, she called the Crown & Spears manager and asked his advice.

"They might hit you with a final charge of several hundred credits per ship," he said. "But if you'd like to arrange a line of credit—I really think you're safer aboard ship, frankly—I know that Vatta Transport has been a Crown & Spears client for decades, and I am confident that your company will take care of it when the ansibles come back up."

"Thank you," Ky said. Once, she would have expected such a courtesy, having seen how the Crown & Spears branch back home treated her father. Now she knew how much he risked, and not only with the Gretnans. "I'd very much appreciate it."

"My pleasure," he said. "I will need your voiceprinted authorization—a moment while I access the form—" He read it to her, and she repeated the relevant authorization paragraph as he recorded her voice. "Now here's what you'll see when you access your account. The balance will drop, and show the overdraft, but we will honor the draw on the account from Gretnan sources. That way you'll know how much you owe, should you come to a system with working ansibles before ours comes back online, and the Gretnans will not know how much your line of credit is."

She had to assume the Gretnans had a hook into financials somehow, because the balance continued to dwindle . . . paused at zero as the twenty-five-hour limit approached. Then—at thirty hours—another charge appeared and her balance dropped below zero. But her financial status report from the Gretna officials still showed green.

Finally, at forty-six hours fifty minutes, the stationmaster announced they were clear for undock, and counted them down.

Vanguard eased out of the docking bay, centimeter by careful centimeter. Ky knew that Argelos and Pettygrew were undocking at the same moment, as ordered.

As the bow cleared the station's hull, Ky let out the breath she'd been holding. "Well, that's over with," she said. "Go on and bring up longscan now."

"I wouldn't be too sure," Hugh said. He pointed to the forward scans, which had just come alive as they cleared the station. "Something's going on—I didn't think there was anything docked that close to us. Of course we weren't allowed off the ship, and they could fox the data station communications sent us. And that ship with the Polson beacon is still out there, near-zero relative motion."

"It's not my concern," Ky said. "That one is—" A small ship, barely shuttle size, was pulling back from an adjoining docking bay on the station hull as well.

Ky called the stationmaster. "We have traffic portside," she said. "Warn them off."

"Not your business," the stationmaster said.

"*Vanguard*, I have a small craft approaching on my flank," said Pettygrew in her other ear.

"So do I," said Argelos. "And I don't like the look of it. We can't kick up the drive until we're a safe distance from the station."

Everything the indentured medical personnel had told her made it clear what was going on.

"They're going to try to board," she said. "In a moment, they'll claim—"

A loud squawk on the official channel nearly deafened her. "Thieves!" said an angry voice. "Stop at once! All three of you! Shut down your engines. Prepare for boarding!"

"Not in my lifetime," Ky said to her bridge crew. "Do they really think they can take all three of us?" She touched the alarm that sent the ship to battle stations. "Prepare to repel boarders," she said into the shipcom. "Unknown number, unknown tech at this time." Then she called Argelos and Pettygrew. "We're expecting an attempt to board; you'll probably have them, too."

"I see them," Argelos said. "I've got my people arming up now. Damned Fishies! Should've known they'd try something. I wish I knew how many . . ."

"If that shuttle was full of them, quite a lot. They know how big our crews are, though they don't know how well we'll fight."

"We're not in position to support one another," Hugh pointed out. "We're still too close to use the beam without risking backflash damage; we can't use the missiles because they're inside the auto-delay distance."

"To keep us from blowing a hole in ourselves, yes. And they know that, because they sold them to us. What do they have for close-in weapons?"

"Well, they can't use missiles, either, until we get farther out, and they won't, if their shuttles are this close to us. They have the perimeter platforms—"

"Light-hours away," Ky said. "We're in no immediate danger there. So how *do* they expect to attack us—with handguns?"

"Tools from their repair facilities to breach the hull and put armed parties aboard. And we don't have any weapons designed to repel them."

"That shuttle's almost touching our hull," Lee put in. "They're evacuating . . . no, it's an EVA crew. In armor."

"If we had rocks," Ky said, "we could at least throw them. The next time I have money, I'm going to put *something* out there we can repel boarders with."

"They've got some kind of tools," Lee said, over his shoulder. "Can't tell what, exactly—"

"They'll be used to boarding hostile ships," Hugh said. "But they'll expect disorganized, incompetent resistance. May I suggest that the captain get into armor?"

"I suggest everyone does," Ky said. "They can't get through the hull instantly . . . I hope . . ." She headed for her cabin, where she kept her personal armor. She and Hugh had made a plan for this situation, if it occurred, but they'd had no time to drill the crew in it. She suspected the others hadn't, either. If everyone did what they were told, let the military crew handle it, casualties should be low—or even nonexistent, she hoped. And when it was over, and they were far enough away, she would enjoy blowing holes in Gretna Station . . .

Over the ship com came Hugh's steady voice: "Battle stations. Battle stations. Prepare for hostile boarding. Remember your assignments. Nonmilitary crew, take cover and stay at your assigned locations. Fighting crew, report now . . ."

Ky's implant gave her the crew reports: where they were,

what weapons they had, what their sensors told them. She knew, through the implant's connection to the ship, the instant an enemy hand touched the hull . . . and exactly what it was doing.

"Emergency air locks are supposed to be easy to exit," she muttered. "Not enter . . ." *Vanguard*'s hatch lock finally deformed and let go under the combined attack of vacuum torches and brute force. "And that's an expensive repair. Damn them." But the attack on the air lock had been only a decoy—on the far side of the ship, a cargo hold opened suddenly, and a string of space-armored bodies drifted into it. Some cargo loader had managed to get the hold lock code. If they had all of them, things could get very difficult very quickly; the boarders would enter behind the obvious defense positions based on air locks and crew passages. Ky wanted to race to the bridge, but Hugh had convinced her that she should stay here, in her office, until an invading force came close. Then . . . then she would find out if Osman's deviousness actually worked.

For the first time since taking his ship, Ky had reason to thank Osman for his piratical ways. The Gretnans had walked right past hiding places and the access hatches to secret passages, apparently in the belief that *Vanguard* was nothing more than the armed trader she seemed. Ky's implant tapped into the onboard surveillance, and she followed the invaders' progress to the bridge, the splitting off of smaller parties to take control of the missile batteries.

She spared a quick thought for the other captains, who would have improvised something, she was sure, as she eeled forward in a conduit just big enough for her and its intended contents on the slick, silent platform meant for just such contingencies. Then she was behind the bridge overhead, looking out the carefully placed fish-eye lens that gave her a view of the whole space. Pilot, bridge officer, communications tech, all seated on the floor with their hands on their heads, while two of the enemy aimed weapons at them, and five more examined the controls, weapons slung. One of them was talking.

"This way, we get the ships already loaded up, y'see. Make a fine addition to our fleet, they will, once we've washed out the stench of you Mudders. We'll just put you in holding until another ship comes and takes you off our hands."

"What kind of ship?" Lee asked.

Another unpleasant laugh. "A ship that trades in such as you. Well, them others. What's a decent man like you doing hanging about with Mudders?"

First things first. Choice of rounds . . . Ky decided on two solid rounds followed by frangibles with low-dispersal chemstun. Supposed to be low-dispersal: Ky put on the emergency filter mask anyway, and pulled out several more to toss down to her crew. It would be inconvenient to have reinforcements arrive . . . yet closing off the bridge physically would warn the enemy. But there was another way . . . through her implant, she slammed compartment hatches at a distance. Sure enough, one of the two guarding the prisoners moved to the bridge entrance and looked down the passage.

"What was that?" asked one of the others.

"Nothin' I can see," the guard said, shrugging. "Doors slamming . . ."

"Doors don't slam by themselves."

"Well, I didn't see nobody. If there was somebody, I'd of seen 'em."

"Call Merin. See if he's got anythin'."

The guard muttered something but spoke into a shoulder mike, then shook his head. "Nuthin' from Merin. He says he's got eight under guard just off the cargo hold." Ky unlatched the little drop-hatch Osman had installed so conveniently near the fish-eye, and with two quick shots dropped the guard at the entrance and the one standing over her crewmembers. Then, as her implant shut the bridge hatch, she took out another two before they even turned around to see what happened, the frangible rounds bursting on impact, releasing the chemstun. Another one, close enough to be affected, slumped down. Before she could take aim on the last two, Lee had thrown himself toward the weapons the Gretnans had taken from them. He took out one. Hugh's moddy arm melted the barrel of the last Gretnan's weapon; the man dropped it and threw up his hands, shaking.

"Don't kill me! Don't! Please—"

Ky dropped the filter masks she had ready. "Mask up, folks. Supposed to be low-dispersal, but—"

"Good timing, Captain," Hugh said without looking up. With his other hand, he had already pulled a filter mask from his belt and slapped it to his face. Lee scooped up a mask for himself and tossed one to Theo Dannon. "What do you want done with this prisoner?"

"It depends," Ky said. "If he offers any resistance whatever, kill him. Otherwise, make sure he's secured. I'll be there in a moment." Surely Osman had planned for the need to have the secret watcher actually arrive in person . . . there. Another drop-down hatch. Ky opened it and eased through, making sure she didn't come in contact with the area in which the chemical should have stayed.

The Gretnan, now with hands bound behind him, stared at her, wide-eyed with what looked like both fear and horror, flinching when she grinned at him.

"You," she said. "You're alive only as long as you behave. Get that?"

"I didn't do nothin'. It's not my fault . . . you're all thieves anyway."

"What?"

"All your kind. You know. You come in and take stuff, you don't work for it."

"I paid for it," Ky said. "Perfectly good credits from Crown & Spears."

"But that's not real work," he said. "You just had them credits, and for all I know—what I think is—it was prob'ly stolen anyway. People like you don't deserve money."

Lee cocked a fist, but Ky shook her head at him. "You don't want his slime on your skin," she said. The man spat. "I think you need to go to sleep awhile," she said, switching to a trank round and shooting him in the buttock. In moments his head sagged and he fell onto his side.

From the bridge to the captain's cabin, their way was clear. Ky led them into the secret compartment and along between bulkheads, aft and down, as her implant forwarded data from the surveillance equipment.

"Bad news from the others, Captain," Hugh said in her skullphone. "Pettygrew says he's making a fighting retreat, but he's cut off from the bridge and from drives; apparently they'd gotten cargo hold codes for all the ships. Argelos still has control of drives, but not the bridge. They've taken casualties."

"So have we," Ky said, looking down at the latest, the number two engineer, sprawled in a pool of blood and splattered flesh. The intruders here were all dead, but she had been just that instant too late for Foxeham, who hadn't stayed in the hidey-hole he'd been assigned. Neither had

Seeley. Just as Hugh had predicted, some of the civs hadn't followed orders. "One dead, one wounded." Seeley would recover, but right now he was in shock, partly from a shattered leg and partly from seeing Foxeham die in front of him. "But the drives are secure now. We've made contact with the aft batteries; we're about to squeeze the bastards between us."

She left Twigg from Environmental with Seeley, with orders to stay put until someone came to help him get Seeley to sick bay. At least she had medical experts now; surely they had stayed where they were told. Now, with Lee at her shoulder, she moved back into the cover of Osman's labyrinth. Just ahead, a cluster of intruders—the most heavily armed, since they had attacked the aft battery and armory—continued their attempt to break through the barricades her aft crew had thrown up. In addition to the chemical rounds for their light weapons, they had two cutters at work on the bulkhead aft of the battery hatch, trying to cut in behind the defenders.

"Jon Gannett reports the forward batteries clear, all intruders accounted for, forward of bulkhead sixteen, all decks," Hugh said. "Do you want reinforcement?"

For a moment she weighed a faster mop-up here against the evident immediate peril to *Bassoon* and *Sharra's Gift*. Her own ship's safety had to come first. "Link me to Jon," she said. "The faster we clear this ship, the faster we can help the others."

As the Gannetts worked their way aft, they reported on two more intruders, detached individually, trying to break into the ship safe. These were now disposed of, and now Jon spoke in her skullphone.

"Captain, I have you in view. Permission to close up?"

"Come ahead," Ky said softly. The intruders had shown no sign of having competent acoustic surveillance, but she wasn't going to take chances. "The intruders are about two meters away, working on the aft port battery bulkhead. Our crew's in position, ready to surprise them now you're here. Starboard battery's got about the same situation, but the enemy haven't started digging into the bulkhead yet."

This time Ky felt a wicked glee as she prepared to signal the attack through another one of Osman's secret panels. She could almost admire him for the way he'd set up the ship. Here they were below the deck level; the panels lifted up. Osman had even installed ricochet baffles, not that those would help much with frangibles.

"On three," she said, and flicked her fingers—one, two, three—and five deck hatches lifted. She had a perfect view of boots and lower legs as they all fired simultaneously; the low-power solid slugs had plenty of punch to knock the intruders off their legs. Their return fire was wild, unaimed; an instant later the aft battery hatch opened and her battery crew poured through to finish them off. Ky knew her shots had gone home, but it was over so fast she didn't feel anything but mild satisfaction.

She and the others emerged, set a watch on the passage both ways, and then she and Martin inspected the intruders' arms and equipment.

"I think they brought only the two drills," Martin said. "That's why the starboard squad is just waiting around . . ."

"They made a mess of that," Ky said, pointing to the deep grooves in the bulkhead. "We'll have to get one of the engineers to check it out, and repair it eventually. But for now—secure these drills, and let's go clear the ship."

The starboard squad of intruders were standing around "like idiots," Martin reported, making loud threats to the battery crew, who made no answer. "Lousy communication among them—they should know their people are being massacred."

"Complacent," Ky said. "We'd better not be." This time they attacked at deck level, using the cross-passage between the two batteries. Martin edged ahead, extending a spider probe on the deck itself, where it would be least visible. As Ky's implant had indicated, the intruders looked careless and complacent, weapons held loosely, the men— they were all men—slouched against the bulkhead with their masks unhooked.

Ky signaled a change of ammunition, to chemical rounds, and checked the seal on her own mask as she slipped out her magazine and fitted another. No one said anything. She checked her implant readings again. Something not quite clear farther aft down that other passage . . . she called in data from the nearest of Osman's fish-eyes, and there they were, a squad farther down the passage, just out of line of sight. Weapons ready, masks tight, half facing each way. So they did suspect something, but didn't know which direction an attack would come from.

Fine. She was in the mood for more of a fight. She signaled again, this time the number and location. Jon Gannett shrugged, grinning behind his mask. She knew she was grinning, too. She took a breath and spun rapidly around the corner, raking the first group with chemstun rounds that shattered on the bulkhead. Two of the intruders fell at once; another tried to seal his mask and fell to Martin's solid round. As the rear guard moved forward, rounds bouncing off the curve of the bulkhead, the battery hatch opened and the battery crew took them in the flank. Ky hit the deck as rounds richocheted around her. Something slammed into her shoulder; her back. The deck felt hot under her. She heard one of the battery crew swearing in his native language as he took a leg wound.

Then it was over, a firefight that had lasted scant seconds. Martin reached a hand down. "You all right, Captain?"

"Fine," Ky said. "Thanks to that expensive stuff I bought on Lastway." The deck was littered with intruders, most of them dead. "Hugh, what's the overall?"

"Ship's clear. All icons green. Still some chem residue, but I'll put a work party on that right away. It'll be safe to unmask in ten minutes."

"That's good." Ky rubbed her shoulder, very glad of the custom armor. "Crew report?"

"Five casualties, three serious, in the ship crew. One in the fighting crew—no, wait, there's that leg in the battery."

"Attached to a name," Ky said.

A brief pause. Then, "Sorry, Captain. Jedrah Puran. No one else has more than minor injuries. What's the enviro reading at your end?"

"We need cleanup—a lot of chemical residue, both ours and theirs, back here, but everything else looks good. There's some structural damage to a bulkhead, but they didn't get through to the circuitry."

"What do you want done with the prisoners?"

"We only need one," Ky said. Then she shook her head; they might come in useful. "Secure them all."

"Good-oh," Hugh said. "And Pettygrew? Sounds like he might lose his ship."

Ky turned to Jon Gannett. "We need a boarding party, EVA-qualified, but we also need the forward batteries here operable. Who can you spare?"

"Number two's capable of operating both, Captain, in a pinch. All us Gannetts are EVA-qualified and experienced."

"And me," Stewart Cavanaugh, from aft portside, spoke up. "I can take three of my people who are good EVA and shipside."

"Excellent," Ky said. "Jon, you're senior. Take whatever you think you need; on your way out, let me know how much damage they did to the hull when they breached the aft air lock. You may need to go on to *Sharra's Gift* after *Bassoon*; keep that in mind." He had already flicked hand signals to his own family, who were moving fast; Cavanaugh waited with his crew. "I'm going to the bridge now; I'll let Pettygrew know you're coming, and relay his communications channel to you."

"Thanks, Captain," Jon Gannett said. With a brisk salute to her, he waved Cavanaugh into motion.

"You're not going, are you?" Hugh said in her ear.

"No—I've learned my lesson," Ky said. Martin, at her side, let out a long sigh. She shook her head at him.

"Thanks be," Hugh said.

Ky ignored that. "Hugh, split the crew of number two forward battery, and get both manned. I'll be on the bridge as fast as I can; we're going to close with the other two ships. And power up the beam."

"Yes, Captain. What about the aft batteries?"

"Standby only for now. My concern is to keep the station from using anything they have."

"They don't have much," Hugh said. "I broke their code ten minutes ago, and they have only one half-power tractor and one LOS. We can pin them—"

"We're going to demonstrate that." Ky strode forward, Martin just behind her. Even though both her implant and Hugh reported the ship clear of intruders, Ky did not let her guard down as she jogged back upship. Martin stayed with her, going ahead at the cross-passages and checking out the lift before she got into it. By the time she reached the bridge, her away party was exiting the ship.

"They made a mess around the air lock," Jon reported. "Idiots figured they'd bring it in for repair, I guess. It won't be hard to do a rough patch, but we'll have to keep the next two compartments at vacuum until we do." He forwarded a visual.

"Did they get the hatch-opening software?"

"Oh, yes. Hardware, software panel, everything." Ky wanted to smack someone. It was criminal, stupid, to damage a ship's air lock. Although she'd accidentally destroyed the forward lock herself, when Osman was attacking *Gary Tobai,* this was different. She moved abruptly, trying to settle the sudden anger, and winced.

"You were hit," Hugh said, eyes widening as he pointed to her suit. "How bad is it? Why didn't you say—"

"It's nothing," Ky said, ignoring the stiffness as she shrugged. "Good armor. I'll probably have some fine bruises tomorrow, though."

"How many rounds did you take?"

Ky tried to remember. "Three, I think. But I took out more than that." She grinned at him.

His look was hard to read. "You've done close-in killing before."

"Yes," Ky said.

"So . . . no more shakes," he said.

"Maybe later. Not now. There's work to do." She settled into her seat; her back twinged again. Yes, she was going to feel it later. "What's the status on our wounded?"

"Teams are working on them," Hugh said. "I hope the stuff we bought is what it's supposed to be; I don't trust this place."

"They expected to get it all back," Ky said. "Sell it to the next ship they were going to rob. It's a neat scam, when you think about it. They don't even need factories: all they need is the initial inventory, since they'll get it back plus the money paid, the ship itself, and the crew for slave labor downplanet."

"Or to sell to slavers," Hugh said. "What you've told me about Osman, sounds like he could have been in that trade."

"If it was bad, Osman was in it," Ky said. On scan, her team was nearly to *Bassoon*. "Have you got Pettygrew on the horn?"

"Channel Two," Hugh said.

Ky flipped over to 2. "Vatta here," she said. "My team's almost at your hull. What's the signal?"

"Fairway," Pettygrew said. He sounded steady again, if tense. "We just can't hold them—they're up to the forward batteries. It's the smoke they're using; we can't see."

"My team has IR and other modes," Ky said. "Full space armor. Jon Gannett's in charge. I'll give him the signal; here's his code for you—" She sent it over.

"You're not coming yourself?" he asked.

"I'm about to give the station what-for," Ky said. "Don't be surprised at anything." On her other channel, she gave Gannett the password; he acknowledged. Then, to Pettygrew again: "You have an open channel here. If you need to tell me anything, don't hesitate. I'll also have someone monitoring my team. Otherwise, I'll be keeping the station busy so they don't interfere. They expected to have control before we'd moved out to a safe range: they're about to find out how wrong they were."

"Right, Captain Vatta."

"Yes, ma'am," Gannett said. "We're about to go in the same hole the rats used."

The tricky thing was figuring out the best angle of attack, given the limited traverse. Her forward beam had only a twenty-seven-degree cone; the forward missile batteries could not track that far forward. Given the station's size, she could hit the disk on one end with the beam, and the disk on the other with a single battery, but that left the middle, where most of the population—and the missiles— were. Which would be scarier to them, a beam or a missile? The beam . . . and it could take out their one weak LOS weapon. They knew how many missiles she'd bought, and what guidance systems, but not the power of her beam.

"Bring the beam up," she told Dannon.

"Yes, ma'am," he said. As the beam's tracker came online, Ky hailed the station.

"Attention. Attention. Attention. Stationmaster, Gretna Station, you are under my guns—" Obsolete language, but the traditional term ought to get their attention. "Your personnel have illegally breached and boarded my ships and injured my crew: you will immediately inform them that they should cease resistance and surrender to lawful authority—"

"What are you talking about?" The stationmaster came onscreen, buttoning his tunic. "You're crazy—turn that thing off or we'll—"

"I am protecting my ships and crew," Ky said. "If you attempt to reinforce your intruders or harm my ships, I will fire on your station. If you do not immediately order your criminals to surrender, they will all be killed."

"You can't do that—you're thieves—they just acted to take back property you'd stolen—"

"Don't even try that," Ky said. "Either comply with my orders or take the consequences."

"You wouldn't dare fire on the station. On civilians—"

"Use the targeting laser," Ky told Dannon. "Half power will take some skin off their noses, but not kill them. There might be some innocents on that station." She hadn't seen any children, but she hadn't explored the station. "Next shot, take out their LOS weapon." It wasn't even warmed up yet, but it was the one thing on the station that might damage them.

"Just scorch 'em for now. Yes, ma'am." He touched the controls. On Ky's scan of the station, a part of the hull in the central disk suddenly showed up as a bright white spot: hot enough to ablate a layer of hull a few millimeters thick.

"Stop!" the stationmaster yelled, eyes bulging. "You can't—"

"I can. I will. How many people do you want to lose?"

"But we're—we have weapons—"

"Not mounted," Ky said. "And you've got only lightspeed communication with your defensive platforms; it'll be hours before you can give them targeting information on us, and I doubt even your best targeting systems can distinguish between us—this close to you—and the station." She grinned at the man, and he flinched. "You're screwed," she said cheerfully. "Do you want to call off your goons, or do you want to hope you can retrieve the parts later?"

"Parts?"

"Parts. I see no reason to be careful with the remains of inshore pirates."

He was wringing his hands now. "We can't—we don't have any way to talk to them."

"Too bad," Ky said. "We'll just have to deal with them ourselves. Dannon—"

"Wait—I can try—"

"You have one minute. In the meantime—" Ky nodded to her weapons officer, who touched the controls; another hot spot appeared on the station's hull, this time at the mounting of the station's LOS weapon. It sagged to one side; a fountain of electrical discharge showed that they'd gotten the main power cables. On her scan, its icon went to black.

It was only forty seconds before Captain Pettygrew called from *Bassoon*. "They're dropping their weapons and begging for mercy," he said. "Are we feeling merciful?"

"Depends," Ky said. "I'll talk to Captain Argelos and get back to you."

Captain Argelos answered her hail with a cheerful, "Are we done yet, and can I chuck the lot of them out the air lock?"

"Are you sure your ship's secure? All of them located and neutralized?"

"Well, two more fell out of the overhead about a minute ago, but I think that's the lot. Scruffy bunch. Apparently they didn't realize that people who buy thousands of rounds of ammo are likely to know how to use it. We got them all with small arms, except the last two." He didn't specify how they'd been taken down.

"Here's the situation," Ky said. "I've got the station under my beam; they're trying to claim innocence, not very successfully. I'm not sure how many we had total—do you have a count?"

"Fifty on my ship," Argelos said. "Thirty-seven are dead; thirteen are alive, but eight won't make it."

"How about your people?" Ky asked.

"Two dead, fourteen casualties, from minor to serious. All should recover, though."

"Pettygrew had it worst," Ky said. "Ship design as much as anything, from what they said." *Bassoon*'s design made deep penetration easier; the defensive positions were more exposed, and the smoke screen the attackers used had worked well. "But he's secured his ship. The question is, what do we do now?"

"I'd like to blow that scumsucking station out of the region," Pettygrew said. "It's outrageous, a contravention of every treaty—"

"*Vanguard, Vanguard!* Please answer!" That hail, on conventional com, carried the ID of *Dryas,* the ship from Polson.

"*Vanguard,* Captain Vatta," Ky said. "Identify yourself, please."

The image on the screen was blurry, badly focused. "Captain Vatta, I'm Captain Partsin. We're in distress . . . we've been sitting here for days, they won't let us dock, because we're humods. Please—can you do something? Make them let us have supplies, at least?"

"What kind of distress?" Ky asked. That would be an easy claim for a pirate ship to make. "And why didn't you call on us when we came into the system?"

The image cleared a little, enough to show a gaunt-faced man with staring eyes and obvious humodifications: chem-sensor probes on either side of his nose, now curled into smooth knobs, and one forearm split giving him a three-fingered hand and a socket into which various tools could fit. His uniform hung loosely on him; it was clear he was malnourished.

"Our system was attacked—by pirates, we think—and I got away with a shipload of survivors, but we're out of supplies. We couldn't take anything but the people, and we're . . . it's bad, Captain Vatta. We're almost out of water; we've been out of food for days. If we don't resupply—"

"Those scum!" Ky said. She felt an exhilarating rush of white rage. Aid to disaster survivors was a basic human value; nothing could be worse than refusing to help them because of their appearance. "Captains—" This to Argelos and Pettygrew as well as Partsin. "Gretna Station needs a lesson it won't forget. Stay tuned; this could be fun." For a definition of *fun* she didn't want to think about right then.

She called the station. "If you want any of your people back alive," she said, "and your station whole and func- tioning, you're going to agree to resupply that refugee ship at no charge, and you're going to pay for the damage to my ships."

"That's—you're threatening human lives! For those— those—*obscenities*!"

"So did you threaten human lives," Ky said. "Ours, if you don't count theirs, which I do." After a moment, she went on. "Let me make it very clear. You have broken inter- stellar law, both commercial and criminal. You have cheated, lied, stolen, and killed. So you can complain all you want, but either you do what I say or I'll start punching holes in your station, beginning with your command deck. And all your people out here will be dead. Most of them are anyway—"

"Murderers!"

"No. You started this. I'm finishing it. You have sixty seconds."

In the next hours, as pieces of the station hull spalled off under sporadic hits from Ky's beam—and a longer burn finished the destruction of the station's one line-of-sight weapon—the station population finally came around. By then, they had no way to communicate with their remote platforms. Ky monitored their communications with the refugee ship, whose captain first thanked her, then said he was afraid to bring his ship in. Ky sighed; she could understand that, after what she'd seen and heard. Clearly, overwhelming force hadn't changed the Gretnans' opinion of outsiders, and the weakened Polsons would be at risk from anyone stronger than a child with an airbat. She called Argelos. "Can you find room for some really big tanks?"

"I suppose. Why?"

"Because I'm a softheaded idiot, just like my family always said," Ky said. "I can't just leave that ship out there without enough air, water, and food, and I don't trust this bunch of wolves not to attack them in dock. I need you to pick up oxygen and replacement cultures for them, water and food, and whatever else they need to make a safe jump somewhere else."

"Can you afford it?"

"Better than living with the memory of not helping them. I've been in their situation, almost. But I'm not paying for it—I'm taking it. The Gretnans are learning to be generous—as long as I have their station hostage, that is. I'm not going in, because I'm the one with the beam weapon. Pettygrew hasn't the cargo capacity, and his ship has the most damage. I'll have him stand off with his batteries hot, and I'll have the beam on them. I know where their munitions are stored, and they know I know."

"Fine with me," Argelos said. "I won't mind a bit dumping their trash and picking up something worthwhile. And if they blow us up—"

"You'll have an honor guard," Ky said. "There won't be a Gretna Station." She would regret killing the Crown & Spears manager who had been so helpful and the other indentured captives, but if they attacked Argelos, she would.

Three days later, Ky's group met the refugee ship out near the jump point. While she and Pettygrew kept watch, Argelos arranged the transfer of emergency supplies onto the transport. Oxygen, water, fresh cultures for the environmental chambers, additional tanks and equipment, food, bedding, personal items. Argelos' crew had ransacked dockside stores for everything from antibacterical soap to children's toys and stuffed it into station shuttles, which they'd put under tow.

"I can't thank you enough," *Dryas'* captain said. He looked even more gaunt and haggard; Ky suspected he had cut his own rations as well as those of the crew and refugees. Her own belly griped as she remembered the situation she'd faced back at Sabine. "I don't know how long we can hold out, but now we have a chance. Where are you headed next? Can we tag along?"

Ky had not thought of that. Now that her group had plenty of munitions, should they go on to Ciudad or somewhere else?

"Where did you want to go?" she asked Partsin.

"Somewhere friendly," he said. "Polson had trade agreements with the Adelaide Group; that's only two jumps from here, one into an empty system. I'm pretty sure they'd let us in, at least for resupply. You can't imagine what it's like for these people. They've lost everything—"

"I can, actually," Ky said. She didn't explain, though he raised an eyebrow. "Let me check with the charts and my captains; I'll get back to you within the hour."

Ky checked the scan of the station again. No communication from them; no sign of more hostile activity. Apparently they were going to behave, though she would not put past them some kind of trickery before her people had left the system. She called a conference with Argelos and Pettygrew.

"*Dryas* wants us to escort them somewhere—their captain suggested the Adelaide Group, two jumps away. I know we had planned to go to Ciudad, but this is the kind of mission that could boost our reputation—and they need the help. They can't pay us—"

"Tell you the truth," Pettygrew said, "I was never that eager to get to Ciudad. As you said, all we have to offer them is that one of their own died to save us. It's not much recommendation when we didn't even recover the bodies. I'd rather go there when we have something to show them."

"I agree; let's help the refugees," Argelos said.

"And your military adviser?"

Argelos grunted. "I told him times have changed and I don't give a whatsis if Slotter Key doesn't approve what I do. We have no communications with them anyway."

"Good," Ky said. "That's what I wanted to hear."

"If you're going to be our supreme commander," Pettygrew said, "are you always going to ask our opinion?"

"No," Ky said. "Just sometimes. When I want it. Now I'll tell their captain."

Captain Partsin was embarrassingly effusive in his thanks. "I don't know what we would have done. I didn't think anyone would take advantage of refugees the way they did—"

"I'm just sorry it happened," Ky said.

"Who are you people?" he asked.

"SDF," Ky said. "Space Defense Force: a multisystem force to defend against these pirates." It seemed like the right time to announce their new beginning.

"I never heard of it," Partsin said. "When did this start?"

"Not that long ago," Ky said. "And it's still growing. We're part of Third Fleet." No need to mention that so far there was no First or Second fleet and that her three ships were the whole of "Third." "Now. Do you have route information for the Adelaide Group? Is your ship capable of microjumps?"

"Yes, I have navigation data, but no, we can't do micro-jumps."

"What's your best insystem speed?"

The answer was depressingly low. They would be another five days to the jump point—another five days of high alert, because Ky did not trust the Gretnans at all. On the other hand, that was five days to gather information about what had happened to Polson, everything that Partsin knew.

"We're a small colony," Partsin said at the first briefing with the other captains. "We're not rich; I don't know why they attacked us, except maybe we have a six-axis jump nexus."

"That would do it," Argelos said, nodding.

"They came in," Partsin said. "Maybe fifteen ships; I'm not sure. Overwhelmed our local protection, occupied the colony, and told everyone to get out within thirty-six hours or expect a bloodbath. We only had two ships docked capable of taking on passengers—it wasn't nearly enough." Ky remembered the panic at Sabine; she could imagine how much worse this might be. "They didn't care," Partsin went on. "Everything our governor tried to say, begging for more time, they just said *Not our problem, get out or die*. A lot of people didn't believe them until they shot a whole classroom full of children." His face twisted; Ky felt her own stomach knot in horror. She waited until Partsin had caught his breath.

"What can you tell us about them?" she asked then. "Any details at all might help."

"They're insane," Partsin said bitterly. "They look like thugs, most of them, but they act like robots—that kind of discipline. They wear burgundy and black—"

"Turek," Pettygrew said. "It's got to be—"

"Go on," Ky said to Partsin.

"The governor asked who they were, where they were from, who they worked for—they just laughed at him."

"Did you get any records of them?"

"No . . . well, nothing really good. One of the kids had a toy recorder; the images are blurry, but you can tell the color of the uniforms and so on. I do have a list of ship IDs, but I'm sure the beacons were faked."

"Anything might be helpful," Ky said. "How are your passengers doing?"

"Better than they were," Partsin said. "Some of them had medical training, so they set up the protocols for refeeding."

Ky, remembering the situation at Sabine, sympathized, but there was nothing more they could do until they reached a friendlier place.

SIX

Nexus II

Ilkodremin was one of the major manufacturing cities on
Nexus; from the air its roofs glittered blue with solar panels.
Rafe took a tram directly to his first call, the manufacturer
of commercial ovens he had noted at Flasic's Bakery Supplies, and entered into a long discussion that became an
unsatisfactory negotiation about the availability of their
ovens offworld, the possibility of sublicensing the plans,
and other details he hoped would bore anyone doing surveillance.

In the afternoon, it was the manufacturer of a machine
that turned out small cylindrical snacks filled with minced
spiced fruit, but that, too, led to no contracts being signed,
since Rafe specified a filling that was incompatible with
their machine.

The next morning, he was off on another regional
transport, headed away from what he thought of as his
target area, to the tropical seacoast city of Maresh. A
small specialty manufacturer there had, he explained to
the apparently bored waiter at dinner, a reputation for
innovative small-batch designs.

The small specialty manufacturer did indeed have such

a reputation; the company's designer was also one of the very few people on the planet outside his own family Rafe felt he could trust. The connection was accessible if anyone looked, but decades old. Lissa had been a student at the same school where he'd been sent.

He watched her scowl over his list of requirements, wondering if she'd remember the simple code they'd used in school. If not, he'd try something else. Her frown deepened; she shook her head once as if to dislodge a fly. Then she looked at him, straight-on as she always had.

"Genson Ratanvi. From . . . Cascadia."

"Quite so," Rafe said. He let his face relax for an instant, Genson's expression of stuffy disapproval shifting, he hoped, to the crooked smile she'd remember. From her change in expression, just as quickly suppressed, it seemed to work.

"These specifications . . . will be difficult," she said. "Expensive."

"I hope not too expensive," Rafe said, back in Genson's persona. "It is because of your known expertise and reasonable prices that I came here at all. Maresh is hardly on the beaten track."

"It can be quite pleasant," she said.

He smiled, Genson's smile and not his own. "Perhaps you could show me? A dinner, maybe?"

She stiffened a little. "I don't usually socialize with clients, Ser Ratanvi. I'm sure Ser Bannat would be glad to show you around—"

"But I was hoping you—" He cocked his head. "I don't mean to give offense, you understand. It is the habit of we Cascadians to maintain politeness; there would be no . . . nothing to object to, in that way. It is just that I would prefer you to Ser Bannat as you are the person who would be involved in the design of any machines, should we come to agreement on price."

"I see," she said. "Perhaps you'll excuse me a moment . . ."

"Of course," he said. "May I wait here—?" The design studio, with its files of projects. "Or would you prefer I wait in the public area?"

"I won't be long," she said. "You can wait here."

Rafe refrained from stripping the data out of any files, since Ratanvi would not have done so, and in a short time Lissa returned.

"My boss has agreed to let me leave early today, Ser Ratanvi, and he's given me permission to entertain you on the company account. I'll just make a reservation at— you do like seafood, don't you? Spicy?"

Something fishy, yes, and yes, he was hot where security was concerned. They were agreed on that. "I'm so sorry," Rafe said. "But something I ate when I landed from the spaceport is still causing me trouble. If it could be something very mild instead?"

"I'm sorry," she said. "Our regional cuisine is known for its spice blends, but I can certainly find a place with good, but blander food."

And either no scans—or no scans she couldn't fox.

"I hope you will pardon the liberty," he said, "but you have beautiful hair."

She touched the red-gold of it and grinned. "Now don't start, Ser Ratanvi. You promised no offense."

"Understood," Rafe said.

The sights of Maresh included, as Rafe remembered from his childhood vacations, the long, rocky promontory forming one side of the harbor, where the seabirds nested in summer. Now, in autumn, only a little of the sickening stench remained, but it was enough to keep most people far away. Lissa led him out to the very tip, where the waves sloshed noisily at the rocks, to watch the lights dancing on the waters of the bay.

"So," she said, when he finally nodded, having checked everything he could check. "What's going on?"

"My family's disappeared," he said. "And someone put a trap on the old home number. Have you heard anything about a shake-up in ISC?"

"Nothing," she said, shaking her head. "Not a shake-up . . . I don't pay attention unless it's something dramatic, you know."

"You do know ansibles have been out all over, don't you?"

"Have they? Where?"

She sounded sincere. "You really didn't know?"

"No . . . our customers are mostly local to this system, and the others are nearby. How bad is it?"

"Generalized failure. Happened almost simultaneously."

"Sabotage." No doubt in her voice at all.

"Yes."

"And you're still working for the same firm?"

"I can't answer that," Rafe said.

"I see." He suspected she saw more than was convenient. She started to speak, stopped herself, and dropped back into the old lingo. "Pretty evening on the water, isn't it?"

He, too, had seen the light from the little boat, distinguishable from all the other lights dancing on the water by the vee it left behind.

"I think perhaps we should go back," he said. He turned and offered her his arm. "You've been a most gracious hostess and guide, my dear, but this damp air can't be good for either of us."

"About the contract," Lissa began, taking his arm and moving slowly back toward the city.

"I will call on your employer tomorrow," he said, as stuffily as possible. "Tonight is not the time. But you may assure him that your services were perfectly satisfactory."

The next day, he shook his head at the estimate Lissa's employer gave him. "I'm sorry . . . I believe that is beyond our budget, though I will keep this in mind."

"You won't find a better price," Ser Bannat said. "Not for what you want; it's quite complicated."

"Possibly too complicated," Rafe said. "I will tell them back home. Apologies for possibly wasting your time."

"No problem," Ser Bannat said. "But if you'll excuse me, I have an appointment." He left the room.

Rafe had a last few minutes' chat with Lissa, and took a chance, asking her if she had kept in contact with anyone he might have known, anyone near Pittville in particular. She had cut herself off from the others in the school, she said, except for two girls who had also made it through university. "You might not remember them," she said. "Colleen and Pilar—both two years younger than me."

"Just barely," Rafe said. He had their images stored in his implant; he had more about the old school than anyone suspected, but this was not the time to brag.

"They made it through university, too," Lissa said. "Colleen married, then it fell apart, then she married again. She and her second husband live about eighty kilometers from Pittville, but I don't think they ever go that way— she's always talking about their summer cottage down on the coast. They have three children; she does pottery. Pilar's an attorney, specializing in family law. She never married, never had a partner that I know of. She lives in Pittville. Colleen lived with her for a while after that first marriage broke up; she might still know people there."

"You have been most kind," Rafe said. "Thank you for your time and hospitality." Her employer was coming back down the hall; Rafe smiled and thanked him as well before leaving.

His next trip took him by train along the coast to Marrn; there he transferred to the line that ran up between rounded green hills to Pittville. On one side, the town looked peaceful and idyllic; on the other, the gaping hole for which the town was named lay raw and red as a wound.

Pilar Metris had an office in a building full of professionals: attorneys, accountants, land surveyors. Rafe did not intend to confide in her; he hadn't known any of the younger girls well. The woman who came out to greet him from an inner office looked nothing like the girl's image in his implant. Dark, elegant, and hard-faced, she looked him up and down as if he were an animal for sale.

"You're a foreigner; you should know that I don't handle international disputes."

"I did not come for representation," Rafe said, "but for general advice. Your receptionist has my credit deposit for an hour of your time."

She grimaced. "Come in, then. Explain."

"I am in food service," he said. "We—the professional organization I belong to, of food service managers—are looking for a location for our triennial convention. We prefer not to be in urban areas, but within an hour of a transportation hub. I was hoping you could advise me whether there is anything in this part of the continent that might suit. I came to a barrister—an attorney, I believe you call them—" She nodded, her face now less hostile, merely intent. "I came to you," he went on, "because I thought you would be more likely to know of any legal barriers to an interstellar gathering of considerable size, and any local legal difficulties that might arise with advance contracts."

"What size?"

"For the triennial, that would be five to six thousand. For one of our smaller conventions, such as the annual local regional, which includes all of the Moscoe Confederation and Nexus Group, only about two hundred. All this is contingent on restoration of ansible communications, of course. Not the regional, because we and you both have working ansibles, but the big one . . . well, I haven't been able to contact friends back at Allray or Sallyon for almost a standard year."

"I see. I'm afraid there's nothing suitable here—or within hundreds of kilometers—for your large convention. We do have several recreational and retreat centers in the hills to the northeast; for business people, I would think Green Hills Conference Center or Chelsea Falls Conference Center would be best. The others are either summer facilities for children or sporting complexes. Should you need to book facilities with one of the conference centers, I'll be glad to guide you through the contract process."

"Thank you," Rafe said. "You've been most kind and helpful. I will look up the conference centers—I presume they have listings—"

"Oh, yes," she said. "But I would expect both to be booked up for the next two years; they're very popular." She cocked her head. "How long will you be staying in Pittville, Ser Ratanvi?" That had a slight edge. Had Lissa contacted her? Lissa might.

"A few days," he said. "My stomach does not like constant travel; I find I need to pause now and then and recover."

"I see. Well, if you need any further assistance while you're in town, by all means ask me."

Rafe spent the rest of the day as a travel-weary businessman might be expected to. He ate a bland meal, went for a walk in the mellow afternoon light, and settled into his room for the evening. The deskcomp connected him to the advertising for both conference centers. Chelsea Falls, northwest of the mines, had two pretty waterfalls in a gorge. Rafe set up a bounce relay with care; he wanted any number he called to connect as if he were in Central instead of here in Pittville. Then he contacted the number given. He spoke to the desk clerk, inquiring about future vacancies, and expressed his regret that they had no space at the time of the regional convention. Its communications codes included the relay sequence, but the originating codes were nothing like the ones he'd noted.

That could be faked, of course. Or his parents might be held in some private residence, in which case . . . he shook his head and called Green Hills with the same inquiry.

As the numbers came up, he had trouble keeping his voice steady in the Cascadian accent. The same originating code . . . the right sequence of communications nodes. He forced himself to finish the conversation with the clerk—so sorry, no, the date of the convention could not be changed to fit Green Hills' only vacant slot—and closed the contact breathing hard. He closed his eyes briefly, willing himself to calmness. From here on, he must be even more careful.

The structure was listed as the Green Hills Conference Center, owned by the Green Hills Development Corporation. Who owned Green Hills? Rafe, flat on his belly on the edge of a vast grassy space, had not been able to winkle that out of the local databases without risking the question being noticed. He stared across the bowl to the cluster of buildings surrounded with shrubs and trees.

One large, three stories at least, the cupola to a small tower peeking out of the trees. One with the extra-large ventilator hoods that suggested a large, institutional kitchen. Small buildings, hardly more than cabins, placed haphazardly around the margin of the wooded space. And beyond, surrounding the buildings, the mown grass. Clear field of fire, up to the tree line, where dense forest surrounded the facility. Here it was a mix of evergreens and deciduous trees now dropping leaves like flakes of gold and bronze with every puff of air.

Two roads in: the staff entrance a narrow, one-lane blacktop bordered by hedges—the only cover across the grassy circle. The public entrance, a generous two lanes edged with bedding plants, all copper and bronze at this season, ended in a small parking area. One vehicle sat there. By its thermal signature, it had been in place for at least six hours.

And the whole place was thick with detection equipment in all modes. If he had not found, and suppressed, one of the section command nodes two hundred meters back, not even his chameleon suit would have kept him safe. The command node's instruction set was ISC security standard, proof that someone involved was ISC—or that ISC's security had holes all through it, another depressing thought.

A white van came into view on the servants' road. Small, any lettering or logo on its sides hidden by the hedges from his viewpoint. It moved at a moderate pace and disappeared behind the cluster of buildings. Rafe extended his probe into the security command net, careful not to tickle any of the internodes, but he could not reach anything useful. The elements within his reach could give him enhanced audiovisual of their detection arc direct to his implant, but nothing more.

The staff parking areas, he already knew, were surrounded by buildings, out of sight of the perimeter or underground. In a benign setting, this might be to keep any utilitarian objects out of view of customers who expected total elegance. Here, such caution seemed sinister. No legitimate enterprise needed this level of security, of secrecy.

Something moved; he saw sunlight flash . . . it was a glass door opening. Tiny figures exited the building, three of them. Two were in gray coveralls. Rafe increased the magnification in his eyepiece. Not just coveralls, but camouflage battledress, its surface now inactive. The third figure wore business clothes . . . but atmospheric instability made wavering patterns in Rafe's eyepiece; he could not see the face clearly enough to be sure of an identity.

That third figure went to the parked vehicle and entered it; after a moment the vehicle moved, leaving by the public road. The two uniformed figures stood together, watching, then turned back to the buildings and entered the largest.

An hour later, another white van entered the area along the service road. He could still see no logo, thanks to the hedges. It—or its twin—reappeared quickly and stopped partway to the trees, blocking the service road. Rafe boosted his visuals; the sun was going down, and long shadows dimmed his view of the road. A short time later, a second white van emerged from the trees near the buildings, followed by a third. The first van moved ahead, on into the trees, followed by the other two; Rafe dared not tap into the perimeter security to see if it went all the way to the public road.

He lay there another three hours. Nothing moved in the compound; no lights came on. Were his parents still there? Had they ever been there? Were the three white vans benign—transportation for cleaning or maintenance crews prepping the facility for another conference—or something else?

By midnight, he was out of the woods, undetected as far as he knew, and back in Pittville, his disguise restored in the cab of the rental car.

"Did you enjoy your drive, Ser Ratanvi?" the doorman at the hotel asked when Rafe had turned the car in.

"It's very pleasant country," Rafe said. "Especially, I would think, at this time of year. The trees where I live are all evergreen."

"You should see it in spring, when the trees are in bloom," the doorman said.

The next morning, Rafe went back to Pilar's office, and this time the receptionist smiled at him. "You are having a pleasant time, Ser?"

"Indeed, yes, though the resorts are all booked up for next year, as Sera Metris said they might be. I have just a few more questions for her, if she is free."

"It will be a short time, but then, yes."

Rafe pored over the local business directory, trying to think of some way to ask what he needed to ask without breaking character. There simply was no way that even his supple imagination could devise . . .

When they were alone, Pilar looked at him, one corner of her mouth pulled in, "Ser Ratanvi, I perceive that you are not entirely what you seem."

"Lissa," Rafe said, to see what she'd do.

"Lissa . . . was not my year. I didn't have much to do with the younger girls."

"No. You were younger."

She scowled. "That time is over. I don't talk about it."

"Nor do I, but some things are never over."

"So what do you really want, Ser Ratanvi-in-food-processing?"

"A name," Rafe said. "Which an attorney might have."

"And if I choose not to cooperate? If I think this is something for law enforcement?"

"Then my family will die," Rafe said. "If they aren't dead already."

She gazed at him without a change of expression for a long moment. "You are serious."

"Completely."

"They . . . were rich."

"Yes."

"Powerful."

"Yes."

"And you think they're in danger. Why?"

"I would rather not tell anyone who doesn't have to know," Rafe said. "I believe the danger is extreme."

"You want to find them . . . rescue them?"

"I need to find a reliable person who does that sort of thing."

"Hostage extrication," Pilar said. "Very dangerous, very much a specialty. There are three firms I know of, assuming you don't want to go to the authorities—since you haven't, I'm safe to assume."

"That's right," Rafe said. "If their disappearance isn't public knowledge, there's a reason, and the authorities could be involved."

"You have asked me if I will serve as the local contact should your association decide to hold its annual conference here," Pilar said. "That is all you have asked me. I asked for a retainer. You paid it; you will pay it when you leave. A name you might know: Gary."

Gary. Rafe remembered exactly one Gary they had in common, the older boy who had made his life hell for two years of his incarceration at the school.

"The best reputation on the planet," Pilar said. "It's a

respectable company providing general and special security services."

"Gary?"

Her mouth quirked. "As it happens, I have his personal contact numbers. Here." She scrawled something on a plasfilm strip. "And now, I believe our business is finished. My receptionist will be glad to take care of the retainer."

"Thank you," Rafe said.

Pilar shrugged. "Lissa was kind to me, and to Colleen. And I have to admire someone who cares about a family who dumped him into that hellhole. Mine can rot, for all I care."

In the outer office, Rafe paid the retainer. He decided to wait until he was away from Pittville to call Gary . . . in fact, he would call while in transit to his next stop. He caught the afternoon train back to the coast, then the night train to Balcock, the nearest city with a commercial airport. The night train had a full directory; Gary's firm came up, with an office number instead of the ones Pilar had given him. And the firm's office was in Balcock . . . why there and not Central, he wondered. Which number to call? Well, Ratanvi would have no reason to call a security services firm . . . he called the private number. He was not surprised when the link icon lit a security bubble.

"S'Gary," said a male voice. It didn't sound like the old Gary, but it had been fifteen years at least.

"Pilar gave me this number," Rafe said. "Lissa mentioned me to her."

"I don't play games," Gary said. "Whatever you're—"

"The door to the steam tunnel could be opened from the other side only with a key," Rafe said. The worst night of his life had been spent on the wrong side of that door. Silence, now. Finally, a gust of air huffing out.

"This wouldn't be that rich boy, would it?"

"Yes," Rafe said. "I need to hire an expert."

"Expert in what?"

"Retrieving stolen valuables."

"Where are you?"

"On a train to Balcock."

"You know where our corporate HQ is?"

"Yes."

"Don't go there. Check into a hotel—the Dorset Arms or the Seaview. Name?"

"Genson Ratanvi."

"Good . . . grief. Cascadian, by your accent. Well, Ser Ratanvi, we'll meet tomorrow to discuss your business. Shall we say ten of the clock?"

Rafe left the station in the morning crowd, and didn't notice anyone following him. He checked into the Seaview—which, despite its name, had only one narrow slice of sea view, and that only from rooms on the right front corner. His room, fifth floor back, looked out onto a parking lot and the blank wall of another building. That suited him. He had slept little; his mind kept churning through the possibilities, most of them grim. He forced himself to eat something for breakfast.

Promptly at ten, the deskcom buzzed; he told the desk clerk that yes, he was expecting a visitor and please send him up.

Despite himself and the years between, Rafe's stomach tightened when he opened the room door and faced Gary. Whatever he'd been doing in the intervening years, Gary had not let himself go: he was as fit and muscular as he had been in his late teens. Almost a head taller than Rafe, massive shoulders in a well-fitted suit, he looked like the tough he was. Or had been. He looked Rafe up and down after Rafe closed the door behind him.

"I hope that's not your real belly," he said.

"I am here in the person of Genson Ratanvi, food service manager," Rafe said, in his Cascadian accent. He let one of his knives slip into his hand and turned his hand so Gary could see it. "But underneath . . ."

"You're the same snaky kid you were before. I suppose that's good." Gary moved to the room's easy chair and sat down. He opened his briefcase and pulled out an array of gear that Rafe recognized as scan detection and stealthing equipment. For a moment or two, Gary said nothing as he set this up and turned it on, Then: "So . . . what do you need?"

Rafe settled into the desk chair. "My parents and sister—my whole family—have disappeared. I can't find my sister's husband. She may be pregnant, or she may have a baby—I've been away for years; I'm not sure of the date she was due. The house is empty but not looted, and there's a police guard out by the gate. The private house line has a trap on it. My father's private number is supposedly out of service. There's been no word publicly . . . I think they've been abducted; I don't know by whom. Or for sure, where they are, I think I know where they were until the day before yesterday."

"And what do you want from me?"

"I want to find them and rescue them, of course. Pilar says you're the best on the planet. I want you to help me. I was going to do it myself, but if something went wrong—"

"You're crazy," Gary said. "No one person—no two people—can extricate hostages if the captors are at all competent. And from what you say, they're professional quality."

"I have to—"

"You have to use your head, Rafe. You asked my advice. Listen to it. You're talking three, four hostages, right? Two seniors—"

"They're not senile!"

"I didn't say they were. But they're not going to be as resilient, as physically capable, as younger people. And a young woman who may or may not be pregnant, may or may not have a child—"

"I don't know—"

"And that's a problem. And you also don't know if any of them were injured in the original snatch, and you don't know why law enforcement isn't on this loud and clear. It's serious gray, if not black, and you aren't qualified to know what it's going to take."

"I—"

"Rafe. Sit down and listen. This is my specialty; if it were yours, I would know that. So it's not. You know covert stuff, I'll grant that; I have no doubt you've done things on the dark side. I have no doubt you're brilliant with any kind of communications or surveillance gear. But you do not know what it takes to extricate hostages, and I do."

"So do it, then."

"Just like that." Gary shook his head. "You show up again after . . . however many years it's been, and it doesn't matter except that we've been out of touch and I have no idea if you're still worth a damn."

"As a killer?" Rafe asked.

"As someone I can trust to pay the bills," Gary said. Rafe opened his mouth, but Gary raised a hand to silence him. "Oh, yeah, we all knew you were a rich kid, good for any amount of money. And what I heard was you were still a rich kid, getting remittance from papa as the price of staying away. That doesn't sound like someone I want to trust with the lives I'm responsible for."

Rafe tried not to glare, remembering Gary as someone who had never, to his knowledge, accepted responsibility for anyone else. "Responsible," he said, testing that.

"Yes," Gary said. His mouth worked as if he might spit, but he didn't. "Things you didn't know, rich man's son. There were other kids I took care of back then. There are men I take care of now."

"You didn't—"

"Do a thing for you for the first year. That's true. You were a cocky little squirt, Rafe; you had all that rich-man's-son gloss all over you, and I hated the rich for good reason. I wanted to see that gloss come off, see if you were worth anything underneath. And you surprised me. You were. Then you left . . . and I don't know this Rafe."

Rafe shook his head. "Too much time between. Too many things happened. It'd take weeks to catch up, if we ever could, and I don't have that time."

"Think you're tough enough to force me?"

"Might be. But that's a waste of time, too. I have more important things to do than prove myself to you, Gary. If you don't want the mission, say so. I'll go somewhere else."

This time Gary did spit, with the same precision Rafe remembered from their youth. "You won't find any better than me. You'll just get in more trouble." He gave a sharp head shake. "I am an idiot, because I'm going to trust someone I know is a snake to the backbone, and I swear, Rafe, if you cross me, I will stake your snaky vertebrae to the hottest griddle in hell, one by one . . ."

"I don't want to cross you," Rafe said. "I want to get those people out safely."

"Those people . . . not your family?"

"If I think of them that way, I can't think," Rafe said. He heard the tremor in his own voice and struggled to control it. Gary had no respect for weakness.

Gary shrugged. "Whatever helps you give me what I need for the team."

"Which is?"

"Info and money. I'm assuming you still have unlimited funds . . ."

Rafe shook his head. "Not at the moment. My account's not available. I don't have access codes for the family accounts, let alone the corporate accounts. That's part of the problem. I can get into my personal accounts locally, but that will be obvious to anyone watching, and I know someone is."

"Tell me," Gary said.

Rafe described the experiences he'd had in the past days, from the phone surveillance of his family's numbers to the difficulty with accessing his accounts. "I should've been able to transfer funds from the deposit account to my alias's without a hitch; I'd done it before. Financial transactions are supposed to be secure, anyway. It's one of the selling points for financial ansibles. This time a team of ISC security personnel showed up at the hotel, and I barely got away."

"So how were you planning to pay for my services?" Gary asked.

"My alias has accounts on Cascadia, and ansible service between here and there is still functional. I don't know if it's enough until you give me a price, though. If it is, then you'll work through a dummy corporation selling baking equipment—"

"Baking equipment?"

"My alias is a food service manager," Rafe said. "I've been all over the planet looking at food processing equipment—commercial ovens, specialized snack production equipment, and so forth. There's suspicion, but so far I think the bad guys are convinced that my alias is a real person with someone trying to use his identity."

"I don't come cheap," Gary said. "What we do is dangerous work, and my team are all well aware of the risk.

I have to provide sufficient medical coverage and death benefits to recruit reliable, skilled team members, as well as training facilities and equipment."

"So how expensive is *not cheap*?"

"There's a per diem or a per mission rate. Per diem seems lower, but you have to understand that it includes the pre-extrication time necessary to assemble, brief, and train the team for this specific task, as well as the time needed for the mission itself. That's always more days than the customer expects, though I give the best estimate I can. Per mission is much higher, but it's a turnkey price. Doesn't matter how long it takes; I absorb any overage."

"How long do you think this would take?"

"Don't have enough data yet. You say they've been moved from Green Hills . . . that's good, because a setup like Green Hills is very difficult. We have to find the new location, assess it, plan a route in and out, train the team on any specific problem areas, and so on." Gary spat again. "I don't take credit; we have expenses up front and I got stung a few times early on when I trusted someone. But I can see you're in a bind. If you can come up with a substantial down payment, I'm willing to trust that you or your family will pay the balance afterward."

Rafe felt a tiny burst of warmth. "You're that sure you can get them out."

"I didn't get the reputation I have for failing, Rafe." Gary grinned. "I can't exactly give you references, but I can say that we've had only one failure in the past six years, and only two before that. Out of . . . quite a few cases."

"So tell me what the down payment is," Rafe said.

SEVEN

The funds transfer from Cascadia went through without a hitch and without—so far as Rafe could tell—arousing any interest from ISC security. With great care, he and Gary routed funds through several company names, and Rafe filed contracts for the manufacture of commercial ovens and food production machines with the relevant offices, and applied for export permits "upon completion of design & manufacture of these machines." As far as Rafe could tell, this seemed sufficiently dull to arouse no interest here, either.

In the meantime, Gary had put his own intelligence-gathering team to work on the problem of location. His files revealed that Green Hills Development Corporation was distantly owned by ISC's Nexus II local development division, along with a string of other resort and retreat properties.

"By talking to various travel agents, we've been able to determine which ones are scheduled for events when," Gary said. "If your parents' captors are corporate, as you suspect, they'd be able to find holes in the schedules and move your family from one resort to another. Most of the places are fairly secure—it's what clients pay for, after all. If we're lucky, this is how they're being held, and we'll locate them in a few days."

"How long do you think they're being kept in each place?"

"Don't know yet. The gaps in the schedules range from a weekend—probably not time enough to move in hostages and move them out again—to sixty days or more, for the hunting lodges. Did you ever stay at one of these places?"

"We went to resorts sometimes, but I don't know if they were part of this list," Rafe said. He looked down the printout Gary had handed him. "Bel Ara, yes. That was the first time I saw a tropical reef. But you've marked it off—"

"It's one of the busiest. All-year use by conventions, corporate training sessions, and so on. Vacant at most for three days, or during tropical storms. What about the ones marked in green?"

Rafe shook his head. "My father may have gone to one of these—I see they're mostly hunting or fishing lodges—but I didn't."

"I think they're the best bet," Gary said. "You said your family was snatched a maximum of three weeks ago, judging by the condition of the house and the plants. Green Hills had an opening starting about then, but a series of religious meetings is starting two days after you think your family was moved out. That's the kind of thing a retreat center can't cancel without people noticing. Maybe they hoped whatever they wanted would happen in that time, but just as likely it was planned as a short-term holding site."

"Still a lot of places to look," Rafe said.

"And a lot of tools to look with," Gary said. "I've got long-term surveillance data to play with. Want to see?"

"Always," Rafe said. The files Gary opened astonished him. "What made you start keeping all this?" he asked, looking at a summary graph of the previous three years' satellite data on travel patterns.

"The need to find people," Gary said. "You'll have noticed that this algorithm allows me to filter out all scheduled traffic—" The graph changed. "—and then to spotlight specific areas. Here I'm entering the locations of the ISC-owned resorts with gaps of thirty or more days in their schedules." The graph changed again. "The colors show total traffic in the past three years . . . file that . . . and now for this year . . ."

Rafe, watching the lines and colors shift, was more impressed than he wanted to admit. Gary had always seemed like a big dull-witted bully. "Big" and "bully" might be true, but not "dull-witted." Rafe wondered how many other misjudgments of character he might have made—and how much those misjudgments mattered in this crisis. The planetary schematic turned, showing the other hemisphere.

"Now let's match the traffic to the schedule gaps," Gary said. He reset the parameters, and they watched the schematic redraw itself. "Now that's interesting . . ."

"What?" Rafe wasn't sure which colors went with which meaning now.

"There." Gary pointed. "High-latitude hunting lodge specializing in ice bear trophy hunting in winter and wildlife ecotourism in summer. Normally it's vacant this time of year—too cold for summer tourists, migratory birds have left, and the ice bears haven't migrated down yet. But you'll notice . . ." He touched the controls again. "Ah. Yes. Traffic there a week ago, and since, and I'll check the infrared data on the next satellite pass."

"You can access the security satellites?"

"Nothing tricky about that; I have a license," Gary said. "Law enforcement doesn't mind as long as I'm not extricating criminals from their prisons. I don't do that; it doesn't pay enough." He turned to another console. "And while we're waiting for that, let's see what else we can find out about . . . what do they call the place? . . . Aurora Adventure Lodge."

Another visual came up, this one a developer's rendition of the site. Against a backdrop of a lake, with mountains beyond, a glacier peeking between them, a massive log structure surrounded by smaller log cabins was rendered in bright colors, windows framed in white and bordered by green shutters. Flower baskets festooned the eaves, and more flowers overflowed planters on the deep porch.

"This must be for summer tourists," Gary said. "Terrain's not bad." It was treeless, lumpy with huge boulders scattered here and there, cut by streams emptying into the lake.

"Above timberline?" Rafe asked.

"Yeah," Gary said. "But plenty of cover in those rocks. If we control the airspace and aerial surveillance—and we will—we can get very close without being detected. Weather's the possible problem here. It's late autumn; the first winter storms should hit any time."

"So how soon can you do it?"

"I still don't know enough. We need to know if they're really there—that it's not a decoy—and how many people are guarding them."

Access to Aurora Adventure Lodge, its website said, was by "the incredibly scenic" train from Brygganha to the high-altitude station at Dobst, from which the train went on to Pergyn, on the far side of the plateau. Dobst Station was just that: a small prefab building with a snack bar, toilets, a ticket counter, a left-luggage room. Beside it was the station staff's dormitory, and adjoining was a bare-bones hostel for high-country hikers. At Dobst, the site went on,

Aurora Lodge guests were met with "a seasonally appropriate vehicle" and transported some eight kilometers to the lake. The summer vehicle was motorized; the winter one appeared to be a horse-drawn sleigh.

The website map showed "public hiking trails" well away from Lodge property, touching the lakeshore kilometers away from the Lodge. "Private hiking trails" led from the Lodge down to the lake and along its shore, up from the Lodge to the glacial margin, to various fishing spots and scenic overlooks. All were color-coded "for the use of Lodge guests only." The property was secure, its brochure said, from all types of intrusion, physical and electronic; the perimeter barriers were "top of the line."

"They're not, actually," Gary said, leaning back in his chair. "They'll certainly stop a curious hiker, or a criminal who'd like to sneak in and pretend to be on staff while robbing guests, or the casual everyday kind of commercial snooping." He leaned forward again, deep in another site. "The latest version of their perimeter security was installed . . . almost two years ago. Reputable company in Brygganha, main concern ice bears in winter and nosy tourists in summer. Good products, but not the best; that cost too much. I know Stani; he supervised installation, and he's good."

"So . . ."

"It's more difficult than some jobs we've done, but not impossible."

"When will I meet the others?" Rafe asked.

"Meet them? You're not going to meet them."

"But—"

"Rafe, for the hundredth time—! You are not part of this op. You cannot be part of this op. You are a *client*, like any other client. You must not be seen to have any connection whatever with what we're doing; it's bad enough that you aren't out there continuing to look for food processing equipment, or being the businessman on vacation chatting up beach girls or boys or something."

"I can't just—"

Gary's look stopped him. Rafe took a deep breath, then another. When he looked down, his left hand was shaking slightly; he went on breathing, willing it to stop. When it was steady, he looked up.

"I'm being an idiot," he said.

"You're being a client," Gary said with a shrug. "Clients are like that."

"I don't like thinking of myself—"

"—as just like everyone else? That hasn't changed, at least." Gary punched him lightly on the shoulder. "Don't worry, son; you aren't like the others except in being anxious and tense and entirely too eager to jump in and help. But part of our security, and yours, and your family's, is a nice thick, tight wall between my people and you. You have no idea what will happen after we get them out—"

"You said *after*—you really think—"

"After we get them out, yes. Yes, it's doable, and yes, we'll do it. If you don't muck it up in the meantime. Now—what was your original itinerary? How long did you plan to stay on Nexus?"

"Not this long," Rafe said. "I planned to visit Dad, find out what was up with the ansibles, see how the land lay, and then—"

"Did you have a reservation?"

"Yes, but now—"

"You have to use it."

"No! I can't leave the planet not knowing—"

"Rafe, you have no reason not to leave—your persona

doesn't, I mean. If you don't leave you'll arouse suspicion—you already have."

"But—"

"Do you have anyone outside who would act as your office manager or CEO or whatever and send you orders to stay?"

"Er . . . no." Stella might, if he explained it to her, but he hadn't explained it before he left Cascadia, and he could not trust even secured ansible transmission now.

"Then you have to go. If you can sneak back in, that's fine, but you have to go, in that persona. It will make our job, and your family, much safer."

Intellectually, Rafe knew Gary was making sense, but he did not want to leave. If something happened while he was away, something that his presence could have prevented . . . "I'm sure I can work something up, something believable—"

"What, break a leg? That's no bar to travel, as you know—"

"I know. I'd need to be in a hospital or locked up—" Rafe stopped. From Gary's expression the same thought had come to him. "I don't suppose—"

"You wouldn't like it," Gary said. "Lockup isn't much more fun than school was."

"It wouldn't be the first time," Rafe said.

"You're kidding."

"No. Not on this planet, but—I do know my way around a jailhouse."

"Something local," Gary said. "Something you could get out of, probably. Just to tide you over, hold you onplanet until your ship's taken off and the op's started."

"I don't even know what gets you temporary incarceration here anymore," Rafe said. "And it can't be with ISC security, or something that a local would report to them."

"Right. On the other hand, they—or someone higher up—has to know that you're behind bars or something else legitimate, so there's an explanation for your not catching your ride out."

"I guess I could get sick," Rafe said.

"It's harder to find cooperative doctors and hospitals than cooperative law enforcement," Gary said. "No, don't look at me like that. I'm on their side now, and favors go both ways. I'm just thinking which one to call."

"May I make a suggestion?"

"I may not take it."

"Of course not. But a traveling businessman, like my persona, is apt to become . . . lonely. He could misunderstand, perhaps, local customs."

Gary snorted. "A Cascadian?"

"Polite amorous insistence is still amorous insistence. And it depends so much on the attitude of the person receiving the attention, whether it is unwanted or not. Such a person might come to understand, at a convenient time, that the incident resulted from a cultural misunderstanding . . ."

Gary shook his head. "Rafe, you are even more devious than you were. But yes, that's a possible scenario, and I suppose it suits you better than a false accusation of theft or conspiracy."

"Since I expect to be guilty of the conspiracy, at least, before this is over, yes."

Gary's directions led Rafe to a mountain village straight out of the tourist brochures. Up a narrowing valley on a steep winding road, mountains already snowcapped looming closer and closer above . . . to the picturesque hotel with its wide porches on three sides, the big airy rooms looking out on nothing but scenery.

Genson Ratanvi thought it was charming, and said so. Rafe allowed his persona's gaze to linger just a little too long on the young woman at the desk when he came down to inquire about places to eat in the village. Then, instead of going to eat right away, he headed for the bar Gary had told him about.

Inside, it was like every other small-town bar Rafe had seen. Noise aspiring to music came from speakers on one side. Two women of a certain age leaned across the bar, chatting; at a table in the corner, three men eyed him as they went on with whatever conversation they'd been holding. One of the women, a redhead, looked up.

"Want something?" she asked.

Rafe compared her to the description Gary had furnished and ordered a drink; he handed her the marked bill.

"You're not from around here," she said.

"No," Rafe said. "From Cascadia. I am sent by my company to find a supplier of food processing equipment."

"Here?" asked the blonde.

"Well . . . not exactly." Rafe sipped his drink. "I have been here on your lovely world for many days, and I needed a break. It is lonely, you know, traveling so far from home at the holidays."

"Holidays?"

"At home," Rafe said, "It is the festival of trees. We put lights in the trees and walk among them." Cascadians did that, anyway. He had done it once, just to experience what Cascadians claimed was the ineffable spiritual power of trees. What he'd felt was chilly and damp from the wet branches dripping on his head. Now he leaned toward the woman and fell easily into the role Gary had given him.

"We don't worship trees here," the redhead said. "But I know what you mean about being lonely."

From there the conversation moved swiftly to the necessary conclusion, both he and the redhead having the same goal. She offered to show him around; he agreed.

On the way up the street to the high end of town she suggested a trip to the town's dairy center, empty at this time of day. Rafe agreed. They spent a pleasant fifteen minutes or so in the hay barn, settling on who would do what, and then Rafe walked back to the hotel alone. They might have enjoyed more, but an essential part of the agreement was that no biological evidence should be produced.

"I understand your concern, Ser Ratanvi," the man in the green uniform said an hour later. "And I mean no disrespect to either your system of origin or yourself. But when we have a complaint—"

"But it wasn't me," Rafe said, thickening his Cascadian accent. "She must have made a mistake. I'm a Cascadian; I would never offer insult to anyone. It's against our culture. And I have tickets. You've seen them."

The man's name tag read SLY LILYHANDS, which seemed entirely too strange, but his subordinates—two of them—addressed him formally as Lieutenant Lilyhands without so much as a twitch of the mouth. He sighed now, obviously a little out of patience with the stubborn foreigner. "Ser Ratanvi," he said a little more slowly. "It is the policy of our government that if a person is detained from travel for an official inquiry, the transport company must refund the price of the tickets or offer equivalent transportation later. You will not be out the cost of the tickets."

"That's something." Rafe pouted. "But it is a disgrace even to be mistakenly thought to have committed such a heinous act. If my company finds out—"

"They will not find out from us, unless you are in fact guilty," Lilyhands said. "Now—if you will agree to make yourself available, and not attempt to flee the community, I will simply retain your identity information." He tapped the ID folder he had taken. "Otherwise, I'm afraid it will be necessary to take you into custody. And I hope you realize that this is a courtesy to a foreign . . . guest . . . and that our laws would allow me to take you into custody no matter what your demeanor."

Rafe nodded. "I understand. It is indeed most kind of you to allow me to remain in . . . more congenial surroundings." He bowed a little, in the Cascadian manner.

Lilyhands laughed. "It was your congeniality that may have gotten you into trouble. A little less congeniality and a little more circumspection would be advisable. Now—you understand that no commercial transportation will be available to you without current ID, is that clear?"

Rafe nodded. "But must I walk everywhere, then?"

"No. Your money is good on local public transport. This applies to long-distance transport only." Lilyhands handed back Ratanvi/Rafe's jacket, the business case, and a little bowl containing what had been in Rafe's pockets: the hotel room key, the small change. All but the ID case.

"Thank you, again, for your generous handling of this unfortunate situation," Rafe said, in Ratanvi's plummy voice. "I apologize for my remarks earlier—it was just the surprise of being accused of such a thing."

"No offense taken," Lilyhands said. "Just settle in for a few days as we straighten this out. The local judicar is on vacation, but she'll be back in ten days or so, and then—and maybe by then the young lady will have changed her mind."

At the hotel, it was clear that his room had been searched; Rafe didn't bother to check for newly planted surveillance gear. He was sure it was there, but it didn't matter. What he ached to know—and could not find out without risking his cover—was whether Gary's contact was Lilyhands or the woman. Or both. Both would make sense, especially if false claims against tourists were part of an established scam of some sort.

He fell asleep, somewhat to his own surprise, on sheets scented with some flower—a few petals clung to a pillow-case—with the window open to let in a draft of cold air off the mountains behind the city. He had nothing to do until Gary contacted him—if Gary contacted him—and he might as well sleep.

Two boring days later, Rafe had chatted up the hotel food service manager, who complained about the inadequacies of the hotel's automated kitchen machinery, and the town's only baker, a Luddite who insisted on doing every-thing by hand. Rafe felt that he had done all he could to establish himself as a genuine food service professional. Everyone in town knew he was stuck there, and most of them thought they knew why. The redhead turned her back on him when he came into the bar; other locals glared. Rafe himself was tired of wearing Ratanvi's plump suit and the disguising facial pads that made him look, to himself, like a constipated rodent.

Another day dragged past. Rafe had walked up the street on one side of the noisy creek, and back down the street on the other side. Though a brightly colored tram trun-dled up to the first ski lift station and back, Rafe preferred to stretch his legs. He needed nothing in any of the few shops, though they were fully stocked with anything a tourist might want, the owners having changed out the summer stock for winter: sweaters, caps, gloves, fur hats and jackets. He had nothing to do. It was like being in deep space, in FTL flight, isolated from anything interesting, except for the smells. His nose wrinkled as a small herd of cattle appeared at the head of the road, up the mountain.

Every day, Lieutenant Lilyhands appeared at the hotel, paused for a polite greeting, and then walked back to the station.

Rafe wondered how much longer he could stand this without going crazy. He had finally given up walking the street over and over, and spent hours sprawled in a swing on the hotel's porch, staring down the valley. Far away, sunlight twinkled on moving vehicles, where the regional roadway and railway ran together for a few miles, sharing bridges across the Meltorn River.

The car was a kilometer up the valley before he registered it. By now he knew the usual ones: the regional post van, bright blue with buff stripes, that came every day, the eight vehicles that left in the morning and returned in the evening from jobs away in the valley, the grocery truck that came every other day to the hotel and restaurants and bars. This car was different. Rafe took his feet off the little table and looked more closely.

The car went past the hotel and stopped in front of the nearest bar. Gary got out and went into the bar without glancing at the hotel. Lilyhands, on his morning walk through the village, nodded to Rafe on the hotel porch and stepped into the bar, as usual. He came out and walked back to the hotel.

"I do believe, Ser Ratanvi, that your accuser may have made a mistake; she seems willing to retract her accusation. On the other hand, I really must have the judicar's permission to release your identification documents. So I remind you that you cannot travel on any commercial vehicles"—the slight stress he placed on 'commercial' went with a twitch of his mouth—"and while I do not feel compelled to forbid your traveling outside the town limits with a friend, I must remind you that your identification will stay in my custody until the justice has put her stamp on the file."

"That's very kind of you," Rafe said, adding Ratanvi's stiff little bow.

"I might just mention that there's a fellow in the bar now, someone I personally know, who says he's willing to take you into town for a short time. I realize that a foreigner might not be willing to just go off with a stranger, but you may find it easier to contact your office back home, let them know what's going on and when you'll be back, from a communications center like Brygganha, which is where this fellow's headed. It's up to you, of course."

"That's very kind," Rafe said again. "I should—I need to contact the office, you're quite right, and also to make another reservation. I should talk to him perhaps?"

"I can tell him you're willing," Lilyhands said. "If you want to settle up with the hotel . . ."

"How very kind of you," Rafe said, bowing again. "I believe I shall take the assistance of this kind stranger, if you will excuse me."

The hotel clerk accepted his money; Rafe rolled his belongings into his duffel and was waiting on the hotel porch when Lilyhands came back with Gary and solemnly introduced them to each other, with a warning to Gary that Ser Ratanvi was on no account to be allowed to use commercial transport without proper identification, which he, Lilyhands, retained.

"He is not a criminal," Lilyhands said slowly, as if Gary needed a full explanation. "There was a misunderstanding, and I do not wish to make difficulties, but the judicial process must be followed. When the judicar comes back, I am sure that his documents will be released."

"I will take care of him," Gary said.

"You have my thanks," Rafe said, with a final bow before he climbed into Gary's vehicle.

EIGHT

"That was a very interesting experience," Rafe said as Gary negotiated the tight curves on the way down the valley.

"I've stashed nervous clients there before, some of them unwillingly," Gary said. "People likely to interfere with the op, cause me trouble . . ." He looked sideways at Rafe. "Truth be told, I did consider just leaving you there until afterward, but I was afraid you might bolt. Lilyhands is good, but I'm not sure he's your match."

"He's not," Rafe said. "But I wouldn't have bolted. You don't need to be worrying about me." His tongue probed the edge of a cheek pad. "Can I get out of character now, or should I stay Ratanvi awhile longer?"

"Stay until we're through Istelhaut. There's a rail station there, a busy one. Buy a ticket to Brygganha, board the train, get off at the first stop. I'll meet you there."

"What about ID?"

"They don't check ID on the suburban part of the line. And you can use this in the ticket machine—" He handed over a small ID chip. On it, Rafe saw his own image, with a different name: Oliver Pierson. Address: 6713 Av. Rets, Apt. 1407.

"It's a valid address," Gary said. "Shouldn't be a problem in a quick inspection, if they even ask. Which they won't."

Rafe went into the train station—as busy as Gary had said, and why was that?—and bought his ticket from a machine that evinced no interest in who he was. It probably had a visual recorder—certainly the station had a number of them—but how often were such records checked? He found the right track and bought himself a snack from one of the vendors. When the gate opened for his train, he boarded with a crowd of others, pushing his ticket into the automated reader. No one in uniform appeared on the short ride to the first stop, where he got off along with at least fifty others and pushed his way out of the exit turnstiles. He didn't spot Gary at first; it wasn't the same vehicle but a utility van, with MARRIN & SONS, CUSTOM DOORS AND WINDOWS on the door. Gary was apparently reading a newsfax like half the other drivers in the lot, his face partly hidden with just enough profile showing for Rafe to recognize.

"Get in back," Gary said as Rafe neared him. Rafe said nothing, but climbed into the back of the little van. Gary drove off and after a short distance said, "Now you can change. Clothes for you are in the blue duffel. Be sure to wear the cap, and come sit by me when you're done. Bring the mugs that are in the rack behind my seat."

Rafe changed quickly, stuffing Ratanvi's paunch, cheek pads, and clothes into his own duffel and putting on the contents of the blue one. Programmable long underwear, lightweight body armor, a loose turtleneck that concealed the armor's gorget, a set of arm and leg sheaths, already loaded with knives—Rafe slid them out to check before putting the sheaths on—shoulder and back holster with the firearms to put in them, a striped jumpsuit to fit over all that, and a cap that—when he felt carefully—had reflex armor sewn in between its cloth layers.

He glanced around the van's interior. Neatly racked and secured tools and other equipment. Two multipaned windows and a door were secured in racks toward the rear, with an obvious invoice taped to the door.

He clambered forward. They were moving along a road lined with light industrial buildings: building contractors, plumbing supply, weatherstrip manufacturing, and the like. The mugs racked behind Gary's seat had the logos of a local drive-through eatery; Rafe picked them up and twisted between the seats to settle in beside Gary and put the mugs in the forward drink holder as a much larger vehicle roared past.

Gary also wore a striped jumpsuit with a logo panel on the breast. "Everything fits?" he said, not taking his eyes off the road.

"Like you measured me," Rafe said. "Changed your mind about having me along, I see. I take it we expect trouble?"

"Trouble pays my bills," Gary said. "I always expect it, though I do my best to avoid the worst of it. Still, if I let you get killed, where's my money coming from? Yeah, your father's rich, but my contract's with you." He negotiated a sharp turn in silence. "About the other—you behaved yourself, Lilyhands said. And it occurred to me, if this is an ISC inside job, as you think, then your expertise may be useful. As long as you do what you're told." That with a warning glance. "You can still use stickers as well as firearms, right?"

"Right," Rafe said. His stomach felt far more uneasy than the vibration of the van warranted.

"We have food in the van," Gary said. "If you're hungry."

"Not really," Rafe said.

"I need you in condition," Gary said. "You're going to

be helping Sid with the communications; I can't afford to have you groggy. You look sick. What's the problem?"

"I'm just tense," Rafe said. "I get this way."

"Well, don't barf in my van. Try some crackers."

"In a bit," Rafe said. He watched the terrain to their right. Up there—ahead, off to the right—his family were imprisoned by . . . by whom, exactly? He still wasn't sure. And how were they doing? He tried to imagine it, then tried not to. His background gave him too many pictures of such things, and it was all too easy to put his father's face, his mother's, his sister's, into those images. "How far in this van?" he asked.

"South side of Brygganha," Gary said. "Three to four hours, if conditions don't change. We're delivering the windows and door there. You don't say anything, just follow orders."

Rafe had never been to this part of his home world; his family home was on the far side of the continent, and they had vacationed mostly in the tropics. Now he saw mountains, ever more mountains, lifting higher and higher, and the sea visible on the left, bright as a mirror. The sun sank westward; gulfs between headlands appeared far to the north as traffic thickened and the usual urban-suburban mess closed in around them. Gary turned into a fenced yard, backed up to a loading dock, and hopped out. Already the yard was dim, the late sun blocked by a taller warehouse across the road.

"Got those windows," he yelled up to the man on the dock. And to Rafe, "Come on, kid, get out here and help."

Rafe climbed down and went to the back of the truck. Gary was already up on the loading dock, opening the van's back doors. The man on the loading dock had gone back inside for a wheeled dolly; Rafe climbed up to stand beside Gary. When the man came back, they eased the windows and door onto the dolly, and the man wheeled them into the light.

"Close up," Gary said to Rafe. "Then get in the cab and wait." Rafe closed and locked the back doors, jumped off the loading dock, and climbed back into the cab. Whose windows and door? Was this Gary's other job, making custom windows and doors? Another truck came in the gate, now with lights on. Rafe slumped down in his seat like any lazy helper, cap tipped forward. Footsteps crunched past him; someone tapped on the window. He looked up. Gary beckoned.

"Sid's going to drive from here. I'll be with the rest of the team. It's about another hour, hour and a half, to our base for this op." Gary waved and turned away; someone Rafe had never seen had opened the other door and was already climbing in.

"Understand you know something about surveillance and com," Sid said. Rafe couldn't tell much about him except that he was dark and lean.

"Something, yes."

"Gary said he knew you back when," Sid went on. "Just so you know, I didn't, so I got no reason to trust you and I'll kill you if I think you're ruining the op. That clear?"

"Clear," Rafe said.

They said nothing more for the remainder of the drive, and it was dark by the time they reached the far side of the city. Sid proved a careful, skillful driver; he attracted no attention, and Rafe did his best to project bored relaxation. As traffic and lights thinned out on the road north—Brygganha, Rafe recalled, was the northernmost large city on the west coast—the air grew markedly colder. Sid made no move to turn on the van's heater; Rafe touched the controls of the programmable underwear. Finally, Sid turned off the main road onto a secondary, and then another, always moving toward the mountains and climbing; it grew colder yet. They came to a cluster of vacation cottages overlooking a stream, and Sid pulled into a lean-to shelter. Before Rafe could say anything, he had touched a control on the dash, and Rafe felt the van shudder . . . then blackness rose around them as the van sank down into the ground and something thudded closed overhead. A jerk, a faint whine, and then lights came on.

The underground garage held three trucks, the van, and several smaller vehicles; it had room for more. Sid drove the van off the lift, parked beside the trucks, and sent the lift back to the surface.

"Come on," he said to Rafe. "You come with me."

Rafe climbed out. "Do I need my stuff?"

"Might as well. Don't worry about the rest; someone else will unload it."

Rafe grabbed his own duffel and the blue one his present costume had come in, and followed Sid's directions through two massive doors and down a corridor; Sid stayed behind him, which Rafe understood all too well.

"In there," Sid said finally. Rafe opened that door, hoping it was not a cell in which he'd be locked for the next few days. Instead, it was a control center, banks of displays curving around a central space furnished with a round table and four swivel chairs. "Your stuff can go in the corner there," Sid said. "Have you eaten?"

"No," Rafe said.

"I'll call the kitchen," Sid said. "Pick a chair. Your headset's number two. The op schedule's on the table— the blue folder."

Rafe dropped the duffels in a corner and tried out all four chairs, just to annoy Sid, who didn't seem to care. He picked one that felt just that bit better than the others— it would matter after hours in it. Sid, meanwhile, had called for "two meals" on what appeared to be an ordinary household intercom. Rafe picked up the blue folder. Now, at last, he'd know how Gary had organized the op. His brows went up almost immediately . . . it started as what he'd have done on his own, but quickly went beyond that. He didn't know it all; he hadn't done this kind of work himself . . .

Someone knocked on the door; Rafe didn't look up, but he heard Sid move across the room, open the door, and mutter something. A tray landed in front of him on the table. "Here," Sid said. "Eat up. It's going to be a long ride. We've got twenty minutes to eat and whatever."

Rafe peeled back an opaque film and found a pile of sliced meat, a fresh salad, and a stack of some kind of cookie. His stomach growled; now he was hungry. Sid ate, too, shoveling in slices of meat as if it were his last meal. "I hope protein doesn't make you sleepy," he said finally. "My metabolism loves it."

"I'm fine," Rafe said. He felt completely awake, fully alive, as he always did before something started.

"Toilet's in there," Sid said, jerking his head at the room's only other door. "No other exit, and I wouldn't try breaking through the ceiling if I were you."

"I wasn't thinking of it," Rafe said.

The displays showed, singly and in combination, the locations of surveillance satellites, the location of aircraft, trains on the railway, and other "items of interest." Rafe found himself looking at a live infrared image of Aurora Adventure Lodge from a high-altitude drone: advanced software had already presented an outline of every room, with labels so far as were known, and the little blobs that represented heat were easily located. The chimney in the main lodge emitted a bright white spot with wavery pattern of colors around it.

"Your temps are on the side panel," Sid said. He wore a headset with two different mike attachments, now both pushed aside. "Can you keep an eye on the HAWATS as well?"

"HAWATS . . ." Rafe looked at the other screens.

"High-altitude weather satellite. Second screen on your right. At its current settings, it's not a problem even though it'll be scanning the area in about a half hour, but if someone tweaks its controls, it can change its parameters, and we need to know if that happens. Watch for a blue flashing light on the bottom of that screen, and if you see it, let me know and read off the numbers that will display."

"Can do," Rafe said. "There's a small heat source leaving cabin eight and heading south . . ."

"Probably a guard taking a pee," Sid said. "Let me see—" He rolled his chair over and looked at Rafe's screen. "I'll tell the guys."

"It's hotter than the other single blobs," Rafe said. "Someone took their jacket off?"

"Could be." Sid pulled one of the mikes forward. "Airtrans flight twenty-one, be advised there's a wild animal detected south of the runway . . ."

"Airtrans?" Rafe asked.

"Just in case," Sid said. "It's a charter cargo outfit."

Gary came into the command center a few minutes later. "Sid?"

"Fine, boss. He hasn't tried anything."

"Good. Rafe, if you've followed the plan, we're on page eleven now, line four. Two minutes from drop. No signs of trouble so far. That outlier you spotted—still there?"

Rafe looked. "There, but cooler . . . cooler than the other outside heat sources."

"Let me see." Gary moved in close to Rafe's screen and

hit some controls. A plot appeared on the screen instead of the image he had been seeing. A curved line, dropping from left to right, with dots not quite on it, but parallel. "That's . . . interesting."

"What?" Rafe said.

"The plot is how fast an unprotected human body will chill to infrared detection at the air temperature on site. The dots tell me that someone is out there without adequate clothing. And whoever it is isn't moving very fast." He looked again. "Not at all in the last twenty minutes. That's not likely to be a guard. Rafe, you don't have any fancy communications method the rest of us don't know about, do you? Did you reach one of your family and tell them to get outside?"

"No," Rafe said. "I haven't tried to contact them—not since that first night I told you about, anyway. But do you really think one of them got out?"

"Barring your intervention, if I were guessing, I'd guess one of them was allowed to escape, to raise false hopes, and they'll reel him or her in shortly. Let whoever it is get really cold, hypothermic, confused, and then—"

Rafe repressed a shudder. On his screen, now back to its original form, a string of tiny dots like sugar grains appeared, then disappeared.

Gary turned away, talking now into his mike. "Confirm drop-one. Confirm drop-two." To Rafe he said. "Did you get that on IR?"

"Yup," Rafe said. "Didn't last long, though."

"Not supposed to. They've all got a heat patch on for drop, then it's off. Our drone picks it up; a satellite would have to be damned lucky."

"I've got Red One," Sid said. Gary nodded. Rafe felt his dinner turn to a solid lump in his stomach. He looked along the bank of screens. The weather satellite, HAWATS, had not deviated from its path, and no blue light flashed. But on the next screen, which Sid had told him nothing about, four icons suddenly appeared: two orange triangles and two red squares.

"Gary," he said. "What's that?"

Gary glanced where Rafe pointed and huffed out his breath. "Well, well, well . . . someone wants to join the party. That's someone setting out from the regional emergency response headquarters—someone must've called an alarm. Rafe, widen your field . . . is there a forest fire or something?"

Rafe moved the controls. Now he could see the heat emissions from those vehicles, but no heat source between them and Aurora. "Nothing I can see. They're moving a fair clip—they have to be aircraft—"

"They are. You have identification routines—"

Rafe found the right controls and the IDs came up—each craft's registration number first, and then its type.

"Personnel carriers, two of them, and two ground attack—"

"Thirty more seconds and we'd have had their com cut off," Gary said. Sid, Rafe noticed, was muttering into both of his mikes, presumably letting the teams know what was coming. "Well, it's always something. Let's see now." He pulled up a third chair and moved to the console at the end. "Baker tango: four buns in the oven."

Now Rafe saw more emissions on his screen, this coming in from the southwest. He opened his mouth, but before he could speak Sid said, "Those're ours. Look at your other plot—they're green squares. Gary—we've got their com."

"I need Aurora's ID code," Gary said. "It's not the one that's in the record . . . Rafe, do you have a clue what a code starting with *BTR* might be?"

"Secure ansible access," Rafe said. "It's an ISC

sequence; it'll be eighteen digits and letters, changed at least daily by a random generator. What time is it?"

"Two minutes to midnight," Gary said. "Why?"

"It'll roll over at midnight. Change your time signature and transmit any eighteen digits and letters; if you're questioned, point out that the system just changed it . . ."

"Gotcha." Gary did that, then began talking into his mike. "Poppyseed, this is Aurora guardhouse . . . we goofed . . . yes . . . perimeter malfunction, just like you said it probably was."

Rafe switched channels so he could hear both sides.

"Ice bear?" asked a masculine voice.

"No, not an ice bear, just one of my guys who didn't turn in time, hit the perimeter, and didn't want to admit it. We owe you fuel allowance; I'm really sorry about this."

"It happens," the same voice said. "Want us to do a flyover just to be sure he was telling the truth this time?"

"We don't want to pay for that much fuel, Poppyseed. I've got guys out there now patching the wires. You can if you want to, but I've logged the time of this call."

"Whatever you say. Poppyseed out."

The icons turned and headed back east.

"Cooperative fellows," Gary said. "Wonder if they'll stay cooperative or if . . . yup, someone decided to tag a little extra flight time."

One of the ground assault craft had slowed, and now, dropping to near ground level, turned back toward Aurora.

"Perimeter's clear," Sid reported. "Blue's on it; Blue Three is looking for the outside blip; we're not getting any thermal from ground level. Red's going in."

Rafe felt cold.

"Laggard's getting reamed by his boss," Gary said. "He says he wants to check something he saw . . . he's flying awfully low and there are large rocks out there . . ."

"Go ahead," Gary said. Moments later, a thermal bloom lit Rafe's screen.

"What was that?" Rafe said. "Did you have stuff on the ground?"

Sid laughed, unpleasantly. "Don't need it."

"But did you—"

"World's full of rocks for idiots to bash themselves on if their onboard scan freezes up," Sid said. "He should have followed orders."

"They're coming back," Gary said. "Couldn't miss that flash. But they're convinced it was pilot error. They're coming to pick up pieces, not look for black hats. The other assault plane's going in; they've sent for medical. Handy, if we need more than we think."

"Red's in," Sid said. "Resistance . . . neutralized. Two females found locked into cabin eight . . . transmitting images. Rafe, are these the right people?"

Rafe stared at the screen . . . he hadn't seen any of them in years, but that was clearly his mother, despite the bruises and black eye. The other . . . might be his sister. Must be her. "Yes," he said, trying to hold his voice steady. "Mother and sister. The baby?"

"No baby," Sid said. "And no male. Blue team's looking but they haven't found him. The whole place is secure now."

"Can I talk to M—to my mother?"

"Not yet," Gary said. "We're not done yet. I don't want to risk it."

"Weather's deteriorating," Sid reported. "Rafe, give me a readout on the HAWATS."

"Temperature's dropping below freezing, frozen precip—sleet changing to snow, flurries at first and steady within an hour, accumulation to sixteen centimeters by morning . . ."

"We've got to find that outlier or he's dead," Gary said. He spoke into his mike. "Blue Leader, you've got weather moving in; we want you all out of there before it closes down . . . find that outlier or we'll have to leave whoever it is . . ."

"No!" Rafe said, half rising. He froze then: Sid, without moving from his place, had pulled a weapon and had it centered on his forehead.

"Sit down," Gary said. "Malcolm's not going to leave him if he can find him, but I'm not going to risk the team having to stay there, in case this mess is run by someone with enough clout to call in heavy stuff on a fixed location."

Rafe's heart hammered in his chest; he sat down. "I just—"

"Sid, put it away. He's not going to do anything."

Sid shrugged and slid the weapon into its holster. "Blue's still looking. He's not where he was, and it's a mess of boulders, lots of hollows and things."

Rafe sat rigidly.

"Patch Rafe to Blue's channel, too, Sid," Gary said. "Rafe, if that's your father, do you have any idea where he'd go? Would he be trying to hide? Would he try to disguise a thermal signature?"

"You said he's hypothermic, by the earlier scan," Rafe said.

"Yeah, but before that. Would he have had a strategy? Did he have any cold-weather or high-altitude experience? We need to narrow the search parameters."

Rafe tried to remember. "He did go hunting—I don't remember exactly where, but it was in the fall or winter. Not trophy hunting, really—or, he never brought trophies home. It was more to spend time with his peers, I think. Uh . . . we used to go for hikes when I was a little boy—

I do remember being caught out in a storm with him once and he said get on the downwind side of some rocks, hunker down . . ."

"What was the wind direction when you first spotted that outlier?"

"Um . . . southeast . . ."

"So he'll have gone to the west side—also more cover from the lights, if he was trying to get farther away—and now he's on the drift-exposed side."

"Blue, look on at the west side of boulders, any hollows—"

"How big is your father?" asked a voice in Rafe's earbug.

"About a centimeter shorter than me," Rafe said. "That makes him . . . one meter eight, maybe?"

"Close enough. He'd curl up?"

"I don't know," Rafe said. "I think—"

"Wait—" A confused noise, then. "We found someone— dammit! He's really cold. Stiff. Not responding."

"Is he—?"

Gary turned. "The rule with hypothermia: they're not dead until they're warm and dead. Our people know how to handle it."

"Here's the video," Sid said. "Is that your father?"

The gaunt, gray, battered face, stiff as a corpse's, looked nothing like his father except for the familiar scar above his right eyebrow.

"Yes," Rafe said. He could not say more.

"First team's airborne with two females," Sid said. "Original course is not feasible; they'll go the alternate route . . ."

"Close to that fire—"

"Second team's loading . . . second team's away."

"Where are they going?" Rafe asked. "I want to be there when—"

"Security first," Gary said. "Pay attention to your station."

His station. Rafe dragged his mind back to the assignments he'd been given. The HAWATS satellite moved serenely on its orbit: no flashing blue lights, no sign that it was doing anything but tracking the winter storm moving across the landscape below. No other unidentified blips on the other screen.

He, Gary, and Sid kept watch; Gary and Sid both muttered into their mikes occasionally, but Rafe had no live circuits. He wanted to argue, but he knew it would do no good. A half hour later, Gary took his earbug out.

"Current status. The bad boys will be here for interrogation in a couple of hours. Your family have been transferred to long-range transport—a mobile medical facility that will be damned near impossible for whoever did this to locate. You have a choice. You can stay here with me and observe the interrogation, or Sid will take you to a transfer point; you'll meet your family in a secure location."

Much as he wanted to get his hands on those who had held and tormented his family, his first priority had to be their safety—and letting them know he was here and ready to do anything that had to be done.

"I'll go to my family, then," he said. "Where—"

"Rafe, I'm sorry; I can't tell you. This whole op has had some parameters neither of us knew about."

For a moment, his gut knotted into an icy ball. Was Gary betraying him?

"You don't expect a clandestine snatch to have a connection to the regional militia . . . if you're thinking this started with something internal to ISC, I'd be looking very far up the chain of command. Very far." Gary cocked his head. "You have any ideas yet?"

"There's a senior VP who's now listed as acting CEO," Rafe said. "I'd have to look at him, though it's hard to believe—"

"Lewis H. Parmina," Gary said.

"You know him?"

"I know of him. It's my business to know something about people at that level—"

"So you would have researched my father—"

"Of course. And before you get your back up, I asked you all those questions because I needed to know what you knew. And to double-check my data." He paused; Rafe said nothing. Gary went on. "Parmina, now . . . very interesting fellow. You know he was adopted?"

"Adopted? No."

"Yes. His official public bio mentions it; he's proud of rising from humble origins, apparently. I've found another source with more details. He was one of a group of children found alive on a derelict spaceship—he was very young, barely more than a toddler, like most of the others. There were no adults on the ship; the presumption was that they'd been taken by slavers who didn't want to bother with the children. It was an ISC repair ship that found them; since the ship's AI was ruined, and its beacon nonstandard, the children were put up for adoption through the company's own internal site. The Parminas both worked for ISC; they took Lew and a girl. The girl died young; the Parminas died when Lew was in university."

"Did he kill them?"

"The girl, certainly not. He was only about seven; she was older, and she contracted whitefever while off at camp one summer. The parents . . . I never looked into it, tell you the truth. It was an accident, is what the report says. He went to work for ISC shortly after that."

"When I was a child," Rafe said, "I remember meeting

him at the office. My father wasn't CEO yet; he was some-where far up in the hierarchy, though I don't recall what. Lew was his personal assistant. When I got out of that place—" He still hated to say the name. "—when I went to college, Lew used to come talk to me. My father was so angry, he said. He tried to give me advice."

"And he ended up a senior vice president, in line for the top job," Gary said. "Very convenient, having the CEO's son disgraced and out of the picture."

"I can't believe—"

"Oh, come on, Rafe. Surely you don't have any lin-gering pockets of naïveté. Yes, there are exceptionally talented orphans who pull themselves up by their boot-straps and rise like oil above the common water. But in our culture? Where everyone knows that birth matters, especially in the upper echelons?"

"I never heard anything against him," Rafe said. "He had that smooth polish all successful climbers have, but that means nothing."

"What I find interesting," Gary said, "is that I can't find any flecks on the gloss. Other than a daughter with psychological problems, that is. Was that you, by the way?"

"Me? No, I had nothing to do with her. I suppose he wanted me kept away as a bad influence."

"Or because you might notice things," Gary said. "She has never . . . what is the phrase? . . . lived up to her poten-tial."

"What does this have to do with . . . ?"

"With your family? Little. With Parmina's . . . a lot, I suspect. There's also his wife. Good family—a social climb for him, but he was already well up in the company at that point, and obviously on his way. As a girl, a lively girl, not exactly wild but definitely headstrong. Finished university and graduate school, was headed, her family thought, for a career in genetic engineering. And then she fell in love with Parmina and married and . . . her older brother says the lights went out. She's the perfect society wife now. She hardly sees her own family."

"So you think he's the villain."

"My research shows the man is ruthless in business, seriously into micromanagement and control, and a master planner. There certainly could be someone else—perhaps someone who wanted to detach your father from Parmina—but Parmina has all the characteristics necessary to pull something like this. If he thought your father was softening toward you, might bring you home and install you in Parmina's place—"

"That wouldn't happen," Rafe said.

"It's what he thinks, not the reality, that drives him," Gary said. "So my point is, I don't want to transport you directly to your parents, not this instant. We need to be sure the op wasn't compromised at all; we need to keep all the clients safe. Can you be patient a little longer?"

Rafe struggled for a moment, then managed a tight smile. "I am patience on a tombstone," he said.

"As long as it's the right person under the tombstone," Gary said.

NINE

Adelaide Group, when they reached it, lay beyond the usual trade routes Vatta serviced. Its ansibles were functioning, shortening the response time of the local officials and giving Ky access to a business directory for the various settlements. She was startled to find that Crown & Spears had no branch here; she had grown up believing that Crown & Spears was everywhere, like photons and gravity. She looked at the list of other financial institutions and wondered which to choose. Perhaps the locals could give her some advice.

Unlike the other systems Ky had visited, here humans lived only in space, on huge stations positioned near the ring system of a gas giant. *Humans* was a term of choice in this case, as most were humods whose modifications suited such a life: geeners, in fact, who had been genetically engineered for it from conception—which was entirely artificial. The first face Ky saw on the com screen bulged with what she hoped were implants, the nose was a spongy-looking blob, and the two eyes did not match. She hoped she didn't look as startled as she felt.

Yet their response to the plight of *Dryas'* passengers was as warmly human as Gretna's had been cold and inhumane.

"Of course they can come," the system Traffic Officer told Ky. "We've been trading with Polson for over a century. It may be hard for them at first—I'll talk to our medical people, but I'm thinking they'd be best on Tria—it's the station where most lowmod visitors prefer to stay. Give me a few hours and I'll have the Tria Council give you a call."

Ky would not have considered the Polson humods "lowmod," but to other humods maybe they were. She could imagine what the Gretnans would have thought of Adelaide's citizens.

Tria's Councilor Malroy was just as cordial when she called. "We have plenty of room; we'll just shift some of our people to Qadro."

"That's not a problem?"

"No—we have plenty of room and we enjoy moving; it's bred in us. But tell me—we've never heard of the SDR," Malroy said. "Who are you—some kind of mercenaries?"

"No—we're not for hire," Ky said. "We're part of a military force—Space Defense Force—made up of units from worlds that understand the threat is greater than any one system can handle. This particular unit has ships carrying three flags, as our beacons show."

"Ah. We're a bit off the beaten path; we don't hear much. Is the threat really that great? Do you know if any other systems have been attacked?"

"Bissonet fell to these people," Ky said. "Polson as well. Slotter Key was attacked but—at last report—still holding." She was not going to explain all that had happened at Slotter Key. "The Moscoe Confederation—you may have known of Cascadia?—hasn't been attacked yet. But the ansible service—"

"—is down in many places. Yes. We thought maybe it was a natural phenomenon—some kind of flare or something."

"No, it's definitely sabotage, probably by the same group that attacked Bissonet and Slotter Key, though we can't prove it yet. Our unit's main mission—besides fighting the pirates anyplace we find them—is to recruit additional systems to support the SDF. It's going to take a lot of resources to defeat them; they have a solid head start."

"We don't have a space navy, per se," Malroy said. "A lot of our people have private vehicles . . . we have small insystem search and rescue craft, and some traffic patrol craft, but we haven't had to worry about piracy much . . . nothing beyond the occasional single idiot who thinks he can rob our miners." From her tone, she thought of pirates as dull-witted ruffians.

"I'm afraid all civilized people are going to find a reason to worry soon," Ky said. "This is no ordinary pirate."

"I don't know how we'd find and train a real deep-space warship," Malroy said. "I suppose we'll need to hire someone . . . you're not for hire, you say, but if you know how we could . . . what we could do . . ."

Go back ten years, twenty years, and start over . . . but saying that wouldn't help. "You might contact other governments, the ones you can reach," Ky said. "Talk to them, find out what they're doing."

With that conversation over, Ky considered whether—no, when—to call Stella. Stella would be worrying, wondering what had happened since Ky had left Cascadia. When Ky checked the calendar, she was shocked . . . 115 days? A lot had happened, but it hadn't seemed that long.

Stella might even think Ky was dead, and she'd probably be as angry about the delay as relieved that Ky was in good health. What had she been doing? Was Vatta Transport making any money yet?

That thought led to the state of their supplies, and Ky decided to wait until she had a shopping list before contacting Stella. A few days' more worry surely wouldn't make Stella's reaction worse. In the few days before they docked at Tria, Ky put together a list of everything her group needed.

"We've got to do something about that air lock damage," Hugh said. "Engineering say they can't do a permanent fix themselves—I see there's a repair yard listed here."

Another money sink, Ky thought. And how long would it take? With no Crown & Spears branch here, with no large stash of valuables . . . should she try to sell off one of the shipboard ansibles? If only she hadn't been in such a hurry to get away, she might have figured out a way to make the Gretnans pay for the damage they'd done. She'd gotten supplies for the refugees out of them; she could have gotten some sort of reparations. But at the time she'd been so disgusted and angry . . .

"Contact the others, put together a package, and get estimates, including scheduling," she told Hugh. "With the system ansible working, I can contact Stella. Maybe she can help."

He was back all too soon. As Ky had feared, the estimate for repairing all three ships was more than she had. "They gave us a good deal," Hugh said. "In consideration of our good works, apparently, they cut ten percent off the original."

"I just don't have it," Ky said. No conceivable value of the remaining diamond stash would cover this and the other things they needed. Repairs would have to wait. Her engineers said the patches were holding . . . they could hold a little longer.

A few days after docking at Tria, Ky was still juggling figures when Malroy called her again. "We have talked more to *Dryas*' captain and we have thought about what you said. Though we have no warships to contribute, we know that fleets need supply and other types of ships. We could contribute such a ship—in fact, *Dryas*' captain would like to give you *Dryas*."

Dryas would be filthy, Ky knew, and need a crew, and anyway the refugees needed something to offer in exchange for the help they were getting from Adelaide. What she really wanted was help with the repairs. But a ship was a ship. Maybe she could sell it to pay for repairs, though it didn't seem likely that Adelaide Group had a large market for ships. Maybe Stella would want to take it for Vatta Transport and pay for some of the repairs in return . . .

Before she could answer, Malroy went on. "We would clean the ship and provision it for you. *Dryas*' captain said he would be willing to command, if you were willing to have him. And some of our people have already volunteered for crew."

"That is most kind," Ky said, with an internal sigh. She couldn't sell the ship off if they were doing so much to make it useful for her. "We could definitely use a supply ship, and though I worried about finding a crew, you have solved that problem, too."

"It is no more than your actions deserve," Malroy said. "We were shocked at the perfidy of Gretna Station. We have traded there in the past with no problems, but we will not trade there again."

The other captains were less pleased about the new

ship than Ky expected. "We'll have to protect it," Argelos said. "It will slow us down."

"I don't think so," Ky said. "It should make resupply faster. We can send one escort in with it, fill it up, and then transfer goods at safe distances from stations—or in empty systems."

"Maybe," Pettygrew said. "But how will we know none of the crew are Turek's agents? Are you going to vet them all?"

"I'm going to have my security check, yes," Ky said. "We do have to assume that not all volunteers are safe. I understand that."

"Would you like the use of my adviser as well?" Argelos asked. "I don't know who you have, what their background is."

"A former Slotter Key military man with security experience," Ky said. "Backed up by my second in command—you've met him—who has mercenary experience closer to this sector. But if your adviser finally wants to let me know who he is . . ."

"He's not eager for that, but he wants to be in on any security screening."

"And I would like to contribute someone as well," Pettygrew said. "I believe that we, being from Bissonet, may have some very useful background."

"There is the matter of courtesy," Ky said. "We should be tactful in our investigation. But I believe the locals will understand the need for our caution."

Ky explained their concerns to Malroy, who nodded. "Of course, after the terrible events, you would want to be sure you had no vermin in your system. We will make available space and clerical support, if you need it, for your investigation. Can you give me a list of personnel who will be involved? And you yourself, I would like to meet hand-to-hand."

"Of course, though I can leave the ship only briefly," Ky said.

Malroy was a cheery, round-faced individual with the usual microgravity humodifications: lower limbs ending in branched tentacles, upper limbs divided at the elbow with one pair of hands and another set of tentacles, these specialized for sensation of chemicals, magnetic fields, and other useful bits. In addition, she had an artificial "eye" in her forehead and a cranial crest suggesting a larger and more elaborate implant than those Ky was used to. She met Ky in a lounge designed for transients who were comfortable in higher gravities: though it was less than Ky was used to, she did not bounce off the floor with every step, and her clothes hung where they were supposed to without tugging on the adhesive tabs.

With Malroy was Captain Partsin of *Dryas*. He still looked gaunt, but less so than he had onscreen when they left Gretna. He strode forward to clasp her hands in his. "My dear Captain Vatta . . . we had always heard of the honorable Vatta Transport, but truly I never expected that I and so many others would owe our lives to your courage and generosity. My own ship is small, a very tiny gift to repay that generosity, and I would hope that it will enable you to win this war against the pirates. You have my thanks and the thanks of our remaining people. I understand your need to question some of them who wish to serve as crew, but I hope you will understand that they do not have all the documentation that they should, because of the conditions under which we evacuated. Those of my crew I can personally vouch for."

"Thank you," Ky said. "You are certainly more than generous, and I do understand about evacuees . . . though you know why we must be careful. My second in command,

Hugh Pritang, and Gordon Martin, my security chief, will be joined by the security officers of our other ships." She gestured Hugh and Martin forward. "I believe the others will be here shortly. You had an office or other space?" She glanced at Malroy.

"Yes. Would you prefer to wait for the others or come with me now? It is in the same gravity as this."

"I should return to my ship," Ky said. "With all respect, with Hugh here, the captain needs to be aboard."

"Of course."

On the way, Ky stopped in at the local bank Malroy recommended to inquire about financial transfers.

"We have a relationship with Crown & Spears, of course," the manager said. "We respect them highly, and we will be pleased to handle any funds transfers from or to them. The financial ansible here has had no problems in the last twenty years—before that, you'd have to ask my predecessor."

"My cousin is CEO of Vatta Transport," Ky said. "I know our routes never extended this far, but I hope you've heard—"

"Certainly, certainly. Well, I hope to be hearing from you soon, Captain Vatta."

Ky intended to call Stella when she got back to the ship, but the temporal chart revealed that local time on Cascadia Station was 0200; that gave her an excuse to delay another few hours until first-shift, the usual business day. In the meantime, she noted that Cascadia's searchable directory gave both home and office numbers for Stella Vatta; Vatta Transport, Ltd. was listed as well. To save money, she chose the audio-only option.

"Vatta Transport, how may I help you?" said a pleasant voice.

"Ansible call for Stella Vatta from Kylara Vatta," Ky said.

"Just a moment . . ." A soft tone replaced the receptionist's voice, and then Stella's voice came through.

"Ky! Where are you? Are you all right? What happened? Why aren't you full-band?" Stella sounded as much annoyed as worried.

"I'm in Adelaide Group," Ky said. "It's a long story, but I'm fine, just somewhat short of funds. How are you? And Toby?"

"Things are going well," Stella said, more calmly. "I've established a new headquarters office; we have five ships, now, counting *Gary Tobai,* which I have out on contract doing insystem runs here. The *Kat* was able to make contact with our ship on the Garth-Lindheimer run; they've accepted me as CEO, for now, and they'll be contacting all the Vatta ships they cross paths with. It looks like the most damage to Vatta was within five jumps of Slotter Key."

"That's good, I guess," Ky said. "Of course, most of us *were* within five jumps of Slotter Key."

"We're not making a profit yet," Stella said. "Not from shipping, at least. But it's not a gaping wound in the accounts, either. So what are you doing way over in the Adelaide Group? What happened with those people you were going to . . . see?" The pause was significant.

"It's a long story, not all good, but I'm alive and the ship is whole. I'm traveling now with two other warships, *Sharra's Gift* from Slotter Key and *Bassoon* from Bissonet; we escorted a shipload of refugees from Polson here."

"Refugees? From what?"

"Attack on Polson," Ky said. "Oh, and don't let any of our ships go to Gretna."

A pause while Stella accessed her implant. "Why not?

Mildly shady, is what I have in my file. Check all bills, inspect all replacement parts."

"They've gone from mildly shady to inshore piracy and trafficking in human lives," Ky said. "I bought eighteen indentured workers—"

"You *bought* them? Ky, how could you! That's illegal— and horrible!"

"Not as horrible as what they faced. Bought them and freed them, of course. But that's part of my cash-flow problem. I'm guessing Gretna's economy tanked when the ansibles went out and trade dropped. Whatever the reason, they've gone rogue: they take your money, then try to take your ship and sell you for slaves."

"You're serious . . ."

"Very. Anyway, they wouldn't even let the refugees have food and air. I forced the Gretnans to provide the necessities, but I couldn't leave the refugees there. So we escorted them here; they said Polson and Adelaide had been trading partners before. Adelaide Group's not on our routes now, but they seem to be good people, so if someone has a hole in the schedule—"

"What do they have to trade?"

"Mostly low-grav manufactures. Pharma and things like that. Oh, and humod adaptive devices; most of them are serious humods, engineered for low-grav and rapid-change environments; they need assistive devices to function well in what we call normal."

"I'll look into it," Stella said. "Can you zip me their directory?"

"Right away," Ky said. She called it up and sent the compressed version on sub-audio. "How's Toby?" she asked.

"Toby's fine. In fact, Toby's a raving genius. You won't believe what he's come up with."

"He's trained Rascal to do ansible repairs?"

Stella snorted. "Not quite. Better. He's making more of that very interesting cargo we found—"

"The shipboard—"

"Yes," Stella cut in. Ky could hear the irritation in her voice. But it wasn't a secret; the pirates at least knew about shipboard ansibles. Before Ky could say more, Stella went on. "He's already made one, and he's made some . . . improvements. Apparently all that time he spent with Rafe, he was soaking up everything Rafe told him. That, and native ability. We can certainly market these, if ISC doesn't stop us."

"Or use them as our competitive edge," Ky said. She hoped Stella wouldn't give it all away before they made a profit off it, if Toby really had pulled it off.

"Or use them as our competitive edge, yes," Stella said. "Rascal, by the way, has earned his keep for the rest of his life . . . Toby's education is taken care of already, and Rascal's picture's all over the place. Apparently he's superfertile with the local female dogs, and they've confirmed pregnancy in one hundred percent of the inseminations."

Ky laughed. "I realize this helps our bottom line, but there's something just a little ridiculous about being saved from financial ruin by a scruffy little dog we pulled out of a trash bin."

"Well, you saved the scruffy little dog," Stella said. "Remember all those fairy tales in our children's books, when the hero was the one who helped the little animal stuck in a trap or whatever?"

Ky started to say that real life wasn't a fairy tale, but refrained. Maybe it was, after all.

"So," Stella went on. "Tell me what's going on with you, besides rescuing some refugees."

"It's been . . . interesting," Ky said. "We now have a fleet. Well, a small fleet. Multisystem, since *Vanguard's* now Cascadian registry; there's also one Slotter Key privateer, and one Bissonet former space militia. What he's told me is that while Bissonet always claimed they didn't have privateers, they actually did. They called them militia, though, and their trading capacity was limited."

"Yes, but what happened? You and that Argelos fellow left Cascadia together—"

"Right. Well, you remember that Bissonet was taken—"

"I know that—"

"Argelos had located three Bissonet ships together. They had heard about my idea of combining forces, and they wanted to try it. Originally we had three of them, Argelos and me, a ship from Ciudad, and one from Urgayin, I think it was. We went to an empty system to do some training, which made sense—"

"You were commanding, right?"

"No." Ky sighed. This was going to be difficult. "There were three *Bissonet* ships, remember? Their senior officer insisted that command belonged with the greatest contribution—in other words, she wanted it. And I agreed, because I cared more about the idea than about the power."

"Mistake, was it?"

"Yes. She may've been good before—one of the other ships claimed she was—but she just didn't know how to command this kind of group. She alienated the man from Ciudad. One of the ships didn't show up—and it turned out to have been a plant, someone working as an agent of the pirates. He told them where we were. Didn't know that at the time, of course. I was worried, but she wasn't. Short form is, they ambushed us, and she didn't have a clue how to get anyone out alive. I'd been discussing it with Argelos, just in case—and we lost the battle but three ships came out whole: mine, Argelos', and one of the Bissonet ships, commanded by a man named Pettygrew."

"Ky . . . I don't know how to ask this, but . . . are you sure you know what you're doing?"

"I got three ships out alive when they all thought they were doomed. My tactics. My commands." Ky's throat tightened, thinking of those she hadn't been able to save, and Captain Zavala's courage in coming back to warn them all.

"I believe you. I just . . . people are going to die, Ky, because of commands you give. Are you ready for that?"

"It's already happened," Ky said. "And I'll never be ready, and I am ready now."

"All right. I'm still terrified, you know. You're the only real Vatta of our generation left, that I know of."

"You are as real a Vatta as I am," Ky said. "And this would be a lot easier if I'd been Osman's daughter, wouldn't it? It fits better."

Stella's voice trembled a little. "Yes . . . and I guess I have to get over it."

"I guess you do." Time to get back to realities. "I tapped out the Vatta accounts at Gretna; in fact, Crown & Spears gave me a line of credit so the authorities couldn't claim I hadn't paid all the fees they added on at the last moment. I resupplied there, before they tried to get it all back, and we need repairs soon, for the damage done there. You'll have to start linking accounts again."

"Well, if Adelaide Group is as useful as you're saying, I can extend a route there—maybe *Gary Tobai*. Can you establish a corporate account there before you leave?"

"I set up one for our fleet," Ky said. "I'll have Adelaide Central Bank send you the account information and let them know you want one for Vatta Transport."

"You could contact me using our . . . uh . . . family code."

That had to mean by the shipboard ansibles. "Oh. You're right." How to tell Stella that she'd made changes to the shipboard ansibles, that the original settings would be known to the pirates? "I didn't want to use a channel the pirates might pick up on; we modified ours to use different ones, but yours isn't."

"Toby thought of that, too. He said it was something you'd need. Wonder if we have the same new channels . . ."

How to convey them without risking discovery? Were the pirates monitoring routine ansible transmissions? Or those to a Vatta family member? Ky rummaged through her implant looking for some concealing data that Stella might also have. "Stella, your implant has the list of family birthdays and ceremonies, doesn't it?"

"Yes, why?"

"That channel thing . . . your mother's, month and day; my oldest brother's year and day."

"Oh! Yes. I'll tell Toby and see if those are the same, and if not, I'm sure he can modify it to fit." A pause, then: "Ky, I'm really relieved to hear from you . . . I know I behaved badly before you left Cascadia, and then I thought maybe you were throwing yourself into danger because of that—"

"No, Stella, please—it wasn't that."

"We're just—there's so few of us left. And I know I'm doing the right thing with the company, but . . . Toby is just not enough, if you know what I mean."

"Me, too," Ky said. "Stella, I meant what I said then. To me, you're always family. Always. It doesn't matter how far apart we are."

"Well, before I start sniffling like a kid," Stella said, "I think we should end this conversation. I'll contact you in a few days, if I don't hear from you first, to let you know what I can send. It's such a relief to have real, functioning ansible service!"

"That it is," Ky said. "Later, then."

She arrived on the bridge in time to see the entire bridge crew staring at the external vid monitor. "What in the world is that?" Hugh asked, staring at the screen, where a steel-blue ship with a bright gold stripe down its long axis and some kind of curly gold lettering on the bow was easing toward its docking space. "I'd say a yacht, but it's too big for that."

Ky looked at the message marker coming up on the armrest of her command chair, tapped for access, and grinned.

"It's the *Courageous,* and its captain says they're Ransome's Rangers," she said. "The other two are the *Furious* and the *Glorious.* They want to join up with us." She put up the video they were sending. On the bridge of a ship—presumably the same one—several officers in light-blue-and-gold uniforms with white facings stood watching over the instruments; crew in light blue ship-suits scurried about busily.

"They look like an operetta chorus," Hugh said. "One of those old revivals with the brave young soldier and the pretty dancing girl the prince falls in love with."

"They are a bit gaudy," Ky said. "On the other hand, they are ships. We don't have anything that size or that speed. They've got excellent scan—light on weapons, as you'd expect . . ."

"Do you really think all of them together could take down one pirate?"

"Possibly," Ky said. "At the least, they might make a pirate die laughing."

"You're actually thinking of signing them on?"

"Not necessarily." From the data they'd sent, she couldn't tell if it was a joke or a serious offer. "I will talk to their commander. Apparently he's filthy rich and organized this bunch all by himself. That alone makes me suspicious, but on the other hand, Vatta used to have dozens of ships and *we* weren't pirates."

"No, and you weren't dressed up like stage performers and pretending to be pirate hunters, either."

"I'm just going to talk to them, Hugh. Promise."

"Well, be careful. You're taking security, right?"

"Of course."

Their commander was as handsome as his screen image, though his coloring reminded Ky unpleasantly of Gretna. But Theodore Albert Driscoll Ransome was as cheerful and open as the Gretnans had been dour and sly. Tall, his shock of honey-colored hair flopping over one side of his forehead, he moved as flamboyantly as he spoke.

"Captain Vatta! In reality as I live! What an honor to meet the hero of Sabine!" He flung out an arm and bowed low.

Ky had to think hard to figure out what he meant; Sabine was many crises back in her personal accounting. "Oh, that," she said finally.

"Your modesty becomes you, but I insist, it is an honor to meet you at last." He gave a half shrug, and his captain's cape swirled out dramatically. "Together, we shall do wonders; together we shall free the universe of this scourge of pirates."

Together, Ky thought, they could sound like a primary school play.

"We have a long way to go," she said. It sounded flat after the man's flowery language, but she couldn't match his tone even if she'd wanted to. "Are you prepared to stay the distance?"

"Oh, death and glory by all means," he said, grinning. "Trumpets shall sound and if we fall maidens will throw roses on our graves—"

"If we fail, those maidens will be dead or slaves," Ky said. "This is not an operetta."

He blinked. "Well . . . of course. I understand that. It's only . . . there's no harm in . . . in seeing ourselves as heroes, don't you think?"

"There's no harm in it as long as it doesn't affect performance," Ky said.

"Oh, no danger there. No danger at all. My people are more efficient in pursuit of honor than anything else. I chose them for that."

Could anything so handsome, so decorative, so . . . so enthusiastic . . . possibly be useful? Ky wondered. Behind her, Martin stirred; she knew without asking what he was thinking of this . . . *popinjay* would probably be the kindest term he'd come up with.

"Tell me something about your experience," Ky said.

He smiled broadly and settled himself on the edge of his seat, like a dragonfly about to take off again any moment. "It all started with Grumnos. You won't know Grumnos. It's a moon of one of our gas giants in my home system, and about a century ago the prisoners— it'd been used as convict exile—overthrew the guards and wardens, stole some supply ships, and began preying on commerce in our system. It was more of a nuisance at first—they'd just hold up a ship for ransom, or steal some food, and the government decided that putting it down would cost too much." He gave a dramatic shrug.

"But then it got worse, as rascals always do if you don't nip them in the bud, and about five years ago some of us decided to take care of it ourselves. My friend André and I bought a couple of ships—my *Glorious* and his *Triumphant*—hired some mercs for crew, and by the time we were done . . . well . . ." he dusted his hands. "No more pirates on Grumnos. And it was a ripping good sport, hunting pirates, we decided. André and I set up the Rangers and invited our friends to fit out their own ships and join us. Our government agreed to pay us a bounty for every pirate ship destroyed. For a while, we had very few outland pirates—I imagine they heard about us . . ." He smirked; Ky wanted to laugh but didn't. "But then some nasty types showed up, first one and then two. We fought them off, not without casualties. Poor André was killed when a beam took his ship, but I am assured he would have had time to feel nothing, not that fear ever touched that noble heart. But then . . . then it was I heard about the vast pirate horde assailing distant systems, and it seemed to me the best way to protect my own was to meet them there, at a distance, and with allies whose courage and honor matched our own. I believe you, my lady—Captain Vatta—are such an ally, one I would be proud to die with—"

"I would rather *they* die," Ky said. "But I thank you for the compliment."

"Our ships are small, but our hearts are great," he went on, gesturing magnificently; Ky still could not think of anything but the more melodramatic stage productions. "You and I together—against the foe!" He looked at her then as if he expected applause for the rhetoric and delivery.

Would he and his ships be any use at all? Surely some use—even if only as scouts or messengers—but what a risk if he proved not to be honest.

"I'm somewhat concerned about the lightness of your

ordnance," Ky said. "We expect to be up against groups of the enemy. When you and . . . er . . . André fought the pirates, were you using multiship tactics, or . . . ?"

"Well, we did read about standard tactics, of course," Ransome said. His voice sounded calmer now, as if—having delivered his set speeches—he was actually capable of normal conversation. "But as you say, our ships are small—what some space navies called escort size, as you noticed. We don't mount as much ordnance as the standard tactics called for, so we pretty much had to make it up. Our speed's an advantage, and our smaller size means we can do microjumps in and out of FTL closer to large masses than bigger ships. I've installed the best available navigational computers, and our drives—insystem and FTL both—are top of the line, of course."

"I'm sure," Ky said. She wasn't, not until she'd seen the specs. *Top of the line* in one system might be mediocre in another. "How did you see your contribution to our organization?" she asked.

"Oh, we don't expect to be part of the *regular* fleet," he said. "We're more suited to independent action, I would think. Can't expect my people to knuckle under to an outsider, y'know."

That didn't sound good. "You would need to train with us to be much use," Ky said. "Wouldn't want to be running into each other, fouling each other's shots, that sort of thing."

"Quite," he said. "I do understand that. I was thinking, size of our ships and all, we could be useful as couriers, as scouts, and in cutting-out expeditions." That was a term Ky had never seen applied to space warfare. The rest was along the lines she'd already thought of.

"Tell you what," she said. "You need to meet my other captains, and I need to meet some more of your people.

What you're offering sounds very generous, but you know how it is—people are either going to get along, or not."

"How about a dinner?" he asked. "Or a party?"

"I think we captains should meet first. A quiet dinner, perhaps."

"That would be great . . . I could host . . . no, you probably want something on neutral ground, don't you?"

"Adelaide Station has several good restaurants in the standard-gravity sections, and there's always the Captains' Guild," Ky said. "We can reserve a private room—"

"Splendid! I'll tell my fellows. This evening, or is that too soon?"

"Let me check with Captain Argelos and Captain Pettygrew," Ky said. "If their schedules allow, this evening would be fine."

TEN

Ransome's fellow captains—introduced by Ransome as Dennis Malachi Quartermaine St. Cyrien commanding the *Furious* and Allan Desmond Joachim Baskerville commanding the *Courageous*—were cut from the same cloth as Ransome, though not quite as flamboyant. All three showed up in formal uniforms, the captains' capes of silk that gave them a fine flair as they moved. They, too, had wealthy families, which came as no surprise. Ky felt old and staid beside them; Argelos and Pettygrew looked like she felt.

"You should've seen him at school," said St. Cyrien. "I remember when we were taking that history class—he took it into his head to learn the fighting styles of every period—"

"Only those with swords," Ransome said. "*Much* more fun than the others—"

"—and one day when our teachers arrived, he and Des and Hal were on the main stairs, whaling away at each other—"

St. Cyrien started laughing so hard he could barely talk. Baskerville stepped in to finish the story.

"They were afraid the blood was real," he said. "We didn't use actual sharps; our mothers would've killed us.

And we aren't stupid. So we'd fixed little squirt bottles of red stuff—food coloring, wasn't it?—on the ends of the blades, so when you made contact it pushed some out. It didn't really look that much like blood, but it was red . . ."

"It was just a lark," Ransome said. "But we all got detention for it. I had to read some moldering old lecture about the evils of violence and the dangers of glorifying war . . . not that it had any effect . . ."

Ky glanced at her captains; they both had the expressions of men caught between horror and amusement, and determined not to show it.

"Not that we think war is good, you understand," St. Cyrien said. "I mean, everyone knows it's bad, and people die and so on. But it's been around for thousands of years, and it's not going away. Might as well be on the side of truth and justice and all that, and go at it with flair, don't you think?"

"Flair is nice. Skill and training are even better," Ky said.

"See?" Ransome said, throwing out his hands to the others. "A lady of intelligence and character as well as beauty." He beamed at her. "We're going to get along splendidly, I can tell. You will be the steadying influence—women always are—and I will be—"

"See here," Pettygrew said suddenly. "Are you serious about anything?"

Ransome's handsome face contracted in an obviously intentional scowl. "I am perfectly serious, sir—Captain Pettygrew—about opposing the scoundrels who now threaten civilization. I am prepared to give my life's blood, if necessary—though I quite agree with Captain Vatta that we would prefer the pirates to die instead of ourselves. No one can be more serious than that."

"How old are you?" asked Captain Argelos. "And how

long do you propose to stick with this war? And what does your family think?"

Ransome waved one hand. "My family? They're all quite mad—"

"I can believe that," Pettygrew muttered under his breath.

"They're in the fourth year of their cycle, and you know how that is—or maybe you don't play evolving rings here?"

"Never heard of 'em," Argelos said.

"Oh. Well. They've given up cause and effect for the time being—they're being Irrationalists . . . that's *intentional* Irrationalism, not accidental."

"Doesn't this cause . . . er . . . problems?"

"Oh, but that's the point, you see. It's part of the doctrine of oppositional intellects. Just as with muscles, where one contracts while another relaxes and stretches, so in our culture we exercise one intellect at a time. In the Irrationalist phase, people are legally mad—Irrationalism *is* insane, you know—and they all have to wear labels to warn everyone else."

"This is all fascinating," Argelos said. "But what I wanted to know was, what does your family think of your spending the family fortune fitting out ships and going off to war?"

"It isn't the family fortune; it's mine," Ransome said. "Settled on me when I reached majority. And as for the other—they don't think. They are absent from thinking in this phase. I imagine if they transition to Reason while I'm gone, they'll be upset, but since no one can predict how long their Irrationalist phase will last, I don't worry about it."

"It runs in the family," Pettygrew muttered.

"Tell me," Ky said. "Is one of these phases Romanticism?"

"Of course. I've only been a Romantic for two years now, but I can't imagine being anything else."

Dead hovered on the tip of Ky's tongue, but she managed to not say it.

When they were alone again, Argelos shook his head. "I thought you were a loose cannon when we first met," he said to Ky. "I apologize. I've now seen the real thing, and you are a model of discretion and prudence."

Ky laughed. "He's not that bad."

Argelos narrowed his eyes. "You're not going to tell me you find him attractive?"

"Decorative, merely," Ky said. "But there's always been a place in war for the decorative enthusiasts."

"Cannon fodder," Argelos said. "That's their place. And your senior crew would tell you the same. Send them to charge the barricades like the fools they are."

"You're in a mood," Ky said. "Let's talk plans then. How can we use cannon fodder?"

"Why would we even want to? We aren't fighting that kind of war."

"Support is support. Why wouldn't we want them? They'd be useful as couriers, as scouts—"

"They stick out like supernovas," Pettygrew said.

"So? Who's going to suspect that people in gaudy ships with gaudy uniforms are actually connected to a serious military force? Let them stick out. Let them swagger about, show off, all the rest of it. It will divert attention from the rest of us."

"As long as you're not just falling for the shiny prince-figurine—" Argelos said.

"Oh, for—no, I am not 'falling for' him or any of them."

"He is handsome . . . and you're . . . uh . . . of an age—" said Pettygrew, with a glance at Argelos.

"If you say the word 'hormones'—" Ky said. She was

furiously angry and moved to laugh at the same time. It was just too ridiculous.

"I didn't. I didn't. It's just—" Pettygrew spread his hands.

"I don't believe this. Just because you're both older, and I'm a young female, you think I'm going to lose my judgment—" She walked on a few paces, trying to regain her equanimity. "It would serve you right if I did fall head over heels for him. And it might make him easier to manage if he thought I had—"

"You wouldn't do that!" Pettygrew sounded shocked.

"Well, thank you for that, anyway. But let me tell you—" She rounded on both of them. "—I would rather do that than act like a silly schoolgirl faced with a storybook prince. Pretending romance is at least a calculated tactic; the real thing is . . . is stupid."

She whirled and stalked off; the memory of Hal's betrayal rose in her memory like bile. She had done that once: fallen in love with someone as handsome as Ransome, fallen in love with the whole idea of romance, of two hearts beating as one, two lives lived for each other. Not again. Not ever again . . . and she wasn't going to tell them why, either.

But she would work with Ransome because right now he had ships she needed, and money she needed, and his aims and hers ran side by side.

She came aboard *Vanguard* in a black mood, not helped by the concerned expressions Hugh and Martin wore when she got to the bridge.

"Don't say a thing," she said. "I can read it on your faces—you think I'm impressed by a pretty face and shiny braid."

"I—"

"No. I just got that from Argelos and Pettygrew. It's

not true. I have no interest in Captain Ransome because of his face or his uniform. My interest is military and practical: he has ships we could use, and money we need. We will work with him because we need him, and he, of course, needs us. He can't fight a war with those little ships; he needs to ally with a force that has real muscle."

"We just worried—" Martin began.

Ky rolled her eyes, and he stopped. "I am not a silly schoolgirl. I am not going to go breathless over every handsome face that comes along . . . and if I were, I'd already have fallen for a lot of men on this ship. You're not the ugliest bunch in the universe."

That got their attention; they both looked startled and then slightly ashamed.

"Now," she said. "Let's think how to use Ransome's Rangers to our best advantage. I'm thinking couriers and scouts. They're so flamboyant, it's a kind of disguise; I'm sure others will see them as we did—rich playboys playing at war. If they connect us, they'll probably think what you did—that I've let my hormones influence my decisions. And though I think they are rich playboys, I also think they are more than that."

"All right," Hugh said. "But can you trust them to follow orders?"

"Probably not," Ky said. "But I don't think it matters. If they're loose cannons, they're still a distraction to the enemy."

"And they'll get killed . . ."

"Yes, they'll probably get killed and die convinced they're achieving undying glory. That's their problem. If they don't follow orders, I'm not going to worry about their survival rate." Ky cocked her head. "So can you quit worrying about the romantic streak I don't have, and waste no more time on it? We have more important things to worry about."

"I suppose we'd better," Hugh said. Martin still looked shocked, but Hugh grinned at her. "I'm glad to find that my concerns were unwarranted, Captain, and I'm sorry to have doubted your maturity or judgment for even a moment."

"Don't go overboard," Ky said, grinning back, "or I'll begin to wonder about *your* sincerity. Now. Captain Ransome made an offer, before the other captains came, to help us with supplies. I realize this puts us in his debt, but we need more munitions. Adelaide Group's not known as a big munitions dealer, but I've been poking around. They do have twelve hundred older SS-V-87s, which we could upgrade using components they stock in another department."

"Twelve hundred! And what will that cost?"

"Well below what Gretna would have charged. I think I can get Teddy to buy them—and yes, I may call him Teddy if that gets the job done, and you will just have to bear it."

"For twelve hundred missiles and the components to upgrade, I can bear a lot," Hugh said with a smile.

ELEVEN

Slotter Key

The new Sub-Rector for Defense, Grace Lane Vatta, climbed out of the official car that had appeared for her precisely at six forty-two, marching up the five steps to the entrance of the Annex and through the tall door that was opened for her. *Turn right,* MacRobert had said, *and go to the leftmost security booth.*

As if she had been doing it for years, she placed her right palm on the plate and looked into the scanner. The tiny flash hardly registered. A voice said, "Both hands on the plate . . . ," then trailed away; she turned and gave the sentry a frosty glance. He was already red-faced, staring at her arm-bud in its casing.

"Anything else?" Grace Lane Vatta asked.

"Sorry, ma'am," he said. His forehead glistened. "It's just we're supposed to . . ." He opened the little wicket and let her through. "Third elevator, ma'am. Fifth floor."

She nodded without saying anything and walked through. She knew which elevator, which floor, which door. The other two elevators, she saw as she neared them, had plain metal doors. Hers had the Rectory seal on an outer grille. She slid her keycard through the slot; the grille swung out, blocking anyone else's passage, and the doors opened. Inside, the elevator was carpeted, walls as well as the floor. The rear wall also displayed the Rectory seal.

Her shoes sank into the carpet—ridiculous, she thought, and the former occupant of her office deserved his demotion. Five floors up, the hall to her office was also carpeted. A uniformed guard—some militia unit, she didn't yet know which—stood by her door. He saluted as she approached and flung open her door with a flourish.

"Sub-Rector Vatta!"

Through the open door, she saw five people lined up waiting. "Good morning," she said, walking through, giving a slight nod to the guard at the door. The five before her, three women and two men, were staff inherited from the former Sub-Rector. From their expressions, the carefully blank faces shown to those in authority, they expected to be fired. Some of them, no doubt, would be. Some of them, no doubt, deserved to be. It was her responsibility to be sure that the second group and the first group were the same. All who survived the winnowing would be working for someone else; she didn't want anyone contaminated by the former Sub-Rector on her own staff. MacRobert's dossiers on them had not revealed useful clues.

"We'll meet in the conference room," she said now, turning to the left. The most junior, Esmaila Turnin, scrambled to get to the door before her and open it. Les Vaughn, the most senior, held the others back until she was through, then led them in as they arranged themselves around the polished tik-wood table. Grace took the end seat, settling into the blue leather. Too soft, and the chair sagged back as if expecting her to lounge in it as Selwin had done. Selwin wasn't lounging now; the bastard was awaiting execution, and there was no chair in death row cells.

Her assistants stood behind their chairs, waiting. Grace let them wait a moment, then nodded. "Be seated. We have work to do."

Vaughn had brought in a portfolio and started to open it. Grace held up her hand. "Just a moment. I have seen your dossiers, of course, but I would like to speak with each of you before we begin the day's work."

"Certainly," Vaughn said. He opened his mouth to say more; Grace stopped that with a look.

"Your former boss is on death row," Grace said. Their faces stiffened; that had not yet been released to the press. "You must realize that you, too, are being investigated thoroughly. Such a person—" She put an emphasis on *person* that denied everything but a genetic connection to humanity. "—such a person will not have worked alone. If you were assisting him in his treason, you will be exposed and tried, do not doubt it. If, on the other hand, you are innocent of any wrongdoing, you should have no concern for your employment."

"Surely you don't think—" That was Armand Politsier, at the far left end of the table. His face had an unhealthy sheen.

"I am not in charge of that investigation," Grace said. "What I think is of no importance to you; what you—any of you—did is all that matters. I believe the new chief of security is quite able to find out without my assistance." The new chief of security, now relieved, perhaps permanently, from his duties at Spaceforce Academy, was happy as a terrier down a rathole.

"Yes . . . ma' am . . . ," Politsier said. Grace looked at him with distaste. Innocent or guilty—and she would wager a considerable sum on his guilt—he was not a man she would choose to work with.

"Today I will review the current items and my predecessor's minutes on them. I am lunching with the Rector and the President at one; I will require a five-minute warning before it's time to leave, if I become distracted." She would not become distracted, but she could feign distraction and see what happened.

"Yes, ma'am," Vaughn said. "In here, or—"

"In my office," Grace said. Rising from the deeply cushioned chair was awkward, but she made it up without lurching to one side, and the others scrambled out of their seats.

Her private office had windows on two sides, looking out on the perfectly groomed lawns and flowering trees of Government Place. Her desk placed her badly, her back to a window, but this was not a time to show fear of assassination.

Behind her desk was another lushly padded leather chair, this one even more tippy than the one in the conference room. Had Selwin spent all his time reclined and snoozing, perhaps with his feet on this desk with its leather-padded edge? The desk was still arranged as he had left it, functions laid out for the use of both hands. She would have to reprogram it . . . but first, she found the icon for the chair. Indeed, it was set to FULL RELAX; she tapped the panel until it read FULL UPRIGHT and leaned back cautiously. It held still.

By the time she had the desktop reset, collapsing functions so all could be accessed by her right hand, Vaughn was tapping at her door. He delivered a stack of hardcopy. "The most current items are on top, Sub-Rector," he said. "I wasn't sure how far back—"

"I'm not, either," Grace said. "Selwin appears to have been taking bribes from someone at least two years ago— so I've been informed." Not least by Selwin himself,

sweating and shaking in the combined grip of the interrogation drugs and his own fear. But her office staff did
not need to know how she knew. "I don't have time to
review all that at the moment; the Rector tells me we have
other, more immediate crises. But I must know what Selwin
was doing in the past half year."

"These cover only the past four weeks," Vaughn said.

"I'll get started, then," Grace said. "Hold any calls; I'll
check with you before lunch." She glanced at the top
memo.

"Should I bring water or . . . or anything?" Vaughn
asked.

"No, I'm fine," Grace said, not lifting her gaze from the
papers. "I'll call if I need anything."

She could imagine what he thought as he quietly shut
the door behind him: Silly old woman, appointed here
because the new President knew he had to placate the
Vatta family. Probably didn't have a clue. Her reputation
was decades behind her, unless he'd accessed certain files.
She trusted MacRobert to find out if he had done that, in
which case . . . well, to work.

By midday, she had cleared the first stack of paperwork
and asked for the next. Selwin might have been up to mis-
chief earlier, but the most recent actions seemed to be
more about setting up lunch, dinner, and weekend dates
with various friends in the department or in other branches
of government. Any wrongdoing would have taken place
at those meetings—and the surveillance of those meetings
was someone else's to analyze.

At quarter to one, she came out into the reception area.
Vaughn looked up from his desk and stood immediately.
A door was open to another room beyond, where Grace
could see two women at desks. The third, she supposed,
was taking an early lunch or off on an errand somewhere.

"Sub-Rector . . . I didn't know whether to interrupt you, but Security took Armand . . . uh, Armand Politsier . . . away a few minutes ago. To help with their inquiries, they said."

She would have to install her own equipment, somehow; she would have liked to watch that. "That's . . . most unfortunate for him," she said. "One hopes he has not done anything rash."

Vaughn looked worried, as well he might, but nothing in his face or bearing suggested he felt guilty. Hard to imagine the senior assistant not being aware of Selwin's corruption, but perhaps he felt no guilt because he approved. "I don't know of anything, Sub-Rector," he said. "Would you like me to call down and see if your car is waiting?"

It was only a ten- or fifteen-minute walk, but protocol—and MacRobert—insisted that she be transported by official car. Grace bared her teeth in a formal smile. "Thank you," she said. "That will be . . . appropriate. I am not sure how long I will be with the Rector and the President, and I have a medical appointment to follow; I will continue working on the same files when I return."

"Yes, Sub-Rector," Vaughn said.

Grace switched her mind from office problems to the possibility of assassination on the way through the building, evaluating each component of her journey in those terms and deciding how to respond. When a junior clerk—a mere child, she seemed, all pink cheeks and bright eyes and a fluff of dark hair—flinched away from her in the lower corridor, Grace almost laughed.

Much more fun to be perceived as dangerous than as a dotty old woman. More dangerous, too, but that was part of the fun.

Nonetheless, as she climbed the pinkish steps of the

presidential palace, she schooled herself back into the identity that had served her so well the past few decades. Elderly, surely infirm with that missing arm, perhaps a little set in her ways . . . she was almost giggling by the time she had passed through the various security checkpoints between the entrance and the small dining room where the new President and the Rector of Defense waited for her.

At one glance, she knew they had already disagreed about something. The Rector gave her a look thick with suspicion; the President came forward to greet her.

"Grace—I'm so glad you accepted the appointment. I believe you're just what we need in this difficult time."

"I'm honored," she said. Was her appointment the problem? She had been told the Rector was neutral about it, but the tension in the room didn't feel neutral.

"Let's eat first," the President suggested, waving Grace forward. Erran Kostanyan, she reminded herself. Ten years her junior, he had bowed politely over her hand at any number of official functions, including the dedication of the new Vatta headquarters. Colorless and boring, some said. A good administrator, others said. What mattered now was the perception that Kostanyan had stood aside from political wrangling for decades. Grace wondered. People did not rise to the top of the cream pitcher without intent.

Lunch had been laid out on a buffet along one side: sliced meats, shellfish on a bed of ice, dark and light breads, fruit. Two attendants stood by to pour tea or coffee or water; Grace noticed that no alcoholic beverage was on the buffet, or offered. That was a difference from the former Administration.

For the duration of the meal, custom prevented discussing business. The Rector asked the President how his daughter was liking her university courses, and the conversation stayed on families—good news only—until the attendants removed the plates, laid out desserts on the buffet, and withdrew.

"Donald and I have had several chats since I took office," the President said to Grace. "So now I'd like your opinion. What do you see as our priorities in defense?"

MacRobert had told her this President came to the point quickly; Grace had been thinking about this for days.

"We must have ansible service," she said. "It's not just the isolation from the rest of human space, though that's hurting us economically as well as militarily. It's also a matter of communications within Spaceforce in our own system."

"We need an ISC technical crew to work on the ansibles," the President said. "Without their permission, and their skills—"

"Skills are replicable," Grace said. "I'm sure we have technical brains in government somewhere who could get an ansible up and running."

"But ISC—no one else is allowed to touch their precious ansibles."

"We can't ask their permission, but by the same token they can't tell us no," Grace said. "I don't know why they haven't sent a repair crew, but the fact is, our security and our economy depend on communications. We can't be held hostage like this. What if another attack comes? Without ansible service, we're limited to lightspeed communications in our system, and our space fleets are hours out of touch with the planet."

"But you know what they do to systems that touch their ansibles or their personnel," the Rector said. "We can't risk an ISC invasion—"

"I don't see that as likely," Grace said. "They must be

suffering some kind of widespread emergency, or they'd have repaired our ansible before now. After all, one of their ships left here to find out what had happened very shortly after our ansible failed. If it were only a local problem, they could have contacted their headquarters by ansible as soon as they reached the next system . . . and they've had time to go all the way to Nexus II and come back. That argues for some widespread trouble—perhaps much like ours. We must have communication; the only way to get it is to find out what's wrong with the ansible and repair it."

"We could send out our own scouts," the President said.

"We could, if we wanted to weaken local defenses," the Rector said. "If I weren't concerned about ISC's response, I'd back the Sub-Rector's suggestion—"

"We've been without ansible service for almost a year," Grace said. "We have a legitimate complaint against ISC, for that matter."

"Well, if you're willing to take responsibility—" the Rector began.

"She can't, Donald," the President said. "Responsibility goes up; authority goes down. If I let her do it, it's on my head."

Grace looked at him, surprised. He had a reputation for honesty, but her long experience in undercover work gave her little reason to trust anyone in power. He looked back, lips pressed tight. Then he shrugged.

"You're right, Grace," he said. "The economy's foundering without good communications for our out-system trade—and even our insystem trade. We have financial assets out of system that we can't use because we have no financial ansible. Our defense is compromised when we can't get immediate response from our outlier plat-forms and ships. I didn't expect . . ." He shook his head, clearly changing direction. "I'll authorize an attempt to repair the ansibles, both financial and general communications, with the proviso that we advise ISC as soon as they're online, direct to their headquarters, what we did and why. Acceptable?"

"Acceptable," Grace said.

"I'll draft the order this afternoon; you have my verbal consent to start the operation."

The Rector looked sour but said nothing. "Donald," the President said. "You know we need your expertise, but things have changed. If you can't work with us, I'll accept your resignation."

"I—" The Rector's round face had reddened; Grace looked at him and it paled again. So. Would the President recognize what that meant? Would it matter to him? "I may find," the Rector said, "that the strains of the past few weeks have told on my heart. In that case—"

"In that case I would not presume to place more burdens on you," the President said. "Perhaps you should check with your physicians and let me know—"

"Yes. I'll do that." And with a vicious glance at Grace, the Rector pushed away from the table and left the room.

"Dear me," Grace said, and bent to sip her tea.

"That's going to cause trouble," the President said. "I think perhaps you should return to the Annex."

"By all means," Grace said. She wanted time alone to analyze what had just happened . . . and she would have time, if she went straight to the Annex now, to dig into different files and see if she could determine why the Rector had chosen to leave. Had he intended this from the beginning?

She had an appointment that afternoon with her rehab team, an appointment she had rescheduled three times already. Her arm-bud's sustaining capsule needed its fluids changed, her doctors insisted. She left the Annex shortly after three, arriving at the clinic by three thirty, and found her doctor pacing the floor.

"I was afraid you'd reschedule again," he said. "And that would not have been good for your arm."

"It doesn't hurt," Grace said.

"It won't hurt until it's too late," he said. He nodded to one of the technicians, who inserted a fine needle through the cap and drew off a sample of fluid. In the analyzer, the fluid produced a series of colored blips, meaningless to Grace.

"Just as I thought," the doctor said. "Electrolytes are borderline. We'll start with a flush. Lie down here."

The flush itself was not unpleasant. Fluid ran out as other fluid ran in; it felt a little cool. The arm-bud looked as if it had grown a couple of centimeters; the doctor confirmed this.

"It's growing normally, but you must make every scheduled visit," he said. "As growth accelerates, there's less margin for error in the chemical milieu. If you want to have a functional arm—"

"Of course I do."

"Then you must cooperate, however busy your schedule. Remember, this is not normal embryonic and fetal development; not only is it a graft onto an adult body, it's being pushed to develop faster, in a less natural environment."

That would serve as a metaphor for her nieces, Grace thought as she was driven back to the Annex. Grafted onto adult responsibilities and pushed to develop faster in a less natural environment. She hoped they were doing as well as her arm-bud.

*   *   *

When she finally got home that night, she found MacRobert waiting for her. He had said he might drop by, but wasn't sure; she was slightly alarmed at how glad she was to see him.

"I thought you might be tired," he said. "How does soup and hot bread sound?"

"Excellent." Grace slipped out of her shoes. "I'm going to go get comfortable."

"It'll be ready when you are," MacRobert promised.

Grace came back to find steaming bowls of soup on the table, and hot bread wrapped in a towel. Custom or no custom, she could not resist telling him about her day, including the meeting with the Rector and President.

"I don't know how to do this," Grace said at the end. She bit off the end of a warm roll.

"Of course you do," MacRobert said. "You've been giving orders for ages."

"Not that," Grace said. "It's finding out who knows what without doing it my way, the back-door way. I need to find reliable communications technicians who might be able to repair the ansibles, and I don't even know whom to ask."

"You asked me," MacRobert said, smiling. "That's a good start."

"That's another thing," Grace said. "This business of coming to you first. I haven't been dependent on a single source of information for . . . years. It's not that I don't trust you. It's just habit."

"And a very good habit," MacRobert said, nodding. "Just as my telling you you're an extraordinary woman is not flattery. We both know it's true. And we both know that this particular setup is stressful for you . . . just not as stressful as being shut out. You're not comfortable working out of cover—and neither am I, for that matter. I hadn't realized quite how much I depended on being the invisible—in my own way—senior NCO at the Academy, pulling strings from behind the scenes. You were behind two layers—well, three, if I count the visual one of acting the batty old lady, which you do so well. How many people in Vatta knew?"

"Two. They're both dead." Grace pushed away the rage she still felt at the former President and his minions, and wished she still believed in an afterlife where an angry deity would torment them for eternity.

"Fortunately, you're not," MacRobert said. "And we're both having to cope with coming out into the open where people know who we are, what our jobs are. But not everything."

"Not everything?" Grace said. "When there are people all around, all the time, watching everything I do and no doubt logging it?"

"Not everything." He grinned at her. "An old spook like me isn't going to open up all the files, and neither are you. All we have to do is act the part."

Grace felt her muscles loosening. "So you don't expect—"

"—you to be totally dependent on me? No, of course not. In this case, though, I do have what you need—I know where the best techs are in Spaceforce, and they're almost certainly the best for this particular job. You won't know that one of Spaceforce's clandestine activities was trying to devise an ansible small enough to be carried aboard ship. We suspected that ISC had them—it explained their quick response to threats against the system—and we wanted them. We had a breakthrough shortly before your niece's little difficulty, and I actually sent her some components, just to see what she'd do. She's quite good at tech, when she puts her mind to it."

"Ansibles aboard ships?" Grace wasn't that interested in Ky's former technical ability, but the implications of shipborne ansibles were obvious. "Do you think the ships that attacked us—that disrupted ansible service—had those?"

"Might have, but they definitely weren't ISC. It's possible that someone else was on the same track. And you're right, we have to get ours back up."

"And on our ships," Grace said. "If your research went that far." The concept unfolded in her mind, opening out more and more, revealing infinite possibilities. "And trade—ships could always stay in touch with headquarters, even if they were in systems without ansibles. Do they work in FTL flight?"

"Not that we know of," MacRobert said. "Nothing works in FTL flight; theory says the ship's in a sort of enclosed kernel. Nothing gets in; nothing gets out."

"Too bad," Grace said. "That could be really handy. But how long do you think it'll take to get the system ansibles up? Assuming we find someone who can do it?"

"Days to weeks. We have to get someone there, physically, and then it depends on what's wrong."

"All right," Grace said. "Now for the big question."

"Yes?"

"If the Rector resigns, and the President offers it to me, should I take it?"

"You? In charge of the entire Defense Department? The batty old lady, the auntie who makes fruitcakes stuffed with diamonds?"

Grace felt herself flushing; she wanted to kick him, but he was too far away. He grinned at her.

"Our enemies should be very, very afraid," he said.

"You didn't really answer me," Grace said.

"Grace, I'd have to be crazy to tell you what to do. You'll make whatever decision seems right to you at the time. And it will be."

Eleven days later, MacRobert stopped by her office with the news.

"They're back up," MacRobert said. "It was software after all. The apparent physical damage was all surface stuff, for show."

"ISC's own people sabotaged it?" Stella had gone off with an ISC courier; at the time, she'd thought that was the safest way to get Stella offplanet, but now . . .

"I don't think so. I think they'd have done a better job of making it look like the main damage. This was mostly to impress flybys, I think, and our people also think it was done from space. Impossible to date it, at this point, but I'd hazard a guess it was the same mission that took out your people on Corleigh. The software end was much more sophisticated, and I'd bet that it did come from somewhere within ISC, a long time before failure. At any rate, our people have both ansibles back up, but not yet patched into the local networks or transmitting readiness. Yes, they managed to block the automatic alert function. We wanted to test the waters, as it were. See what's happening before we broadcast anything."

"You know the President wanted immediate notification of ISC," Grace said.

"He would," MacRobert said. "But this is safer; ISC isn't our enemy." He smiled at her, the smile covering all that had happened in the intervening days. The former Rector, citing reasons of health, had resigned. Grace, with only three days' experience as Sub-Rector, had been named Acting Rector.

"Go on," Grace said. He knew what she most wanted to know, and she was determined not to ask.

"You'll be interested to know that Vatta Transport lists a new headquarters, in the Moscoe Confederation—"

"The idiot tree people!" Grace said. "I was there once—"

"S. Vatta, CEO, the listing says. They're running four ships: *Katrine Lamont, Gary Tobai, Marcus Selene,* and *Mary Alice.*"

"So Ky decided to work for Stella," Grace said. "That surprises me."

"She isn't listed as captain of any of those ships," MacRobert said, amusement shading his voice. "However, the newsfeeds mention a Ky Vatta who is apparently recruiting for an interstellar military force, who's on a ship called *Vanguard* that used to belong to—you won't believe this—one Osman Vatta. One of our other privateers is with her—"

"Ky took Osman?" Grace felt her heart stutter and then go on. "Osman Vatta?"

"It says she's on a ship that used to be his. Who is Osman Vatta?"

"The worst piece of slime my family ever had to deal with," Grace said. She could hear the loathing in her voice. "If she's got his ship, she had to kill him to get it." She didn't want to imagine the circumstances that had brought Ky and Osman together, but someday she would have to hear how Ky had bested him. Osman! After all these years, that bastard was finally dead. Surely he was finally dead.

"The news said she claimed the ship was hers by right, that it had been stolen—is that true?"

"Oh, yes," Grace said, remembering those days all too clearly. "The family threw him out, disinherited him. He snatched a ship, one of the new ones, just commissioned. Killed three people getting away, and that's not a tithe of what that man did in his time. And his children—" She stopped just in time. Even MacRobert didn't need to know about Osman's bastard children and what became of them. Of the ones they could find. She hoped that secret would never come out.

"There are rumors, out of the Moscoe Confederation. Apparently one of your captains challenged Ky's identity on the grounds she was really Osman's daughter." MacRobert looked at Grace.

"Ky? Good gracious no. I was there when she was born. She took after her father—after Gerry as he was in his youth—much more than her mother."

"Oh, well, newsfeeds always get things half wrong," MacRobert murmured. "You wouldn't have known of a Captain Furman, would you?"

"Furman? Stick-in-the-mud, dull as lukewarm dishwater. He made a play for . . . who was it, someone's daughter in the family, and she wasn't about to marry him, especially after he threw up on a carnival ride. When Ky went off on her apprentice voyage, he was her captain; they did not get along. No one really expected they would. Was he the one who challenged her identity? She hadn't changed that much, to my eyes."

"Apparently. He was executed by the Moscoe authorities on grounds of 'intractible rudeness in a court of law.' "

"I wonder what got into him," Grace said. "He was always polite, unctuously so, the times I met him. Made my skin crawl." She shrugged. "Well. I do need to get in touch with Stella, at least, and find out what she's up to."

"As soon as we allow transmissions, whoever's out there will know the ansible's up, and ISC will know someone else worked on it," MacRobert said. "On my end, we'd like to snoop a little longer, and Spaceforce would like time to rearrange the system defense."

"How long is 'a little longer'?" Grace asked. "Not just for me, but all the others who depend on interstellar trade."

"Three days," MacRobert said.

"I suppose I can wait that long," Grace said. "Though knowing my nieces, they can probably manage to get into trouble between now and then."

"I suspect Ky is making trouble for someone else," MacRobert said.

Power flowing through the circuitry of the main ansible created, as power does, a magnetic field . . . and though the ansible's automatic signal of availability did not come on, that magnetic field attracted a small, unimportant magnet on the ansible platform's outer surface, making another connection, this one visual, completing a pattern that before had seemed to have a gap, a missing paint chip. Far away, the detector planted by ISC on a small chunk of "space debris" matched pattern to pattern every six hours. It had not been noticed by those who did the physical damage, and those who created the software problem knew of its existence, but not its location: such detectors were installed in systems where the platforms had no resident crews.

On its next cycle, it noted the completion of the pattern, stored that information, and attempted to communicate with the ansible. When that proved unsuccessful, it launched a tiny messenger drone preprogrammed to reach ISC's regional headquarters and inform ISC that an ansible out of service was now receiving power but not operating normally.

Spaceforce detected the drone on routine review of the

day's surveillance; it had been too small to trigger an alarm at launch, and by the time it was discovered, it had long since gone into FTL flight.

Grace initiated the ansible call to Stella as soon as she'd figured out the temporal differential between Slotter Key and Stella's reported location on Cascadia. If the idiot girl had moved, it would serve her right to be wakened in the middle of the—

"Vatta Transport," said a pleasant female voice, not Stella's. "How may we help you?"

"Grace Vatta for Stella Vatta," Grace said. "This is an ansible call."

"Just a moment," said the same voice.

Then Stella spoke. "I've got it, Gillian, thank you. Aunt Grace? How lovely to hear from you. I didn't realize the Slotter Key ansible was back up."

"Just now, dear," Grace said. "Of course I had to call you first and tell you the good news."

"Yes?"

"We laid the cornerstone of the new building. There've been some changes in government."

"I should hope so," Stella said. "You should know— I've opened an office here. Well, you heard—"

"Yes. An excellent idea, especially since you had communications, I gather."

"Ky said I should. Aunt Grace, there's something—I don't think you know. About me."

Grace squeezed her eyes shut a moment. Had Stella found out? And how? With Osman safely dead, according to report, there should have been no way . . .

"There's almost nothing about you I don't know," she said. "If you're speaking of the past, that is. Everything in our . . . um . . . heritage was part of my brief."

A silence that seemed to stretch as long as the light-years. "You knew," Stella said. Anger edged her voice.

"Not that I thought it mattered," Grace said. "A few shared shreds of genetic material—"

"So I got to find out in open court," Stella said. Her voice had gone cold. "In front of everyone."

Grace had not imagined that; she wanted to know how, but this was a time to listen. "That must have been a shock," she said.

Stella gave a sound that might have started as a laugh. "A shock, yes. You could call it that. All my life I knew who I was, Stella-second-daughter-of-Helen-and-Stavros-Vatta. Blonde because Mother's relatives were blonde. Now I'm Osman Vatta's bastard."

"No," Grace said. "You're Stella Vatta. The Stella Vatta whom everyone has always known . . . Helen thinks of you as her daughter—"

"Her adopted daughter."

"Her daughter. And so did Stavros. Everything you know about your past is real except for that one thing—where the genes came from."

"And you think that doesn't matter?"

"Not as much as most people think, though your beauty probably came from your biological mother . . . I must admit, however, that the young Osman was a handsome beast. I mean both those words literally."

"I can't believe—dammit, Aunt Grace—"

"Stella, I'm sorry. It was a horrible way to find out. I did mention to your parents years ago that they might consider telling you about the adoption. But they were concerned to give you a solid background, as much security as they could."

"Because they were afraid Osman's traits would come out in me. And they did."

"Nonsense." Grace put all the force she could into that. "Your fling with the gardener and all the rest of it had nothing to do with Osman. Do you know how many young people, boys and girls both, living in privilege, do something that stupid? And they aren't all Osman's bastards. Osman was cruel; you were just young and stupid."

"Well, that's a comfort." Stella's voice was shaky, but underneath the shakiness Grace heard relief.

"It should be. Stella, you aren't cruel. He is. Was. And I really want to know how that happened."

"No, you don't," Stella said. "It was horrible."

"I'd expect it to be. Osman wouldn't go peacefully. Ky did it?"

"Yes. It's a long story—and I'd better start at the beginning." Stella launched into it, starting with her discovery of Toby Vatta in protective custody, traveling to Lastway where she'd found Ky, the military escort, Ky's insistence on answering an apparent distress call from a Vatta ship.

"She's an idiot," Grace said. "Didn't she realize it could be a trap?"

"Yes—and the Mackensee escort warned her as well. But she had her mind made up." Stella continued with the threats, Ky's response, what had happened, in all the detail she could muster.

Grace found herself wanting to grab both younger women and bash their heads together. Ky should've known better; Stella should have . . . but then, in the end, she had taken Osman's ship and he was dead, and that was the right outcome even if the means had been . . . incredibly risky.

"She was covered with blood," Stella said then. "It smelled—I don't want to remember that smell. Or the look in her eyes."

"The look?"

"Ever seen a hawk mantling over its prey, Aunt Grace? Ky was trying to hide it, but she was . . . excited. Happy. She'd *enjoyed* killing Osman."

Grace was not surprised, but how to explain this to Stella? "It shocked you," she said.

"I know, it's terrible," Stella said. "I can't bring myself to talk to her about it . . . it's why I thought she might be Osman's by-blow when Furman said she was."

"And then you found out—how, by the way?"

"There was . . . tissue . . . from Osman, on the ship. Genetic analysis said I was very closely related to him, and that he could not have been her father . . . and that Ky and I could not be first cousins."

"Where is Ky now? Is she still on his ship?"

"Yes, but she's re-registered it as the *Vanguard*. I talked to her only yesterday; she's somewhere way across space, a system called Adelaide."

"Have you located other Vatta ships? And what happened with Furman?"

"He's dead."

"I know that, but why? What did he do?"

"Among other things, he lied to Vatta for years, Aunt Grace. He was running some kind of scam—we still haven't got it all worked out—and Ky and I both suspect he was somehow connected to Osman."

"Furman? He was lukewarm dishwater when I knew him. The only spark of emotional intensity he ever had— and I'm not sure it was real—was falling in love with that girl. I can't imagine Osman bothering with him any more than she did."

"We think it was her turning him down that drove him to it. But there's evidence of a long-standing plan to sabotage the family, all the while acting as one of our senior captains. He had secret accounts under false names all over the place; he was transporting unlisted cargo. I'll forward what we know to you. I've been too busy to follow up on most of it."

Grace felt stupid. She'd never liked Furman, but she'd never suspected him of anything that bad. He was so efficient, she'd always been told. Always at the top of the list for on-time deliveries, with very low customer complaints. But now he was dead; whatever she'd missed was over and done with.

"So what do you want me to do now, Aunt Grace?" Stella asked. "I've organized an office here, and for the purposes of doing business we've called this Vatta's headquarters—nobody could contact Slotter Key—"

"You did the right thing, Stella," Grace said. "And I suppose you're acting CEO?"

"Well . . . yes. Ky and I traded back and forth for a while, but she said I'd be better at it, and she wanted to take direct action against those responsible."

"Eventually, you'll need to come back here—when the new building's finished—but for now I think you're quite right to establish a headquarters where we still have ships. You've shown more initiative than the family remaining here . . ." Should she tell Stella now, or wait for another call, a less emotional call?

"Who's going to be the new *real* CEO?" Stella asked.

"You're doing the job; as far as my shares are concerned, *you* are." There: now how would she take it?

"Me?" Stella's voice squeaked, then steadied. "You can't be serious. I'm too young; I don't have the experience—"

"You're getting the experience. How many ships are reporting to you now?"

"Uh . . . four. No, five. *Galloway* came in yesterday."

"And you've reestablished contact with insurers?"

"Yes. The rates have gone up, but I've insisted ours be no higher than others. However, two big companies have ceased operations."

"That's understandable. The ships are carrying cargo?"

"Yes. Overall, trade is down, but we're finding routes that work."

"How many employees do you have?"

"Besides security, just two in the office right now—the budget's still really tight."

Grace grinned to herself. Stella, for all her glamour, had always been a tightwad.

"Part of that's the need to help Ky . . . I never realized how much even one missile cost. And she has more crew on one ship than three tradeships—"

Then again, Stella had definitely learned about the right priorities, if she was funding Ky's war. She was going to be a good CEO. "You remember that meeting right afterward? Just before Gerry died? No one was making sense—"

"You were. And we were all in shock—"

"And too many of them still are. I hadn't realized the extent to which the Vattas with initiative and brains went off in ships, while the ones who stayed here—not the ones who went and came back, but the others—were timid and fog-headed."

"Not Mother!" Stella said, sounding shocked.

"Helen's completely engaged in taking care of Jo's children; she's told me she wants nothing to do with the business. No, that's not being timid or fog-headed, but it's also no help. What I'm getting at is that nobody here has taken over—"

"But you," Stella said. "You have. And you're older. You should be CEO, at least for the transition."

"I have other work now," Grace said. "And I don't mean

my work for Vatta. I'm in the government." She almost hoped someone would intercept that message. Let the bad guys ponder the fact that a Vatta was not only alive and thriving, but had power. "You're doing a good job, Stella. I don't know anyone who could have done as well, let alone better. Count on me to back your decisions, if anyone has the gall to criticize."

TWELVE

Adelaide Group

"I'd be honored to assist, Captain Vatta," Ransome said when Ky asked him. "I told you, we admire you excessively, and anything we can do to help, we are eager to do. You have only to ask."

"It seems very crass, Captain Ransome, to mention so soon after meeting you, but—we are short of missiles, and I've discovered that Adelaide has a supply of outdated missiles and the components to upgrade them. Unfortunately, our recent activities depleted my reserves."

"Your generous aid to desperate refugees," he said, nodding. "I've heard how you ransomed them and asked for no return. It is entirely in keeping with your noble character. Please, allow us to help. My funds are at your disposal."

"Here—" Ky showed him the figures.

"Oh, that's no problem; 'tis a paltry sum." Ky just managed not to gape at that. She had grown up in a wealthy family, but the cost of twelve hundred missiles didn't seem at all paltry to her. "Will you need assistance upgrading the missiles? I'm sure your crew is fully capable, but the task might go quicker with more help."

She could just imagine what her weapons officer and battery crews would say to strangers doing the upgrades. "I appreciate your generosity," Ky said. "But no, I have yet another favor to ask. Adelaide Group has given us permission to do some training in this system. Training exercises can make us vulnerable to . . . to anything that might show up unexpectedly. What I'd particularly like you to do is keep a close eye on longscan, and assign one of your ships to observe our maneuvers, and at the end of each session give us your observations. I realize that's a boring assignment for you, but as you said, your ships are not suited to mass engagements—"

"That would be delightful," Ransome said. "It will suit our abilities. I'll tell the others. We'll start immediately; you will want us well out into the system, I'm sure. Oh, but wait—I need to transfer those funds. To Captain Vatta, or—"

"Kylara Vatta," Ky said. "My account's at Adelaide Central."

"I'll do it immediately," Ransome said. "Then we're off, flags flying and all that. Don't mind if we move about a bit. The lads get bored just hanging about in one spot. When do you think you'll depart?"

"We'll have to get those missiles loaded," Ky said. "I'm not sure. I'll give you a call."

"I can't tell you how wonderful it is that we're going to be working together," Ransome said. "Thank you!" He bent over her hand and then was away, his cape flaring behind him.

The funds transfer cleared within the hour; Ky put a hold on the missiles and components, and went back to the ship.

"You look smug," Hugh said when she reached the bridge.

"Do you want to send crew to pick up our missiles, or do you want them delivered?"

"You got them all?" he asked.

"Yes. I'm thinking two hundred each to Argelos and Pettygrew—that will bring them up to ninety percent—and the rest for us."

"I'd rather we had them all," Hugh said. "You gave them more at Gretna, and now our percentage is a lot lower than theirs."

"I could be convinced," Ky said. "But I need to keep our fellow captains happy."

"An undersupplied flagship won't keep them happy. *Vanguard*'s the most powerful ship; missile tubes aren't worth diddly if you don't have missiles to put in them," Dannon said.

"All right," Ky said. "We'll be selfish and keep 'em all. How long will it take to reconfigure them, do you think?"

"Won't know until we do one. Somewhere between a half hour and three hours each."

Ky grimaced. "I hope it's nearer a half. Ransome offered help with that, but I thought we shouldn't have unknown hands tinkering with our ordnance. I gave him another task—watching for bogeys while we practice maneuvers, and critiquing us."

"I like the first idea, but not the second. What do any of that bunch know about warship maneuvers?"

"If I told them to sit still and watch, so they could learn, do you think they'd be willing?" Ky asked. "But if they think they're being asked to critique us . . . they'll pay attention."

"Oh." Hugh looked thoughtful. "You're right. That might work."

The rest of that shift and the next, crew and hired cargo haulers moved the missiles into *Vanguard*'s docking bays.

One by one, the missiles were upgraded . . . an average of forty-five minutes per missile per tech. Six crew had the skills, but there was room for only four to work at one time. Ky let Hugh determine the most efficient use of their time and space; she needed to convince her other captains of the value of Ransome's Raiders.

"I know why you're keeping all those missiles," Argelos said as they sat down to lunch in the Captains' Guild dining area. "I agree—you need them more, and we need you to be fully supplied. But this fellow Ransome and his schoolboy chums—"

"I think they'll be useful," Ky said, dipping a spoon in her soup. "I've told them to go out and keep watch while we do some training, and one of them will be watching us, supposedly to critique, but actually to learn something about multiship maneuvers."

"I suppose that can't hurt," Pettygrew said.

"We're understrength and vulnerable," Ky said. "You know that. Even with the supply ship Adelaide and the refugees gave us, we have only three warships, less than half what we had before. Ransome's three gives us at least three more sets of ears and eyes."

"I just don't see him—or those friends of his—being much use in a real fight."

"I'm not counting on them for that. They might surprise us, but even if they don't, the enemy may waste some time on them. It's an advantage, even if a tiny one. And they paid for the missiles."

Argelos' eyebrows went up. "All of them?"

"Yes. All of them. The one thing we know they have is money, and they're willing to spend it on us. I don't want to overdo it, but right now we are short, as you know. What we really need is system governments to chip in, but until that happens—"

"If it ever does," Pettygrew said.

"It will, though possibly not before we're random space dust. However, in the meantime, we need to make use of every economic opportunity, and it strikes me that this is an economic opportunity. They want to play, and they're willing to pay."

"I see your point," Argelos said. "It's fine with me, then. We still don't have enough munitions to waste any on target practice, though—not until we're somewhere we can resupply."

"I know. But we can work on calibrating our navigation systems, our scans—and using our communications devices. And I don't know about your ships, but my crew can use more drills on everything from inboard emergencies to boarding situations."

"We worked on that on the way here," Pettygrew said. "But yes. What about EVA drills?"

"Certainly," Ky said. "I made a preliminary schedule—preliminary because we're still upgrading and loading missiles, and also because I wanted your input." She handed over the hardcopies.

"This looks good," Argelos said after a moment. "My military adviser wanted to be sure there was practice in precision microjumps . . . you've got that . . . and scan calibration . . . you've got that . . ."

"We're going to look like idiots at some of this," Pettygrew said. "But I notice you don't have any close-formation practice."

"With so few of us, we can't risk it," Ky said. "You'll find I've suggested close approaches—slowly—for the EVA work. But we can't fight in close formation, where a hull breach of one ship could take out the next. What we need to know is how to position ourselves in open formation to cover one another."

"Makes sense," Pettygrew said.

"And I have a surprise," Ky said.

"What's that?" Argelos asked.

"Remember we'd planned to get ship patches for the new organization at Gretna? And some kind of official-looking seal for the gangways and such? I used some of the money Ransome gave me for that." She signaled a waiter. "Here's the tag for my bag in the cloakroom," she told him. "Please bring it."

When he returned and set the bag beside her chair, Ky opened it and pulled out two patches, handing one to each of the others. "You already have ship patches on your personnel . . . these can be sewn above them."

"That was Bellinger's design, wasn't it?" Pettygrew asked, eyes alight.

"Yes. All I did was add the lettering for Space Defense Force, Third Fleet. You like them?"

"Impressive," Argelos said, fingering the one she had handed him. "My crew will like it, too."

"There are plaques for the ships, as well," Ky said. "Three for each ship, at this time. One should go at the gangway, one on the bridge, and one wherever you think best."

"Same design?"

"Not exactly. They were too big to bring with me; they're being delivered to your ships. I did tell Ransome about this, by the way."

Over the next few days, as the missile conversion went slowly forward, Ky noticed the new patches on the crews of all three ships as they went about the station. To her eye, they moved more confidently, more purposefully.

"Captain! There's something on the onboard ansible!"

Ky rolled out of bed, her eyes sticky with fatigue. They

had finally finished the missile conversions, but she had stayed up to supervise. The other captains knew that; no one should be calling her now.

"It's supposed to be first-shift where you are," Stella said when Ky made it to the console; she looked as beautiful as ever, perfectly groomed, and wide awake. "I checked. And this is a secure connection, by the way."

"I've been up two days," Ky said. "You couldn't have known." Trust Stella to use the onboard ansible to chat, just because Ky had given her the new channel codes. She yawned.

"Trouble?" Stella frowned.

"No. Just some urgent business. You have news?"

"Slotter Key's ansible is back up. Have you noticed?"

"No . . . when did that happen?"

"Just a couple of days ago. Aunt Grace called me. She's in the government somehow. Defense Department."

"That doesn't surprise me," Ky said. "What did she do, kill off all the traitors?"

Stella looked shocked. "She didn't say that . . . and if she had, surely she'd be in jail."

Ky snorted. "Not our Aunt Gracie. She could've just fed them fruitcake with rocks in it or something. What else?"

"They've laid the cornerstone for the new Vatta headquarters. She says it won't be ready for occupancy for a standard year or more, and I should just stay where I am. And Ky—she thinks I should be CEO. Permanently."

"So do I," Ky said.

"But I told her I was too young."

"And she said don't be ridiculous, didn't she? I can just hear her saying that."

"Something like that yes. She thinks I'm doing well so far."

"You're doing far better running the company than I am fighting a war," Ky said. "And much better than I'd do with the company. Are other ansibles coming up? Did ISC say anything?"

"ISC didn't do the repairs on Slotter Key's ansible, Aunt Grace said. Slotter Key Spaceforce did. So far ISC hasn't said anything at all."

"They will," Ky said. She rubbed her forehead with the heel of one hand, trying to wake all the way up. "Especially if there's something seriously wrong in ISC. Speaking of that, have you had any messages from Rafe on Nexus? He was going to ask his father what was wrong."

"Not a word," Stella said. "I haven't tried to contact him myself, either. He was going incognito; I didn't want to arouse any interest."

"Oh . . . that's right. But ISC must have something dire going on internally. I'm glad we're not dependent on them anymore. If they've really lost control of their people— and Rafe thought they had, at least of some of them—"

"Which brings me to Toby's latest fit of genius," Stella said, looking smug. "He's managed to create an interface between his version of the shipboard ansibles and system ansibles. And as near as he can tell, it's not detected by the system ansibles."

"What? That's . . . that's impossible."

"I'm beginning to think that with Toby, nothing technical is impossible," Stella said. "I know his talents were supposed to lie in space drives, but seeing what he's done with ansible technology, I wonder if that doesn't mean he's going to invent an instantaneous space drive, like, two days ago or something."

"Good . . . heavens." Ky realized that Hugh was looking at her oddly; her face must show the astonishment she felt.

"Of course it means his mess is spread over half the apartment as well as a sort of lab at the office here, and I keep telling him that the next time I step on something that crunches or goes *sping* under my foot I'm going to throw it all out, but he knows I'm not serious. He thinks all this is fun . . . I have no idea how they contained all his energy back on his apprentice voyage. Scutwork, I suppose. At any rate, it gives us an enormous trading advantage, if we mount this technology on Vatta ships."

"And an economic advantage if we sell the units . . . how fast can you manufacture them?"

"At the moment, Toby's making each one by hand. I have three—this one in the office, two more at home. I don't have the capital yet to manufacture them in quantity, and if ISC finds out, I expect trouble."

"Rafe knows we have the basic models," Ky said. "He said those conformed to ISC designs, though he was sure they were being made by someone else. If Toby's advanced the technology, the least you should do is get patents on it."

"I'm looking into that. Because the Moscoe Confederation is so close to Nexus, though, they look with some suspicion on anything that might infringe on ISC territory."

"Mmm. Did ISC ever patent the shipboard ansible technology?"

"They must have; they're not stupid. At least the components, if not the final product. And intellectual property lawyers cost an incredible amount. I've got one, but I'm running out of funds to pay him. I'm going to ask Aunt Grace . . ."

"No—wait. Just let me think." She hadn't yet told Ransome about the shipboard ansibles . . . and she had enough left to give him one for each of his ships. She'd planned to do so, in fact. But if he bought them . . . She gave Stella a quick outline of Ransome's Rangers and her agreement with them. "Give me a price," she said finally. "This is the old version, the ISC version, but—"

"But you're the only source except the pirates, Ky. One-of-a-kind items . . . let's see, I need at least fifty hours of legal representation . . . divided by three . . . and a cushion you can bargain down from . . ." Stella named a sum that made Ky blink.

"That much?"

"If we don't ask, we don't get it. We can try, anyway. It's Vatta trade goods, right? And you're a Vatta captain. So that's the price I authorize you to sell at."

"Actually, at this point I'm the commander of a detachment of Space Defense Force's Third Fleet," Ky said.

"What is Space Defense Force? I never heard of it."

"We have pretty patches," Ky said, grinning. "And big fancy plaques hanging on the bulkheads."

"And if I said I'd bet on the first and second fleets existing only in your fertile imagination?"

"And the imaginations of a few other people," Ky said. "But you'd be right, in principle. Nonetheless, I will sell the ansibles at the price you recommend, boss. We need those patents, and then we need those advanced ansibles. ISC will just have to eat our dust. Since they still haven't fixed all the ansibles they've got, I'm betting they have enough other problems to worry about."

"I hope so," Stella said. "Aunt Grace also mentioned that she's met your Master Sergeant MacRobert and approves of him. She said not to worry about your letter of marque."

"With her in the government, of course not. We'll be on maneuvers here in Adelaide Group for a little while,

Stella; I'll let you know how the sale of communications equipment goes."

Ky had consulted with Argelos and Pettygrew, making sure she fully understood the performance characteristics of their ships; now the three set off for the first real training they'd done as a group since that disastrous battle.

Right away, she noticed that the new patches made a big difference in both morale and discipline. Those who really didn't want to be in a space navy had already left, but the remaining civilians—former civilians now—had sewn on their patches eagerly and moved now with more decision. The other captains reported the same thing.

It was three days before they had their scans calibrated to Ky's satisfaction. "I'm being picky for a reason," she said, when Pettygrew complained. "If I take a shot at someone with my beam, telling you the bearing of that beam, and you microjump four light-minutes in front of me and don't microjump out within four minutes because on your scan you think my beam's going to pass you a kilometer away, what will happen?"

"I'll . . . oh."

"And the same with missiles, to a degree. We're not doing close formation; we're going to be loose. That means we must know *exactly*—or at least consistently, from one ship to the other—where each ship is. Our navigational computers must be in sync; our targeting computers must be in sync. Errors of thousandths of a degree quickly expand to tens of thousands of kilometers—"

"All right. I understand now. I just—"

"It wouldn't have happened the way Admiral Andreson wanted us to fight," Ky said. "That's an advantage of the formations you *were* using. The disadvantages, you know."

When the equipment had all been calibrated, Ky had

them practice precision maneuvers, first with only one ship at a time. Accelerating on a mark; decelerating on a mark, while the others charted the movements and compared charts. Microjumps to specific coordinates. Repeated microjumps, or "skip-jumping." *Sharra's Gift* lacked the capability for calibrated and repeated microjumps; Ky and Argelos rewrote tactical plans to allow for the problem. Then the ships maneuvered in pairs, matching velocity, matching course. Meanwhile, she ordered drills for the crews inside, including every emergency she or Hugh or Martin or the other captains could think of. Fires, leaks of all kinds, injuries, illnesses, damage from weapons . . .

Every day ended with a critique session in which Argelos and Pettygrew came to *Vanguard* to give their report on the day's training activities, and Teddy Ransome, bright-eyed and eager, appeared on the vidscreen to give his version.

On the fifth day, he said, "I've started my lads on some of those drills, Captain Vatta. We always did have fire drills, of course, but I never thought of leaking coolant fluid. And it sent us all into a tizzy, I don't mind telling you, but we have it sorted out now. Not much you can't handle with gaffer's tape and a bent pin, you know . . ."

Captain Argelos put his head in his hands.

"I assume you're talking about ingenuity and initiative," Ky said. "Not actually fixing a leak in a high-pressure line with gaffer's tape . . ."

"Oh . . . well, yes. Matter of fact, we don't even have any gaffer's tape aboard, and I'm not sure I've ever seen any . . . it's just an expression. Anyway, I thought you should know we aren't just sitting about with our feet up watching you work."

"Excellent," Ky said. "By the way, I've got something

I'd like to talk to you about, not on an open channel. I'm sure your people are looking, but just in case there's a pirate lurking somewhere—"

"Certainly, certainly," he said. "I'll just bring the skimmer over, shall I? Whenever you wish."

"How about tomorrow, after the day's work is done? It won't take long, perhaps an hour or so."

"I'll be there, Captain Vatta. And now, adieu!" He waved as he closed the connection.

"He is a total and complete *idiot*," Argelos said, looking up. "What are you planning to do, saw off the top of his head and pour in a sack of brains?"

"At least he's started drilling his crew," Pettygrew said. "He may not be entirely lacking in intelligence."

"I want to sell him some shipboard ansibles," Ky said.

"You gave us ours free," Pettygrew said.

"That was you. You had just escaped from an enemy that destroyed your home system. This is different," Ky said. "You weren't bragging about how much money you got away with. Ransome's thrown his around without restraint—I don't see why he shouldn't pay for them. Stella—my cousin, who runs the business—suggested a price."

"Should I know how much I'm beholden to you?" Pettygrew asked, brows raised.

"No. You aren't beholden to me at all, Dan." She rarely used his given name; she noted his reaction—surprise, first, then a subtle relaxation. "You saved my ship as much as I saved yours."

"Thanks," he said, a little gruffly.

"Teddy Ransome's a newcomer, and unknown, and for all I can tell as rich as the entire Vatta family used to be. He hasn't earned any special consideration yet, and Stella needs the money."

"What's ISC going to think of your selling shipboard ansibles?"

Ky shrugged. "I don't care. The ship and its contents were adjudicated to my possession. They certainly haven't advertised any as missing, so I don't think they'll claim they were stolen."

The others looked at her. "You're becoming devious," Argelos said.

Ky laughed. "*Becoming*?"

"And she seemed like such a nice girl when I first met her," Argelos said, shaking his head. "So—when do you think we'll be ready to go chase down some pirates and get this war started?" He held up a hand. "Sorry . . . *finished*."

"Another few days," Ky said. "You're all shaping well. If we had the resources, I'd want some target practice, but we need every missile in stores. I will want your weapons crews using simulation patterns, though."

"And where do we go next?"

"Talking to Councilor Malroy, I think we're most likely to get support from systems like this—those that don't maintain much in the way of system defense but are beginning to worry about the pirate menace. I'm also planning to send Ransome's ships out as scouts a system or so ahead of us; with shipboard ansibles, they can report if they find any small groups of pirates, something we could reasonably hope to destroy. If we can prove that we can destroy small groups, that will get us some support—and more ships, I'll bet—but we really need a good solid victory the next time out. The more Turek grabs, the more he'll have to spread his forces to maintain control . . . there will be small groups, I'm sure."

"Sounds good to me," Pettygrew said. He grinned. "This is a bit different from what I'm used to but . . . I like it."

"I'd like you to go out to a several-light-minute distance, Dan, so I can demonstrate the ship's ansible to Ransome."

Captain Ransome's personal vehicle was as ornate as his ship, and he himself as resplendent as ever. He dove through the docking tube like some fantasy hero, right arm stretched out ahead.

"It's such an honor," he said. "Your ship—" He looked around, then smiled at Ky. "And you have something important to tell me—I am all ears, Captain Vatta."

The general tone of his speech was so absurd that Ky had a momentary vision of a thousand ears all over his uniform. She fought back a snort of laughter. This would never do.

"Let's go to my office, Captain Ransome," she said formally.

"Oh, do call me Teddy. All my friends call me Teddy," he said.

"All right . . . er . . . Teddy. This way."

Once settled in her office, he seemed to relax a trifle, looking around the compartment.

"I've been impressed by your performance," Ky said. "You and your friends have been a help to us, and I can see how you will continue to be . . . but there's additional technology that would make you more effective, and I can supply it."

"What's that?"

"Shipborne ansibles," Ky said.

"That's—that's impossible! They've always said it was impossible!"

"It's not," Ky said. "The pirates have them and are using them; it's one reason their attacks are so well coordinated. We obtained a number of the devices when I captured this ship."

"Do they work just like system ansibles?"

"Not as I understand it," Ky said. "I'm not a specialist in the technology, but I have been told that they will not interface with system ansibles. It's strictly a ship-to-ship tool at this time, but a very effective one. The pirates use it; we must, too, to fight them."

"Do you—is it possible for me to obtain a unit?"

"Teddy, I'm sorry to say that I can't afford to give you one . . . but I can sell you one. In fact, I can sell you three, one for each ship. Then you can communicate ship-to-ship without a time lag."

"It seems incredible . . ."

"Come up to the bridge," Ky said. "I'll show you." As she came through from the passage, Hugh called the bridge crew to attention. Ransome looked around, by his expression impressed with the size and complexity of *Vanguard*'s bridge. "Take a look at longscan," she said. "That's *Bassoon* over there, see? What's the scan range say?"

"Four point two minutes," Ransome said. "So scan lag's actually light-minutes . . ."

"Yes. Now—" Ky nodded at Hugh. "Let's light up the ansible." To Ransome she said, "We know what channels the pirates are using; we don't use the same ones, even though transmissions are supposed to go only to the designated node." She turned to Hugh. "Hail *Bassoon*."

"*Bassoon* from *Vanguard*—"

"*Bassoon* here—"

"Testing, *Bassoon*. Confirm receipt of the following course data—"

"Confirmed receipt, returning—"

Ky glanced at Ransome. His mouth had dropped open; now it snapped shut.

"It—it really works! Ansibles on ships! Fantastic!"

"It really works, and I'm sure you can see the implications for military work—"

"Oh . . . yes," he said. "We can reach each other instantly, anywhere . . . well, except nonspace . . . and—and coordinate maneuvers—it's wonderful!"

"It would be more wonderful if we were the only ones to have it," Ky said. "But at least we do have it; the pirates no longer have a monopoly on ship-to-ship instantaneous communication. Now—you need to know the technical details, how much power it drains, and so forth. That will help you decide whether to purchase—"

"I want it," Ransome said, flushing a little. "I don't care what it costs; if I have to refit my ships entirely, I want it. What fun it will be!"

"Here are the specs," Ky said, handing over the hardcopy she'd prepared. "Do not—understand me, do *not*—discuss any of this on conventional com, do you hear?"

"Oh—yes. Of course."

"Let your engineers look it over, decide if the ships need any modifications to handle the power drain, and then contact me again without mentioning anything openly. In fact, it might be better if we all went back to Adelaide for a . . . a final dinner party, say . . ."

"Of course. Brilliant," Ransome said, glancing at the specs. "I must have this—I must—it *will* work, I'm sure of it."

Back on Adelaide, with three of the remaining ansibles stuffed into Ransome's ships—a job that had taken two and a half days—Ky transferred almost all the credits to the Vatta account at Cascadia, less the bank's fee for transfer. The small remainder paid for the dinner she hosted for the captains and senior crew. The next day, they would set off for what Ransome insisted was "the adventure of a lifetime" and Ky hoped would be the next step toward victory.

THIRTEEN

Nexus II

Rafe had not believed he could sleep, but once he lay down on a cot in Gary's underground headquarters to wait for his transport, the relief of the rescue sent him under. Gary woke him only two hours later.

"Sun's coming up. Time to hit the road. You're still a new helper in the business, same ID as what I gave you yesterday. We're going to my workshop—"

"You really do make windows and doors? And why there instead of Balcock?"

"My people need salaries even when we don't have a specialty job. And I have a legitimate small business within two hours of each of my . . . secure ops command posts, like this. The people at the nearest business don't work that op. And so far, that's worked for me. Enough chatter . . . you should pretend to sleep in the van. You're lazy. Once we're at the shop, you should have time for a real nap before you shower and change back into your Cascadia persona. We need to have you seen coming back to pick up your ID, which should be free by late afternoon. I'll take you in, then you and I will head for the next transfer point. And don't ask me where."

"How are they? Have you heard?"

"Alive. Signs of maltreatment, but they're not in danger of dying—at least not from that. They're still being assessed. I know you won't relax, but I don't cut corners on medical stuff."

By the end of that day, Rafe felt as confused as he hoped anyone trying to trace him was. Sid had driven the van to Gary's shop—a typical light-industrial shop with ventilation hoods rising from its pitched roof. Everything about it looked completely legitimate, from the sign out front to the fence around the paved yard, where another van with the same logo and a heavier truck with a load of wood were parked. Inside, it smelled of sawdust and machine oil; saws screamed and routers snarled as at least a dozen workers, all in similar coveralls and wearing safety glasses and ear protectors, worked on what Rafe assumed were actual windows and doors.

Gary's office, at the back, had a wide table piled with samples of wood, design displays, and paperwork; through a side door, there was a tiny efficiency apartment—a cot, a cooler, a bathroom with shower and toilet. In the afternoon, Gary appeared—looking rested himself—and Rafe, back in his Genson Ratanvi disguise, got into Gary's car for the drive to the village. They arrived near sunset; Lilyhands met them outside the bar and handed over Rafe's ID with a smile.

"Judicar got back this morning, Ser Ratanvi; she said to apologize to you for the inconvenience. And we all wish you the best."

"You were most gracious hosts," Rafe said. "And I do apologize for the misunderstanding."

"I'll be glad to run you into the city," Gary said.

"That's very kind," Rafe said. Probably everyone in the

village was in on the ploy, but it never hurt to be courteous.

From there, Gary drove him through the night as Rafe struggled out of Ratanvi's disguise once more and put on the sweater, slacks, and wool jacket Gary provided. At a private airfield Rafe boarded a small craft, and spent two uncomfortable hours wedged between crates, and a pilot who never spoke. Outside, just before they landed in the early morning, he could see lower hills rising close to a wide brown river they seemed to be flying along. He spent the last leg of the journey locked in the back of a bread truck making deliveries, and obeyed the driver's instruction to walk around from the loading dock and present himself at the front door of the clinic.

It reminded him unpleasantly of the Green Hills Center with its broad green lawns, its exposed public drive to the front, and the concealed drive up which the bread truck had come. On black glass doors etched with a pattern of leaves, the clinic's name and specialty was embossed in ornate gold script: ALARO CLINIC. SUBSTANCE ISSUES.

Inside, behind a dark stone enclosure, a uniformed man gave him a sharp look and then opened the door beyond. "This way, please. You'll want to see Doctor Alaro." Tension knotted Rafe's stomach. He trusted Gary; he had to trust Gary, but this could be a trap.

The hall beyond the door, carpeted in dull olive, appeared to stretch the depth of the building. A man came out of a doorway ahead and turned toward him. "Ser Dunbarger, isn't it?" He was taller than Rafe, trim, with dark hair becomingly streaked silver.

"Yes," Rafe said.

"I'm Doctor Alaro. You'll have many questions, but you'll want to see them first, I'm sure." Without waiting for an answer, he turned and led Rafe down the hall to a

cross-corridor, then turned again. "We're going down—
there's a lift just here—" The sign by the lift said STAFF
ONLY, and it required a key. Once in the lift, Alaro kept
talking. "There's been no evidence that anyone knows
they're here. Apparently there's quite a bit of activity up
north, and in the northwest, but nothing to worry about.
If you're wondering, this is—most of the time—a private
and very expensive clinic for moneyed individuals who
habitually poison themselves with undesirable chemicals.
We also take in the occasional wealthy psychotic who
refuses treatment elsewhere." The lift stopped; he led the
way out. "Just down here . . ."

It looked like every hospital corridor Rafe had seen,
very clean and—for something underground—very airy.

"Your mother and sister first; they're conscious. Talk to
them first, then come talk to me," Alaro said. "There are
decisions to be made. Be gentle; don't try to interrogate
them, but let them talk if they want to. When you're
through there, Doctor Kinjon will take you to your father.
He's assigned as your father's primary physician while he's
here."

Rafe's mother and sister both wore thick fleece robes
incongruously printed with bright pink flower shapes that
looked ugly against the bruises. Following doctors' instructions, Rafe kept his tone light and soft.

"Mother? It's Rafael—"

"Rafe? Oh, my—" She burst into tears and reached
toward him. Rafe moved closer and took her hands in
his, careful not to dislodge her IV line. "Raffi, why weren't
you here? He could never have done it if you'd been
here."

"Shhh . . ." Rafe stroked her hands. *Don't ask questions,*
the doctor had said. *Don't disturb her.* But she was already

disturbed—how could she not be? "I'm here now, Mother," he said. "And you're safe." She clung to him, her eyes still desperate. Rafe fought down the rage she must not see; his anger had frightened her so before.

"Is he . . . they won't tell me . . ."

"Father is alive," Rafe said. "He's very weak." How much to tell her? How much did she know, or guess? "He escaped; he tried to get out and find help, but it was too cold."

"They hurt him," his mother said. "They hurt all of us. I can't believe he'd do such a thing—he was going to be CEO anyway—"

"Father?" Rafe asked.

"No, no! I forgot, you don't know. Lew. Lucky Lew, your father called him. A fine young man, we thought. He always seemed like a fine young man . . . a good family, nice manners, a hard worker . . . I can't understand it. Why—"

"I never liked him." The voice from the next bed startled him. Rafe turned to look at his sister Penelope. Her dark hair hung lank and stringy beside a pale, gaunt face; she looked nothing like he remembered, or like the formal portraits displayed at home. "You told me how wonderful it was for Father to have such a reliable, competent successor, but his daughter was scared of him." She looked at Rafe. "I knew her at school."

"You never told me that!" Indignation lent a touch of color to his mother's cheeks.

"I tried to. You told me not to meddle, that all children get crosswise with their parents on occasion."

"They do, but—of course you couldn't have realized. But Raffi—why did it take you so long?"

"So long?"

"You didn't get your father's messages?"

"No, nothing. That's one reason I came back to Nexus to visit. I didn't know anything was wrong until I tried to call and didn't get an answer." Best not tell her about the trapped phone connection; she didn't need something else to scare her. "Then I went to the house, and it was obvious—"

"What—what did you find at the house?"

"My room," Rafe said. He hadn't meant to say that. "You kept my room the same."

"Oh, Rafe . . ." Tears rolled down her cheeks. "You saw . . ."

"I expected you to clean it out. You told me not to come back."

"I knew you would," she said. "I knew you would someday come to your senses and be our son again. And then you'd come home, and your room would be ready for you just as if . . . as if it had never happened."

But it had happened, and all his life since, and theirs, had been changed forever that night the invaders tried to kidnap him and his sister, and a young boy had taken a lucky swipe with a display weapon and killed a man twice his age and size.

"I saw it," Rafe said. "You even kept my old models. I wish you'd been there with me. Anyway, I didn't know where you were, or what was wrong—just that something was."

"They told him—your father—that they'd set traps for you, that you couldn't possibly get through. Was it you who got us out? I didn't recognize—"

"I hired the team," Rafe said. "I wasn't on it myself; I'm not trained for that."

"I thought we were going to die," his mother said. Her grip on his hands tightened. "I thought they'd kill us. I thought nobody would find us even if they were looking.

He said they wouldn't, that he had convinced the police it was for our safety that we were sequestered."

"He convinced someone," Rafe said.

"How did you know that we needed help?" his sister asked. "Or where we were?"

"The house, for one thing. The plants were dying. I couldn't imagine Mother leaving the house without arranging for their care—in fact, without leaving servants there, if only to guard it from thieves."

"Did you water them?" his mother asked. She had always loved her plants; the big tigis in the living room was her pride, raised from a nub only a finger tall.

"Mother!" his sister said. "Don't be ridiculous!"

"No," Rafe said. "I didn't. I could tell something was wrong; I was afraid if I turned on the water, it might bring . . . trouble."

"You always were the smart one," his sister said. "If I hadn't been so scared that time—"

"You were only a little kid," Rafe said. "Of course you were scared."

"You were only eleven."

"Eleven-year-olds are big kids," Rafe said. "At least, eleven-year-olds think so. Penny, don't feel guilty, please. None of this is your fault." Tears spilled over and ran down her cheeks; he couldn't stand it. "I'm going to check on Father," he said. "I'll be back."

His father would live. They had promised him that. His core temperature had been dangerously low, but the outside temperature hadn't been enough to cause serious frostbite. Rafe stared through the glass panel. His father lay still, IVs dripping into both arms, a warming blanket over his body and other tubes coming out from underneath. Rafe didn't want to think about what had caused those marks on his hands, his feet, his face . . . his first hot rage had turned cold, colder than the glacier above Aurora Adventure Lodge.

"You shouldn't try to rouse him yet," Dr. Kinjon said, coming up beside Rafe. He was Rafe's height and almost as plump as Rafe's Cascadian persona. He glanced at Rafe's face, took a step back, then turned away. "He's sedated right now; his core temperature has stabilized, but with his other injuries and the drugs he had in his system, we felt mild sedation was a good idea. He was also dehydrated and clearly has been malnourished for some days."

"But he'll recover?"

"Yes. But it will take time."

"Fully?"

"We'll just have to see. The stresses . . . his age . . . there is the possibility that complete recovery will be prolonged, or . . . not entirely complete. When someone's implant has been tampered with . . . the neuropsych specialist will be here tomorrow. When we know exactly how much damage the implant took—and possibly delivered— we'll know more."

His father had been intelligent—more than intelligent, brilliant in many ways. Intelligent, charming, commanding . . . and now he lay almost comatose, his body battered, his brain . . . Rafe shook his head sharply. "He has to recover. It's important—"

"It's always important," Kinjon said.

Before he knew he had moved, Rafe had the doctor's collar in his hands; the man's face went white with the shock of that sudden attack. "You don't understand," Rafe said. "It's not just him; it's not just my father . . . he was snatched for a reason, and that reason affects not just Nexus but a thousand other systems. Someone's trying to bring down ISC—do you have any idea what that means?"

"Gggghhh . . ."

"Sorry." Rafe let up the pressure, but didn't let go completely. "Do you know who he is?"

"A hostage that . . . that Gary rescued. That's all I know; that's all I'm *supposed* to know."

"And you rightly assume rich and powerful, and you wonder that you haven't heard anything, am I right?" The man nodded; Rafe went on. "That's the CEO of ISC. He was abducted on the orders of the next in succession . . . who certainly has hooks in the government, judging by their complicity in this. What you may not know is that hundreds, at least, of ansibles are out of service, and ISC personnel are involved in that . . . I believe on the orders of the man who kidnapped my father. People are dying because my father is here"—he nodded toward the room—"and not in his office. If that man isn't stopped, none of us is safe."

"That still doesn't give you the right to choke me," Kinjon said.

Rafe let go. "You're right. I'm sorry. I've been . . . distraught."

"I gathered." To his surprise, Kinjon even chuckled. "Gary did warn me about you, but you just don't look like the type. I'm sorry I upset you; we'll be easing up on the sedation over the next twenty-four hours, and you should be able to talk to your father then."

Rafe had been given a room in the staff wing of the clinic; the next day, when he went down to the hospital level, Alaro met him outside his father's room. "Let's go see what the neuropsych says about your father's implant. He's done an initial neural assessment. He's in the lab."

The neuropysch expert, introduced only as Tony, stared at the trace from Rafe's father's implant. "Mmm. Not liking this a bit."

"What?"

"Well . . . they tried to probe the implant before they removed it. In lay terms, they ran too much power into it, trying to force it to work, and caused damage—and enough power that it heated up part of his brain."

"And that means—"

"It means he has brain damage, possibly permanent but certainly something it's going to take time to repair, and his implant cannot be replaced. Most people depend on an implant for a good part of their knowledge base: he can't."

"But you can install another one, can't you?"

"Not anymore," Alaro sighed. "Not with the brain damage. If we boost the signal enough to pass the damaged portion, we risk the same damage to something else. For now, we're leaving the damaged implant in: it gives him some function he would not have otherwise. But it has to come out so we can start the repair of the brain itself, and at that point he will seem worse than he is now. How much worse, we won't know until we take out the implant. Basically, he's like a stroke patient, and in his case a serious stroke patient. Luckily, he chose to have his implant on the right side, so his language centers are relatively unaffected, but you're looking at a long, slow, incomplete recovery."

"But he can talk?"

"He can talk now, a few words at a time. He tires quickly; he's still somewhat confused. It's too early to test all his cognitive functions, and with the sedation he's become disoriented. We've changed the setup of his room, which should help. I've tested his facial recognition: that's intact, too. He recognized your face in a picture we showed him. So if you want to go in and talk—keeping it calm and not asking questions and not upsetting him—you can do that."

Rafe entered his father's room with what he hoped was a pleasant expression.

"Rafe . . ." His father's face, with eyes open and focusing, looked more like his father, and yet unlike: for the first time, he was looking down on his father, and for the first time he had no fear, no anger, and no contempt, only a great sadness.

"Father—you're looking better."

"I can't—I can't sit up by myself." His father's voice sounded weak and querulous. "My left arm—"

"Father, don't worry. You'll get better."

"Rafe, you have to know. It was Lew, Lew Parmina. He's—I don't know why, entirely, but he's gone completely insane. That's the only reason I can think of . . . he knew he would succeed me; I was going to retire in five years. He's been my friend for years—I thought my friend—"

"Father, don't wear yourself out—"

"But you have to know; you have to help me—"

"Help you how?"

"I told you, in my message—"

"I never got your message. I came back because I hadn't heard from you in too long and I was worried."

"You never got—" His father looked stricken. "But you came anyway . . . Rafe, I always knew you'd . . . but he said . . . but maybe . . ."

Rafe felt old memories, snatches of overheard conversations, sequences of events, coming together in his mind. "Father, was it Lew who first told you I was dangerous? Was he the one who recommended that therapist?"

His father's gaze wavered again. "I—I can't quite remember . . . I know later, when you were in trouble at that school, he was sympathetic. Said he knew it must be hard to be disappointed . . . and I was sure you'd come out of it, you'd been such a sweet child . . ."

Sweet? Rafe had no memory of being sweet, even before the home invasion. Polite, well mannered, that was expected. But sweet?

"You used to be so affectionate . . . when I came home you'd climb in my lap and butt your head against my chin . . ."

His father's expression now was pleading; he clearly wanted Rafe to remember those times, but he didn't. "Mmm," he said, just to make a soothing sound.

"But Lew said it was rare for children who killed to change, that it was usually a sign of deep-seated personality disorders . . . he had references. The therapist agreed. He said I had to be realistic, be concerned for the welfare of ISC, both employees and those who depended on our services. Then when I was given the job of CEO, and you were . . . on remittance . . ." His father's voice trailed off. He looked suddenly grayer.

"I'll come back later," Rafe said. "Just rest."

The next morning, Dr. Alaro spoke to Rafe in the corridor. "I don't know what you're planning, and I don't need to. But if it involves, for instance, transporting this patient and expecting him to . . . oh, to speak to a group about business, for instance, you had better do it within the next ten days. We can't risk leaving the damaged implant in longer than that."

"Can he survive travel so fast?"

"With the right supports, yes. He's getting a little stronger each day. You can expect that his concentration will vary, however, and your visits should be short."

"I think," Rafe said, "that Lew has had something like this in mind from the beginning."

"He couldn't," his father said. He had said it before. "It's impossible—"

"They never traced the intruders that night," Rafe said. "They never found who hired them, right?"

"Well . . . no . . ."

"Lew found that therapist for you, I would bet on it. The therapist and Lew chose the school you sent me to. I know for a fact that Lew set me up with girls when I went to college—"

"I didn't know that!" his father said.

"I thought it was with your approval, since he was your assistant. He gave me money; he gave me names and numbers. When he sent me money later—my remittance—he used to tell me how disappointed you were, and then give me contacts to . . . elements I found surprising."

"But he was always so nice . . ."

"To you, I'm sure he was. You were his ladder, to be kicked away when he thought he had his hands firmly on the top of the tree." Rafe shook his head. "And I didn't see it. I was too hurt, too angry, and mostly I was not here. Which I'm sure was his intent."

His father's gaze had sharpened, almost to the intensity Rafe remembered. "I think . . . you may be right. I can't quite . . . this blasted implant thing. There's information in there that would help me think clearly about it but I can't . . . it's not working right. I need a new one."

"You can't," Rafe said. "Not yet, anyway. When they've done the neural repairs to your . . . head . . ."

"My brain," his father said with surprising energy. "I know . . . I can't think. That's why I need your help. And you're as sharp as ever—it didn't take you long to find Lew's trail in our lives. You're going to have to take over—"

"Take over?" Panic swallowed him; Rafe struggled to stay calm. "You can't mean take over ISC?"

"That's exactly what I mean. We can't let Lew have it. I don't know all he's planned, but what they did taunt me with, while I was hostage, was bad enough. He's determined to maintain the monopoly and he's working with some kind of military leader, someone named Gammis Turek. The ansible outages—"

"—are his fault. And I know something about Gammis Turek—"

"You've met him?"

"No. But a bad guy we—uh, more on that later—ran into over in Sector Five had a suicide circuit implanted to keep him from revealing the name. And supposedly it was Turek's people who attacked Bissonet and took over its system government. I suspect something similar almost happened at Slotter Key."

"Lew has friends on Slotter Key," his father said. "The Vatta family—Vatta Transport, Ltd. You must know their ships."

"They're mostly dead," Rafe said. "I've been traveling with a couple of them."

"Probably his spies," his father said. "Fed you any number of lies."

"I don't think so," Rafe said. "I've known Stella for years, and it wasn't through Lew. Her cousin Kylara—very much the straight arrow, Ky."

"I thought Lew was," his father said. "Right now I wouldn't trust anyone Lew called a friend. The Slotter Key ansible's still down, isn't it?"

"As far as I know, yes." No use trying to explain how he was sure that Stella and Ky weren't lying about their families—or that Vatta had been an innocent dupe, not complicit.

"So you can't check what they told you. But that's another problem for another day. Right now, Rafe, you simply must get to the Board and convince them of Lew's perfidy. You can't let him take over. At the least, your life and ours will be in danger."

"But—I don't know anything about running a corporation—let alone one as vast as ISC." Even as he said it, he knew that wasn't quite true. He'd had his own businesses; he understood how business worked. He had grown up in ISC, he had done work for them. "And I can't—why would you trust me? Why would they?"

"Because," his father said, "if I was that wrong about Lew, then I assume I was that wrong about you, too. If I think of the little boy you were, all that intelligence and fire and sweetness—yes, sweetness, don't flinch like that—the way you never did a single underhanded thing other than the usual 'She broke it' when a dish dropped, and that was only the once, then I see the potential in the man to be as intelligent, capable, honest as you were then."

Tears sprang to Rafe's eyes; he blinked them back. "I'm not that little boy anymore, Father."

"No, and a good thing you're not, or we'd all be dead," his father said. "You've had a hard life; you've learned hard lessons, harder than some of mine. It will take someone like you; I'm sure Lew has collaborators on the Board and elsewhere in ISC. I want you to find a secure way to reach the next Board meeting—what's the date?"

Rafe told him. "But, Father—I'm just not cut out to be an executive—"

"Nonsense. You're my son. You're also the only weapon I've got. You have to do this, Rafe. Or millions—probably billions—of people will die, and more will be ruined, because of Lew and his allies."

He had never wanted the job. He had told himself that over and over: he was a freelance, a lone wolf, a wild rogue adventurer, able to go and come as he pleased, only partly dependent on that remittance credit once he found he could support himself one way and another. He felt the weight of it pressing on him now, all that responsibility he didn't want. And yet—

"I trust you, Rafe," his father said. "Not just because you saved my life—our lives—just now. Not just because you were a good child. But in part because you killed those intruders, and in part because you have survived on your own and developed skills I never needed—or thought I needed. I am trusting you with this, and you will not let me down."

Whatever his father had lost, he had not lost the ability to inspire loyalty and delegate . . . Rafe took a long breath, feeling now the full weight of what his father wanted him to do firmly on his shoulders.

"All right," he said. "I'll talk to Gary—and we also need to get the accounts open so I can pay him and his team."

"When you are sure you can get to the meeting without being killed, I will make a shielded video call . . . I have to show myself to them, to convince the ones Lew hasn't already corrupted. He'll probably try to tell them that you kidnapped me and have pressured me—"

"Thought of that," Rafe said. "I'll bring them here, one at a time, by roundabout routes, to talk to you."

"I think most of ISC's loyal," his father said. "I just don't know who."

"Where are your implant backups?" Rafe asked. "Did you have them?"

"I did. He got them. But although they might contain information to convict him, they wouldn't tell him anything he didn't know."

"My . . . er . . . cranial ansible," Rafe said. "The access code for it?"

His father's eyes closed briefly. "I'm sorry, Rafe. They got that out of me when they threatened to kill the baby . . . and then they did anyway."

"What about Linnet and Deri?" His older sisters, who had never married as far as he knew. The night of the attack, they had been off at boarding school.

"Dead," his father said. "Supposedly both accidental, though now of course I wonder about that. Linnet had gone on a ski trip with her boyfriend . . . Lew's cousin, now I think of it. She was a good skier, but there was an avalanche . . . no one's that good."

"The cousin?"

"Also died, along with fifteen others who were on that slope. Deri—Deri had taken a commerical flight with several friends to go to a wedding; it crashed with no survivors. Pilot error, the safety board ruled: a night landing and the pilot undershot the runway—altimeter wasn't set properly, and there was a little hill, hardly a hundred meters high . . ." His eyes sagged shut, then opened again. "I see now . . . either one could have been arranged, if you didn't mind killing a lot of other people."

"So there was just Penelope left. And me. What about Penelope's husband?"

"He died when we were taken. Tried to defend her. Nice boy. Lew hadn't thought much of him; he wasn't ISC at all. His father was a wholesale grocer, decent fellow, very down-to-earth. We got along fine. Penelope adored Jared; they were so excited about the pregnancy—" Tears rolled down his face.

Rafe let him cry a moment, turning aside to look at the cheery picture of a woman cradling a child by a window that overlooked a pleasant green field.

"All right," his father said, a few moments later. "Let's get to work."

Lew's tentacles had reached far into the government as well as ISC's power structure, as Rafe's discreet inquiries proved, but Vaclav Hewitt Box, one of his father's oldest friends, was clean of that taint.

"Garston!" he said the moment Rafe's father called. "Where in thunder are you? Lew's been telling us you're in safekeeping for fear your demon son will kill you, but he won't tell us where."

"I'm at a secure clinic, recovering from the treatment Lew Parmina's goons gave me. Ardath is alive, and so is Penelope, but Jared and the baby are both dead."

"What!"

"Listen. I don't think any communication on this planet is truly secure, Vaclav, so I don't know how long we can talk without the call being traced. If it is, your life is in danger, too. I believe that Lew engineered the deaths of my other daughters as well. Rafe saved our lives—"

"That sounds like hogwash, Garston. He went bad; bad boys stay bad."

"Poppycock," his father said. "He didn't go bad without help, and he's not bad now. He saved our lives; he got us out of the hellhole where Lew put us with his goons. Vaclav, remember Christine?"

"Ah, yes, Christine of the flowers . . ."

"Christine of the owls, you nitwit."

Vaclav's expression changed. "All right. What do you want me to do?"

"I want Rafe to take over for me, for now. I've got serious injuries, and my implant's fried."

"You sound sane enough."

"Right-sided installation. No speech damage, and yes, I can think. But my left side is involved, and I can't change implants until they've done some repairs."

"Good—grief. You really were—"

"That close to death, yes. I don't know who on the

board are Lew's plants . . . Termanian, probably, Oster, maybe Wickins? But Lew's the real danger. I need to meet you in person—you'll know then that I'm not some zombie plant of Rafe's."

"Where is Rafe? Do you know?"

"He's here, with me. Like I said, he got us out."

"By himself?"

"No. But this is going on too long, Vaclav. Will you come? Quietly?"

"Yes. Anywhere. Tell me."

"I can't. But I can tell you what to say."

Rafe had never been in the Boardroom. As a small child, he'd been taken to headquarters, shown the office his father had then, had seen assistants and secretaries scurrying to do anything his father asked. One of them had given him candy. Now, armed with ID and credentials Vaclav had provided, wearing a new suit altered overnight to his measurements by one of Gary's contacts, he pushed the float chair with his father up to the entry. They were flanked by four of Gary's people.

"Ser Dunbarger!" the guard said. "The rest of the Board are all here. Ser Parmina said you wouldn't be in today again—he said—"

"As you see, I'm here," his father said. "Only a little the worse for wear. You won't remember my son, Rafael— and these are my security—"

"They're not ISC," the guard said.

"No," his father said. "For the moment, I'm using a private service."

"I don't know if I should—"

"You should," his father said. "I vouch for them—can't come from higher than that, can it?" He managed a grin; the guard finally smiled back.

"All right, Ser Dunbarger, if you're sure. They'll need tags once they're inside."

"Waiting for us," his father said. He looked past the guard. "Vaclav—over here." Vaclav Box, taller than Rafe by a head, waved and came forward.

"You said four tags . . . here they are."

"Go ahead," the guard said. Rafe pushed the float chair forward. The guard would no doubt report this to someone—possibly someone in Lew Parmina's pay—when they were past, but that shouldn't matter. The executive elevator was just ahead, its doors already open. They all crowded in.

Vaclav gave him a sardonic look. "You've changed, Rafe."

"Time does that," Rafe said. The edge in his voice would have sliced a ship hull; he tried to soften it. "I believe the last time I saw you, I was fourteen or fifteen, wasn't it? Not my best year."

"No, it wasn't," Vaclav said. He looked away. "This is going to be interesting. Are you ready for any . . . surprises?"

"Surprises surprise because one is not ready," Rafe said. "I expect trouble, if that's what you mean. He's had years to set this up; we've had only a short time to unravel it. We're bound to have missed something." His hand wanted to slide into the suit, be sure of his weapons, but he made himself stand relaxed.

"You always were a confident so-and-so," Vaclav said.

"He got that from me," his father said. "Only in his case, the overconfidence was beaten out of him early."

The elevator rose smoothly past floor after floor, coming to rest at last. The doors opened onto a carpeted space with a receptionist's desk angled to give a view into the elevator. The man there was scribbling something on the desktop; he looked up, and his brows raised.

"Ser Box . . . the meeting started several minutes ago; didn't you hear your page? And—" His face changed as he looked at the man in the float chair. "Ser Dunbarger! I had no idea you were coming! Ser Parmina said—"

"I know what Ser Parmina said," his father said. "But I'm feeling better, and I decided to come in. Vaclav waited for me downstairs. No, don't bother to announce us. We'll just go on in."

One of Gary's people had stepped to the desk and had the receptionist's hand in a grip that, Rafe knew, could tighten in an instant to excruciating pain. He nodded at Rafe.

The Boardroom double doors were not locked during meetings; there had never been need. Now two of Gary's people pulled them open and stepped inside while Rafe pushed his father through. Vaclav walked beside him.

Lew Parmina, at the head of the table, had been pointing at a display hovering over the group. Rafe tipped his head; one of the guards stepped that way. Lew had gone white, but he recovered quickly.

"Ser Dunbarger—Garston—we didn't expect you today. What a pleasant surprise!"

"Is it?" his father asked. Rafe didn't look down at his father; he was watching Parmina's hands. "It wasn't a pleasant surprise when your goons abducted me and my family from our home, killed my son-in-law, and spent the next several tendays torturing us."

"My goons? What do you mean? You're confused; you—"

A stocky redheaded woman on the far side of the table spoke up. "You said Garston had to go into hiding for fear of his life, Lew. You said you knew where but couldn't tell us, for security reasons . . ." Rafe's implant informed him that this was Madeleine Pronst, senior vice president for human resources. Headhunter, hatchet woman, and yet not universally hated. Madeleine, his father had said, was ruthless with the incompetent, as willing to chop off a VP or division head as a terrified new hire, but oddly compassionate with those who had real problems, and fair-minded with everyone.

"He—I thought—that's what I was told." Rafe could just about see the gears whirling in Parmina's head, trying to cover himself.

"Interesting," his father said. "The men who killed my grandson—my daughter was forced into induced labor while captive, and the men then murdered the infant in front of me and my wife—told me with great pleasure that you had ordered it. And what you planned to do with the power you would gain as CEO of ISC."

"I—*he* did it!" Parmina pointed at Rafe. "He's been bad from the first; he's jealous of me; he wants the power himself. He came back; he had you abducted; he had his hirelings tell me you were in hiding, told them he was acting on my behalf, and then he fooled you by pretending to rescue you—"

"It wasn't pretense," Rafe's father said. "I would have been dead in a few hours if he hadn't come. And I think I know my son better than you do. A lot of things make more sense now, Lew."

Rafe watched Lew's hand slide under the table. That would be the panel for the emergency response, his father had told him. "It won't work," he said, surprising himself by his own tone of voice: light, relaxed. "You have no communication with the outside world, Lew. No, not even your skullphone, as you've no doubt been noticing while you tried to buy time."

"This is ridiculous!" That was Oster; Termanian and Wickins hadn't yet moved, though they were sweating more than the innocent would. "Lew is a respected member of this corporation; he has been handling things since you disappeared. You can't just walk in here and expect us to fall in line—" His hands, below table level, jerked up suddenly.

Rafe felt a surge of glee, drawing and firing his pocket needler before Oster's weapon was clear of the table. Oster slumped forward, his face thudding onto the table's polished surface. He had hardly taken his eyes off Parmina; he had *felt* Oster's move as much as seen it.

"You!" Parmina said. All pretense gone now; teeth bared, he glared at Rafe. "You disgusting little leech! Why didn't you die?"

Rafe pretended to blow smoke off the end of his needler and slid it back into its holster. "Only the good die young," he said. "And you're older than I am, Lew. Feeling lucky today? By all means, go for that pocket blaster. It's a messy way to commit suicide, and it will make things hard for your family, if they care. I understand your daughter's not fond of you . . . so my sister says. But you might be able to set it off before one of us drilled you." He let his smile widen. The directors nearest Lew at that end of the table leaned away, ashen-faced.

"If I surrender," Lew said, hands wide.

"Oh, I don't think you'll surrender," Rafe said pleasantly. "I think you'll do something stupid, and we'll have to kill you."

"That's murder!"

"Is it? Wasn't what you did to seventeen skiers murder, when you set off that avalanche to kill my sister and her boyfriend and it also took fifteen others? Wasn't what you did to the passengers in that plane murder, when you tampered with the instruments so the pilot flew into a hill and killed another of my sisters? I think it was."

"You can't take the law into your own hands!" Lew shouted. "It's illegal—it's—"

"Scared now, are you?" Rafe asked. He pulled out his needler again and pretended to polish it with his handkerchief, all without taking his eyes off Lew.

"You have to let me explain," Lew said, standing awkwardly, trying to back away from the table. "You have to listen."

Rafe cocked his head. He could feel everyone's attention, including his father's. The rush of anticipation merged with the rush of pleasure from shooting Oster.

"No," he said, pretending to sigh, thumbing the selector over. "I don't have to listen," and he fired.

FOURTEEN

"Murderer!" screamed Termanian as Parmina stiffened and slid down the ornate cabinet at that end of the room.

"Not yet," Rafe said. "I merely use more efficient knockout drugs than most. You, on the other hand—" He thumbed the load selector again. Termanian threw himself back in his chair, hands over his face.

"He made me do it . . . he said if I didn't . . ."

"Oh, be quiet." Rafe nodded to the guard nearest Termanian. "Secure him, would you?" He looked down. "Father?"

"I think we might adjourn to the room next door while someone picks up the fallen," his father said. The rest of the Board turned to look at him. "Now," his father said. Rafe waited until the near side of the table was clear before moving his father down the room toward that door. Their last firm suspect lingered, looking around uneasily.

"I do know about you," Rafe said. "But it's up to you whether you want to cooperate or cause trouble."

"I . . . I should've said something," he said. "When Lew first came to me, I should've . . . but it seemed to make sense in a way—and he promised—and suddenly all my pet birds died, and he said how easy it was for pet birds to catch something, and I knew what he meant . . ."

"Did you know his plans for me, Wickins? For my family?"

"No," the man said. "I swear I didn't. I wouldn't have—even scared, I'd have told someone. It was just *Vote like this* or *Let this project run* or *Terminate that one*."

"I see," his father said. "You will forgive me if I must delve a little deeper than that . . . I had not suspected Lew myself, and it makes me suspicious of others."

"I understand. I'm sorry, I really am. I had no idea he was capable of anything like . . . like . . ."

"Torturing people and killing babies? Neither did I. But he did, and those who helped him in any way, knowing or unknowing, are going to be held accountable."

"I will resign from the Board at once . . ."

"Of course you will, but I commend you for saying so quickly. I'm afraid you'll have several unpleasant days, but I assure you they will not be as unpleasant as mine were. If you will go with these gentlemen—" His father nodded at the two of Gary's people who stood ready.

"Y-yes. I'm sorry . . ."

"I'm sure you are. Rafe, let's go in."

The room looked more like a lounge, with couches and chairs arranged around the room and a bar at the end. The faces turned toward his father were all, as far as Rafe could tell, full of honest concern and shock.

"I want you all to know," his father began, "that I had begun an internal investigation into some irregularities about two years ago. At no point in that investigation did I suspect that Lew Parmina had anything to do with the irregularities. I had known Lew for years, as all of us have. He was my protégé; I brought him into management myself, when he was an eager young intern. When we were abducted, I could not believe, at first, what we were told—that he was behind it. However, I was wrong. He was acting against the intent of this Board, and against me. In the days since Rafe rescued us, he and I have been able to crack some of Parmina's files and see what he had in mind. This evidence—where it does not compromise our internal security—will be turned over to law enforcement. I wish to apologize to the Board for having brought Lew into our confidence, for not having realized what he was. I hope you will agree that I have been sufficiently punished . . ."

"Of course, Garston," Vaclav said; others nodded. "None of us spotted it. He must have had incredibly good luck, or an accomplice within the firm, to keep it all so quiet."

"He's very intelligent," Rafe's father said. "My own guess is that his first goal was simply to rise in the company and end up as CEO; I'm not sure when his other goals became involved. But it was not recent. I'm now convinced that he was behind the attempted abduction of Rafe and his sister Penelope—the incident in which Rafe killed the invaders and saved himself and his sister. And behind the advice to send Rafe away. He wanted to eliminate the competition, as he saw it."

"So . . . I'm assuming Oster was one of his people," Madeleine Pronst said. "Termanian? Wickins?"

"Yes," Rafe's father said. "We have some of the other names, but not by any means all. However, more immediately, there's the matter of the running of the company. As you can see, I am physically impaired. Doctors are unsure if I will regain all function. I am also mentally impaired due to damage to my implant, which propagated into the brain. It does not affect my language functions, and I have passed a competency test, but I am not at full capacity and in this crisis ISC needs someone who is. They tell me that for full recovery—if it's possible—I must have my damaged implant removed, and I will be much more impaired then for some considerable time. No new implant can be installed until the brain damage has healed."

"And we are all suspect," Madeleine said, glancing around. "Perhaps not in your mind, Garston, but everyone on the Board must be, at least for a while."

"Yes," Rafe's father said. "And that's why I want you to agree to my next request." He paused, glanced around, and went on. "I want you to approve Rafe as my successor, at least on a temporary basis."

"Rafe! But he's not . . . he has no background!"

"We need someone who knows the business—"

"He can't possibly understand the complexity—"

Rafe's father raised his hand, and the hubbub died down. "Hear me out," he said. "Rafe was brought up in the business; his university studies, to the point at which he left, covered business topics—and ISC was the model used in classes. I know, because I checked at the time. He has done work for us as an undercover agent from time to time, especially in the last five years, investigating situations important to ISC in a number of systems. This has required him to live under an assumed name. Some of which—fortunately—Lew Parmina did not know."

"Was he on the payroll?" Madeleine asked. "I don't recall—"

"No. As some of you know, he received a remittance on condition of staying away from Nexus except for brief visits, not more than once every year. In part to protect his cover, I did not put him on the payroll. I found his data to be accurate, and there was no indication that he had ever breached our confidence."

"I see. Well . . ." She gave Rafe a challenging look. "Do you think you're up to this, young man? You'll have your father's advice, but—"

"In many ways, I'm not up to it," Rafe said. "As several of you pointed out, I haven't been working openly in the company, I don't know all the right people and procedures. Any one of you—any division head, for that matter—knows more about how things work here at headquarters than I do. In other ways, I agree with my father that I am the only person for the job right now. I know things about ISC and its employees—out in the systems where our income originates—that none of you can. I can untangle the mess Lew Parmina left faster than you can, because I have not only the background but also offworld contacts you lack. ISC is in crisis, not only because of Lew Parmina. You don't know this yet, but shipboard ansibles are now being used both by a hostile force intent on domination of systems, and by the force that opposes it. I saw the ansibles myself; I know they work. I know that they are being manufactured somewhere off Nexus II, though not yet where. Once technology like that gets loose, as I'm sure you appreciate, it can't be stuffed back in the closet. We are in a fair way to lose our monopoly, to be seen as an obsolete, inferior system of communication, useful only for those systems too poor to afford better."

The shock he saw on their faces now was economic; all of them could see the implications of that.

"We have ruled the universe within hundreds of light-years by virtue of controlling communications," he said. "We wisely did not bother with planetary governments— we simply maintained open communications and insisted on our monopoly. It was a great idea, and it worked brilliantly . . . until technology advanced. When every ship carries its own ansible—"

"But they don't link with ours," someone said.

"They *didn't* link with ours," Rafe said. "The ones we manufactured didn't. But there was no technical reason why they couldn't . . . it was ISC's decision to limit connectivity to maintain control of the technology. We've lost that. At present, I haven't personally seen a shipborne ansible with the capability to connect directly to our net, but if you believe it won't happen, you believe in fairy tales."

Stunned silence. One of the men—Bennett D'Argent, his implant informed him—raised his hand. "You talked about a hostile force. Do you know anything about that?"

"Quite a bit, but that's not the first order of business. The first order of business is whether or not you'll confirm me to my father's role. I certainly can't do what needs to be done without your support, and I believe I can if I have it."

"You have mine," Vaclav Box said. "But you knew that."

"And mine," Madeleine said. "I can see we've got a crisis; we need all of Garston's input we can get, and Rafe seems to have skills none of us have."

The rest fell in line with almost no more resistance; when they moved back into the main boardroom, all its messes cleared away, Rafe sat at the head of the table, with his father's float chair at his left hand, and called the meeting to order.

The next morning, Rafe woke in his own room, on a bed that he had not realized his body remembered. This would not do, he realized. He wasn't that young boy. He had been moved to tears that they'd saved his room, kept it for him, but he was no longer the person for whom these mementos had meaning. He ignored the robe his mother had put out for him—obviously his father's—and padded down the hall to the bathroom. A quick shower . . . into the suit . . . *A suit*, he muttered to himself. It felt more like a costume.

The car would be waiting . . . he glanced outside. It was.

He tapped out the code Gary had given him, and the lights flared and died. So it was the right car. He was sure it would be. Gary had been paid his fee, with a bonus, and he was using Gary's people for the house security as well as his own.

"You're not leaving already—" That was his sister. Her bruises had gone an even uglier yellow and green, with a few magenta marks where the injuries had been bone-deep; in the hall light, she looked fragile and ill.

"I have to," Rafe said. "I have to be at the office on time." He made himself grin at her. "Can you believe it? Your bad-boy brother getting all dressed up to go to the office on time?"

"Don't," she said. She put out her arms, and he pulled her into a quick, fierce hug. "You're not bad," she said, against his shoulder. "You were never bad. I shouldn't have cried, that night—"

"It's not your fault," he said. "You were young; you were scared; I killed our pet—"

"But if I hadn't—"

"This would still have happened," he said. "It wasn't you. It was him." That charming, intelligent, clever snake of a man. That monster, now locked in a cell deep within ISC headquarters. Rafe pushed her gently back. "I have to go; I have to take over. Father said so."

"Will he ever be the same?"

"I don't know, but I know we'll do all we can for him."

In the car, in the darkness of an autumn morning with cold rain drizzling down, Rafe turned on the light and looked at the data chips, glittering blue-violet, that his father had given him. Backups to the implant his father had had . . . or, if Lew Parmina had found them first, traps for anyone who used them. He needed the data . . . Lew would have known he'd need the data. Be careful, his father had said. He put the chips back in his inner pocket.

ISC's headquarters building was lit top-to-bottom two hours before most employees were due at work. At the main entrance, Rafe's bodyguard—still one of Gary's people—stepped out first, looked around, and then opened his door. "You did remember the body armor, sir?"

"I never leave home without it," Rafe said. "But I'm hoping that the snake had only one head."

At the door, the security guard recognized him and would have passed him through, but Rafe stopped him. "Son, I've had more faces than you have years." That wasn't true, but it got attention. "Don't you *ever* skimp on validating ID, not with me, not with anyone. Now check my bioscans properly."

"Yes, sir . . ."

He chose the lift for ordinary employees, transferring at the seventh floor to the stairs. He needed the exercise, he told himself. Later, he would have to find some way to work exercise into his daily schedule, not only the executive gym but also someone to spar with, someone to shoot against. His bodyguards, one a flight ahead and one a flight behind, would probably be ideal.

At the eleventh floor, the stairway door opened around the corner from the elevators. Rafe's forward guard stopped before turning and produced a small flat screen connected to a fiber-optic wand with a lens in the end. Rafe peered over his shoulder as he extended it around the corner. Someone was waiting, positioned to watch the elevator . . . someone suited, but with an ominous bulge under his jacket. A receptionist, pale and immobile, sat perched on the edge of her chair to one side. The bodyguard glanced back at Rafe and cocked his head. Rafe shrugged and ran a finger along his own throat.

A moment later he heard a soft *phut!*, then the sound of a body hitting the floor, and a cry, quickly cut off. The guard extended the wand again. The man was down, not yet dead but clearly dying; the receptionist had both hands to her mouth and looked about to faint.

The bodyguards both went ahead. No one else was in sight; no one popped out from behind one of the ornamental plants. Rafe followed, smiling at the receptionist.

"Sera Contado? Most upsetting for you; I'm so sorry. You'll want some time off to recover—"

"Please—I don't want to look—"

"Of course not. Come over here." He took hold of her chair and swung it around so she faced the striped curtains at the windows. "Was he here when you got here?"

She nodded, her mouth trembling. "He—he must have been hiding . . . around the corner . . . I was in early; I always come in early, and I knew . . . I thought . . . you're new . . . I wanted to be here . . ."

"That was very thoughtful of you," Rafe said, in his gentlest voice.

"And I was sitting here, sorting the calls that had come in, just as I always do . . . did . . . for your father. I mean, I'm not his assistant or anything, but the calls do come to me first, and I do my best . . ."

"I'm sure you do. So you were sitting here sorting calls . . ."

"Yes. By urgency, you understand. Things you'd need to know about immediately. And . . . and then . . . I just saw a sort of shadow and he was beside me, and he had a weapon . . . he said he'd kill me if I moved, and I didn't move; I couldn't move; I was so scared . . ."

"Of course," Rafe murmured. Whatever his guards were doing, the sound of harsh rattling breath had stopped.

"And you're still frightened, of course you are. I'm going to call down for some tea—"

"Don't leave me!" Her eyes, as well as her voice, begged him.

"I'm not leaving."

"There's . . . there's hot beverage service here always . . . I could make . . ."

She would fall over if she tried to stand; she was trembling.

"Just tell me where it is," Rafe said. "I can make tea."

"Not you! You're—you're the Chairman!"

Rafe grinned at her, keeping it friendly. "Even chairmen can boil water. Is it there? In that cabinet?" He had spotted the concealed doors. She nodded. "Then you sit right there—I'll just be a few meters away—and we'll start this day over with a nice cup of tea." Into which, if he was lucky, he could pour the something stronger he expected would be in the same cabinet.

He glanced at his bodyguards; one was still kneeling beside the corpse; the other was watching him. When he opened the doors, he saw immediately where the man had hidden. The cabinet was intended to house not only a hot drinks service, but cleaning supplies for the reception area as well. The marks of a vacuum and bucket were clear on the floor, but that side was empty. The hot drinks service was in working order, and in less than a minute Rafe handed Sera Contado a fat gray mug with the ISC logo in blue and gold. The intruder had emptied the bottle of brandy he'd hoped to use, but the sugar he'd poured into her tea should help.

"We'll need to get this to forensics," one of the bodyguards said.

"We should give law enforcement a chance," Rafe said. "They're probably not all bent."

"Whatever you say, sir."

"One of you come with me. I want to get Sera Contado out of here before you . . . move anything."

His father's office looked the way Rafe had always imagined it, the way vid shows depicted the offices of senior executives in major corporations. The outer office, with two desks for the assistants and a small seating area for those waiting a meeting with the CEO. The inner office, a large carpeted space with a desk that seemed, at first glance, as big as some of the ship cabins Rafe had traveled in. The seating area, with its small couches arranged around a low table . . . the vase of fresh flowers there . . . the bookcases . . . the windows, with their curtains. A door led into a small passage with a bathroom—a full bath, he noticed—on one side, and a compact kitchen on the other. Beyond was a meeting room, smaller than the Boardroom but still big enough for ten people to sit around the oval table.

And now it was his space. His domain. The domain he had never wanted . . . or the domain he had not let himself want, knowing it was impossible. It felt too big and too limited at the same time. He handed Sera Contado to one of the soft couches, putting her mug down on the table for her, and crossed to the desk. The top was bare, a smooth expanse of flame-grain wood with smoked-glass inserts for the desk displays.

"I'm going to call down to the infirmary," he said to her. "They can send up a nurse . . . and of course you'll take the day off."

"Oh, but I can't," she said. "I can't afford—" Her cheeks turned red.

"It won't count against you," Rafe said. "Think of it as . . . as a reward for your bravery. You should be proud of yourself. You didn't scream; you didn't faint."

Her mouth dropped open. "I—I didn't, did I? I thought I would. I thought, *I can't stand this,* and then . . . I'm still here."

"I think you should at least rest in the infirmary for a while," Rafe said. "We need to check the building, and make sure you will be safe when you leave. Is that all right with you?"

"I'm feeling much better . . . I don't think I need to rest." But her breath still came too fast; her color came and went.

"Just for a little while," Rafe said. "You don't have to lie down, if you don't want. Just give us a chance to check things out."

By the time the nurse arrived, Rafe was already engulfed in the day's crises. The police were on the way; nothing should be moved. The building security staff, with rough guidance from Gary's people, were moving through every space—every space they knew about, Rafe thought—with speed that he hoped wouldn't let them miss something important. No other intruders had been found yet.

FIFTEEN

Adelaide System

As her small fleet moved slowly to the outer reaches of
Adelaide System, Ky sent Ransome's Rangers to scout out
three different systems within a one-jump range. She didn't
expect to find pirates in any of them; it was more a test
of the Rangers' ability and willingness to do what they
were told—and of the ansibles' performance across much
greater distances.

The Ranger ships jumped out as soon as they had cleared
the mass limit; Ky did not expect to hear from them for days.
She had ordered all the larger ships to move slowly so that
there would be ample time to receive reports before reaching
the mapped jump point. Five days later, *Furious* reported
from its target system. The ansible signal was as clear as if
they were alongside; the report, as she'd expected, was of
an empty system with a single relay ansible, nonfunctional.
Ky put a note in the navigation tables and told *Furious* to
return to the group. *Courageous* reported in only twelve hours
later, with the same news, and Ky called them back as well.

Glorious had gone the farthest: it was the direction Ky
wanted to take the fleet, heading back toward the area
where Vatta had trade routes. In the navigation database,

that system was also uninhabited, with a relay ansible now off-list. Because of the six-day jump lag, a report from the system would be at least twelve days out of date before they could arrive, but Captain Ransome still needed the practice in using the shipboard ansible. His report was the same as the others: empty system, as expected.

Furious reappeared in Adelaide System; Ky watched the scan as Captain St. Cyrien dumped excess velocity, micro-jumped to realign his vector, and reappeared precisely where she had asked him to go.

"Very neat handling," she transmitted to him.

"Thank you, ma'am," he said. "Have you heard from Teddy?"

"What we expected. He should be back here within the next twelve hours."

Courageous also reappeared on schedule, and came into position neatly on their other side. Finally, only two hours from their planned jump into FTL, *Glorious* reappeared.

"Great news, Captain Vatta!" Ransome looked indecently boyish as he threw her an elaborate salute. "There's no problem at all. In fact, you have friends there—"

"Friends?"

"Yes. Mackensee Military Assistance Corporation just arrived as I was getting ready to jump out. I have their transition profile if you'd like to see it. We also picked up a bit of chatter. They're going to be training there. Brilliant of you to anticipate where they'd be."

Ky blinked. She'd had no idea Mackensee would be training in that system.

"Did you contact them?" she asked.

"Oh, no. You said we should act as scouts, and scouts should not announce themselves—or should we have?"

"No, you did quite right," Ky said. "Though you could have contacted me by ansible with that update." She noticed that Ransome's crew had moved *Glorious* quickly into position with deft microjumps. These little ships might prove useful after all . . . "Their scans probably picked you up, but if you were on the way out they might have ignored it."

He made a dramatic gesture. "I should have thought of that—they wouldn't have known if I'd used the ansible. I was thinking they might intercept, and we were being scouts, so I shouldn't risk being overheard."

"That's all right," Ky said. "It's a new technology to you; you'll think of it next time. We're about to jump out, then, if you're ready."

"Quite ready, I assure you. Mapped point to mapped point, it's exactly six point three days of FTL transit."

"Switch to Channel F, then," Ky said, and gave the order to the other ships. "We want to exit with low relative velocity," she said to them all. "Captain Ransome reports that Mackensee Military Assistance Corporation is training in that system; they will have their own scouts out, and we don't want to be attacked as pirates before we have a chance to explain. I'm going to assume that—despite Captain Ransome's care—they might have spotted his out-bound jump and might have planted mines at the jump point. Synchronize navigation computers—" She hoped this would work with ships of such disparate mass. No reason why it shouldn't, but . . .

They reached transition simultaneously, and during the next six days of FTL isolation Ky kept her crew busy. If they were to meet Mackensee in that system—if the MMAC ships were still there—she wanted to present a military appearance without, however, getting killed out of hand.

They all emerged from the jump point within seconds of one another, still in formation. Ky heaved a sigh of relief as the last ship reported in, even before scan cleared. "Captain Ransome, detail one of your ships to stay with our transport," she said. She could not leave the unarmed transport with no protection. "Everyone else, formation Zeta-blue, but slowly—when your scan clears, watch for mines."

The mines showed up when scan cleared: five clusters, spaced to allow lanes between them for those who either knew the locations or were slow enough, with good enough scan, to avoid them.

"Is that Mackensee's standard toss-out?" Hugh asked her.

"I don't know," Ky said. "But it's not like what I saw at Sabine. Of course, I didn't have the scan capability then that we have here. It's an effective distribution, though . . ."

Other scan data came in; at first glance the system was full of ships of all sizes and types.

"Mackensee?" Ky asked.

"No. The Mackensee ships are there—" Hugh pointed. "They've got clear beacons; they're not hiding who they are. These are something else. That new software you loaded thinks most are bogeys—drones, signal emitters, stuff tossed out to be confusing. There's at least four actual ships, but with fogged beacons, which doesn't look good. And microjumping—here—here—there. Looks like an attack pattern to me. They've pincered the Mackensee ships . . ."

Ky's mouth went dry; she swallowed. "Pirates, then. Attacking Mackensee—they'll get a surprise—"

"Maybe not. Look at the numbers." Whatever they were, they outnumbered the Mackensee ships at least two to one, and when the weapons analysis came up, they out-gunned them as well.

Ky hit the alarm. "Whatever it is, it's trouble," she said. Lights flashed for alert status; she saw the boards light with acknowledgments from Weapons. Number one battery was first, as usual.

"We jump out?" Hugh asked.

"Not yet," Ky said. "I want to know what's going on."

"There's more of them than us," he pointed out.

"I know," Ky said. She was not going to repeat the mistake she'd made with Osman. Ship ID beacons began to register. "Mackensee," Ky said. "The two together there—" She pointed. "I know that beacon logo."

"Right," Hugh said. "I recognize it, too. But who are the others?"

"They have shipboard ansibles—they've got to be the enemy." Her stomach tightened into the familiar knot. "And they weren't expecting us."

Clearing scan showed that four of the enemy were in the same attack formation they'd used before, their ships converging from either side, both pairs in echelon, with the Mackensee ships at the crossing of the X. "Tactical conservatives," Hugh said.

"And we're in position to hit them on the flank," Ky said. If she wasn't being rash again; if she wasn't missing something deadly. This time she had to get it right. "Except for those—"

She indicated the other icons, still marked UNKNOWN TYPE, UNKNOWN ORIGIN.

"Those may not be ships," Hugh said. "Like I said, we used to get scan data like that from drones or from holos. They don't carry ID beacons, drones. They're just there to be scary."

Ky eyed them suspiciously. "I'd hate to discount them and then find that they're firing up my tail."

"True. And there are such things as towed arrays, or

armed drones. But considering the way they're arranged, I think they're fakes. What's our mass detector say?"

"We're too far out still." Ky chewed her lip. Four pirates against two Mackensee ships . . . the Macs might fight free; they were certainly capable, as she knew. And she had no duty to them. On the other hand, she did have a duty to destroy the enemy, as long as it didn't mean losing her own ships. And she had wanted them as allies. "If those other icons are harmless drones or fakes of some kind . . . we'd make it five to four, not even counting the little ships, and I know the Mackensees aren't going to sit there doing nothing."

"Battle stations?" Hugh asked.

"Yellow only," Ky said. "We have hours to go before we're in range, and I don't want to jump until we're well clear of the mines and sure we aren't jumping into worse. I hope Mackensee can hold out that long. Signal the others with the new code." That now seemed a brilliant idea. Her spirits lifted. They had tactical surprise, secure communications, and a superior position. "We can take them, and if we get Mackensee on our side—"

"Crossing fire," Hugh warned her.

"We're far enough out to track it and avoid it," Ky said. "We can define their plane." The X-attack made things simpler for the attackers, who knew exactly where their own fire would go, but a third party could attack from off-plane, avoiding the original shots and also the intended victim.

She explained her plan to the other captains, who agreed with her analysis. "Three to four's not bad odds," Argelos said cheerfully.

"It's five to four in our favor, really," Ky said. "Not even counting our scouts. The Mackensee ships will fight, and fight well. We do have to let them know we're on their side, though. And we can't really communicate with them until we're close enough for lightspeed to make sense. In the meantime, they have no reason to believe our beacons are honest, even if they notice us in the confusion."

"When do you think the pirates will notice us?"

"Depends," Ky said. "This isn't a heavily used transfer jump point, so they may be concentrating on the Mackensee ships. And"—a thought suddenly hit her—"if they're monitoring their drones or holos or whatever those other signals are, their scan tech may be too busy to notice new signals in the system. I wonder why the Mac ships aren't moving faster—"

"Already disabled?"

"Or they had personnel on EVA," Ky said. "If they were on a training mission, practicing EVA, they'd want to recover their personnel before they moved."

"That just makes targets out of 'em," Hugh said. "They can get roasted by passing fire . . ."

Vanguard and *Bassoon* had military-grade microjump capability, but *Sharra's Gift* did not. Argelos could jump his ship only in longer hops, with less precision. Ky made a mental note to find out what it would take to bring his ship up to military specs—later, maybe much later. Now she considered the relative advantages to keeping her little group together, and decided it was worth the risk to disperse them. "We can talk in real time all the way across the system," she said. "There's no reason for us to stick close. If we can position *Sharra's Gift* on the exit side of their attack, to take them in the opposite flank—"

"Crossing fire," Hugh said again.

"Different plane," Ky said. "If we're all above their plane, our fire will cross, but not on one another, nor theirs on ours."

"Right," Argelos said. "I can make that in one hop, pretty close. I think, anyway." Ky hoped he was right.

"And we can come in with short hops," she said to Pettygrew. "Here's where we want to end up." She pointed to the display. "With any luck, they'll be too busy monitoring their own decoys or drones, and we'll be able to blindside them."

"What about us?" Ransome asked. "Where do you want us?"

Where he and the others wouldn't interfere, but she couldn't say that. "We need someone watching our backs," she said. "*Furious* has to concentrate on the transport; we need someone watching our backs and also helping to trace weapons tracks. But you're so maneuverable, I want you close enough to get off some shots if needed. I'd like *Courageous* here"—she pointed—"and *Glorious* there."

"Do we announce ourselves, or just hope that the Mackensee ships assume we're friendly?" Argelos asked.

"When we blow their attackers, I think they'll get the picture. But I'm planning to tell them as soon as we're close in, to less than a one-light-minute range. Oh—and have your communications personnel check the channel we know the pirates use, at least twice a minute. If you pick up anything interesting, record it and pass it on later."

"Attention all ships." Ky had no way of knowing if any of them would pay attention to the broadband hail, but someone would hear it. "This is Space Defense Force, Third Fleet, First Squadron. We recognize ships of Mackensee Military Assistance as under attack by unlawful forces, and we order you to desist or be fired upon." By the time the pirates heard that, her first rafts of missiles should be impacting their shields. Mackensee, she could see, were firing bursts of missiles, but only one of their ships seemed capable of using a beam weapon, in short bursts.

Sharra's Gift reappeared on scan, almost perfectly positioned. Ky had her communications tech monitoring the pirates' ansible channels, and a burst of incomprehensible jargon came from the ansible.

"I think they heard us," Ky said. She nodded, and Hugh changed the ansible to their private setting.

"Captain Argelos, do you have a firing solution?"

"I do," he said. "My primary target is the number one first crossing the X."

Ky nodded to her own weapons officer. "Get 'em, Dannon."

Their forward beam weapon stabbed out, raising a flare on the shields of the nearest enemy ship just as its shield and the second in that echelon sparkled with the impact of their missiles.

"Not getting through," Hugh said.

"Not expecting to yet," Ky said. "This is to get their full attention off the Mackensee ships . . ."

"Space Defense Force—who the hell are you?" That came from a Mackensee ship. "This is MSS *Metaire,* Colonel Kalin commanding. Who's your commanding officer?"

"A combined force formed to defend against the common enemy . . . the pirates commanded by Gammis Turek," Ky said. "We have representatives of various planetary systems . . ." Never mind that one of those systems had been destroyed, one was an exile, three were wild-eyed adventurers, and her own ship's Cascadian registry did not really represent the Moscoe Confederation's support.

"You're on our side?"

"Yes. You're legitimate," Ky said. "They aren't. Excuse me a moment . . ." She turned to her weapons officer. "Phase two, shall we?"

"But who's commanding?"

"I am," Ky said. It was harder than she'd expected to say both that and her name in the same utterance. "Kylara Vatta," she said after a pause. Then quickly, before he could comment, she said, "Can you maneuver? I notice you're near drifting."

"Troops outside," he said. "We're trying to bring them back aboard, but this way we can at least offer them some protection." A pause, then, "Are you *that* Kylara Vatta? The one who—"

"Yes," Ky said.

"I see. Talk to you later." And the contact cut off.

On the display, the battle shifted abruptly from what had seemed like the easy destruction of an outnumbered static force by a larger mobile one, as the pirates realized they themselves were caught in a pincer formed of the Mackensee ships and Ky's force. Though Ky could not understand any of the commands their commander gave, it became obvious that they considered the Mackensee ships' missile batteries less dangerous than the others', and they tried to close in enough to use the Mackensee ships for a screen.

But Ky had anticipated this; she and Pettygrew both microjumped in much closer. Close in, *Vanguard*'s missile launchers achieved a rate of fire Ky would have thought impossible, hammering at the pirates' defenses. Shields on the nearest pirate ship brightened to an actinic flare, and the next launch sent a hundred into her unprotected flanks. The optical monitors blanked; others indicated hull breach, fragments blown wide . . .

"That's not going to be going anywhere," Hugh commented. He sounded calmly pleased.

"Good," Ky said. "Though I wouldn't mind if we disabled one and captured it."

That ship's partner decelerated abruptly.

"Not the maneuver I'd pick," Hugh said.

"Me, neither," Ky said. "The debris cloud will be broader when he reaches it. I think he's hoping to duck it, but it's not going to work."

One of the pirate ships ran full into the barrage *Metaire* had launched shortly before, and its shields flared. "I'm on it," Pettygrew said. He pursued, and a salvo up the bustle breached the after shields. The resulting explosion indicated that at least one insystem drive had blown. The ship yawed, then began a sickening tumble.

"Lost their stabilizers," Hugh said. "Probably lost all insystem, and all internal power . . . talk about vomit comet . . ."

"Is it reparable?" Ky asked.

"By a good shipyard, yes. Jury-rigged, probably not. It'll never go through jump."

"Might as well blow it, then," Ky said. "It's a navigation hazard as it is. Too bad; I'd have liked another armed vessel." She looked at Hugh.

"You're right," he said. "It's too bad, but I don't see any way to get it repaired out here, not with our resources."

Ky nodded at Dannon. "Forward beam." The beam stabbed out, finding the tumbling ship, and a few seconds later it exploded in a cloud of debris.

The fourth pirate ship, disabled, drifted on its way. Ky sent Ransome to keep watch on it. "Stay out of its range," she said. "If we can capture it whole, it'll be useful, but we don't want trouble while we're waiting." If the pirates had contacted their friends by shipboard ansible—and she was sure one of them at least would have—trouble might drop in at any time.

For the moment, though, her concern was for the battered Mackensee ships. She contacted Colonel Kalin aboard *Metaire*.

"Can we assist?" Ky asked.

"Do you have medevac capability for zero-gravity, micro-atmosphere situations?"

"Er . . . not much," Ky said. Her medical personnel had been reading the manuals and working on simulations, but had no actual experience. "We have medical personnel and supplies, but not expertise in EVA work, though they've been doing simulations."

"Then no, you can't. You can keep any more trouble off us, though, if you would. *Verain*'s holed. Internal damage. She's not going anywhere . . ."

"If you need crew space," Ky said, "we have room."

"We prefer to take care of our own people," Colonel Kalin said, a bit stiffly.

"Understood," Ky said. "We'll take high guard."

She moved her ships back, except for the transport, which might prove useful. Her scan crews mapped the expanding debris fields and the tracks of live weapons. Though missile drives would run out after a few minutes, the missiles themselves continued as live warheads.

Recovery of personnel outside the ships took agonizing hours. *Verain*'s captain reported worse news: both insystem and FTL drives down, several onboard fires, no power to deliver the fire-retardant foams. The weapons bay crews shoved unused ordnance out the hatches as fast as they could, racing the approaching fires. Finally the captain ordered his crew to abandon ship . . . and most made it into shuttles or onto the rope tows before the ship blew.

Ky felt helpless and guilty both as they stood off listening to the mounting damage and casualty reports, watching for more trouble that never arrived. Meanwhile, she sent Argelos to the drifting pirate hulk.

"Definitely some hostiles alive aboard," Argelos

reported. "We can pick up the transmission of short-range communicators. Nothing on the ansible—I'm hoping its power source is down; it should be. Can't understand what they're saying, though, except for a word now and then. Wait—they're using regular ship channels now . . . they want to surrender."

"Do they indeed," Ky said. She called the Mackensee ships. "Colonel, the remaining pirate ship is disabled but whole, and they want to surrender. Could you make use of that hull?"

"Chances are they'll just ambush any boarding party," Kalin said. "And I don't have the resources to use right now. We certainly could use the space, if the hull's airtight, but you blew the engines, didn't you?"

"I don't know the full extent of damage," Ky said. "But I don't want to leave a shipful of pirates loose, even if they seem to be disabled now."

Kalin grunted. "I must say, Captain Vatta, that you saved our skins, and I'm grateful. And your tactics were competent. So I guess it's up to you. You're a privateer, aren't you? You'd claim her as a prize?"

"I *was* a privateer," Ky said. "Now you might want to think of us as another military unit. And you have need. If that ship would be of use to you, and if we can capture it without undue loss, I'd certainly let you use it to get back to a system where you had resources. Then, yes, our force could always use more ships."

"I don't know what advice to give you," Kalin said. "And from what I've heard about you, you don't always take advice."

"True, but I'm listening," Ky said.

"Well, then." From his expression, he was trying out approaches, discarding them. "It's very, very tricky, doing a hostile boarding. I know you've been boarded once—"

"Twice," Ky said.

"All right. The advantage is with the defenders, usually. They know their ship best. And that ship's tumbling, which is going to make it harder. You don't know how big the ship's company is, so you don't know if they're all out, even if you get some of them to evacuate onto tethers. They've had plenty of time to set booby traps, too."

"So your recommendation would be to blow it away?"

"Ordinarily, yes: without hesitation. But you're right: we are short of space, especially with our wounded. We expect a resupply force in about fifteen days, but until then—"

"Colonel, we have a transport ship insystem; she's not fully loaded, and there's space aboard her you could use."

"Had you planned to be here that long?"

"I was planning to do training exercises here, the same as you were."

"Did you know we were here?"

"Just before we jumped, one of my scouts reported that he'd seen your ships in the system, and nothing else. It was just over a six-day jump. I didn't know if you were about to leave, had just arrived, or what—but I didn't consider you hostiles."

"I see. If you can take some of our personnel aboard until our other ships arrive, that would be a big help. And if you have extra medboxes and medical personnel—" He turned away for a moment. When he turned back, his shoulders had slumped a centimeter. "Our casualties are very high, Captain Vatta. Any help you can give—"

"Of course." Ky spared a thought for the remaining pirate ship. With her people out there watching it, it wasn't going to cause trouble, and the casualties were more important. The plight of the pirates themselves didn't bother her at all. "Tell me where you want the transport: I don't want to cause more trouble."

He gave her the system coordinates; Ky passed them on to the transport, and then ordered *Furious* to stay far out and keep watch over the jump point.

"Do you expect more pirates?" Captain St. Cyrien asked.

"No, but they didn't expect us," Ky said. "And anyone downjumping there is in danger from those mines. We may have to blow them up . . ." Which would create a debris field wider than the minefield, but a lesser hazard. Only weakly shielded tradeships would be at risk of a hull breach or serious damage.

Their supply ship, unable to perform precision microjumps, followed Argelos' pattern to place itself within a few hours of the location Colonel Kalin had requested, then edged in with insystem engines.

The first shuttle load of Mackensee personnel that eased up to *Vanguard*'s larger air lock swam the tube with helmets sealed. Ky waited for them herself, with armed guards beside her. Friends they might be, but she was not a naïve space cadet anymore.

The first person into the ship had a row of stripes on the suit arm and PITT stenciled on the helmet. Ky fought back a grin. This was entirely too good to be true.

"Master Sergeant Pitt requests permission to come aboard—" Clearly, Pitt was having the same trouble; the corner of her mouth twitched.

"Permission granted," Ky said. "I understand you have three wounded with you?"

"Yes, ma'am. They're coming through next."

"Chief Martin will escort them to our medical facility. Our medical staff is set up and waiting. You and the rest of your personnel will be in our starboard crew compartments. Sergeant Crayle will guide you—" She gestured to one of her escort, who stepped forward. "I'll be in to speak with you later, when I've reported to Colonel Kalin about the status of your wounded."

"Thank you, ma'am," Pitt said, saluting. She stepped aside. Next out of the transfer tube were the wounded, in enclosed litters; Martin led them away. Ky, glancing through the transparent shields, tried not to show what she felt. It was one thing to imagine what being hit by projectiles when outside a ship might mean . . . quite another to see the human wreckage up close. She followed the last of the litters to the medical suite they'd set up.

Here, her medical teams had already opened the first seal; the stench of blood and burned flesh and bowel contents filled the compartment until one of the techs lowered the exhaust hood.

"I'm a combat medic," one of the *Metaire* crew said. "Can I help?"

"Scrub in," one of her own crew said. Ky flattened herself to the bulkhead as the other man came by.

"Down that way; spare jumpers in the locker."

Of the three injured, two went immediately into medboxes for supportive care while the medical team worked over the third. Ky stood by, making sure she was out of the way, until all three had been treated and her team had handed over the medical data Kalin's people would want. Then she headed for the bridge to talk to Colonel Kalin.

"They're all alive," she said. "I'm transmitting the files to you now."

"Thank you," he said. He looked drawn; Ky multiplied what she had seen in her own sick bay by . . . however many casualties there'd been . . . and understood. "If only we hadn't had so many out in EVA. Now—where did you people come from? And why?"

Ky started in again. "We jumped in from Adelaide

System. Our scout—you should have his beacon as *Glorious*—had reported the system empty except for your two ships."

"And that was about twelve days ago, you said? We have a brief scan contact from back then, but no hail. The enemy . . . you say you know who they are?"

"You don't?" Ky asked.

"No. Never heard of pirates attacking armed ships like ours before."

Ky summarized what had been happening.

"They've taken whole systems? And we don't know . . . oh. Yes, of course, the ansibles being out. They must be part of that, too . . ."

"Possibly," Ky said. "Certainly they're making good use of communications being disrupted."

"So . . . who's paying for your bunch? The . . . um . . . Space Defense Force or whatever you're calling it? Organized pretty fast, wasn't it?"

"It's multisystem," Ky said.

"Yes, but the last I heard, Slotter Key's ansible was out . . . so how did they let you know they were in on this?"

"Colonel, I'm not comfortable discussing this kind of thing over an open connection, even with scrambling. My scouts don't think there's anyone else in this system, but what if there's a stealthed observer ship somewhere?"

"I see your point. All right. We'll talk later, in a more secure location."

Down in the starboard crew area, Pitt and her people already had their area ready for inspection. Sergeant Crayle had shown them the mess area, and Ky found them cleaning up after a meal.

"Officer on deck!" Pitt called out, and the others all came to attention.

"At ease," Ky said. "Have you found everything you need?"

"Yes, ma'am. Nice ship you have here . . . bit more than the other one."

"Thanks. It's a repossession; this ship was stolen from Vatta decades ago, and I got it back."

"Yes, ma'am, I did hear something about that. Was a pirate ship, wasn't it?"

"That's right. I re-registered her, after we got her cleaned up and refitted. Good to see you again, Master Sergeant Pitt."

"Good to see you in the role you were meant for, ma'am, if I may be so bold. 'Specially since we really needed some help out there."

"Wish we'd been a bit sooner," Ky said. "What happened to your sentries?"

"Blown away before we knew it. They knew exactly where to look, apparently. First I heard, it was 'Abort exercise, return to ships.' "

"So . . . there's probably an observer here somewhere. Stealthed . . . we haven't spotted anything . . ." The suggestion she'd made to Kalin, because she didn't want to discuss the tenuous nature of the Space Defense Force, might have teeth.

"Almost certainly. And a spy at our last stopover, too. Not that our people are loose-lipped, but we went into the Powdern jump point with the right vector to come out here. It's only got the two endpoints, where we'd come from and this one."

"Come up to my office with me for a bit," Ky said. Pitt sent her people back to work and followed Ky. When they reached the office, Ky waved her to a seat and sat down herself, behind the desk.

"Nice," Pitt commented, glancing around.

"If it was a spy where you were, communicating with someone here, where the system ansible doesn't work, how do you suppose the message went?" Ky asked.

"Is that a trick question? Without an ansible, it would have to be . . ." Pitt's expression changed. "It's . . . it would be impossible."

"Yeah," Ky said. "We're all so used to universal ansible access—to having real-time communication—that the implications of not having it can slip by. If there was no working ansible where you were—Powdern?—and no working ansible here, then a spy there couldn't communicate to ships here. Without another kind of ansible."

"But there isn't another kind of ansible," Pitt said. "Everyone knows that . . . oh." She stared at Ky. "There is? And you know about it?"

"The pirates have a way of communicating instantaneously across interstellar space," Ky said. "It's a ship-mounted ansible."

"But that's . . . everyone's always said—"

"It's impossible, yes. But it's not. It's technology that the ISC tried to keep under wraps. I don't know how it got out but it did, and it explains the coordination of the pirate attacks."

"It would," Pitt said. "Real-time communication in combat? Fantastic." Then her expression changed again. "You . . . certainly showed up in time. How do you know about this?"

"When I captured this ship, it was full of all sorts of goodies," Ky said. "Among them, sixty shipboard ansibles. One mounted ready for use, the rest crated and ready, I presume, to sell or hand over to the other pirates. At that time I had aboard an ISC agent, who just about came apart when he saw them. He knew what they were, and what they did, and he wanted to impound the lot."

"I'll bet he did," Pitt said.

"However, I persuaded him that if the man who'd run this ship had them, the tech was already out of the bag and couldn't be stuffed back in. I refused to turn them over or destroy them."

Pitt cocked her head. "You have grown up a lot, you know?"

"It's been an interesting time," Ky said. "What you don't know is that most of my family is dead."

"What?"

"Someone—I think this same group of pirates, in collaboration with someone in the government of my home planet—set out to destroy my family and my family's business. My parents and siblings are dead, along with many others; ships and crews were attacked as well as the corporate headquarters and some of the homes."

Pitt looked stunned. "When did this happen?"

"Shortly after I got back to Belinta . . . about the same time the ansibles started going out. I didn't find out about all of it until I got to Lastway." Ky shook her head. "Not a good topic of conversation, actually, but yes—I've changed. Not entirely . . . for the better."

"I wouldn't wish that on anyone," Pitt said. "But I'm damned glad you showed up when you did."

SIXTEEN

"I want you to go back and tell your commander about this personally," Ky said. "I don't want to transmit it over conventional radio."

"He's not expecting me back," Pitt said. "I'm supposed to take care of our people here—"

"Will he let you come back, d'you think, if I tell him I'm sending you with an urgent message?"

"Probably. But why don't you go? Or send one of your own crew?"

"He knows you," Ky said. "He knows of me, but he knows you—"

Her office com binged. "Captain, Captain Ransome wants to speak to you. Shall I patch it through?"

"Go ahead," Ky said. To Pitt, she said, "Ransome's someone we met on Adelaide. I'm using him and his ships as scouts." She tilted the vidscreen so Pitt could see it.

"Captain Vatta!" Ransome's broad grin went with the tone of delight. "Guess what! We found the observer!"

"Where?" Ky asked.

"At . . . uh . . . ." He turned, and someone handed him a note. "24-893-2217. Fully stealthed, as you suggested, and transmitting on its own ansi—" He stopped, seeming to notice Pitt for the first time. "—thingie," he finished.

"Anyway, we . . . er . . . we recorded it, and we stripped the beacon, and I just thought, you know, we could blow it away if you like. It's quite close, well within our range—"

Pitt was staring at the screen with an expression of horrified fascination. "What—"

"Just a minute," Ky said. "Captain Ransome, do I understand you to say that you have stripped that ship's beacon?"

"Oh, yes. Neat as an oolun sucking a pinkfish off the hook."

"You are aware that they will know their beacon's been stripped?"

"I don't think so," Ransome said. "We were very careful. You said you didn't want—"

Losing her temper would accomplish nothing at this point. Ky fought it down. She hadn't told them to go looking for the observer, but she hadn't told them not to. She'd told them to go about their business . . . and for Teddy Ransome, that meant sneaking up behind stealthed enemy ships for the fun of it. "Do you think you could ease away without being detected?" Ky asked.

He looked hurt. "I could . . . but where's the fun in that? Why can't I just blow it away? I'm in the perfect position."

He was in the perfect position to be blown up himself if he didn't get out of there, Ky thought. If she didn't blow him up herself. "We may have need of it," she said instead. "We're not getting any other prizes out of this, you know."

"Oh." His face sobered briefly, then returned to that expression of glee. "So . . . if I offered to buy you another ship the same size, *then* could I blow this one away?"

Ky just managed not to let her jaw drop. "I . . . suppose so," she said finally. She glanced at Pitt, whose face had gone unreadable again, though she had a very intentional glint in her eye. "Go ahead then, Captain Ransome." She closed the connection and put her head on her desk for a moment, then looked up at Pitt.

"And I thought *you* were a potential loose cannon," Pitt said. "Who is that decorative character and why are you having anything to do with him?"

"His name's Theodore Albert Driscoll Ransome," Ky said. "He and his friends—who all have long names and about as much sense as wild rabbits—got together in their personal ships to hunt pirates in their home system."

"He is good looking," Pitt said. "If you like that kind."

Ky scowled. "What matters to me is that he has three ships with superior speed and maneuverability, he's richer than stink, and he's willing to use his ships and his money to help us. I don't care about his looks."

Pitt gave her a long look, then nodded. "The major thought you were too susceptible, but I can tell you're not. Not now, anyway. Is he trustworthy?"

Ky shrugged, still a little annoyed that Pitt might think she'd been affected by Teddy Ransome's looks. "He went where I told him to go, and did what I asked him to do during the fight," she said. "I haven't known him long enough to assess his long-range reliability. I suspect, though, that he'll stick it out as long as it's exciting and suits his sense of adventure, and then go do something else."

"I've seen that kind before," Pitt said, nodding. "They can be useful cannon fodder as long as they do what you tell them." She looked around again, as if assessing the décor. "So . . . you want me to convince my commander that this marvelous technology exists and . . . and what?"

"See if he wants it," Ky said. "By the way . . . Teddy's forty-seven point three light-hours away. Did you notice any lag?"

"He was what? That's . . . a long way."

"Yes. And you know this system's ansible isn't working."

"Can you confirm the distance?"

"Your own scan can do that," Ky said with a shrug. "I agree, the timing of his call was convenient, but he's out there."

"Can you just call our ship on that thing?"

"No. Each node has to have a unit, and ships are movable nodes. That's how it was explained to me."

"Can it interface with system ansibles?"

"Not at present. Our units can't. But I don't expect that to last, frankly. And if the pirates get that technology before the rest of us—"

"—we're all in serious trouble. All right. I'll need to call and get permission to return."

"I'll take you up to the bridge," Ky said. "Tell him I'd like to talk to him about this, and other things," she added. "But when we're in a secure location."

"I'm sure he'll be interested . . . though you still haven't answered his question about who's footing the bill for this Space Defense Force we never heard of before . . . surely not the gallant Captain Ransome . . . ?"

"That, too, is something I'll want to talk to him about," Ky said.

Pitt shook her head. "With all due respect, ma'am, you are getting entirely too canny for one of your tender years."

"Captain Vatta!" That was Ransome again, this time with his mop of blond hair in an untidy muddle. "I am delighted to report that the observer ship has been immobilized without injury to *Glorious* or her crew."

"Immobilized?" Ky asked.

"Well . . . in a way. I know you would like another ship, and so we . . . er . . . fired our EMP mines at her, the whole salvo. She fired back, but our anti-missile missiles intercepted most of theirs and our shields held against the rest. And now she's dark—not transmitting at all, not moving."

"That may not last," Ky said. "Some ships have self-repairing AI systems."

"I know . . . I was going to ask your permission to board and secure her."

"Board—! How big is she?"

"Larger than *Courageous*, but not as large as *Vanguard*," he said. "My crew have done hostile boardings—we took back ships from those criminals in our system." From his expression, he might start saying *Please, please, please!* any moment.

"I can't stop you," Ky said, "but I don't want to lose you or your crew, and I can't spare one of the larger ships; we're all involved in recovering Mackensee casualties. Do you think you should have *Furious* or *Courageous* over there?"

"If you could release *Courageous*, that would be perfect," he said, brightening up. "Just in case . . ."

"Go ahead, then," Ky said. "But keep your scans on. Just because you found one—"

"—doesn't mean there aren't others. I understand, Captain Vatta."

Ky called *Metaire* on tight-beam and spoke to Colonel Kalin. "In about forty-eight hours, you'll pick up warhead detonations here—" She recited the coordinates. "One of our people out there found a stealthed observation ship and immobilized it. They're trying to board; I'll keep you informed."

"Master Sergeant Pitt's told me about your . . . uh . . ." Ky could see the struggle to find another word. "We do need to talk, Captain Vatta. Assuming Master Sergeant Pitt's report is accurate, there are . . . um . . . both tactical and strategic implications . . ."

"Indeed there are," Ky said. "But since this is not a secure location, I think that talk should be deferred to a better place and time, where we can demonstrate the object."

"You would not consider coming aboard *Metaire*?"

"Would you consider coming here? I am not comfortable leaving my ship while the situation is so uncertain."

"Point taken. No, I can't come. Our regulations forbid my leaving my command."

"We both know Master Sergeant Pitt. I would like to use her as a courier, if that's acceptable. I realize she has duties to personnel, but—"

"It's acceptable."

"Good. I'll be sending along some tactical analysis you may not have yet, and some suggestions based on that, for your consideration."

Ky looked at the system plot as she waited for Pitt's return. If a large pirate force moved in, they were clumped too close. "Move *Bassoon* out," she told Pettygrew. "If trouble jumps in, we want to be set up to defend *Metaire* as well as ourselves. I need to stay physically close for a while, because I'm using a courier to share sensitive data."

"Right," he said. "We'll keep an eye out. What's Ransome up to?"

"Let me get Argelos on, too—" Ky waited until Argelos come into the contact. "Ransome's found and immobilized a stealthed observer ship," she said to them both. "It was transmitting on the pirate channels; he's stopped that. Now his crew and the *Glorious* crew are trying to board and capture it."

"He's an idiot," Argelos said. "A shipful of pirates? It'll be a disaster."

"Well, he's done all right so far," Ky said. "It seemed worth a try to me. If he gets the ship relatively undamaged, we'll have a chance to learn more about the tech the pirates had."

"More than Osman left you?"

"I don't know how close Osman was to the power structure of the current bunch," Ky said. "It's said thieves fall out with thieves, and certainly there wasn't stealth tech aboard *Vanguard*. We need to beware any others; they might have had more than one."

"Right," Pettygrew said. "I'll keep a careful watch."

"Kalin expects a relief group of Mackensee ships to show up in . . . what is it now, ten days? Anyway, I'll find out if we need to do something about those mines at the jump point. I know we mapped a safe route through, but if they come in fast—"

"What about trying to fix the system ansible? It's only a relay; maybe its inbox is just stuffed."

"We don't have Rafe," Ky said.

"No, but I've got Dozi Lattin. She thinks it's possible she might be able to unstick it, if it's something simple like that."

"You can try," Ky said. "But the watch is more critical right now."

"Understood. We'll just ease up to it and see what she thinks."

Pitt arrived back within the hour, on a shuttle with more wounded and a senior sergeant to take over as NCOIC of the contingent billeted on *Vanguard*.

"The colonel thinks you're part brilliant, part crazy, and part scary as hell. That's a direct quote, ma'am," Pitt said, handing over a hardcopy packet. "And he told me to say that."

"What I am now is hungry," Ky said. "How about you?"

"No thank you, ma'am. I ate when I came aboard, you'll recall. But I don't mind waiting while you—"

"Good." Ky turned to Hugh. "Hugh, have them send something light to my office, please. And patch my office comunit through to the ship's ansible again. I need to check on Ransome."

By the time she and Pitt got to her office, a tray with soup and a pile of sandwiches was on her desk, along with a carafe of water and another of coffee. Ky flipped open the packet Pitt had handed her and sipped from the mug of soup. Colonel Kalin had given her his main concerns: time insystem until the other Mackensee ships arrived, the mines at the jump-point entry, the possibility that more pirates would arrive before the relief ships did . . .

"How likely do you think another incursion is?" Pitt asked.

"Less likely now than before," Ky said. "Their observer will have reported that their forces were wiped. If they'd won . . . they might have brought in more to attack your other ships when they came. Of course, they may see this as a chance to attack us. *Metaire*'s suffered some damage, expended a lot of ammunition—and no, I'm not asking how much is left. It's not my business. But I'm guessing that full as she is of wounded and over-crowded with the rest of the other crew, she won't fight at her best."

"That's true, unfortunately." Pitt sipped at the glass of water Ky had poured her. "So that leaves your three larger ships and the little ones . . . what's happened to Ransome's boarding attempt, by the way?"

"I don't know. He hasn't reported in. I'll check now." Ky turned to the ansible, entered *Courageous*' code, and the screen lit with the face of a crewman.

"Captain Vatta," he said. His gaze slewed sideways, clearly to another screen on the bridge. "Captain Ransome's not here . . ."

"He left the ship?" Ky said.

"Yes, ma'am. He led the boarding party, like he always does."

Ky managed not to say what she was thinking; Pitt's expression said it for her. "I see," she said instead. "Do you have any word on the progress of the boarding?"

"There's resistance," the man said. "Uh—but they just now got through an air lock—"

"You will keep me informed," Ky said.

"Oh, yes, ma'am. As soon as they take the ship, I'll let you know."

Or as soon as they didn't, and were dead. Ky closed the connection. "That idiot," she said, shaking her head.

"Cannon fodder," Pitt said. "Brave, though. I hate hostile boardings, myself."

Ky finished reading the material Kalin had sent. "I've put together a packet for you to take back," she said. "And it does not escape my irony detector that we are sending messages by hand in an era when instantaneous universal communication is—was—common."

"Well . . . it's secure if no one takes it out of my hand, which no one is going to do," Pitt said. She took the packet Ky handed over, slid it into a pocket on her suit. "If I could just make the suggestion, ma'am . . . I know some very reliable people in my unit, and we could spread this duty around."

"I know," Ky said. She had, in the course of reading Kalin's report, finished the soup and eaten half a sandwich. Her mind felt as if she had just walked through a veil into clear air. "I was just—a bit fuzzy. Tell me who you'd like to have on the job; I'll accept your assessment."

"It'll keep my people busy if we rotate it. When you call for a courier, someone will be there."

"Captain Vatta! Captain Ransome wants you to know that they're in the ship but resistance continues!"

"Thank you," Ky said.

"He'll let you know when he's completed the capture," Ransome's crewman said.

"Tell him to watch out for people dropping out of the overheads and coming up through the decks," Ky said.

"How did you—he said something about that."

"It's what I did the last time *we* were boarded," Ky said.

"Oh . . . I'll tell him," the man said, and cut the connection.

"The last time you were boarded?" Pitt said. "When was that?"

"Gretna Station, before we went to Adelaide. They've got a nasty little scam going: first they charge the earth for dock privileges, local identification, and air, and then, just as you leave, they attack. Their idea, as near as I can tell, is to get back everything they sold you to resell to the next unfortunate, hand your ship over to the pirates, and take your crew as indentured workers on trumped-up charges. And in the meantime, your credits are in their account."

"Slavers," Pitt said.

"Good as," Ky said. "My medical team came from there—medical personnel on their way to some kind of meeting, sold as general labor."

"You *bought* them?" Pitt said, looking horrified.

"It was the only way to get them out," Ky said. "Freed them as soon as they were aboard, of course; some elected to stay in Adelaide, but the ones I have now stayed because they wanted to." She finished off another sandwich. "Anyway, they attacked all three of our ships. They weren't amateurs, either. They knew how to go about it—attacked while we were too close to the station to use the beam weapons, and their shuttles were inside the fusing limits of our missiles. Luckily, this ship's full of useful passages, and though it got messy, we evicted them handily. They expected to be in control before we got far enough away to use our forward beam . . . but they weren't."

"You blew the station?"

"No . . . not everyone there was part of the scam, I'm sure. The other indentured workers, for one thing. But I scorched 'em and destroyed their communications masts, so they couldn't tell their remote platforms to burn us on the way out."

Pitt shook her head. "I know I told you, back then, that you were cut out for the military, but now I think I underestimated you . . . must've been that head injury. You're implant-linked now, aren't you?"

"Yes," Ky said. "That was another . . . interesting moment. But a story for another day. You'll want to see your people and set up a rotation, I'm sure."

"That I will. Thank you, Captain. I can find my own way—"

When Pitt had left, Ky stared at her desk for a long moment. The clarity a meal had given her had worn off. She started to call up to the bridge just as Hugh put his head in. "Captain—you're still up?"

"Of course I'm up," Ky said. "Why?"

"Because you've been up more than a day. May I suggest a few hours' sleep?"

"I haven't had a final report from Ransome. And we know the enemy might be jumping in—"

"And you'll cope better if you're even more exhausted?"

"You're right," Ky said, pushing back from the desk.

She felt as if the artificial gravity had been notched up. A lot.

"I was off for four hours . . ."

She barely heard him as she headed for her cabin.

When she woke, she realized she'd fallen asleep in her clothes and had a kink in her neck. Muttering, she went into the shower, emerging in a few minutes awake and eager to find out what had happened to Teddy Ransome. Her implant reported all ship functions normal. She dumped the clothes she'd had on in the 'fresher, dressed, and headed for the bridge.

"Captain Ransome reports he has the enemy ship under control," Hugh reported. "He was a little disappointed not to speak to you personally from its bridge once he figured out how to reset their ansible for our channels, but I explained that you had important other duties and would get back to him."

"Sleep is a duty?" Ky said, grinning.

"For combat commanders, yes. Whenever they can get it without imperiling the mission."

"I think it's a duty for executive officers, too, Hugh. I know you're made of tougher material than the rest of us, but it's your turn—"

"And I'm going," he said. "Shall I send up something to eat?"

"An excellent idea," Ky said.

"Oh—and no other stealthed ships have been located," Hugh said as he left the bridge.

She contacted Colonel Kalin, who looked as much more rested as she herself felt, on tight-beam.

"If you left now, could you intercept your people before they jumped in here?" she asked.

"Not likely. They were going—well, I can't say where,

but coming here they'd be doing serial jumps through several points."

"Well, it was a thought," Ky said. "Do you want me to blow those mines at the jump point?"

"No . . . it's our habit to come in carefully. You aren't leaving, are you?"

"Not while I have your personnel aboard several of our ships."

"I still need to talk to you about your base of support—"

"And I still prefer to wait until we're in a secure location."

"Your people didn't find another stealthed observer—"

"Colonel, I am perhaps too suspicious, but I do not think that not finding something means it's not there."

"Wow!" That was her com officer. "They did it!"

"Who did what?" Ky asked, turning to look.

"Bassoon. They got the system ansible on. Look at the icon."

"The ansible came on!" Colonel Kalin said in her comunit. "Was that your people?"

"I think—just a minute, I'm getting a report." Ky clicked off on that circuit and switched on the shipboard ansible. "Captain Pettygrew?"

"Sorry it took so long, Captain Vatta, but my tech said it was a bit more than a stuffed mailbox. She had to go EVA and get physical with it. I wouldn't let her go until she'd had some sleep."

"That's fine—I'm impressed. Tell her so for me. Have you tried making an actual call?"

"I don't know who—I guess we can call up the index . . . there. We can talk to Adelaide, and from there to anyplace they're connected."

"Colonel Kalin," Ky said to him. "The ansible is indeed

up—Captain Pettygrew's best technician fixed it. You can try contacting your people—"

"And we can expect ISC to come down on us like a storm," Kalin said, frowning. "We had a huge assessment over that Sabine mess, even though it was only held in escrow. This time—"

"You didn't do anything; my people did," Ky said.

"Yes, well, I don't suppose you'll get off lightly, either. And they may assume we're part of that."

"I doubt it," Ky said. "We've been involved with ansible repairs before—with an ISC agent who was traveling with us, until he went back to Nexus to report. As near as we could tell, ISC didn't even notice that their ansibles were repaired, though I'm sure they will eventually. He thought they were probably overwhelmed by the amount of sabotage."

"He probably had an authorization code," Kalin said. "Did he give it to you?"

"No," Ky said. "He never said anything about a code."

"I wouldn't expect him to," Kalin said. "Our people asked, when the ansibles went down, about using our techs to help with repair. The local ISC office told us that we couldn't—that we must not, in fact—because we didn't have the correct authorization codes and they weren't about to give them to us."

"Well, they can come after me," Ky said. "And I'll tell them about Rafe. Besides, they're going to have more to worry about than someone being overhelpful—"

"So I gather from that material you sent. Is this something we can talk about, since we're on tight-beam?"

"I would think so—as close as we are, laser com should be secure enough even if there is another observer in the system. I would prefer we not name the articles, even though they know I have them."

"Good," Kalin said. "I have a few questions. Did the articles originate with the same firm?"

"According to my informant, yes. But the articles as they now exist were modified, by an unknown source, and distributed to the persons you'd least like to see have them."

"Did the ships that attacked us have them?"

"Almost certainly," Ky said. "The stealthed one did. The ones that attacked us before—long story, details to follow—did. I found a supply of them on this ship, sufficient to suggest that a regular trade in them was ongoing."

"Oh . . . my." From his expression, that had not been his first choice of words. "What will be the original firm's official reaction to their use, do you think?"

"My contact was horrified, but recognized the reality that the tech was already out in the universe, in use. I expect they'll adjust somehow; they always have."

"I still worry about ISC's reaction to anyone's messing with system ansibles, even to repair them. We've assumed the outages weren't their fault, but if they had some reason for it—"

"I know that one of my surviving relatives on Slotter Key got the Slotter Key system ansible repaired," Ky said. "If they go after Aunt Grace, they'll put their hand in a buzz saw."

Kalin raised his brows, then shrugged. "I hope you're right. We don't need any more trouble. Still, I've had my communications techs send messages to the intermediate jump points. We might catch our people that way, let them know what happened, though it's uncertain. There do seem to be more system ansibles up and working than when we left."

"If enough systems get impatient and fix them, ISC won't have the resources to punish them all," Ky said.

"We can hope," Kalin said. "Meanwhile . . . I'm not sure I've thanked you properly for your help. You saved our skins, that's for sure."

"We were lucky this time," Ky said.

"I don't know about that," Kalin said. "You made all the right moves. Economical and tidy, as battles go. That's unusual with an inexperienced officer commanding. Pitt says we tried to recruit you, back at Sabine . . ."

"Yes, but I had a contract to fulfill," Ky said. She tried to imagine what it would have been like to be in Mackensee when her family was killed, and shook that thought away quickly.

"Yes—Pitt said your refusal was for honorable reasons. And now you're in another military organization. I rather wish we'd caught you in the interim."

"Then I wouldn't have been here," Ky said. "But thanks for the sentiment."

"Point taken. All right, back to the . . . articles. Pitt said you wanted to know if we were interested. Of course we are, but are you interested in sharing? What does your command think about that?"

"Considering that the pirates already have it and our side needs it," Ky said, "we're more than just 'interested' in sharing. There are a couple of possibilities: direct purchase or license to produce . . ."

"You hold the patents? I thought you said the . . . um . . . original firm—"

"I can put you in touch with the office working on that issue," Ky said. Stella wouldn't be overjoyed about that unless she'd gotten the answers she wanted, but she might be able to satisfy him that they had some legitimacy. "You might be able to relay through to them from here."

"I'll have to talk to my commanders first," Kalin said.

"We have procedures—and I'm sure the Old Man wouldn't want us using illegal technology—"

"Not even if it gave your enemies such an advantage?" Ky asked. "After all, you were attacked by these pirates."

"I know, I know," Kalin said. "But you have to understand—surely you have rules in your organization as well. Discipline is the core of military success; we can't just do whatever we want."

Unlike Slotter Key's Spaceforce, Pettygrew's tech didn't know that system ansibles had an auto response when restored to service with or without the proper authorization code. As the ansible's onboard AI regained control of its functions, its first message went out to all functioning ansibles, with relay-to-headquarters headers. Setting up the linkage from there to Adelaide to Nexus II took only seconds; the message itself took immeasurably less time. At ISC headquarters, in the status room, the watch staff noted that relay ansible Boxtop-zip-figaro 112 was back online, restored to service by an unauthorized intruder. They already knew about the Slotter Key ansible repair.

Pettygrew received the return message from Nexus II requesting identification within minutes. His comtech reported that Captain Vatta was in conference with the Mackensee commander; he shrugged and decided to answer the query himself. "Tell 'em it's Space Defense Force, Third Fleet, light cruiser *Bassoon*," he said. "They won't have a clue who that is." Almost immediately, a response came back.

"You are in violation of the Uniform Commercial Code, which prohibits any tampering with ISC installations, including attempts to repair faulty ansibles. This message is your legal notice of violation, and will be forwarded to the appropriate jurisdiction for adjudication. Note: ISC has no reference documentation for the so-called Space Defense Force; as of this date, it will be listed as an outlaw organization. To change this listing, supply documentation proving legitimacy under a recognized system and a legal business address."

"Oh . . . dear." Pettygrew and his bridge crew looked at one another. "I'm afraid we kicked an anthill. Captain Vatta isn't going to be happy about this."

"Well, we sort of knew ISC didn't like people meddling with their stuff . . ."

"They should fix it faster, then," Pettygrew said. "Let's see if I can shake some sense into them." He thought a moment, and sent: "This is an emergency situation. Pirates attacked helpless ships in this system. Many casualties. We attempted emergency repair of ansible to call for help."

The response was not encouraging: "There is no legal justification for tampering with ISC equipment under any circumstances. As we have no record of any Space Defense Force, we have no reason to believe that this so-called report is anything more than a fabrication, an attempt to evade the legal consequences of illegal actions."

"Something just stripped our beacon," one of the bridge crew said. "I think it was the ansible . . ."

"Your beacon data have been appended to the charges we are filing," the message went on. "You will be apprehended in any system and held for adjudication. Further attempts to contact this facility will result in additional evidence being stored against you. That is all." The contact blanked.

"Do you think they'll turn the ansible off?" someone asked.

"No," Pettygrew said. "Oh, they might, but if it's working, it's a source of income for them when anyone else uses it. I think I'd better contact Captain Vatta right away, even if she is busy."

SEVENTEEN

Aboard Vanguard

"Captain, *Bassoon* wants you," *Vanguard*'s comtech said.

Ky switched to that channel. "Vatta here."

"Captain Vatta, I've just had a disturbing message—via ansible—from ISC. Apparently my repair tripped some kind of automatic signal, and they've threatened to have *Bassoon* arrested anywhere we go, for violation of the Commercial Code."

"Did they get your ship ID?"

"Yes. They stripped our beacon. I'd explained it was an emergency situation, with ships attacked and casualties, and they said that was no excuse. I . . . er . . . I shouldn't have, but I did say I was part of the Space Defense Force—"

"No reason you shouldn't," Ky said. "What happened?"

"They said they had no record of any such organization. Of course they don't, but . . . then they said it must be an illegal organization and they'd report that, too."

"That's not good," Ky said. "Not that I'm blaming you, Dan. It's my fault, if it's anyone but theirs. If they'd repaired their ansibles in a timely manner, none of this would've happened. I wish I knew if Rafe—the ISC person we had aboard for a while—was at ISC headquarters by now or not. He might be able to straighten this out, but trying to contact him could be tricky."

"They said any attempts to contact them would result in gathering more evidence against us," Pettygrew said.

"Well . . . I may have a roundabout way of doing it so they don't know it's us," Ky said. "It'll take awhile to work out, though. Meanwhile, we should get in a better defensive position in case something unfriendly comes through the jump point."

"Do you expect anyone?"

"Not really. But we don't want to be unpleasantly surprised, either by pirates or by an irate ISC ship. We can protect *Metaire* best if we're not sitting on top of either the ansible position or *Metaire* itself."

"You know we expended a lot of our missiles—"

"I know. We don't want to fight a serious battle, but we could manage a fighting retreat. *Metaire*'s worse off than we are, and they're still picking up their dead."

"There's a lot of junk out there," Pettygrew said. "It'll take them days to find all the remains, if they can."

"Kalin's hoping one of his messages got to the relief convoy so they can call in a hazmat ship," Ky said. "But he's not prepared to abandon the search just yet." She had already added minesweepers and post-battle hazmat teams to her wish list, with the wry thought that Spaceforce Academy hadn't really prepared her to organize a fleet. "You'll need to reposition, and I'll contact Argelos—we'll have a brief all-ships conference in two hours." If nothing happened before then. "Meanwhile, I'll also tell Colonel Kalin what we're up to."

"All-ships including Ransome's Rangers?"

Ky rolled her eyes. "I suppose . . . for the part of it they won't think too boring. They served us well, whatever we think of them."

"True. Well, then, I'll be on my way," Pettygrew said.

Two hours later, Ky convened the conference. "This will be short," she said, "since we know that hostiles were undoubtedly made aware of the defeat of their people and may decide to attempt retaliation. We can't leave, because *Metaire* is still retrieving casualties and several of us have Mackensee personnel, including wounded, aboard. I've discussed *Metaire*'s situation with the Mackensee officer in command. He's expecting a group of Mackensee ships in ten to twelve days, but those ships think they're bringing troops to change out for training exercises. He is unwilling to leave until they arrive. They will be armed, of course . . . and our first concern is that they not attack us, thinking we're the enemy. We know these ships are coming, and approximately when. We don't know about the others—the pirates and, unfortunately, ISC. Pirates are likely to attack in force, if they come. They will know we expended ammunition and there's no place here to resupply; they will know that a Mackensee ship was seriously damaged and that Mackensee had many casualties . . . they may realize that we're still here and more vulnerable than before. But since we don't know if they're coming, or when they might get here, or with how many ships if they do come, our ability to plan for them is limited. Our discussions earlier, you recall, led to some excellent suggestions for situations like this, so—" Ky put up a diagram. "This is what we're going to do—"

Nexus II,
ISC Headquarters

Rafe looked out the window at the swirls of snow and wished he were out there somewhere, anonymous, going about his business—whatever that might have been—able to stop in to any shop, ride on any carrier, without arousing attention. He had come to work in the private car, as usual, with his own private bodyguards; it was now the only way he could go anywhere.

He had dealt with the first of the morning's work, and now he could not put off any longer the problem his father insisted was urgent. Here and there, in the vast territory where ISC had once held an unbreakable monopoly on long-distance communication, ansibles out of service were coming back online . . . but not because ISC repair crews had fixed them. Economically, in the short term at least, this was a good thing: the more ansibles, the more traffic, and the more traffic, the more profit. He had made this argument with his father. If they didn't have to send a repair team, it saved costs; if the calls went through, they were paid.

But his father insisted that it was a dangerous precedent, that letting systems fix their own ansibles was tantamount to giving them part ownership in them. It violated the old licensing agreements; it ran counter to those sections in the Universal Commercial Code that ISC had insisted on putting in.

And what exercised his father most was the Slotter Key repair, which had been done—no secret about it—at the behest of Grace Lane Vatta, now Sub-Rector of Defense. In his father's mind, the line of guilt from Lew Parmina ran straight to anyone he'd befriended . . . and he had befriended the Vatta family. Vattas were at least suspect, his father insisted. He had been appalled to learn that Rafe had spent time—a lot of time—with two surviving members of that family, that Rafe expressed anything other than suspicion of their motives.

And now ISC's legal staff were scrambling to deal with requests from an intellectual property lawyer on Cascadia who wanted to know where patents relevant to "mobile ansibles" might be filed. Rafe knew exactly where that request came from. Ky had said flat out she intended not only to use the shipboard ansible installed on Osman's ship, but also to share the others with allies. Stella . . . Stella had seen the economic side; clearly she was preparing to manufacture and sell them. And Toby . . . whether the rest of the family knew it or not, Toby was one of those rare tech geniuses, and Rafe had recognized it. If Toby had been tinkering with the design, who knew what might come out of it?

He hadn't yet told his father about this, but he would have to soon. Though his father was progressing slowly in rehab—the brain damage had been more severe than they first hoped, and neural regeneration proceeded at its own measured rate—he insisted on being kept up to date on the main issues at ISC. If Rafe didn't tell him, one of his old friends might—even though they had been told, by the doctors, not to talk business with him.

He could imagine the response. His father had seemed, when he was a boy, so calm and reasonable . . . but now, in the wake of Lew Parmina's betrayal and his own injuries, he had formed this one unshakable, irrational conclusion. Lew had counted the Vatta family as friends; therefore the Vatta family was, most likely, an enemy. The whole shipboard ansible mess was their fault—hadn't such ansibles been found on a Vatta ship? And wasn't it another Vatta who insisted on using them? And now Stella Vatta was trying to find out about the relevant patents.

"Excuse me, sir." Emil Borcaster, borrowed from the family's own legal firm as his personal assistant, tapped on the door frame. Emil had checked out clean, according to Gary's people . . . unlike some of the other candidates for the job.

"Yes, come in."

"There's a new report on the ansible repair situation. A relay ansible's been brought online by something calling itself the Space Defense Force, Third Fleet. We don't have them in our records—they don't have an account with us or anything—but I did a little digging. Our people on Adelaide report that a group of three ships showed up there, calling themselves the Space Defense Force, and made an ansible connection to the offices of Vatta Transport on Cascadia."

"Surely you jest," Rafe said, swallowing the urge to scream and slam his head on the desk. Ky. It had to be Ky. What she was doing in Adelaide when she'd started off in the opposite direction, he didn't know, but clearly she'd created that multisystem force she'd been talking about. The "Third Fleet" part sounded overdone, though. He was willing to bet it was a ruse, and all she had was what came with her.

"No, sir; it's not a joke. And the commanding officer of that group of ships was a Kylara Vatta. With an account at Adelaide Central Bank; the records on the financial ansible at Adelaide show a funds transfer to Vatta Transport on Cascadia."

"And I thought the day couldn't get worse," Rafe muttered.

"Sir? But this makes it clearer, doesn't it? The Vatta family *is* working against ISC."

"Where did you hear that?" Rafe asked.

"Well . . . down in Enforcement, they're saying that's three. Grace Vatta pushing to get Slotter Key's Spaceforce to meddle with their ansible. Stella Vatta trying to infringe our patents on ansible technology, and now Kylara Vatta and this illegally constituted organization calling itself Space Defense Force tampering with another ansible. Four if you count the shipboard ansibles on Osman Vatta's ship. I know you don't, but some do."

"There's something you don't know, Emil," Rafe said. "As my assistant, you have to be in on this, but you must keep it quiet . . . besides us, only Legal knows, and they aren't talking."

"What's that, sir?"

"We *have* no patents on the shipboard ansibles."

"What? Of course we do! ISC patent attorneys are famous for patenting anything and everything—"

"Yes. And the decision was made, years back, to use that reputation, not actual recorded patents, to protect the mobile ansible technology."

"But . . . but that was stupid! Why—?"

"The danger of letting it be known what was possible, even if it was protected under law. We'd have had to file the plans, including the details of how the design was kept from interfacing with system ansibles. At that point, someone somewhere could have accessed them, taken them to some system that wasn't entirely within the law, and started manufacture."

"Did your father make that decision?"

"No. But he concurred. What we have now is an attempt to stonewall while we see if there is any way at all we can claim rights in the technology, or if someone else—the pirates who are using it, for instance—managed to file patents on it in some out-of-the-way mudball where our staff doesn't usually troll for inventions, because there aren't any."

"Then—then Vatta Transport *isn't* trying to infringe?"

"No. They're trying *not* to infringe—they actually inquired—and if they went on and manufactured onboard ansibles by the shipload, we'd have no legal complaint. Not at the moment, anyway."

"But if they're just small, lightweight versions of system ansibles—I know ISC holds the patents on that—"

"They're not," Rafe said. "I've examined them—and I already knew, pretty much, how they differed. It's a mess, is what it is, and we're not doing ourselves much good by stonewalling. I'm going to try to convince the Board of that."

"They won't like it."

"*I* don't like it. But with so many systems angry that we haven't restored their communications, and our income stream still dropping, I don't see that we're going to get much satisfaction in the courts if we try to fight it." Rafe shook his head. "The legitimate members of the Vatta family—and no, I don't count Osman—found and used the shipboard technology that originated in our research labs. But they didn't steal it from us; it had already been stolen because we didn't protect it, either physically or legally. None of those units had been manufactured here. It's one of the things I checked. Moreover, we didn't take out the necessary patents, so . . . legally . . . there's nothing underhanded at all in what Stella and Ky Vatta did about those."

"But the other—"

"Vattas aren't the only ones to do unauthorized ansible repair," Rafe said. "We have a dozen, don't we, on the list?"

"Fourteen today, sir."

"Right. And only two of them remotely associated with Vattas."

"That we know of," Emil said, scowling.

"That we know of. Fine. But still . . . if Lew Parmina hadn't made such a point of being friendly with them, would anyone seriously suspect them?"

"No . . . I suppose not. But he did, and you said we still haven't found all his people in the organization."

"Vattas aren't his people. Just an ordinary—well, ordinary for rich—family he chose to be friends with. For all we know, as cover." Though, now that he came to think of it, why *had* Lew Parmina chosen to get close to the Vatta family? And how close?

Unfortunately, he couldn't call Stella and ask her. That would raise an even bigger stink.

"So—did Enforcement send a message on this latest repair thing?"

"Of course. They stripped the beacon off the ship involved—*Bassoon,* with Bissonet registry. In fact, it's listed as part of the Bissonet Free Militia, which is—or was, until the recent unfortunate events—what Bissonet calls their privateers."

"And the captain is Kylara Vatta?"

"No, no. *Bassoon's* captain is Daniel Pettygrew. Vatta's ship is the *Vanguard,* Moscoe Confederation registry. Anyway, Enforcement told Pettygrew that they didn't recognize the organization as a legal entity, and that they'd stripped his beacon and filed a complaint against him in every available jurisdiction."

"Who's in charge down there this shift? Oh, right, Jessie Squires. Get her for me, will you?"

"You're not going to rescind it, are you?"

"Not personally, no. The more I can do through established channels, the better. I will convince Jessie it's in our best interest to rescind it. Bissonet's fallen to the pirates and their allies; Pettygrew's a refugee. Yes, he probably knows our rules, but he's actually done us a service. And if Pettygrew is with Ky Vatta, they're hunting pirates—which is exactly what someone needs to do before they're walking into this office and blowing our heads off."

"You don't really think that could happen, do you, sir? We have our own space forces."

"Emil, you have never been in real danger in your life, have you? Ever been on a space station when someone blew a ship, or a hole in the station? Ever been in a ship someone else was trying to blow? Ever had even one weapon fired at you in your whole life?"

"No . . . sir." Emil looked confused.

"I have. More times than I care to remember, someone has tried to kill me personally, or me along with a lot of other people they didn't care about. I know we have, on the books, more armed spacecraft than anyone else we know about, and we have a lot of people assigned to Enforcement Division. And I know exactly what the reality is: this planet is as vulnerable as any other, this office is as vulnerable as any other, and *you* are as vulnerable as any other."

"And you, sir?"

Rafe had two of his weapons out before Emil finished speaking. "I, Emil, am one degree less vulnerable because I believe I can be killed." Emil, he was glad to see, had turned an unpleasantly pale shade of his normal coloring. "Don't panic, boy; I'm not going to kill you. But anything as big, as rich, as powerful, and as centralized as ISC has TARGET written on it in large glowing letters." Rafe slid the needler back into its holster and the blade back up his sleeve.

"But we've never been attacked—" Emil stopped as he saw Rafe's expression. "Have we?"

"The short answer is yes, but not for a long time. Aside from things like abduction, like my father, and attempts at assassination." Rafe reached for one of the folders on his desk. "Let me read you something. Remember I asked for an update on Enforcement's resources?"

"Yes . . ."

"ISC maintains an armed fleet—everyone knows that.

The thing about armed fleets is that they cost a lot. Then you have to crew them: ships without crews don't do you any good. And that costs a lot. Then you have to train the crews and keep them in practice: crews that never go on maneuvers are easy meat for those that do. And that costs a lot, not only for the munitions and fuel and other supplies to go on maneuvers, but also refitting and repair . . . because anything you use deteriorates, and rough use wears it out faster. Are you following this?"

"Yes . . ."

"So . . ." Rafe opened the file and started reading. "Average age of ISC armed vessels: sixty-eight years. Average age of ISC group commanders: sixty-four years. Average time from last weapons upgrade: thirty-seven years. Average interval since last maneuvers with live fire: six years. Percent of armed vessels deemed battle-ready—are you ready for this?—eleven."

Emil stared back at him, a mix of confusion and fright on his face. "That's . . . not good, is it?"

"That's *pathetic,*" Rafe said. "We might be able to scare a backward colony planet into thinking we're all-powerful, but any competent military force that knew what I now know wouldn't hesitate to take us on. What's protecting us right now is our reputation. Enforcement doesn't understand that; they haven't actually done much in a long time, so they think having thousands of ships on the books is the same as having thousands of ships that can actually fight. The back of this report is one long self-serving explanation of why the damning figures up front— that I insisted on seeing—don't matter. But they do matter."

"Your father—"

"Apparently accepted Enforcement's view of our military might."

"Were you . . . uh . . . in another military while you were . . . uh . . . gone? Is that how you know so much?"

Rafe laughed. "No, I'm not soldier material. But despite folk mythology that you have to do it to understand it, even the sterile can understand how babies get made, and even a pacifist can understand supply, tactics, and the chain of command." Emil looked shocked this time; Rafe sighed and excised the irony from his tone. "I had a friend who was a soldier," he said instead. "I learned a lot by listening."

"Oh. All right. But if ISC is so vulnerable, what are you going to do about it?"

That was the sticker. "I'm not sure," Rafe said. "It will probably involve, like most things military, a lot of misdirection and the expenditure of enough money to make Accounting blench. Hopefully no one will find out how feeble our resources are until we've had time to strengthen them, but we can't count on that. Parmina may have taken the reports at face value, like my father, or he may have known how weak we are—and if he knew, he might have told his pirate allies, or he might have kept it to himself, something he could use later on. We have to assume, worst case, that the pirates do know. At the moment, I'm sending you down to Enforcement to hand-carry a note to Squires that she's to come up here. You will not—repeat after me, *not*—tell her what I've been telling you."

Emil nodded and left. Rafe felt like sneaking out and disappearing into the snow, which had now thickened to blizzard proportions. The task was too big, the difficulties too many and too complex. He was fit for the little jobs, not this one.

But here he was, mired in an expensive suit in a vast office where most people seemed to think the purpose of their job was to feed him comfortable lies. He looked at the notes Emil had put on his schedule. Meetings with a cabinet official at 1100, with another government department head at 1300, with the senior representative of Crown & Spears at 1500. They all wanted to meet him, get to know him, tell him how much they respected his father and how sorry they were and if they had only known . . . or so yesterday's meetings had gone.

And all because of ISC's reputation as a powerful, necessary monopoly, which was now—though they didn't know it yet—shattered and gone: that incredible wealth, that reputation for toughness and strength. When they found out how hollow the gold statue really was, he knew who would get the blame. The old man's son, the bad boy who wasn't, after all, up to the job.

He knew what to do—unpopular as it would be with the Board, the bankers, the government. If he called Stella himself, he could probably get her to deal with him, maybe even put out the shipboard ansibles under ISC's label, which would give them an immediate market advantage. But—could he do it? Would the Board back him? Would his father?

Cascadia Station

Stella Vatta listened to the lawyer's recitation of ISC's delaying tactics with mounting anger. "I thought it was illegal now to register patents in obscure jurisdictions—"

"It's supposed to be, certainly, though it was common practice before the Commercial Code was approved. And Nexus is a signatory to the code, so it should apply to ISC for all patents issued within the past hundred-and-seventy-odd years. I've searched all the relevant databases; no patents relating to shipboard ansibles are in any of the five systems where patents are supposed to be registered. But ISC's legal department claims that some of the technology could have been patented before adoption of the code, or could have been registered remotely, as their research labs are widely scattered—but they won't tell me where, for reasons of security, they say."

"I'll bet they don't even have patents," Stella said.

"I find that hard to credit," the lawyer said. Like all Cascadian attorneys, he was studiously courteous.

"If they had patents, they'd be eagerly telling us what they were," Stella said. "I don't think they've lost them; I think they never had them. Rafe said they were practically paranoid about secrecy, and were convinced that the technology involved would endanger their monopoly. They'd know about patent searches; they'd be worried someone could figure out how to pirate the tech, produce it remotely somewhere—"

"Then, if you're convinced of that, let's go on and apply for patents here," the lawyer said. "From the little you've told me, this is revolutionary stuff."

"It will blow the top off communications," Stella said. "And it's time you knew all about it." She took a data cube out of the pocket of her suit. "Here. Look at this on my machine, right here." She handed it to him, then sat back and watched as he read from the screen.

"Oh . . . my . . . trees and leaves and roots and branches," he said. "This really works?"

"The pirates have the old form," Stella said. "The stuff that someone stole from ISC's research lab—don't know who, or when, or how. We've improved it considerably, as you see."

"It makes system ansibles obsolete," the lawyer said. "Or almost."

"Not really," Stella said. "All regular communications

nets tie into them—planetary and station communications, for instance. What this does is give ships the ability to go ship-to-ship even when a system ansible doesn't exist, and ship-to-ansible at distances where lightspeed communication to and from a system ansible is slow and difficult. System ansibles will still carry most traffic."

"But if they can be mounted on ships, they can be mounted anywhere—on stations, even in offices and homes."

"True. But I still think the existing communications networks will keep system ansibles in business."

"You need to apply for patents right away," the attorney said. "Today. Is this the only complete dataset?"

"No. But it's the only one that's out of secure storage."

"I assume you'd rather I didn't take it with me?"

"Correct."

"Then I'll contact my office, download the appropriate forms, and—may I see one of these in operation?"

"Yes, of course. We do in fact have one here." Stella took back the data cube and led him into the back office, which now connected to the "research lab" where Toby worked. She had finally gotten all the parts out of their apartment living room. Toby looked up from his workbench; Rascal, at his feet, looked up, then lay his nose back on Toby's foot.

"Toby, we need a demonstration. What's the time in Aunt Grace's office?"

"I'll look it up," Toby said.

"Conventionally, I'd use a regular long-distance service, call the system ansible, and set up a call to Slotter Key's ansible. That ansible would route my call through local call centers to the code number I specified. There would be delay at both ends, attenuated by something ISC refers to as a 'system booster' to near-natural conversational pauses. From the effect, we're guessing these are smaller, less powerful ansibles placed in orbiting satellites, but we don't actually know."

"Nine in the morning," Toby said. "We're back in sync for the next few days."

"Slotter Key's rotation isn't the same as the standard day length here," Stella explained. "But we're lucky, because I can call Aunt Grace right now. In fact, we'll place two calls—one by conventional, and one using our own ansible—and you can observe the difference. Toby, you start the connection on my mark. I'll be calling on the ordinary one."

Stella picked up the desk phone, said "Now" to Toby, and entered the origination codes for an ansible call to Slotter Key. She handed the headset to the attorney so he could hear for himself the familiar clicks and buzzes that went with an ansible call. The status lights went from red to green, and there was a brief display of Slotter Key's logo.

"She says what do you want, she's busy," Toby reported, from his side of the room.

"I'll take that," Stella said as she heard a voice on the attorney's headset.

To that one, she said, "I'm Stella Vatta, calling for Grace Vatta. I know she's on another line, but ask her to confirm that the other line is an ansible call from Vatta Transport headquarters."

The attorney listened in as a male voice came back on. "Yes, she is on such a call. What's going on?"

"Just a test of our equipment," Stella said. "Tell her Stella sends her love and things are looking up."

She walked across the room and gestured Toby aside; he was pink to the ears. Aunt Grace, who had turned on her video pickup, glared out of the screen.

"Stella! What are you playing at? Why two calls on two lines from your office?"

"Good news," Stella said. "But I can't give you details yet."

"Young lady—"

"There are a few legal threads to tie down," Stella said. "And that's all I can say."

"You were born a tease," Grace said, still scowling. "So—how's the business?"

"Growing," Stella said. "No more ships lost, and the ones we have are moving at ninety-seven percent capacity. And how are things on Slotter Key?"

"Calm," Grace said. "Except of course where I've been stirring the pot. Your mother and Jo's children are fine— growing like weeds and showing every sign of being Vattas to the core. Anything else? I do have a full day, and I'm already running behind."

"No, that's it. Thanks, Aunt Grace." Stella cut the connection and looked at her attorney.

"Most impressive. I'll certainly be able to attest to the efficacy of the device. So if you'll let me have a terminal, I'll get busy. We should be able to file for patents today, as organized as your data are." In his eagerness, he spoke almost as directly as a non-Cascadian.

"Good." Stella led him back to the main offices, installed him at a terminal in her own, and left him to it. A few hours later, he called her in and presented a sheaf of hardcopy for her to sign.

"And what name did you want those patents in? Vatta Transport?"

"No. Toby did the work; he should get the credit."

He shook his head. "He didn't do all the work; you said he started with the pirated design. I'd recommend Vatta Transport for the rest, with Toby—if you insist; he's still a minor in law, and you as his guardian could be named instead—listed only for those things he actually designed himself."

Stella agreed. Even if he held only those patents, he would be secure for life, assuming the pirates didn't blow them all away.

By the close of business, the patent applications were filed: "Patents Relating to the Design of a Working Prototype of a Small Ansible-Based Communications Device Mountable on a Ship and Interfacing with Existing System-Ansible-Based Communications Networks." The Moscoe Confederation, as one of the five systems in which patents were registered for recognition under the Uniform Commercial Code, had a reputation for speedy processing, but Stella was surprised at how fast that could be. Shortly before mid-first-shift the next day, her assistant told her she had an incoming call from planetside.

"Stella Vatta?" The man on the screen wore a Patents Office shield clipped to his lapel.

"Yes," Stella said.

"We have examined your . . . remarkable patent application. I see you took the advice of Brinkles, Patrick, and Stansted as intellectual property attorneys . . ."

"Yes," Stella said. "Is anything wrong?"

"Not at all. They have an excellent reputation; I'm sure that if they say a search for prior patents was made, they did in fact make it. And I see that your attorney attests that he personally observed the . . . er . . . device in operation and is satisfied that it does in fact work as claimed. I did have a few questions for you. Were you planning to manufacture the device in this jurisdiction?"

"Yes," Stella said.

"And were you planning to manufacture and sell the device without ISC knowledge?"

"Without their knowledge? Not at all. We had asked

them, when we couldn't find any record of patents they might have held . . . so they know what we're doing."

"I see. And were you planning to manufacture and sell the device under the name of Vatta Transport?"

"No; I planned to designate a separate entity for that."

"Very well. I am pleased to tell you that we were all impressed by the . . . device, and its likely scope for manufacture and sale. We would expect a reaction from ISC, of course, but the device could benefit many, which . . . is another reason to approve the application. I will forward the relevant numbers and papers at once, and proceed with registration. Congratulations."

"Thank you," Stella said. She could hardly catch her breath. It had worked. It had worked, and so fast. It wasn't, she reminded herself, anything but a start—but it was a strong start.

She found Toby glowering at a monitor. "Aunt Stella, I only made eighty-seven on my history exam. And I think I was right."

"On what?"

"First Expansion was from Old Earth to its system satellites, right?"

"As far as I know."

"And Second Expansion was from Old Solar to Central Sector only?"

Stella shrugged. "I don't know, Toby. I don't remember. And anyway, we have something to celebrate."

"If I don't get a higher grade in history, Zori Louarri will beat me out for class honors," Toby said.

Stella paused. Toby had been topping his class easily until now, and he'd shown no interest in class honors. She'd urged him to find friends, go places with other kids—which he sometimes did—but mostly he stayed in the lab, working.

"Who's Zori Louarri?" she asked.

"She's . . . just a girl," Toby said, going pink.

Even geniuses had hormones. And he was still a teenager. Stella sighed to herself; being Toby's guardian might turn out to be more of a challenge than she'd thought.

"Why don't we go out to lunch, and you can tell me more about her?" she said.

"There's not much to tell," Toby said, sliding off the stool. "She was top of the class before I got here; everybody likes her except the doormops—"

"Doormops?"

"You know. Kids that don't like anybody but each other."

"What does she look like?" Stella asked, leading the way out of the offices, and tapping her wrist to indicate lunchtime to the receptionist.

Toby turned pinker. "She's . . . kind of . . . well, she's a girl, you know. She has soft hair. And . . . and things . . ."

He was sunk. He was completely sunk. Stella remembered, all too well, her own first crush. It had been the boy's jawline, just that angular, bony shape, which made her knees weak. And Toby was old enough for it to be more than a simple crush.

Phrase by broken phrase, on the way to the restaurant where she'd made reservations, Toby told her more than enough to make Stella both sympathetic and amused. Zori was smart, she had a laugh that made everybody laugh, the "soft hair" was thick and black and shiny, she had eyes as black as her hair, she played on the wally team— wally, Toby explained when Stella asked, was a ball game where you bounced two balls off the walls of a small room and scored by a complicated system that made no sense to Stella, even after explanation.

"And her family's been here since forever, and they don't

like newcomers that much, but Zori's nice to them anyway—"

"I'll have the mock duck à l'orange," Stella said to the woman in the black smock. "Toby?"

"Oh. Anything—" He looked at the menu finally. "Can I have that lamb thing, Aunt Stella?"

"Of course, dear. I said this was a celebration."

"What are we celebrating?"

"I'll tell you later. Rack of lamb," she said to the waitress. "And we'll want dessert later," she added, grinning at Toby.

When the waitress had gone, she leaned closer to him. "We have the patents," she said.

His face lit up. "All of them? Already?"

"Yes. And the ones you invented are in your name; the rest are in Vatta Enterprises."

"Is it going to make us rich?"

"Toby, we *are* rich. Compared with most people, anyway. But yes, it will make us a lot richer. If I don't do something stupid."

"You won't do anything stupid, Aunt Stella," Toby said. "You're much smarter than you think."

"I'm glad you think so, Toby," Stella said, her mind racing ahead to all the things she had to do to get the ansibles into production, through sales, before the profits she hoped for would roll in.

EIGHTEEN

Nexus II,
ISC Headquarters

Rafe glanced at the windows of his office. A lowering gray sky, the warm, almost brownish, tone that meant more snow was on the way. Winter in Nexus City . . . not a favorite time of year at all. But he had vanquished Parmina and many of his stooges; he had the board's acquiescence, if not their approval, for the licensing negotiations with Vatta Enterprises.

"Emil?"

"Yes, sir?"

"Check with Enforcement and make sure they've sent that message rescinding threats to . . . whatever that place is where . . . Space Defense Force is."

"Yes, sir."

"And get their chief up here. We need to have a serious talk." Rafe looked at the sealed message from Termanian and turned it over and over. He could anticipate what it said, and reading it would only reinforce his own bias about the man. He didn't need biases; he needed clear thinking. Had the man said anything, done anything, that had value he should recognize? He looked at the window again and saw the first flakes drifting past.

"Sir? They said they sent the message, but they couldn't stop the ships . . ."

Rafe stared at his assistant. "Ships? What ships?"

"Uh . . . they said . . . it's standard procedure. They sent ships to see if they could catch the wrongdoers—didn't you know that?"

"No," Rafe said. "I did not know that. No one mentioned it. What ships? How many?"

"I don't know . . . should I ask?"

Rafe looked at him; Emil paled and disappeared from the doorway . . . to ask, Rafe hoped. Not that he'd wait. He made his own call to Enforcement.

"This is the CEO. Let me speak to your chief, now."

"I—he's on his way up to your office, sir."

"Then let me speak to whoever's left in charge."

"That would be . . . Assistant Director Malaky . . . but he's busy."

"Now," Rafe said.

"Er . . . yes, sir. Just a moment."

"Yes, sir, Chairman." Malaky's tone, bored and annoyed, set Rafe's teeth on edge.

"I understand your division dispatched ships to system ansible Boxtop-zip-figaro-112," Rafe said. "Yet I gave the order to stop any further action against those people hours ago."

"Well, yes, you did, but the ships were already en route—"

"In FTL flight? That was fast."

"Well, no, they weren't in FTL yet, but they were far enough out we didn't think a message would reach them until they jumped—"

"So you didn't even try?"

"Well, it would've been a waste of time, wouldn't it? If they weren't going to get the message before jump anyway? And we're always being told to save expenses . . ."

Rafe clenched his teeth; the words that wanted to come out would not help the situation. He took a breath. "How many ships?"

"We had information from our agents in Adelaide that this so-called Space Defense Force had three warships of patrol and cruiser size and three fast courier ships, so we basically threw the whole sector force at them. We don't want to lose any of our—"

"How many?"

"Uh . . . fourteen, sir. That should take care of them and not cost us anything."

Rafe took another careful breath. "The point is, Malaky, that we don't want to 'take care of them'—that's why I had you send that message rescinding the warning."

"That's not what it said."

"*What's* not what it said?"

"Well . . . you just said to tell them to disregard the previous messages. You said not to institute action against them. That's not the same as rescinding the warning or telling us to quit what we were already doing. They're still illegals, aren't they? They still meddled with our equipment, didn't they? And they can't be allowed to get away with it. I figure you'd have sent the force along later, but sooner's better if you want to catch them with their pants down."

"Malaky, you will shortly realize that your reasoning is completely and utterly wrong," Rafe said. He was aware that his voice had changed; he knew that if Malaky had stood in front of him, he'd have been hard-put to keep from strangling the idiot. "Tell me now exactly where those ships are, where they were, and what their ETA to that system is. And I'll need their beacon IDs."

"I don't see what you're so upset about," Malaky said. "They're the standard sector force; they left sector HQ when we first notified them, boosted hard to the jump point, and exited . . . seventy-nine minutes ago, local time. They're in jumpspace now; they'll arrive in two point three standard days."

"Sir?" That was Emil at the door. "Chief of Enforcement Denny Cuthen is here, sir."

"Ping my assistant with the beacon IDs," Rafe said to Malaky. "Now." He switched off, his mind racing. Fourteen ships, to Ky's three? Even old, outmoded ships with less trained crews . . . at fourteen to three, and hers without a full load of munitions . . . he had to do *something*. And killing the chief of enforcement wouldn't be the right something.

"Show him in," Rafe said, settling himself squarely behind the vast desk.

"I'm glad you finally have time to see me." Enforcement's director was a head taller than Rafe, his head shaved bald, his implants bulging on both sides. The access flaps had complex tattoos on them. "You've been upsetting my people, nosing around, and you didn't even see me in person first—"

Rafe looked at him; the man glowered back. He probably thought he looked tough, Rafe thought, but Gary or any of his commandos could have taken him down in seconds. Telltale softness below the ears, the jaw, where muscle had gone to flab.

"You have made a mistake," Rafe said, in his mildest voice.

"No, it's you that made mistakes, sonny," Cuthen said, leaning forward to put his hands on the desk. "You think just because your father ran this company and wanted you to sub for him for a while, that you're the man he is. Well let me tell you something—" He stopped abruptly, his face paling.

Rafe smiled at him, the nose of the weapon he much preferred to a needler—noisy as it was—pointing steadily at the man's face. "You need to sit down and be quiet," Rafe said, in the same calm tone. His hand didn't move. He really did like the feel . . . it was one of the things that had impressed him about Ky; she, too, carried a Rossi-Smith with bloodbeast-tusk grip. He needed not to think about her right now; he needed to think about this . . . person . . . whose face now gleamed with sweat.

"You wouldn't—" Cuthen said, almost a whisper and definitely pleading.

"Waste a round on you?" Rafe said. "That depends. Sit down. Now." He let his voice carry more bite on the last word, and the man sat as if that word had cut his hamstrings. Rafe rested his elbows on the desk and brought his other hand up to brace the first. "You must realize, Denny, that I've killed quite a few men—using the term loosely—and it doesn't bother me. So in your position, you might wish to be careful to answer what I ask without any unnecessary delay or insults."

Emil poked his head in the door. "Sir, there's some data up from—" His eyes widened.

Without taking his gaze from Denny Cuthen, Rafe said, "Later, Emil. And close the door." He felt a chuckle trying to emerge and stifled it. This was more fun than he'd expected, but he couldn't afford fun. Not with fourteen ships aimed at Ky.

"You're . . . crazy . . . ," Cuthen breathed.

"Now, you see, that's the sort of thing you shouldn't say to someone who's holding a gun on you," Rafe said. He took his left hand away from the other, shook his arm a little, and the hilt of his knife slid into his hand. He flicked it around. "Or a knife. You see, Denny, the first mistake you made was thinking I was some witless playboy pretending to be my father. I'm not a playboy, and I'm not like my father at all . . . in some ways." He flipped the knife up, caught it, all without moving his other hand.

Cuthen's mouth worked; his eyes had moved to the knife but were now fixed on the gun muzzle as if he could see through the barrel into Rafe's intent. Rafe hoped he could.

"The second mistake you made was thinking that you could keep fooling the company forever, pocketing the money that should've gone to our fleet—"

"I didn't! They kept cutting our budget; it's not my fault—"

"Even a divisional director's salary doesn't cover your expenditures," Rafe said. "Or did you think no one would ever think to look at your financials?"

"You *spied* on me? On a division director?" Indignation overcame fear, for a moment: a flush of color, but then he paled again.

"It was my assigned job, to learn all I could about the corporation, so I could make the best decisions," Rafe said. "So yes, I followed the money trails where they led." He paused. Cuthen squirmed in his chair. "And one of them led to you. Money came into your department; money left . . . but not all to the fleet. You paid Despardeaux Materials more than their going rate for spare parts, for instance. Ten percent more. That's . . . over five hundred thousand a year, and you probably split it with them, didn't you?" Rafe shook his head, waggled the point of the knife. "Naughty boy, Denny. Some men I've been around would carve their initials in your most intimate areas before they killed you, very slowly, for something like that."

"You—you can't. You won't . . ."

"Oh, I don't know. You fellows down in Enforcement have some nice quiet rooms, I understand . . ."

"Please—"

"Let's go on to your next mistake. Once I was named CEO, and you figured I was a stupid playboy, you thought you didn't have to follow orders . . . so when I told you— told you, specifically—to inform all those who had repaired ansibles that they need not worry about our response, you chose to interpret that . . . loosely."

"I told my people to send messages—"

"How many places did you send ships?"

"Uh . . . I'm not sure . . ."

"Really. Are you in the habit of not knowing how you're distributing our resources?"

"No, but . . . but this was a special case, see. Some of those places, systems we've done business with for years, I could see your point, maybe. They're frustrated, and they're friendly. We can let them go, maybe, though I still think that's the wrong approach. At least they ought to pay a fine. But illegals, like that whatsit you were calling about— that's ridiculous. We can't authorize every privateer or renegade merc company to go meddling with our property."

"This is not 'every privateer,'" Rafe said. His finger wanted to twitch just that few millimeters; he forced it to hold still. He could feel it, the darkness rising to a primeval shape of fury that delighted in Cuthen's fear and would gladly delight in his blood, given the chance. "In point of fact, that is another mistake of yours. The Space Defense Force is new, yes, and small, yes, but it is a legitimate attempt to combine system resources to resist and eventually destroy the menace that attacked and captured Bissonet System."

"How?" Cuthen had moved past that first fear to defiance; Rafe read his physical signs as easily as if they were

printed on his face. He was going to try something; Rafe
hoped it would be enough to justify serious violence.

"That is my business," he said, knowing it would infu-
riate Cuthen more. "On my father's orders, I did a lot of
undercover work for ISC, offplanet. I have sources you
lack, and I know these people are reliable. Now: your
deputy tells me that you have sent an entire sector's
resources—fourteen of our ships—to attack them. Your
life, Denny, depends on what happens. Your physical life,
I mean. Your life with this company—your job, your
income, and whatever assets we can retrieve from what
you embezzled from us—is gone."

The shock on Cuthen's face was almost worth it. Rafe
pressed a button on his desk, and Emil opened the door.
Rafe was impressed: he not only opened the door, but also
remembered which way Rafe's firearm was pointed and
positioned himself out of the direct line of fire.

"Emil, have Security escort Cuthen to a secure room; he
is not to have any communications device available to him."

"Yes, sir. I have Security standing by . . . uh . . . do you
have a preference?"

Emil definitely had potential. "Yes," Rafe said. "My personal bodyguards." He was still sifting through ISC's
Security personnel records, and another two problems had
been found only a few days before. Emil nodded, and two
of Gary's finest came in. Rafe didn't mention their names
in front of Cuthen. "This is Denny Cuthen," Rafe said.
"He has embezzled from this company and he has acted
counter to my direct orders in matters that will affect the
company adversely. I want him held in a secure location
in this building, and I don't want him communicating
with anyone."

"Very well, sir," the man Rafe knew as Stan said. He
had drawn his own weapon. "Limits, sir?"

"Keep him alive, for the time being," Rafe said. "I suspect he may have concealed communications equipment on his person. Search him carefully." He lowered his weapon to the desk, and slid the knife back up his sleeve, pressing the sheath clip when it was in place.

"You can't—you can't do this!" Cuthen said, his gaze shifting from Rafe to the two guards.

"I think you will find I can," Rafe said. "It would be advisable to go quietly with these gentlemen and co-operate with them."

"If you please, sir," Stan said. "Stand up now, put your hands behind your head, and turn to face the windows." Slowly, Cuthen did as he was told. Rafe, alert to the physical signs, saw the moment when he realized he'd lost everything. It wasn't as satisfying as if he'd beaten the man to a pulp himself, but it was a start.

When Cuthen had been taken away, Rafe looked at the information Emil gave him on the ISC fleet. On paper, it was formidable, even knowing what he knew about the poor maintenance, the lack of upgrades, the mediocre to poor training. He knew what *Vanguard* was like; he knew Ky had hired competent ex-mercs for her fighting crew. But he knew nothing about the other two ships in her fledgling fleet; he didn't count the courier vessels worth much. And even if the other ships were larger than *Vanguard*, and even if the courier ships had weapons and could use them, that was six against fourteen . . .

He called Malaky again. "Here's what you're going to do. You're going to send a priority message to that ansible, with urgent instructions not to attack Space Defense Force ships."

"But why—"

The faint whine in Malaky's voice sent Rafe over the edge. "You are relieved of duty," Rafe said. "Stay where you are. I'm on my way." He stood, unable to sit still, and called for Emil as he crossed the office.

"Yes, sir?"

"I'm going down to Enforcement. Tell my people to meet me at the elevator on that floor—" If anyone tried to kill him between here and there, he relished the thought of what he could do.

"Sir, do you want me to come along?"

Rafe looked at the earnest young face, and for a moment his rage receded. "No, Emil," he said almost gently. "I need you here."

His guards gave him a brief reproachful look when he came out of the elevator but said nothing, flanking him as he strode down the corridor to Enforcement's warren of offices. "Malaky," he said to the first person he saw. The woman paled and backed up a step, but pointed.

Malaky was standing in Enforcement's communications suite; Rafe's implant gave him the face, in its bland official-image expression. Now the man looked tense, worried, glancing around uneasily. The four on-shift communications operators ignored him, concentrating on their consoles. When the door to the com suite slid open, he looked up.

"Sir—Chairman, I'm sorry, I—"

"You're relieved," Rafe said.

"But sir, I—"

"I said, you're relieved. Sit there." Rafe pointed. His guards took a step forward; Malaky almost fell into the indicated chair. Now the operators looked from Malaky to Rafe. One started to stand, then sank back to his seat. "Who's monitoring ansible Boxtop-zip-figaro-112?"

"Me, sir," said one, raising her hand.

"Do you know who I am?" Rafe asked.

"Er . . . yes, sir. The chairman, sir. Ser Dunbarger."

"Good. Then you know I have authority for this order." He waited a moment for that to sink in. "You will immediately transmit this message, while I observe. 'To the ISC fleet: Do not attack Space Defense Force vessels. Repeat: Do not attack Space Defense Force vessels under any circumstances'." Rafe watched as the woman keyed in a series of identification and validation codes, and then the message he had ordered. He had seen a lot of ISC fleet orders in the past few days; he recognized many of the codes, and these looked legitimate.

"Sir . . . ," the woman said, glancing back over her shoulder.

"Yes?"

"Sir, you should know they may not get those orders right away. Our system stats indicate that the jump point is many light-hours from the ansible, and there are no relays in that system. Considering downjump turbulence and communications lags, they could engage those ships before they receive it."

"Put it on broadcast," Rafe said.

She paled, with a quick glance at Malaky, but spoke. "Sir . . . that will put our classified codes out for anyone to pick up—and if I broadcast without them, the fleet commander may decide the broadcast is a hoax."

He wanted to think that was nonsense, but she was right. They should not broadcast the codes, and a prudent commander would reasonably assume that orders without the codes were faked.

"Don't they try to pick up messages when they come in?"

"Yes, sir, but . . . but not if there's a hostile force. Or"— with another quick glance at Malaky and then at him— "what they think is a hostile force."

"So what you're telling me is that they may not get this message until it's too late."

She looked down at her hands, motionless now on the console. "Yes, sir. I'm sorry, sir, but really—once we send a fleet, it's pretty much out of our hands."

"Very well," Rafe said, trying for an even tone. It was not the operator's fault. "Thank you for the explanation." That came out in a rasp; he cleared his throat. When he glanced at Malaky, the man cowered visibly in his chair, but he had no time to savor that. Ky was still in danger of being destroyed by his own people.

He had to contact her directly; he had to warn her. His imagination raced: she would have known the first message, she would have known the second. She would think ISC had given up pursuit, maybe. When fourteen ships came through the jump point, would she even believe they were ISC? Would she think they were pirates? What would she do? Run, he hoped. He knew in his heart she wouldn't run.

Aboard Vanguard

Sleep, as Hugh had said, was a duty for ship officers. Ky thought about activating her implant's sleep function again; her thoughts raced, and she felt as relaxed as a steel bar. Instead, she tried visualizing the color pattern she'd been taught as a child, struggling to find the harmony again. That didn't work, either. She tried inventorying every ship component she could think of, but found herself concentrating too hard on that, worrying when she couldn't remember them all.

Good news, then: that could put people to sleep. Stella seemed to be doing well, and Toby. She grinned, thinking of Toby and Rascal. Quincy had said Toby was ferociously bright; she remembered that he had helped install the defensive suite, and then had figured out that it was defective and how to fix it. Thinking of Toby brought up the memory of Rafe, and Rafe was definitely not a soporific thought. Her implant provided a crisper image of that rakehell face than memory could provide. Where was he now? Had he made it safely to his family? Had they rejected him again? Their last conversation—his story about what made him what he was, that attempted abduction, his defense of himself and his sister, the consequences—ran through her mind, word for word. What a thing to have in common with the man you . . . well, not loved. Were intrigued by, maybe. Felt more alive around, maybe.

"Captain?"

Sighing, Ky fumbled around the head of the bed for the com button. "Yes," she said. "What is it?" She'd been lying in bed for three solid hours, the chronometer told her, and she hadn't slept yet.

"Signal that *Bassoon* relayed to us. ISC sent another message and said to disregard the previous ones."

"Did they say why?"

"No. Just that."

"That's odd," Ky said. "A relief, but odd. I wonder what's going on with them." Suddenly she felt sleepy; she must have been more concerned about ISC's possible intervention than she'd admitted to anyone, even herself. "Thanks for letting me know," she said. "I'm going back to sleep."

Next shift, she woke feeling much less anxious about the days until the Mackensee relief convoy arrived. If the pirates had been planning to move in after a successful attack, ambush the returning Mackensee convoy, either they had changed their minds or . . . she didn't think they would attack now. Not that she planned to let down her guard.

After breakfast, she visited Master Sergeant Pitt in the quarters assigned to the Mackensee refugees. "I'm going to visit the wounded; I thought you'd like to come along," she said.

"Thank you, Captain," Pitt said.

As they walked, Ky asked, "How are your people doing? Anything I should know?"

"My best card player won some money off some of yours; if that's a problem—"

"No," Ky said. "Unless they end up owning the ship."

"I don't have much else for them to do, you see," Pitt said. "If you have any lengthy chores—I'm sure there are things you don't want our people to see or touch, but we've cleaned the spaces assigned to us beyond our own standards—not that they were dirty . . ."

"We have a gym, you know," Ky said. "There's plenty of room for them to exercise; I wouldn't want to expend our ammunition on the firing range, but you could use those facilities in rotation with my people."

"That would be a help, Captain," Pitt said. "They're good people, but just sitting around is not what they do best."

Ky paused and tapped into the ship's internal com. "Hugh," she said. "Would you check the schedule for the gym, and put the Mackensee troops on the rotation? Master Sergeant, how many would you want to send at a time?"

"Half of them," Pitt said.

"Two groups," Ky said to Hugh.

"Will do," he said. "Do you want me to contact you about this, or Master Sergeant Pitt?"

"Me—she's with me now; we're going to visit their wounded."

"A few minutes, Captain," Hugh said. "I'll have a list

of what machines are available and all that. Firing range, too?"

"No, not that. But everything else."

In the sick bay, two of the wounded were now in bed, wired and tubed extensively. One was conscious, only lightly sedated. Ky let Pitt approach him while she spoke to the medical staff.

"He's in the best shape," the surgeon reported. "He needs some tank time, and I expect they'll want to revise some of the emergency repairs, but he'll be out of bed in another twenty-four hours. The other one—" He glanced over at the bed where soft snores indicated the inhabitant was asleep. "—had some implant damage and he hasn't come back to full consciousness. The medbox can sustain him, but we think he's just aware enough to start physical therapy. The others—the chest injury's in fast-heal mode; he'll be in the box another three days, and of course he's kept sedated there. The one with the pulped legs— we've been in contact with the Mackensee medical team on *Metaire,* and they want us to try to save as much as we can for direct tissue transfer after implanting limb-buds. We're doing our best, but I'm concerned that one of the legs is developing anoxia. See here—" He put up a visual that meant nothing to Ky, bands of color on an outlined leg shape. "I'm going to tell Doctor Santino on *Metaire* this morning that I think amputation is necessary. He may want a transfer back to their facility, now that things have settled down. I presume that won't be a problem?"

Only a matter of microjumping a couple of light-hours and then easing into position near enough for *Metaire*'s shuttles to make the transfer quickly . . . but that wasn't the medical team's problem. The communications lag might be. "You know we've moved away from *Metaire,*" she said. "Will his condition be stable long enough for them to reply, or do we need to reposition the ship now?"

"I need an answer within an hour," the surgeon said. "Or it may be too late to do anything but amputate."

"We'll move the ship, then," Ky said. She turned to Pitt. "We're going to move closer to *Metaire*," she said. "Our surgeon needs to talk to your surgeons about some of your people. You can stay here if you like; I need to get to the bridge."

The precision microjump was no problem, with all the practice Ky had insisted on, and Ky reassured *Metaire* the moment they reappeared nearby that the move was not in response to an enemy threat. When she explained the circumstances, one of *Metaire*'s surgeons and his medical team boarded a shuttle; as Ky had *Vanguard* ease toward *Metaire,* the shuttle approached.

Ky went down to the lock to meet them, wondering if there were any way a shuttle bay could be retrofitted to *Vanguard*'s hull. This business of having to transfer personnel by tube made it obvious that *Vanguard* was just a converted cargo ship. The big cargo bay hatches would admit a shuttle . . . but that's where her missile batteries and missile storage were. What she needed was a purpose-built warship, designed from the start for war. What she really needed was a government or two to fund such a purchase.

"We want to evaluate him ourselves," the surgeon said after Ky greeted them.

"Of course," she said, leading the way to sick bay. "This is Doctor Moshalla—" The doctors eyed each other a moment, then dove into medical jargon where Ky could not follow. She returned to the bridge and checked in with the other ships.

"We haven't found any other stealthed ships," Ransome

reported. "We're fairly sure there aren't any, as I've had one of our people monitoring the channels the pirates used, and they've been silent."

"Excellent," Ky said. "Though that doesn't prove no one's here, it does indicate that if someone is, whatever they know isn't going to the enemy." Or that they knew the enemy was somewhere in FTL flight, on the way. "Keep monitoring, just in case. You have a crew aboard that stealthed ship you boarded, right?"

"Yes, I do, but if you could give us a relief crew—it's pretty unpleasant over there, they say. A bit of a hovel, actually. They cleaned it up as best they could, but it's not up to the standards of *my* ships."

Ky considered. Mackensee were the ones with spare people, but she didn't want to give them possession of a ship she felt entitled to. But if she let Pitt's people do some of the work aboard *Vanguard*, she could send a prize crew to . . . whatever its name was. She'd want to have Pettygrew's tech Lattin along, too, to modify the ansible and see what kinds of scan the pirates had been using.

"We're about to do a medical transfer," she said. "When that's done, I'll come out and put my people aboard her with thanks for your efforts in the meantime."

"That's fine, Captain Vatta. We're honored to be associated with you, and we will keep the ship secure until you arrive."

Before she could contact Pettygrew to ask for the loan of Dozi Lattin, a message came up from sick bay that the surgeons had decided to transfer two of the Mackensee casualties back to *Metaire*. Preparing them for transport took over an hour; Ky called Pettygrew and Argelos both, and each agreed to lend her one or two people. Argelos recommended his Slotter Key military adviser for temporary captain.

"Will he do what I tell him?" Ky asked. She had still not met the man who had been so negative about her in the beginning.

"Oh, yes," Argelos said. "He's admitted he misjudged you, based on biased reports after you . . . left the Academy. He was there only one term before being yanked away to be an adviser to privateers. His name's Yamini."

The name meant nothing to Ky. "I'd still like to meet him—at least see his face on the screen."

"Of course," Argelos said. "Bistaf, come over here. Captain Vatta wants to talk to you face-to-face."

The face on the screen was only vaguely familiar. Ky's father's implant had no catalog of Spaceforce Academy's faculty; she finally remembered that he had been a new tactics instructor her last term. No wonder he'd had a negative view of her. "I'm Major Yamini," he said. "You won't remember me—I didn't have you in class."

"You taught junior tactics, didn't you?" Ky asked. "You were in the catalog . . ."

"Yes. I need to apologize for my attitude, Captain Vatta. When Captain Argelos first told me you were trying to get an organization of privateers together, I thought—well, I thought you were as wild and irresponsible as they'd said when you were asked to resign."

"My question now is whether you feel able to follow my orders, if you are chosen to captain the stealthed ship we found," Ky said.

"Absolutely, Captain Vatta. I have no qualms at all now. And I do have skills you might find useful: that ship's computer may well contain information about the pirates' tactical capacity. I know that so far we have seen them use only fairly simple—but effective—attacks, but if they have something else in their arsenal, I might be able to find and analyze it."

"Very well," Ky said. She was glad not to have to give up any of her own bridge personnel except a pilot. "When we've completed this medical transfer, *Vanguard* will jump to your position; we'll pick you up. Then we'll go get Lattin, Pettygrew's talented communications tech, and the environmental tech he's offered me, and we'll take you all out to the ship. I expect to be making your transfer within the hour; I look forward to meeting you in person."

"And I you, Captain Vatta," he said.

Ky went on to set up the transfer time with Captain Pettygrew; he offered instead to jump out to the stealthed ship and transfer Lattin directly.

"I worry about clustering our ships like that," Ky said. "But if you want to do it now, that's a good idea. Just be sure to tell Ransome that you're coming in, so he can alert his skeleton crew."

"I'll do that," Pettygrew said. "Then you want me back on station, I presume?"

"Yes," Ky said. "I know nothing seems to be happening, but that's when things do."

NINETEEN

Aboard Vanguard

Even with precision microjumps and the shipboard ansibles, it took the rest of that day to complete all the transfers and get everyone back on station. But Lattin reported that the enemy prize had a complete suite of advanced scan, passive, active, longscan, and nearscan. "Everything you could want," she said. "All wavelengths—I'd say they spent a fortune on it, except that it's clearly stolen from somewhere. There's a lot of physical damage to what were probably the serial numbers."

"What about the ship herself?" Ky asked.

"They did something screwy to the beacon," Lattin said. "Of course it's damped—all stealth tech does that—but I don't believe the current ID as it shows in the onboard is correct. There's a . . . it's kind of technical—"

"Never mind," Ky said. "But you think it's not the real ID?"

"No. But I can't tell if it's a stolen ship chip or one they programmed themselves. Most beacon readers won't pick up what I'm talking about, but you really should have it re-registered with a new chip somewhere."

"I intend to," Ky said. "Can you tell if the rest of the AI is reliable?"

"I'm running checks on it now, Captain Vatta. Captain . . . er . . . Yamini . . . he asked the same thing. He said he wanted to be sure the ship didn't do something weird on its own. Oh—do you want me to check the stealth function?"

"Not at present," Ky said. "It's working now; let's leave it alone. Just get that ansible rigged to our frequencies so we can use it without the pirates finding out."

"Yes, Captain," Lattin said.

Ky looked at the arrangement of the ships in the system plot again before she went back to her cabin. The stealthed ship had moved, on her orders, and now was far from where the pirates had stationed it—and where they would presumably expect to find it if they invaded. No single attack, however lucky, could take out all her ships at once. *Metaire* was still in danger, but Ky had persuaded Colonel Kalin to keep the shields up constantly.

Once in her cabin, she fell asleep almost at once, only to wake in the middle of that shift to a terrible stench that almost made her gag. "Light!" she said; the bedlamp came on. She looked at the bed, half expecting to see a piece of spoiled fruit, but nothing . . . the inside of her head seemed to tingle and itch, the smell was so strong.

Her implant popped up a message: CONTACT Y/N?

Implant. Implanted ansible. Rafe . . . he'd said he wouldn't ever use it, but who else could it be? A quick fumble through that folder in the implant and she knew what she should do. But not before securing the ship.

"Hugh," she said, when she had him on the intercom. "I need you to meet me in my office."

"What's up, Captain?"

"I can't discuss it. I'll be there momentarily."

By the time Hugh arrived, she was dressed and had splashed cold water on her face. Hugh looked worried, unsurprisingly. "Are you sick, Captain? Has anyone . . . done anything?"

"I'm not sick. But I will be . . . unavailable for a time, and you needed to know that. I can't explain it . . . not now, anyway. You will need to take over until I am . . . back. I'll let you know. I'm sorry, that's all I can say, and I need to hurry—"

"Are you going to try to change implants or something? You really should have medical assis—"

"It's not that. I can't say. I could have done this without telling you but that wouldn't have been right . . ."

"All right, Captain. I won't press you further, but . . . I get the strong feeling someone should know what's going on." With that he left.

Ky secured the door, retrieved the power cables Rafe had given her, and followed the implant's directions. She did not like the idea of plugging into the ship's power supply—it took an effort of will to make herself close the connection.

And he was there, as if he were standing beside her. The stench faded, replaced by a smell rather like wet leaves. As before, the urgency of his transmission felt like a shout inside her head.

"Ky! Are you there? Answer me!"

"Not so loud!"

"Sorry. You do have volume control . . ."

She found that and brought the volume down to a manageable level. "I thought you said you wouldn't ever use this thing," she said.

"Except in a dire emergency," he said. "Which this may well be. Are you alone?"

"Yes. Hugh's in command; I told him—"

"About the ansible?" Rafe's voice sharpened.

"No. That he was in charge and I was unavailable; he's puzzled but coping. What is it?"

"A long and miserable story, and I'm afraid you're going to have to listen to quite a bit of it."

"The story of your life," Ky murmured.

"Something like that, yes," Rafe said. "I'll try to keep it as short as I can. When I got to Nexus, I found that my family was missing, and someone had a great interest in anyone who inquired about them. It took me an unfortunate length of time to figure out what had happened, find them, and arrange a hostage rescue."

"Hostage!"

"Yes. My parents and my remaining sister had been abducted; her husband had been killed. My delay in reaching them . . . resulted in the loss of my sister's baby. Killed by the abductors in front of her and my parents."

Ky could think of nothing to say. After a moment, Rafe went on.

"My father was badly injured; he suffered neurological damage and is in rehab. He wanted me to take over as CEO of ISC; the Board agreed, though some of them probably wish they hadn't. You need to know that the person who instigated the abduction of my family was Lew Parmina—I believe you knew him."

"Lew—but he came to visit us. My father brought him home; he liked him—"

"So did my father, to his cost. I don't know whether he was involved in what happened to your family, but I know what he did to mine. Unfortunately, my father got it into his head that Parmina's friendship with your family made your family suspect. He has drawn a line from Osman Vatta's possession of shipboard ansibles, through your insistence on using them, your aunt's repair of the Slotter Key ansible—"

"She didn't—"

"Our sources say she authorized it; that's enough for him. And then there's Stella's pursuit—now successful—of patent rights to the improved version of shipboard ansibles. He's convinced himself that Vattas were involved in Parmina's treachery. I'm hoping that as his recovery proceeds, he'll think more clearly and understand you had nothing to do with it, but right now—he is a problem, and the people in ISC who were his people are a problem. More immediately, there's an ISC fleet—fourteen ships—headed for the system you're in, with intent to kill or capture you."

"But . . . we got a message saying—"

"I know. I told them to send it, though my wording was different; the idiots in Enforcement changed it. But they'd already dispatched the fleet, on their own initiative, and I didn't find out about it until now. I've put an urgent message for them on the system ansible, but they may not stop for it before they start shooting. You've got to get out of there now. They're less than sixteen hours out, and that's if Enforcement told me the truth. Since I just arrested their head, they may not."

"We can't leave, Rafe. We're guarding a Mackensee ship full of wounded and our supply ship; the pirates might come back."

"Pirates might; ISC will. Ky, listen—fourteen ships. Including two full-size battle cruisers. I know you've just fought a battle; you can't have a full munitions load. You haven't got a chance—"

"I'm not leaving helpless ships behind for your goons to shoot up," Ky said.

"They're after you, not Mackensee," Rafe said. "I didn't realize—my father's not supposed to be interfering with my management but he called someone in the department, told them about his suspicions, and they've picked *you* as the primary target." No need to explain his father's dementia or the internal politics at ISC. "You and that Space Defense Force you've put together. It's all a mistake; I can call them back once we're in contact, but they could blow you away before that."

"Do you have their IDs?" Ky asked.

"Yes, but it won't do for you to blow them away, either. That would prove that you're the enemy. You have to get out of there."

"Send me their IDs—and I presume you know something about what armament they carry?"

"Yes, but I can't tell you that. Ky, if you'll just listen to me and get out—"

"Or you could listen to me, when I say I'm not going anywhere."

"Ky—"

"No, listen. The Mackensee ship has had some damage, and it's stuffed with casualties. They're waiting for their relief convoy, which is due in . . . I forget how many days, but several. It's in transit; they can't contact it. The pirates not only attacked Mackensee—we happened to arrive in the midst of that fight—but they had a stealthed observation ship in the system. We captured that, but not before it reported on the battle, and I'm not sure there's not another one. If I leave, and there *is* another one, then the Mackensee ship could be a prime target for another attack—and so might the relief convoy."

"Protecting mercs is not your job!"

She felt a wave of heat rush up to her head. "*You* do not define my job," Ky said. "The way I see it, my job is to protect those who need protection. And this ship does, and I'm doing it."

"You are the most stubborn, idiotic—"

For some reason, that quenched the anger. She made her voice calm. "Rafe. We're wasting time. I need the data on those ships, if only to evade them. Send me the data first. Then we can try to figure some way to ensure that neither my people nor your people end up splattered across space."

"Ky—all right." A moment later, a datastream spit out in the implant. Ky was able to route it to the regular ship interface of her implant, and thence to the bridge.

"Now just a moment," she said to Rafe. "I'm going to try to talk on an external channel." The pervasive smell of wet leaves changed to something peppery—whatever that meant—as she used the implant's interface to the ship intercom.

"Yes, Captain?" Hugh said. "Are you available again? What's this datastream about?"

"I believe those are the ship IDs of fourteen ISC ships that are believed to be on the way here," Ky said. "If the data are correct, someone may have the ship specs in their implant databases. Please check that."

"On the way here to . . . deal with us?"

"I believe that's the understanding," Ky said. "I have to go now; I'll be back with you shortly." She disconnected the in-ship channel.

"I wish you'd change your mind," Rafe said. He sounded tired, now, tired and worried.

"I can't," Ky said. "Now—quit arguing and tell me everything you know about those ships . . . and if you need more time, why not contact Stella and relay through her so we can use the shipboard units? It's a lot more convenient."

"She wasn't there," Rafe said. "I did think of that, but she was en route from Cascadia Station down to planet-side to inspect manufacturing facilities. And the watchdog at her office wouldn't let me talk to Toby." He sighed; his voice was rough at the edges, as if he were exhausted. "I can't send you much more anyway—it's proprietary; it would be a breach of company security—"

"And talking to me on the ansible I'm not supposed to know about, let alone have, isn't? Rafe, be reasonable: I'm not out to destroy ISC. I have no desire to blow up your ships. But the best way to ensure I don't is to tell me what their performance capacity is, so I can evade them until they've had time to get your messages via ansible."

"All right. All right, here—"

Another datastream flowed into Ky's implant. Range, insystem maximum velocity, FTL engine type, weapons types and numbers, munitions types, range . . . She blinked. Surely a lot of those data had to be wrong. "Rafe . . . some of these ships look . . . a little outdated."

"They are," Rafe said.

"I don't see a minimum-radius microjump listed—"

"It's not in their specs that I could find."

Ky felt her spirits lifting. "When is the last time this fleet went on live-fire maneuvers?"

"I'd rather not say," Rafe said.

That wasn't surprising, if her surmise was correct. "Are their munitions . . . have they been stored in the ships all this time?"

"All what time?"

"Rafe, those Model R-ZM-200s haven't been manufactured anyplace I know of for over thirty years. And they're incompatible with current guidance systems." And, she did not add, the warheads deteriorated over time . . . probably half those things wouldn't detonate at all, and the rest might detonate anywhere, any time, once they were unlocked.

"They still outnumber and outgun you," Rafe said. "Numbers count."

"It's true that enough ants can eat a camel," Ky said. "But a camel can walk away before they do." It was too early to feel what she felt—but she couldn't help it. Fourteen ships, yes, but . . . not particularly dangerous ships.

"You think you can evade them?"

"It's a possibility," Ky said. "Thank you for warning me, Rafe, but I think I need to disconnect now and get busy with my officers."

"I still think—"

"That I should leave. I know. I'll talk to the Mackensee commander, but he's even more stubborn than I am, so don't expect that to happen."

"Ky, please . . . take care." This time she heard something in his voice she had not heard but once, during that last serious talk.

"And you also," she said, before pulling the plug to the ship's power. A last strange smell, and it was over. Her head felt odd, as if it were too big, but after a few moments the sensation faded and she was able to put away the cables, stand up, and move without any difficulty.

As she'd expected, Colonel Kalin was unwilling to leave the system. "We are supposed to be in this system, and you assure me that ISC has no intention of attacking *us*—"

"That's what my informant said. But it's still dangerous—"

"Yes, but . . . the one thing I'm sure of is that my relief will be coming here, expecting to find us here, and if we are not here there will be hell to pay."

"It will not help either Mackensee or ISC if they shoot holes in you by accident."

"True. I will tell our captain to move us a considerable distance away from you."

"That's a start, at least." Ky hesitated, then went on. "There's still the pirate problem. I'm not convinced they won't return . . . and the longer it is before they return, the more ships they're likely to bring with them. If it ends up as a three-cornered fight—"

"That's very unlikely," Colonel Kalin said. "It would be an amazing coincidence—"

"True. But coincidences happen, and we can't afford to ignore them. I'm going to give you the data I have on those ISC ships—"

"You got this from that . . . device . . . on your ship, did you?"

Ky reflected that an ansible in her head was in fact on her ship and thus fulfilled the criteria. "Yes," she said.

"I know we're going to want that technology," he said. "But in the meantime—what you're describing is very dangerous for you, and you have no contractual obligation to us—"

"I'm not leaving," Ky said. "If worse comes to worst, if we're losing . . . maybe. But not now, not before any shots are fired."

A few hours later, a message came through the system ansible for *Metaire*. Colonel Kalin contacted Ky—though the lightlag meant she got the message six hours after it came in, two hours after he received it. The Mackensee convoy had picked up one of the messages he'd sent at an interim jump point and had changed their route; they would be insystem days earlier than expected.

"Early enough to be here when ISC arrives?" Ky asked. She wouldn't get an answer to that for four hours.

"Possibly; they said they'd go to full power. By my calculations they could be here a few hours before, or within six hours after. They know about the mined jump-point entrance . . ."

Ky had another conference with her captains. "We may have an interesting time," she said. "ISC's due to arrive in . . . something under ten hours. If they don't take care, they'll run into those mines; they may assume we placed them. Mackensee's relief convoy might be here just before or just after them—or hours later. And the pirates—if there are pirates—may show up at any moment. Kalin told Mackensee we were on their side, so we know Mackensee ships won't shoot at us—but whether they'll shoot at ISC if ISC attacks us is another question. I didn't bother to ask Kalin; he wouldn't know. And lightlag in communications is going to be a royal pain, with at least three and maybe four sets of ships."

"You want us to hold our present alignment?" Argelos asked.

"Yes. The pirates are the only ones who might risk coming in on some strange vector. The others will use the mapped jump point, and I expect both of them will come in warily, knowing the jump point might have been mined. Even if the pirates do something odd, we're in a good arrangement for them. Set your crew schedules so the crew you'd most want for battle are rested when we expect things to get interesting."

Ky woke with the knot already in her stomach. Calculations or no calculations, fourteen ships to three was higher odds than she had ever imagined facing. Ransome's Rangers would be effective gadflies, faster and more maneuverable than anything in that ISC fleet, but their armament was pitiful in comparison. She had only two beam weapons on her own ship; any two of ISC's larger warships should be able to blow her entire fleet away.

Except that ISC's ships should not be as effective as their paper statistics suggested. "Should not" was a slender thread to hang all those lives on . . . was she crazy to think it might work? If she could slow down the attack long enough, if the captains of those ships downloaded the waiting message Rafe said he'd sent . . . no one need fire a shot. "If" was an even more slender thread. Had Rafe told the truth? Had he really sent such a message? Were the ISC ships really so outmoded? Or was Rafe playing the role of ISC's chief officer, luring her into a situation she could not survive? Was his apparent concern for her just an act? They had been allies in the past, but he'd always insisted his primary loyalty was to ISC.

She had no alternative, really, other than abandoning *Metaire* . . . though with the Mackensee relief force coming so soon, they wouldn't be uncovered long.

"Captain?" That was the comtech again. "It's Captain Yamini."

"What's the problem, Captain Yamini?" Ky asked.

"Lattin picked up something on the shipboard—on a channel the pirates use. She doesn't know the language, but the coordinates of this system were given. And she thinks she's got a direction on another stealth ship in the system. Here—" A string of numerical data came in; Ky shunted it to her navigator. "She doesn't have any data on range, of course."

"And we really don't have time to set up for triangulation and try to capture another signal," Ky said. "Call Captain Ransome and ask him to assign one of his ships to a quick search pattern along that vector, but carefully. That ship may be trying to lure one of us into range."

"Yes, Captain."

"And let's hope that ship doesn't have microjumping capability. I know we can detect the disturbances it'll leave that way, but a stealthed ship hopping around is . . . not my favorite thought."

"We have contacts," her scan tech said suddenly. "Not at the jump point."

Longscan showed fifteen ships in three-ship formations at that distance. They'd emerged from jump hours ago—the uncertainty smudges were elongated ovals—all immediately red-tagged as armed, weapons live. Ky's stomach knotted tighter. "That's not ISC," she said. "And it's not Mackensee—they were coming into the jump point. Tell *Metaire*; make sure they have the scan coordinates." Though a message was probably on the way from them to her, as well.

Moment by moment, scan refined the position from first acquisition, the ovals shortening behind and lengthening in front, narrowing as the data showed no deviation in course, no slackening of velocity.

"They came in really fast; they know where they're going; they know they have no minefields to worry about," Hugh said.

"Yup. And where they've been is safe for us," Ky said. "They can't lay mines at that velocity, or reverse vector on insystem. They'd have to microjump—"

"Found it!" That was Teddy Ransome, breaking in on the shipboard ansible. "It *is* another stealthed observer, and we're taking it out! *Furious,* your turn! Oh, good shot!"

"They've all left station," Ky said, rolling her eyes. "Give me another all-ships channel—I need to talk to Argelos and Pettygrew."

"Is that ISC?" Pettygrew asked. "They look at lot more formidable than you said . . ."

"No, that's not ISC," Ky said. "That's the pirates. If we're incredibly lucky, ISC will come barreling through the jump point and run headlong into them, but I don't think we'll be that lucky. Ransome's taking out the other stealth ship—I hope it's the last one—and we're all going to play hide-the-thimble until ISC or Mackensee arrives—or both. Once that stealth ship is gone, we'll start micro-jumping on those courses we discussed. *Metaire* knows where to go, and our transport's already in hiding. If it gets too hot—we'll have to leave. Be sure your FTL engines are warmed up."

"They're almost in range to use beam weapons . . ." Argelos said, looking worried. "You know we can't jump with your precision . . ."

"Jump now, then, your first vector. Just don't deviate from your plan—we don't want to land on top of you accidentally." *Sharra's Gift* disappeared from the scan; she would reappear half a light-hour away, in a direction the fight should not propagate. Three minutes later, the pile of garbage she'd jettisoned as a marker sparkled and flared as a beam hit it.

"They're really annoyed," Hugh said. "That was maximum distance; shields would've held."

"But flared," Ky said.

"Got him!" came another cry from Ransome. "All to smithereens, he blew, to the great delight of all the crew!"

"Not all that fancy stuff and poetry, too," Lee said, making a face.

"If they blow up our enemies, they can make up all the silly songs they want," Hugh said. "They're definitely a case of the clock on its side." Lee looked confused; Hugh didn't explain, but Ky chuckled.

"Congratulations, Captain Ransome," Ky said. "Excellent shooting. Do you have the attackers on scan?"

"Yes, we do . . . I'll bet we could take one from behind; I believe we have the legs of them."

"It may come to that, but right now it would be most

useful if you could slip in behind them and give us real-time data on their movements," Ky said. She was watching scan. *Metaire,* moving in the right direction, had still not microjumped. Kalin had said nothing about problems with the FTL engine . . . was it functioning? It disappeared from scan and reappeared almost at once, having jumped less than a light-second . . . that would have been two hours ago, before Ky's crew had detected the pirates. Were they testing the FTL engine? And was that tiny hop evidence of precision, or of a problem?

She should have pushed harder to get Kalin's permission to install a shipboard ansible on *Metaire*—at no charge, if necessary—so they could communicate in real time.

"Beam discharge, vector data—" Ransome again, sounding as cheerful as ever. Ky's navigator converted the vector data into a line on the screen. The pirates were still over four light-hours away; the beam was aimed at where *Vanguard* would be on her present course.

"That is the weirdest thing I ever saw," Hugh said. "We know they've shot at us; we know where it's going and when it will get there—and unless it's more powerful than any beam I know about, our shields would hold against it if we let it hit us at that distance. It's child's play to evade it . . . they're much too far away; I wonder why they're taking these long shots."

"They don't know we've got someone on their tail who can communicate with us in real time. They're trying to take us out before we think we're in range . . . hoping we don't have our shields up yet."

"And we don't."

"True. Without shields—it could at least knock out a lot of our scan and com equipment on the outer hull." Ky looked back at scan. "I wish *Metaire* would get out of there. We can't protect her from fifteen of them. That little hop worries me . . . is she all right?"

"She may be playing stupid," Hugh said. "Trying to lure them in."

"Broken-wing act?"

"Something like that. Dangerous, though—"

"There's something on the pirates' channel, Captain," the comtech said suddenly. "I'm recording—"

"Let's hear it," Ky said.

"ALL SHIPS INSYSTEM! HEAVE TO AND IDENTIFY YOURSELVES! THIS IS THE BLUERIDGE DEFENSE ALLIANCE!" The voice was heavily accented; the face on the screen was of a clean-shaven dark-haired man in a medium blue uniform with gold braid on the collar and epaulets dripping gold fringe. Behind him, they could see what looked like other officers in the same shade of blue, with similar collar markings but no epaulets.

"What the—?"

"Who's the Blueridge Defense Alliance?" someone said. "I never heard of them . . ."

"Someone else with the same bright idea?" Hugh asked, his brow furrowed. "It's not unheard of for even legitimate forces to fire a warning shot before hailing."

"Who just happened to have shipboard ansibles with the pirates' channels? I don't think so," Ky said. "I think that's the pirates trying to act legitimate. Give me Captain Ransome."

When Ransome came on, Ky said, "Can you strip their beacons yet? They're using the pirates' channels to claim they're the Blueridge Defense Alliance. I don't believe them." He should understand that without being told, but she wanted to make sure.

"Of course, Captain Vatta. Just a moment—got 'em. At least, we've got the first three—here—"

The beacon data indicated that the first three were *Blueridge Battersea*, *Blueridge Belinda*, and *Blueridge Backfin*. Next came *Blueridge Alba*, *Blueridge Ardent*, and *Blueridge Asera*. All had supposedly been built by Blueridge Space Industries, on Blueridge, where all were registered on dates that varied across fifteen years.

"That's not much like a real space militia's way of naming ships," Ky said. "There's a heavy and two mediums in each triad . . . everywhere else I know about, related names are for related hull designs. And why would *Alba* be registered thirteen years before *Asera* when they're the exact same hull type . . . and look at the serial numbers . . . squirt that over to the others, see if anyone has any ideas. And where is Blueridge? I never heard of it. Is that their real home base, or have they captured another system?"

"PIRATE VESSELS BASSOON, VANGUARD, SHARRA'S GIFT. HEAVE TO OR YOU WILL BE FIRED UPON. VESSEL METAIRE, HEAVE TO AND PREPARE TO EXPLAIN YOUR ASSOCIATION WITH THESE PIRATES."

"They *sound* like a legitimate space force," Dannon said. "That might fool traders or even a system defense force."

"How long would it take pirates to get themselves some pretty uniforms and patches and so on?" Ky said. "No longer than it took us, I'm betting." But would the ordinary tradeship captain think of that? If she'd been hailed on normal channels, back when she was a novice captain, she'd have believed the transmission legitimate.

"There's something about that fellow on the screen," Ky said. "I feel like I've seen him somewhere."

"Blueridge isn't in the directory," her navigator said suddenly. "If it's legitimate, it's outside this whole region."

"Captain Vatta!" That was a call from Pettygrew, on one of their channels."

"Here," Ky said.

"One of those serial numbers is—was—on a Bissonet Defense Force heavy cruiser. A friend of mine commanded her; that's how I know. It wasn't built on Blueridge, wherever that is; it was built by Masawa Fabrication, in Bissonet System. I don't know about the others, but I'd bet that all those beacon IDs are faked. And they could all be captured Bissonet warships."

"Aha," Ky said. "So it's our old friends Gammis Turek and company. You have the weapons specs for Bissonet ships of those classes, Dan?"

"Yes, but the short answer is we're in trouble. Kev's ship was built only five years ago; the 'tronics are all up to date as of the time I left. We can't possibly fight them and survive, let alone win."

"That's most unfortunate," Ky said. "And we have to assume they know how to use what they've got, though that premature shot suggests incomplete familiarity. I wonder if that talking head is Gammis Turek after a haircut." She turned to Martin. "Pull Turek's image out of our files and compare, please. If we've got a chance to wipe out Turek—"

"ISC should show up on our scans any moment," Hugh reminded her. "If your source was right about the down-jump time."

"Contacts," said the scan tech. "Jump-point entry, low relative velocity, five . . . eight . . . twelve . . . fourteen. High-powered beacons . . . yep, that's the ISC contingent. It's tightening up; they didn't come in fast, and this shows them working their way through the minefield."

"I think our dance card is about to get full," Ky said. "I wonder what they'll say to each other. With any luck, one set will turn tail and run—preferably the pirates. And I hope the ISC ships pick up their messages from the ansible before they do anything else."

"We have lightspeed data coming in from the Blueridge pirates," her comtech said. "Same message . . ."

"They aren't sure we have the ansibles; they don't know if we all have them. I wonder what ISC ships will make of it."

"ISC doesn't heave to for anyone," Lee said. "Er . . . sorry, Captain."

"It's not that message I'm worried about," Ky said, "but the one where they label us pirates. ISC doesn't know that the Blueridge Defense Alliance is actually pirates."

TWENTY

Large battles in space, Ky remembered being told in advanced tactics, had two main problems: command and control, when ships were far enough apart to suffer lightlag in communications and scan; and debris fields that rapidly made large volumes of space very unpleasant places for ships.

Weapons continued until they ran into something; debris from damaged ships did the same. In the long run, that something might be a gravitational sink, like a planet, but in the short run—in the period of the battle itself—microjumping around anywhere near a space battle risked returning to normal space right in front of—or attempting to occupy the same space as—something lethal.

Already, the tac computer had marked out swaths of the system as potential killzones where it would be extremely dangerous to come out of jump, just from Pettygrew's data on the pirate ships.

"We're going to have to jump out farther," Ky said. "Dan, would Bissonet ships' computers display our view of things?"

"Yes," Pettygrew said. "To anticipate our movements."

"So . . . they will, or already have, filled what now look like safe zones with bad stuff. I think it's time we put a good healthy distance between ourselves and them . . . say, a couple of days . . ."

"That'll put us a long way from the jump point, if we need to get out of the system," Argelos said.

"I don't think we'll need to leave the system entirely," Ky said. "ISC will figure out soon enough that we're not the enemy, and Mackensee already knows it. If Mackensee and ISC team up against the pirates—" She shook her head suddenly. "Wait. We need to tell the ISC ships that the Blueridge bunch are the real pirates. They may not believe us, but we have to warn them. Send it as text, not audio," she said to her comtech. "Tight-beam, from Ky Vatta to the ISC commander: 'Blueridge ship IDs are faked; former Bissonet militia personnel with our force recognized serial number as from Bissonet defense forces. We believe these are the same pirates who attacked Bissonet and other systems. Extreme caution; the Bissonet ships are modern and well equipped. Specs follow.' And then squirt them the weapons specs we got from Pettygrew."

"Yes, Captain. It'll be hours before they get this," he said as he sent it.

"And it may be too late. I understand that. But the evidence that we tried will be around for a long time."

"Message from *Metaire*," her comtech said. Hours old that would be, too, but better than nothing. "They said get out now; they're jumping to that place you talked about."

"That's no good now," Ky said. "Not with ISC already in the system . . . I hope they changed to the alternate—" She looked at the tac computer's plot again. "Captain Argelos—you can do a two-day jump, right?"

"Yes, that's no problem."

"All right. Ransome! Are you there?"

"Right here, Captain Vatta. Want us to blow one away for you? I've got him in my sights. That'll shake 'em up a little."

"No, I want you to microjump to these coordinates—" She sent them, one for each of his ships, safely separated by a couple of thousand kilometers. "On my mark. All ships in Space Defense Force prepare to microjump to assigned coordinates—" She counted down, and at "Now!" the monitor screens blanked momentarily, then lit again as *Vanguard* skipped two light-days away from its previous position.

Here they were safe—for a while—from any weapons that had fired at them before they jumped, and their position would not register on those ships' scans for days. Only the luckiest of random skip-searches would locate them. Unfortunately, they could not see what was going on; their scan lag was the same as the others'.

Within a few minutes, Ransome called Ky. "Why don't you let me go take a look closer in? I can relay scan data to you—you'd know what was going on. I can find *Metaire* and make sure she's not in danger, or even get really close and tell her where we are. It was helpful before, wasn't it? And it would be much more fun than sitting out here wondering and worrying."

"It's really dangerous," Ky said. "If the pirates and ISC start shooting at each other—and I expect they will—a very large volume of space will be a killzone. Including hanging out behind one of the pirate ships."

"Oh, I'm not worried about that," Ransome said. "None of us are."

"You should be," Ky said. "Have you ever been in a large multiship battle? It could overwhelm your computing capacity." His offer was tempting, though. She wanted very much to know if the ISC contingent would collect its message from the ansible, if the pirates were taking on ISC or fleeing, if the Mackensee relief convoy had arrived.

"There's risk in everything," Ransome said. "And we're small, and harder to find and hit. It would be great sport, eh? Sneak in behind those Blueridge fellows again? And if I blew one up, then ISC would know we weren't the enemy, wouldn't they?"

"Not if the pirates have convinced them that Blueridge is a legitimate military organization." Ky looked into Ransome's eager face. She had the distinct feeling that he was going to do something rash no matter what she said, and after all he had insisted that they weren't completely under her command. "Look, Captain Ransome, your Rangers are very valuable to me as scouts. Now that the larger ships are safe for some hours—as long as we're not located—I appreciate your offer and agree that we should have some closer-in observation. But I want to be sure you're fully aware of the hazards. Scan can't detect everything, in a crowded battle zone. Precisely because you've proven yourselves so valuable, I don't want to lose any of you."

Ransome grinned at her, already eager, she could tell, to throw himself into something risky. "Thank you, Captain Vatta. But I'm sure we can get the information you need without getting caught. We'll toss for the honor; I went last time, and it's only fair to give the other fellows a chance at glory."

Or death. Ky had seen what ship weapons could do; some of the casualties still clung to life in sickbay. But they needed the information, and Ransome and his fellows were all adults. "Go ahead then," she said. "If you can disperse safely, and give me more than one observation point."

"Oh, splendid!" he said. "I'll just tell the fellows and we'll be off."

"Cannon fodder," Hugh said, when Ransome disappeared from the screen. "But he's right and you're right—we need to know what's going on. Especially if some of them start hopping around the outer system looking for us." He shook his head. "I'll say this for him and his bunch: they're brave and they're good ship handlers. No more sense than a bunch of schoolboys, but that much they have."

Ky called the other ships and explained that the Rangers would be going back to provide more current data on the situation. "Do you want to be linked to the reports as they come in?" she asked. "If you'd rather take a shift off and rest your crew, I'll have it recorded for you to play later."

"I could go back as well," prize-captain Yamini said. "After all, this ship can be stealthed."

"No," Ky said. "I don't want to risk my last scout ship. If you want to move back about one light-day, fine, but no closer."

"Then I might do you more good taking high guard," Yamini said. "Looking for anything coming in away from the jump point."

"Good idea. Since we know the pirates have onboard ansibles, they could call in reinforcements." Reinforcements could even be in the system, but far out, able to jump in within seconds to minutes. Ky shivered at the thought of the entire pirate fleet showing up, smashing ISC's fleet and the Mackensee relief convoy, and then coming after her little group. Would ISC—even Rafe—believe it had been pirates who destroyed their fleet when they knew it had come after her?

Before she had time to worry more about that, the Rangers began to report in. *Furious*, with St. Cyrien in command, tucked in behind one of the Blueridge pirate triads. "We can pick up the pirates' ansible transmissions

on their channels," St. Cyrien said. "But we only understand a word every now and then; they speak the most
awful jargon. I think it must be a private language or
something. Here's a sample—" He forwarded an audio
file; Ky shunted it to storage for later analysis. "They're
also active on regular com, not tight-beam, to the ISC
fleet. Same thing they told us about themselves—a regular military outfit chasing pirates. Claiming you're a
notorious privateer turned pirate, on a stolen ship, con-
victed in absentia of a whole string of crimes. Asking ISC
to join them in hunting you down. The ISC commander's
answered that he has to pick up any messages on the
system ansible first, and they're trying to get him to ignore
that. Our jumping out is evidence of guilt, and all that
rot. One of the ISC ships has left their initial formation
and looks to be headed for the system ansible. If the
pirates have an inkling what that message is, I'll bet they
scupper him."

"Good work," Ky said.

Glorious, positioned just outside the jump point, offered
an analysis of inbound tracks. "No more ships have entered
since the ISC ships, and they're now under acceleration;
we can't pick up their transmissions easily, but the ship
that seemed headed for the system ansible should be there
in another four hours. We'll stay here so we can monitor
jump-point usage."

Courageous, with Baskerville commanding, was standing
by *Metaire.* "They've had no damage so far, but Colonel
Kalin says the captain would like to move farther out.
That's a long way from where the action is; unless you
need me for direct communications with them, I'd just as
soon stay in close."

"We need the communications," Ky said. "When the
Mackensee convoy shows up, we need to be able to tell

them where their ship is. At least they know, from that one message, that we're on the same side."

Baskerville did not quite pout, but Ky could tell he was disappointed.

"Besides," she said, "*Metaire* may be a warship, but at the moment she's out of ammunition and full of wounded. She needs protection. She's safer alone than with us at the moment, but you're the only way she can have real-time communications to call for help."

"Oh . . ." Baskerville's expression changed. "So we might be attacked anywhere—"

"Yes," Ky said. "And you will be an enormous help to her. I understand it may seem like just standing out of the way—"

"No, no, that's all right. I understand now. Of course, I'll be glad to escort *Metaire*."

"Good work, Captain," Hugh murmured from out of pickup range.

"Everyone but bridge watch, stand down and get some rest," Ky said. "I want extra people on scan and communications, power up and weapons on standby."

Time passed, then Ransome appeared on the onboard ansible's screen again. "Mackensee ships just arrived," he said. "Six . . . I think two troop carriers, two cruisers, a supply ship, and something small—not sure what type. Weapons hot, slow insertion; they're broadcasting a call for *Metaire*."

"What's your distance on them?" Ky asked.

"About ten light-seconds."

"Give them a situation update while you relay their call to Baskerville so he can pass it to *Metaire*; the two of you can assist with their communications after that." To Martin, she said, "Ask Master Sergeant Pitt to come to the bridge, please. If the Mackensee relief commander wants to talk to me, I'd like Mackensee representative standing by."

"Captain Vatta!" That was St. Cyrien on *Furious*. "They just fired on the ship approaching the ansible—I detected discharge. If that ship doesn't change course, in two minutes it'll be a goner. Their cross-ship chatter has increased a lot."

"Either they suspect what's in the ansible message, or they think Mackensee and ISC will automatically hook up—now they'll run," Ky said. "They won't want to face odds against."

"Not until they've done some damage," her weapons officer said. "They might blow the ansible or attack any of the ships out there."

As if to underline those words, St. Cyrien reported again. "They've accelerated; we're sticking with them. Looks like they're going for the ISC ships—which aren't responding . . . wait . . . transmission from ISC, Dopplered . . . I'll get it stretched and send it along . . . there. ISC got your message, Captain, that Blueridge were pirates, and they're asking about that. That must've triggered—" St. Cyrien's transmission ended.

Ky waited. No one on the bridge said a word; they all looked at her. "Something happened, and I doubt it was good," she said finally, when he didn't come back.

"They spotted him," Hugh said. "If they switched to nearscan as they came closer to the ISC ships, it's got better rear-facing capacity, even under acceleration."

"Captain Vatta, we've lost contact with *Furious*." That was Ransome, looking less than ebullient for the first time.

"So have we," Ky said. "His transmission ended abruptly. We'll hope for the best."

"I can't believe—" Ransome began, then changed his tone. "Still, whatever, it's a death in battle, isn't it? Straight to the Heroes' Halls."

Ky felt a sudden urge to smack him, even though it was his friends who had just died. She said nothing; Ransome's face changed again.

"He's—he was—a good fellow."

"An oblique shot could've knocked out his communications without blowing the ship," Ky said, though she didn't believe it.

"That's true . . . that's very true," Ransome said, smiling again. "I'd better take his place, hadn't I? You still need up-to-date information—"

"That's not necessary," Ky said. "I don't think—"

"And if he or the crew are still alive, then I can perform a rescue before . . ." His voice trailed away.

"Or you could end up dead just like them," Ky said before she could stop herself. From the sudden stillness around her, she realized that she'd shocked everyone. She took a deep breath and let it out. "Look—we have fifteen ships out there eager to kill us, fourteen—"

"Thirteen," said Ransome. "The first ISC ship just blew. I don't know if it picked up its ansible message or not." He paused. "And the Mackensee commander wants to speak to you. There'll be a twelve-second delay between us; I'll record and then transmit."

"Thank you," Ky said. She glanced around; Master Sergeant Pitt was just inside the bridge; Ky beckoned, and Pitt came nearer.

This Mackensee commander was dark-skinned, thinner-faced than Colonel Kalin. "I'm Colonel Bandes," he said. "We received Colonel Kalin's message; we understand that your group assisted him when he was under attack, and I am now informed by him as well as Captain Ransome that you are able to communicate with your ships in real time without detection by the enemy. We accept your assessment that the so-called Blueridge Defense Alliance is in fact a pirate group. The situation here looks grave: those ISC ships are using obsolete munitions and ship for ship are no match for the pirates. We have been able to contact their commander, and he asked our assistance; together we may be able to drive the pirates off. However, are you able and willing to give assistance beyond communications? Your scout ship did not have complete information on your remaining munitions . . ."

"We can't sustain a long fight," Hugh said before Ky could answer. "We're down to forty-seven percent of our missiles. *Bassoon*'s at forty-two, and *Sharra's Gift* at thirty-eight."

"If both ISC and Mackensee are defeated, all we can do is run away," Ky said. "That still leaves *Metaire*—"

"They could jump out."

"They shouldn't, except at the mapped jump point. The uncertainty could add days or weeks to their time to full medical facilities. And we'd have to go along; we all have Mackensee personnel on board. If the others are destroyed, I see no chance that the pirates would let us all get to the jump point unmolested. All they'd have to do is sit there until we tried to sneak in. Sure, some of us might make it, but . . . we need them gone."

"That still doesn't change our munitions situation," Hugh said. "And we could get out before the battle's over. So could *Metaire*."

"*Metaire* leaving now is a good idea," Ky said. "She's the most critical; she needs to be on the way with her casualties, but Kalin will probably insist on talking to the other Mac ships about it. I'll talk to Kalin first—no, Ransome first.

"Captain Ransome," she said. "Will you stay with the Mackensee ships, to relay communications? I'm going to talk to Colonel Kalin on *Metaire*, via *Courageous*, and try to convince him to leave the system now and get those wounded to a permanent facility. I'm sure he'll want to talk to his colleagues."

"Of course," Ransome said.

Baskerville, on *Courageous,* put her in touch with Colonel Kalin at once, and Ky explained why she thought he should make for the jump point at once, taking his wounded home.

"You make excellent points," he said, lips pursed. "I'll have to clear that with the relief convoy commander before I agree, however."

"*Courageous* and *Furious* are both ansible-equipped and can relay your communications in near real time," Ky said. "They're at your disposal for this."

"I'm sure we're going to want this technology," Kalin said. "Thank you again for your assistance—we'll let you know."

"Lattin was so right that we wanted more than one additional channel," Ky said to her com officer. "I never thought we'd need so many, but . . . it makes sense now." She checked with Pettygrew and Argelos on their munitions status.

"Two more ISC ships blown," Ransome broke in suddenly, his face stern. "One of them from its own munitions, apparently."

"Eleven ISC, four Mackensee . . . that puts them just one up on the pirates . . ."

"Nowhere near equal, if those ISC ships are as underweighted as your source told you," Hugh said. "Which, from their performance, I'm beginning to believe. They're big enough . . . good targets . . ."

Baskerville's face popped up in its window. "Colonel Kalin says he has permission to withdraw, and requests my escort to the jump point. He says he has mapped the

minefield and will make one jump to a few kilometers
from it, then proceed to the jump."

"Thank you," Ky said. "I recommend that you do as
he asks, but take position on the far side of the minefield from him, where you have clearer scan range. He
should be able to give you coordinates—"

"He has, already. Back in a flash!" Baskerville's smile
looked tense, but he was still smiling. Ky gave herself a
mental shake as his image disappeared. Now she had to
reply to the Mackensee convoy commander, Colonel
Bandes.

"We're all low on munitions," she said. "I have the only
ship with a beam weapon, in the bow, and I have only a
twenty-seven-degree arc. We cannot sustain a long fight, and
if we're all involved in that, and don't achieve a decisive
victory, getting out of the system could be . . . difficult. I'm
thinking our best use is as Labienus—the unexpected
reserve."

Ransome must have moved in very close; the delay was
only a couple of seconds before Bandes replied.

"You know military history," he said with a tight grin.
"I remember—you were in a military academy, weren't
you? Yes, you could be very effective as a surprise reserve,
if we need it. I appreciate your willingness—otherwise
we'd be abandoning this ourselves, as it looks entirely
too close . . . I'm afraid ISC would blame us for losing
their fleet, but we can't do what they haven't. My suggestion is that you come in from behind the jump point—
even microjump just beyond it if you can—and broadcast
a message to those following you—not that there are
any—"

Ky grinned. "We can definitely do that. We'll move in so
we can respond very quickly indeed. You could set it up
with transmissions they'll intercept, about the reinforcements

you expect. Maybe that we went off to meet other units of yours and lead them here?"

"Grandmother. Eggs. Sucking. Do you have that expression?"

"Yes, Colonel, we do. My apologies."

"Never mind. We're engaged now. Damn, they're good. Lucky for us our shields are stronger than they thought—"

Ky spoke to her other captains. "If I knew where to send our transport, to meet up with later, I would. But as it is, we'll leave her here, and the three of us will jump here—" She gave them the coordinates. "Weapons on standby; don't bring them live until we jump into the fray."

They emerged from that microjump only light-minutes from the battle; scan monitors filled almost instantly with the data pouring in. Their com was stuffed with backed-up messages from ISC, the first few demanding that they surrender . . . then the preliminary conversations with the pirates' assumed identities . . . then with Mackensee, a plea for help that included a plea to Ky if she was within hearing. Communications between ISC and Mackensee . . . all lightlagged to the point that messages on both sides were obsolete before they could be received.

ISC had lost another ship in those few seconds of transition from the outer system to the region of the jump point; the remaining ten were in two groups of five. The pirate ships had gone into the familiar X-attack formation, two triads—one of them short its heavy component—on each arm. The fifth triad had positioned itself at a distance, on a vector where the pirate shots would not endanger it.

"That's their commander," Ky said; she had channels open to Argelos and Pettygrew so they could listen in.

"Looks like," Hugh said.

"Would your Colonel Bandes catch that?" Ky asked Pitt.

"I don't know, Captain," Pitt said. "You've seen their attack patterns before; he hasn't. He might think it's a reserve force."

"I don't think so," Ky said. "I wonder how close we could get our captured stealth vessel to it . . ." She called Bandes. "That outlying triad—I think that's their commander, and it might be the head of the whole mess, Gammis Turek."

"You think we should go after him?"

"No—you've got enough going on where you are." From this distance, scan could pick out the flare of shields, even the launch of missile flights. "I'm going to try to sneak the stealthed vessel we captured up to it and find out."

"Good luck," Bandes said. "Aha! Got one!" He transferred his own scan image to Ky; she saw that two ships in one triad had been knocked out; the third appeared to be damaged. "Their missile defense AI isn't as good as ours."

Ky called Yamini on the prize ship. "Can you maintain stealth while microjumping?"

"Not as well as when holding still. We'll leave mass anomaly footprints."

"I'm hoping they won't have time to analyze every little mass anomaly, not with all the ordnance flying around," Ky said. "That outlying triad . . . I think that's their command group. If we can knock that out—"

"This thing doesn't have weapons to speak of," he said.

"I know. But you should be able to confirm if it's the command group or not by timing its transmissions to the behavior of the other triads. It'll have to say something. They just lost some ships; there'll be adjustments. From there, you'll see what they see. And you may be able to spook them into leaving: when our group comes in as if we're leading reinforcements, transmit on their own channels that you have located the command group and here they are. Have your microjump out programmed in, and hit it—I don't think they can react fast enough to hit you, if that's the first they know of you."

"That's not bad," Yamini said. "If we survive, I'll say it's a great idea."

Ky's scan did not pick up Yamini's movement to the outlying triad; she hoped their scan didn't. Another ISC ship blew; Mackensee's superior shields and defensive suites kept them whole in the maelstrom that now covered hundreds of thousands of cubic kilometers, but that wouldn't last forever. Even military ships had power limits, and enough impact could overload the best shields.

"Looks nasty in there," Pettygrew said. Even as they watched, another pirate ship and two more ISC ships vanished in a scatter of debris. "You aren't going to try to use your beam, are you?"

"Intermittent," Ky said. "My bow shield will be open only as long as the beam's on, and it'll erase anything in its path. I'm not dropping the shields to gain beam time. The rest of you keep your shields up full, and we'll try to stay on the edges." The edges looked almost as unhealthy as the dense interior of the fight; her scan showed red zones in shades indicating the probability of a shield-ripping encounter—most of it at 100 percent.

"I don't care that Bandes hadn't called yet. That's too edgy. We go now," she said. "On my mark, this formation—"

They emerged into chaos, proximity alarms pinging, shields flaring almost at once as debris impacted. Ky had the com on general broadcast. "Labienus, Labienus, follow on . . . Labienus, Labienus, all units follow on! Target Blueridge beacons!"

She had one of her comtechs monitoring the channels the pirates used in the onboard ansible, and within seconds she heard Yamini say, "Enemy command group in view: enemy command group. Labienus units, mark these coordinates."

A burst of pirate jargon followed, chatter crashing into chatter until one voice shouted something and the channel went silent. Ky microjumped nearer and decided to make another jump before reorienting the ship for the best angle for her forward beam. Another short jump and—that triad disappeared from scan as Lee brought the ship around to line up the beam.

"I should've taken the shot anyway," Ky said. "It was long but it might've done something—"

Pirate chatter returned, this time sounding more frantic than cheerful.

"He ran," Pitt said, brows raised. "That was their commander and he ran off and left them—"

"Microjumped to somewhere else," Hugh suggested. "He's got an onboard ansible; he can communicate just as well from anywhere except FTL space."

But one of the pirate triads, poised for another attack, now fired a salvo at Ky's group, from far too great a range to be effective, and also disappeared from scan.

"They're pulling out, or they're regrouping?" Ky said, considering. The remaining two triads completed their next attack run but then kept going, boosting to higher and higher velocities.

"Can't catch those," Hugh said. "Not even with the Ranger ships. And they won't get back into position for attack for a long time, the way they're going. If that's not a prep for jumping out of the system, I don't know what is."

"We're not out of trouble yet," Ky said. On scan, yet

another ISC ship blew, from what cause she couldn't tell in that mess of danger signals. Then a Mackensee ship, the smallest, disappeared from scan. Ky called Ransome. For once he didn't look eager and happy; his face was pale and streaked with sweat.

"We're in between two bigger ships," he said. "Their shields are helping but . . . I never saw anything like this."

"The pirates are gone, at least for now," Ky said. "I think we spooked their commander enough that he got out, and now the thing to do is get you and everyone else out of that killzone. Do you still have contact with Colonel Bandes?"

"Yes," Ransome said. "I'll tell him."

The relay continued to work, somewhat to Ky's surprise. "You say they're all gone?" Bandes said. "Our scan's so overloaded, we're having trouble picking out ship beacons."

"If you can microjump out a few light-hours, we can regroup," Ky said. "Can you contact the ISC commander?"

"Not easily," Bandes said. "It's one of the things—their damned protocols, and the lightlag—but I'll try."

In the end, only six of the ISC ships made it out, and two of those had serious damage. The incoming Mackensee convoy had lost its scout ship and had damage to both troop carriers and the supply ship, with a number of non-fatal casualties. Five pirate ships had been completely destroyed; Baskerville, in *Courageous,* located another limping along under stuttering insystem power, shields down and the missile pods on one side half melted off. Not worth salvage or the risk to personnel if they tried to capture her.

"We can take care of it," Ky told Bandes. "Or, if you want, you can have the honor."

"Did you ask the ISC commander?"

"I'm not sure any of the ISC ships could take it," Ky said.

Bandes chuckled. "Go ahead, then. You've earned the right."

"It's shooting fish in a barrel," Argelos said when Ky told him what they were going to do next.

"Nasty fish. Poison fish. If it bothers you . . ."

"Me? Not at all. I was gloating, actually." Argelos' first salvo breached the hull, and moments later Ky's and Pettygrew's met in the center of mass and blew it apart.

As the scan for that area filled with multiple tiny returns, Pettygrew said, "Mapping this system is going to be a mess for a while. We'll have to warn someone—I don't even know who—to mark this system off limits for a while."

Ky said nothing; Pitt glanced at her. "What is it, Captain?"

"Just—acknowledging their humanity," she said. "Bad though they were, they were once people. Tiny babies, maybe even children someone loved. People who might have been something other than scum of the universe, if things had been different." She met Pitt's gaze squarely. "I'm quite willing to blow them away, but not to pretend it meant nothing."

Pitt nodded. "I understand that, Captain. Doesn't surprise me."

When they got back to the others, close enough to communicate nearly in real time, Ky found that the ISC commander was particularly angry with her.

"It's all your fault," he said. "I lost ships, crews—all because you had to fiddle around with an ansible you had no right to approach, let alone touch. And as for that—thing—you're using to communicate, it's illegal. You're going to be arrested and tried—"

"I don't think so," Ky said. "Have you picked up your messages from the system ansible yet?"

"What business is that of yours?"

"One of them concerns me, and it comes from a high source in your company. I suggest you retrieve it now."

"You can't give me orders—"

Ky fought her temper down. "I didn't give you an order; I made a suggestion. If you want to ignore it and risk the consequences—"

"What consequences?"

"What would've happened if my ships and Mackensee had jumped out and left you to the pirates?"

That silenced him for a moment; his jaw worked. Finally he said, "All right. I'll look. But I assure you that I am thoroughly familiar with ISC rules and regulations, and with the Uniform Commercial Code as it applies to ISC installations—"

"I'm sure you are," Ky said. She looked at the scan of the system. "As it will be hours before you can retrieve your messages, we're going to set up a defensive perimeter just in case. There will be no call on your resources during that time." When she glanced at the ansible screen, Colonel Bandes' image looked as if he might burst out laughing. She turned to that console.

"I'm impressed, Captain Vatta," he said. "And you certainly picked the right moment to come in. I had just opened my mouth to ask you when you appeared on scan close in. And going after the commander alone—that was overly risky, don't you think?"

Ky explained what she had told Yamini to do. "I hoped it would panic them either enough to let me get a good shot at them, which I almost did—or make them move, or even leave. They'd lost a third of their ships; our doctrine said most forces wouldn't stay cohesive with quick losses that high."

"That's what our research shows, too," Bandes said. "And I have recordings of ISC transmissions that show they were falling apart after they lost the third ship, but couldn't figure out where to go. Their fire was never that effective, but some of them quit even trying to attack the pirates. If they'd had a coordinated fire pattern—but that's post-battle analysis."

"They're really annoyed with me," Ky said. "I hope they'll be less so when they get the message that's waiting for them."

"You know what's in it?"

"In substance, yes. In words, no."

He tilted his head. "You're a very interesting person, Captain Vatta."

Ky could think of nothing to say to that.

TWENTY-ONE

At the time he'd calculated the ISC fleet should arrive in the system where Ky was, Rafe found he could not sit still. He left Emil to forward messages and went down to Control, where the feed from ansible Boxtop-zip-figaro-112 was already shunted to a station set for him. If only this had been a system ansible, with its array of sensors to monitor activity in its area, he could have seen for himself what was going on. But this ansible, intended only to relay messages from other ansibles, lacked such enhancements. The only thing he could tell about it was that it was online. Control had a record of the message he had sent earlier. Rafe could not resist adding another. *Do Not Attack Vatta Ships. Do Not Attack Space Defense Force under any circumstances.—Dunbarger, Chairman.*

How long would it take them to retrieve their message? Had Ky at least moved away from the jump point, so they would have time to retrieve the message before they had a shot at her? She wasn't stupid, but she was . . . *just as stubborn at you are,* something whispered in his head.

"Are you worried about our fleet, sir?" one of the technicians asked. "I'm sure they'll be fine. We've never had any problem with privateers and such, once they recognize the ISC ship beacons."

It would not help his authority to tell her there was always a first time. "No," he said. "Or not the way you think. It's a complicated situation out there."

"Is it, sir? We haven't had any alarms from the ansible." Rafe glanced up. She stood just to one side and behind him, and seemed to have nothing to do but watch over him. Perhaps that was it. Even the Chairman couldn't be left alone with Control equipment—after all, he wasn't supposed to know how to operate it.

"We won't have, from this ansible," he said. "Relays can't do anything but tell us if they're tampered with. If it had the sensor capability of a full-service ansible, we could see exactly what's going on."

"But they might tamper with it again—"

"Who?"

"The people who tampered before—"

"They wouldn't. All they did was fix it when it wasn't working. That means they wanted it to work, so why would they turn it off?" From her puzzled expression, she wasn't used to thinking that way. "If anyone does tamper with it, it'll be someone else." The pirates Ky had worried might come back, for instance. If they did, the ISC fleet—his fleet—would be in trouble. Statistics on that sector fleet were no better than the average—old ships, outdated equipment, inadequate training schedule.

Emil pinged him. "Your guards want to know what to do with Cuthen. He's told them he's going to sue—"

"He can't do that if he can't call out," Rafe said. "But you may notify his family that he's been unavoidably detained. I'll speak to the guards myself." He called down to the cells. "This is Rafe—I understand our friend is threatening?"

"Yeah. Says he's going to have us all thrown in jail for unlawful imprisonment. Demands we let him out of this shielded room so he can use his skullphone."

"Tell him that his family has been informed that he's been unavoidably detained, but that he's perfectly safe," Rafe said. "Tell him that his safety still depends on the outcome of events now taking place, and I will let him know whether he's got a future life when I know what that outcome is."

"He says he needs rest," the guard said.

"So do we all," Rafe said. "He can rest when I'm satisfied. Are you . . . um . . . getting anything good out of him?"

"Oh, that pocket com you thought he had was full of data. I squirted it up to your office; Emil has it for you, or I can squirt it to you now."

"No, that's all right," Rafe said. He stared at the screen in front of him, which remained obstinately blank. Time was passing, things were happening—things he could imagine vividly in sixty different varieties of disaster—and he was stuck here, out of contact. He wanted to use his internal ansible—he wanted Ky to use hers—but if she was in the middle of a fight, he couldn't afford to distract her. Someone offered him a mug of something hot; he sipped it without noticing a flavor. His eyes itched and burned with staring at the console so long.

To distract himself, finally, he let himself think about his own family. His mother, his father, Penelope. His father's behavior could be explained by the damage to his implant and to his brain, and the years of insidious conditioning by Lew Parmina. As predicted, his mental status had deteriorated after removal of the damaged implant, and neural regeneration was proceeding very slowly, in part due to his age and partly because the damage was extensive. His attitude toward Vattas had hardened from suspicion to outright paranoia, but his doctors said many brain-injured patients became suspicious and somewhat irrational until they recovered . . . if they recovered. Brain injury as extensive as his father's often produced permanent changes in personality, one of the neurologists had said.

His mother, arbiter of family standards . . . she had seemed to come back rapidly after the rescue, but now, to his eye, she was looking more and more brittle. She scarcely ate that he could see, and her energy seemed more frenetic than natural. She called him daily at the office; she hovered over his father, over him, over Penelope.

Penelope . . . he could not imagine what it was like to lose a husband and a newborn by violence in such a short time. But he had no idea what she had been like before, as a grown woman. His clearest memories were of that night when she had been so frightened and he had been so . . . so mean. Why had he slapped her? He wouldn't have done that when they were playing together, no matter how annoying she was. He had known better; it was something good children did not do. So why? He had a vague memory of watching a video of some kind—at home, at a friend's house?—in which a man slapped a hysterical woman and she stopped crying. Was that why? Or was it his dark side, as the therapist had said? Even knowing the therapist had been incompetent didn't erase that doubt.

The screen lit suddenly; his attention snapped back to it. "ISC scout ship *Beremund*. Message received. No Vatta ship located. Blueridge Defense Alli—" The message cut off.

"Did you touch anything, sir?" asked the comtech standing by.

"No," Rafe said. He watched the technician manipulate controls.

"Ansible's still up, but there's no contact. Their equipment must have malfunctioned."

Rafe felt cold inside. "They were blown," he said.

"Blown, sir?" The comtech's expression was utter confusion.

"Attacked. Blown up. Pirates," Rafe said as she continued to look blank. "The Mackensee ship insystem wouldn't have fired on ISC. Neither would Vatta. Whatever this Blueridge Defense whatsis wants people to think, it's our enemy; most likely it's the same pirate force that overthrew Bissonet System. And others."

"But how can you tell that just because the message was cut off?" the technician asked. "Equipment fails for all sorts of reasons."

"When you know you have the potential for hostilities, the safer bet is enemy action," Rafe said. He called Emil. "We have trouble, almost certainly hostile action against ISC. Get me a conference call with all the sector commanders in Enforcement. Then I'll want to contact Mackensee—locate their headquarters system, and if their system ansible isn't working, dispatch a repair crew immediately, fastest route. And get me a list of the most reliable mercenary companies in our files. And—let's see—get hold of our own System Defense, and tell them I want a meeting with whoever's at the top."

"What's happened, sir?" Emil asked.

"I don't yet know, for sure," Rafe said. "But it's bad, and we don't have what it takes to handle it by ourselves."

"What about Cuthen?"

"His life hangs by a thread," Rafe said. "I'll get back to you."

By the time Emil had located the sector commanders

and set up the conference call, more data had come in. The Mackensee ship insystem, Ky, and the Mackensee relief convoy commander had all squirted data to the ansible, tagged for ISC headquarters, but the varying lightlags meant that data came in out of order in chaotic lumps.

Rafe did not wait for computer analysis to sort things into chronological order; he didn't need to.

"We have a serious situation," he said to the sector commanders, using another of Control's modules. Two techs now hovered over the console, aligning the images for his convenience. "An ISC sector fleet has been nearly destroyed, and the only reason it wasn't was the presence insystem of other ships that assisted our fleet."

"Are you sure?" asked one.

"The data will be squirted to you in code as soon as analysis puts things in order," Rafe said. "We've lost at least five ships—"

"Sorry, sir, new data, it's now six . . . no, seven . . ." a third technician murmured.

"Seven ships," Rafe said. "I expect that number to rise as more data come in. Our ships were hit by something calling itself the Blueridge Defense Alliance, but the ships have false IDs. By a lucky chance, the captain of one of the friendly ships recognized a serial number as belonging to a ship from Bissonet System, which as you know—I hope you know—fell to a pirate coalition."

"How many of these enemy ships?" asked one of the other commanders. "Any data on their weaponry?"

"Fifteen," Rafe said. "And the technical data will be in the same squirt." He paused; none of them spoke. "Now: in my short time as acting CEO, I have found that your maintenance, upgrade, and training budgets have been cut, and as a result our ships are markedly less able than those of other organizations, including this enemy. Some of you, I have no doubt, were colluding with Chief of Enforcement Cuthen to divert funds. I don't care, at this point—it's too late to worry about that. What I do care about is that you and your people aren't thrown in the meat grinder to no purpose." Another pause, longer this time. One of them—his implant informed him it was Bian Tarleton—opened his mouth and then shut it again.

"Go ahead, Tarleton," Rafe said.

"Sir, I—there's no way you can upgrade eighty percent of my ships at this point. They're approaching the end of their structural reliability; they'd have to be completely rebuilt."

"I know that. I also know that you have obsolete weaponry and some of you have dangerously old munitions. And your people haven't done live-fire training for an average of six years."

Now the resentment he saw on all the faces was replaced by dawning respect on some.

"How'd you know that?" Tarleton asked.

"I do my homework," Rafe said. "Here's the situation as I see it. All of you have what are essentially paper fleets: they look good on paper, they even look impressive in formation. As long as we had people convinced we were invulnerable, it didn't matter . . . but there's no way we can hide what happened. The enemy knows we're a soft target, and we're now a soft *rich* target."

"I told headquarters years ago!" one of them said.

"Years ago isn't our problem," Rafe said. "Placing blame won't get us out of this, though it certainly comes in later. So what I need from you right now is this: bring your fleets to what readiness you can, and start training your people for combat now. Review the data you'll be getting, and revise your plans accordingly. By tomorrow, I want a list from each of you of the most critical needs. We can't

meet all of them, but we might meet some. Pick your best
ships, however few that is, and get busy improving them.
By tomorrow I want your assessment of the battle that
cost us those ships; I want your plan for training that will
address the weaknesses that made things worse."

"By tomorrow?" asked one.

"Or if you can't do it, I'll find someone who can," Rafe
said. "If any of you feels unequal to command, I presume
you have someone down the chain of command to whom
you can hand over this onerous duty." His voice, he realized, had hardened.

"What about our regular duties?" asked one of the
others.

"Your top priority now is getting your command in as
good shape as you can. Next is informing all legitimate
governments that any entity calling itself Blueridge Defense
Alliance is actually a swarm of pirates. Do not waste any
time on routine enforcement; if systems want to repair
their own ansibles, all the better. We get income from message traffic, and the more complete the communications
net, the harder it will be for the pirates to evade detection."

Heads were nodding now, all but two. "If anyone has
comments, make 'em now, and then get busy. My assistant will set up another conference call tomorrow." None
of them spoke, and he clicked off.

"Another ship gone, sir," said the tech who had spoken
before. She looked very pale; glancing around the room,
he saw that everyone was tense. And so they should be,
but panic wouldn't help, either.

Rafe stood up and raised his voice. "We've lost ships;
we've lost people. Some of them may be your friends, or
relatives, or just people you contacted regularly. It's a blow,
no doubt about it, but it's not the end of ISC. I told our

sector commanders to prepare for more trouble. But I'm hoping that we will find allies to help all civilized, legitimate governments and organizations survive and defeat these pirates."

"But . . . but could they attack here?" came a timid voice from the back.

"They might, but I'm not going to let that happen," Rafe said. "I'm going to meet with our government, warn them of the danger, and assure them that ISC will support system defense to the fullest extent possible. Some of you, I know, are aware of my decision that we will not prosecute or interfere with systems repairing their own ansibles. We need as much communication as we can get; these pirates used the lack of ansible access to hide, organize, and attack."

He looked around. Too many scared faces, too many people looking for a way out. He smiled at them. "We will get through this," he said. "ISC has survived challenges before, and we'll do it this time. You are all intelligent, skilled people . . . you can help us pull through. There will be changes, yes: we have to meet this challenge, not just sit and let it happen to us. But you're the kind of people who can do that."

Better now; they were listening, they were not as tense, not as frightened.

"The ships that hit our fleet did not escape unscathed, and they are far away—even if they headed directly here, which they won't, they're not going to hit Nexus today or tomorrow. It's not physically possible. We are going on emergency schedules; I want doubled watches posted here, so that every change in ansible function, every bit of data we can gather, will be noticed as soon as possible. If someone is able to locate and identify the pirate fleet . . . well, that would be an enormous help."

"Who was it that helped us?" someone asked.

"Mackensee Military Assistance Corporation. I'll be contacting their chief, to thank them and ask for some more help. And the new group, Space Defense Force."

"Weren't they the ones who . . . ?"

"Fixed that ansible? Yes. Neither of those two had many ships in the system, but they did assist our fleet and finally drove off the attackers. From what I gather, Space Defense Force figured out where the pirates' commander was and attacked that ship directly. They weren't able to destroy it, but they did chase it out of the system, and the surviving pirate ships followed."

"So they're not really against us?"

"Not at all," Rafe said. "Now. I need to go back up to my office and contact the government and Mackensee. I trust you'll all keep at your stations here, and let me know if there's anything new—"

The chorus of "Yes, sir" and "Of course, sir" sounded firm enough. Rafe waved to them and headed back upstairs. He was tempted to stop off at the Enforcement safe rooms, but Ky was alive and he had no excuse for roughing up Cuthen himself. More urgent matters awaited. He needed to get ansibles onboard all ISC ships, for one thing, not those pitiful booster units.

"You've got a call from home," Emil said as Rafe came past him. "Your mother sounds upset; she wants to know when you'll come home."

Outside, the day had already darkened into night again. A clear night; the glowing cloud of the Arctan Nebula hung over the city. He shouldn't go home; he had too much to do. Those calls to the government, to Mackensee. He could make them from home, but then his parents would want to know what was going on.

"What about the government?" he asked Emil.

"The office was closed by the time I got your message, sir. I didn't know how urgent it was."

"Urgent—but probably not worth interrupting the secretary at dinner." And he himself was tired; he could feel it in his shoulders, in his eyes. When had he last slept? Before the blizzard began? "What about Mackensee?"

"I've contacted their local office; the ansible in their system is still down. I've directed the nearest ISC repair team to go there—it'll be several days."

"Good work," Rafe said. He noticed that Emil, too, had dark circles under his eyes. "Take a shift off at least, Emil. Get a proper meal, somewhere off the premises, and a good night's sleep."

"Are you sure that's all right?"

"You have a skullphone—I can always wake you if I need you. I'll go home tonight; call the car. We can drop you somewhere if you like."

On the drive across the city, Rafe tried to sort out how to tell his father what was going on. He shouldn't; the doctors had said to limit business talk. But every time he came in the door, his father had a hundred mumbled, semi-coherent questions along with a stream of advice. He felt smothered, trapped in his father's expectations, his father's . . . he hated to say it even to himself . . . his father's limitations.

How could his father not have seen what Lew Parmina was? How could he have let ISC's fleet slide into obsolescence? He'd always thought of his father as completely competent, all-knowing; even when he was angriest with the man, he'd felt pride in being Garston Dunbarger's son. Now . . . he felt pity for his father, for what had happened to him, for his struggles in rehab, but his admiration had dimmed as he dug into ISC and found so many things so badly awry.

What he should do was move out, separate himself from the family. At the thought of having his own place, a place without the associations of so much misery, he felt better immediately. If he lived closer to headquarters— even *in* headquarters; the guest suite could be rearranged for him—he would lose less time traveling back and forth. Weather conditions would matter less.

By the time the car turned into the drive, he had decided that moving out was the best possible solution to the whole family entanglement. The house loomed ahead, the familiar pattern of its façade, the windows, the portico. How, he wondered suddenly, did it seem to his family? Twice this house had been invaded, once successfully. Yet he could not imagine his parents living anywhere else.

He paused outside the door of the house, scraping his feet carefully. This was not going to be easy. He put his hand to the reader, and the lock opened; a chime sounded inside as he pushed it open. He wished he'd been able to persuade his parents that they needed to have someone in the house to answer the door, but he hadn't. At least they hadn't balked when he upgraded the house security system and hired more external guards to patrol the grounds.

"Rafe—I thought you were never coming home—" His mother came from the music room.

"The snow finally stopped," he said.

"You could work from home; your father did some-times."

"He knew everyone, and everyone knew him," Rafe said, unwrapping his scarf, slipping out of his coat. "I need to be visible, on the job. Parmina had a lot of people confused, and his departure has left . . . holes . . . in various depart-ments." He glanced at the door to the library, where his sister Penelope stood, wrapped in a big shawl, her shoulders hunched. "How—"

"Don't ask," Penelope said. His mother drew in her breath; his sister came forward with a quick, angry glance at their mother. "I lost my husband," Penelope said. "I lost my baby. How do you think I'm doing?" Her gaze swept the entrance hall, and *in this house* carried to him without words. In this house where she'd been the night they were abducted, the night her husband died. Where she'd been the night Rafe had saved her, and terrified her, and the night he had not saved her, and the terror went on too long.

She needed to go somewhere else, too . . . but would she? Could she?

"What's for dinner?" he asked, retreating from that dilemma. His sister's face twisted a moment into a knowing look that recognized his retreat.

"A well-balanced meal designed by a medical nutritionist," Penelope said. Her voice matched her expression: cold and scornful.

"Dear—" his mother said.

"Well, it is," Penelope said. "It doesn't matter what it *is*, that's what it tastes like. The right amount of protein, carbohydrates complex and simple, the right amount of fiber and vitamins and minerals . . . they sent a cook with a list, Rafe. What father should have, how much, and so on."

"It's not that bad," his mother said. "Quite good, really—"

"I've been told it tastes that way to me because I'm depressed," Penelope said. Rafe eyed her. She looked far worse than she had when they first came back.

"It's probably too early," he said, as they went into the living room. "But I was going to ask if you could possibly do a little work for me."

Her expression shifted a little. "Work? What kind?"

"Rafe, she can't possibly; how can you ask?" his mother said.

"Mother, please. I have nothing to do all day around here except . . . what I do. Mope. Cry. Go to therapy. Mope and cry some more. Have nightmares."

"I'm sorry," Rafe said. "I don't remember what it is you studied, if I ever knew, but you are family, and I know I can trust you. There's a ton of data to go through, trying to untangle Parmina's relationships in the company. I need someone to help me with that. Even a couple of hours a day would help."

"Do you think I could?" she asked.

"Rafe, you can't be serious," his mother said. "After all she's been through, she doesn't need—"

"Mother, please—I need to get out of this house!" Penelope said. She turned to Rafe. "If I just have something to do, something useful . . . I may not do it well . . ."

"Be ready to leave when I do in the morning," Rafe said, keeping his tone light. "I'll take you in with me. We'll see how it goes." Clearly, Penelope couldn't be expected to leave tonight, as he had planned to, nor should she make her own way to ISC headquarters . . . he would have to spend at least another night here, and tell his parents in the morning that he was moving out.

Dinner was not as bad as his sister had said, but nothing like the meals he remembered. His father, propped in a float chair, seemed barely able to feed himself; a medical attendant sat beside him, murmuring suggestions. His father's left eyelid drooped almost shut, and his mouth sagged. Rafe felt his stomach tightening. They were all worse than they had been even three days ago, before the storm. Was something wrong with their medical care? Had Parmina somehow arranged to mess with that?

Rafe ate steadily, silently, glancing now and then at his

mother. She ate little that he could see, perched like a bird about to take flight on the edge of her chair. His sister ate even less . . . one or two bites of each offering, that was all.

His father tried to speak, his one good eye fixed on Rafe, but managed only a rough jumble of noises. Supposedly the left side of his brain hadn't been damaged; why was his speech so impaired? Like everything else, it had worsened over the past weeks. Rafe struggled to hide his worry and concentrated on the sounds, trying to parse meaning from them.

"Everything's going well," Rafe said, interpreting this as a request for information, information he was not about to impart. "We've found a few more of Parmina's cronies and we've taken care of them."

"No business worries . . ." the attendant said to Rafe, with a warning glance.

"Sorry," Rafe said. "I'm glad to see you up and around, Father. That was quite a snowstorm. When the weather is bad, I may spend nights at the office—please don't be concerned if I don't come home." He shot a glance at his mother. "In fact, I was thinking of getting a place near the office—or even bunking in that guest apartment."

His father's hand twitched, sending a spoonful of the steamed greens flying onto the carpet. The attendant bent to wipe it up.

"I want to do a good job," Rafe went on, hoping his face matched the tone he was trying for. "I want to take care of the company—as you asked me—"

"Yuh . . . duhnuh . . . dih-wih-vvvvatttah . . ."

"You'll be better soon," Rafe said. No one else might have understood that, but he knew that *You do not deal with Vatta* was what his father wanted to say. "If you rest, if you do what they tell you. I know you'll be all right,

and I will take care of things for you in the meantime."
He finished his own meal, all he could eat, and looked at
his mother. "Mother, I need to take a long, hot bath, if
you don't mind."

"Of course not," she said, her brow furrowed a little.
"Are you coming down later?"

"Not if I fall asleep in the tub," Rafe said, forcing a
smile. "Don't wait for me, I beg you."

When he emerged from the bathroom, rubbing his hair
dry, his sister was waiting in the hall, shoulder propped
into the corner between a case of antique porcelain belt
ornaments and the wall.

"Were you serious? About giving me a job?"

"Yes," Rafe said.

"I hate this house," she said with quiet intensity. "I've
hated it since . . . and then what happened made it worse.
I can't sleep here. I keep seeing . . . what happened. Jared's
face . . . when they shot him . . . and . . . then it comes
back, that night when you saved me. It's always cold; I'm
always cold. I tried to tell Mother I wanted to move out,
find someplace. She thinks I'm better here, or I should
go back to our—to Jared's and my house—and I just can't.
And *you're* getting out, aren't you? I can tell. You don't
want to live in that little boy's room; you're not that boy
anymore. You'll get your own place, or stay at the office,
and I'll be here with . . . with all this." She waved again
at the surroundings.

"It . . . would be easier to do my job if I lived closer,"
Rafe said.

She gave him a long look. "Would Father be happy if
he knew exactly what you were doing?"

"What kind of a question is that?" Rafe asked. "Why
would you think not?"

"Because you're you," she said. "You're not like him . . .

you have that other . . . that other flavor. What are you doing, Rafe?"

"Come and see," Rafe said, trying to keep it light.

"Is it all going away?" she asked, her eyes shifting now from his face to the hall, to the pictures on the walls, the carpet on the floor. "Is something wrong with ISC?"

"You are in deep grief," Rafe said. "You are seeing all the darkness there is, and that's perfectly normal—"

"But there is something wrong, isn't there—I can feel it—"

This was not a conversation he wanted to have here, in the hall, where anyone might hear. Yes, his father was supposed to be having a final series of exercises before bed, but houses had been bugged before.

"You are upset," Rafe said. "Tomorrow will be different; tomorrow you won't spend all day here. And if you can show me that you have a definite plan in mind, I'll help you move away, if that's what you need."

She stared at him now . . . was she as irrational as she looked? He didn't know; he had no idea how to interpret her expressions, her quickly changing moods. "But I'm . . . I'm not like I was . . . I never will be . . ."

"Doesn't matter," Rafe said firmly. "Yes, you'll need to stay in therapy—you've had terrible things happen, and everyone needs help after something like that. But I'm here, and I'll help you." She looked as if she might cry again; Rafe was too tired to deal with that, he told himself. "Good night, Tinkabear," he said, softly. For a moment, her face lit up: it had been her nickname as a toddler.

In the morning, she was dressed and ready by the front door, holding a small suitcase, when he came down. He didn't comment; he, too, was carrying a suitcase, packed with two of his new suits and other necessities. The house was silent; his parents, he hoped, were still asleep. Rafe tapped out the security code; the car outside answered. He opened the door for her, nodding as she went past, and called softly into the silent house "We're on our way!" as cheerfully as if they were headed for a picnic.

On the ride into the city, she settled herself warily into the wide backseat; her face was pale and her fingers tightened on her case every time they went around a corner. Finally, in the last stretch up to the entrance, she said, "I'm not going back."

"No one can make you," Rafe said. "Certainly not me."

"No one can—you just said that."

"So I did. Now, what time is your usual therapy appointment, and do you go, or does someone come?"

"The doctor comes. At eleven."

"We'll call, to be sure the doctor comes here . . . unless you'd rather go to someone's office—and by the way, do you like this therapist?"

"It doesn't matter." Her voice had gone soft.

"Of course it does. You'll get better faster with someone you like and trust."

"Not . . . really. He's all fatherly and comforting, but I can tell he thinks I'm just a spoiled girl who will always be too weak."

Whether the therapist really thought that or not was not as important as his sister's belief. Rafe felt the family bond tightening around his shoulders, a noose that would hold him here longer, keep him from Ky. And yet—this was Tinkabear, Pretty Penny, Pennyluck . . . all the silly childhood pet names came back to him. This was the little sister he'd smacked one time, and much good it had done her. She was his only remaining sister, all he had, really. He could not abandon her just because she was so unlike Ky.

"I'm sure that's not the only good therapist in the city," he said. "But first, let's be sure Mother doesn't panic when she finds you gone and the therapist is coming. Then we'll find you a place to stay. Do you want an apartment, or would you feel safer here?"

"I won't feel safe anywhere," Penelope said. "But—I'd like to be near you for a while."

He was not going to have her in his apartment . . . which meant they should both stay at headquarters for the time being. "Did you visit Father at work much?" he asked.

"No. Not at all since I married, and not much before that."

"Well then: welcome to the executive life." One of his bodyguards preceded them up the steps and through the door; Rafe led her to the security desk and spoke to the middle-aged woman there. "Hi, Sylvie. This is my sister Penelope; you will have her biometrics on file. We'll need an all-shift pass for her. She's going to be helping me out for a while."

"Of course, sir." Sylvie glanced up at Penelope. "If you would, please, put your hand in here and look into the hood. We need a current image for the tag." In less than a minute, the machine spat out a laminated tag; Sylvie punched a hole in it, attached the clip and a lanyard, and handed it over. "There you are."

Penelope clipped the tag to her jacket. Rafe waited as his bodyguard checked the lift and his fellow upstairs, then nodded. Rafe ushered Penelope into the lift with a low bow.

"Stop it," she said, turning pink. "You're being silly . . . people will look . . ."

"You used to like it when I played prince to your princess," he said, leaning against the wall. "Don't you remember the time you made me wear Linnet's dance tights and that coronet?"

This time she giggled. "I'd forgotten that. It must have been a scene out of one of the videos. And you kept wrapping Mother's evening cape around you, when it was supposed to trail out behind."

"There are reasons," Rafe said, putting on a scowl, "why I needed that cape . . . those blasted tights were too big."

The elevator coasted to a stop; Penelope stepped forward, but Rafe blocked her. "Why—" she began, but he caught the nod from his guard and stepped back.

"After you, Princess."

"You aren't going to call me Princess—"

"Only when you deserve it," Rafe said. "Now let's find you a desk—"

"Are you serious? You're really going to put me to work?"

Rafe shrugged. "Sitting around here doing nothing won't help you any more than sitting around home . . . the house. Emil, this is my sister Penelope. Find her a place to work, will you? On this floor, close to me. She's going to be helping me with some research. In the meantime, Penelope, come into my parlor . . ."

She gave him a weak, wavering smile.

TWENTY-TWO

By the time Rafe had rescheduled Penelope's appointment with the therapist, Emil had found her a quiet place to work, shifting an assistant one door farther away. Rafe cocked his head at Penelope. "Do you want me to call Mother, or—"

"Please," she said. "And tell her . . ." Tears spilled over.

Rafe felt helpless. Any of the usual comforting phrases would be an insult. "I'll tell her that you and I are both staying here for the time being. I think we can find a therapist who agrees that's best for you, if yours doesn't."

"Th-thanks," she said, swiping at her eyes. "I'm sorry—" She stood up. "I—I want to find a room—"

"Emil will show you," Rafe said. "If you need a restroom, or something to drink, or anything—"

When she had left his office, Rafe called home. His mother answered. "Rafe—where's Penny? Did she go with you? Is she all right?"

"Yes, she's fine. She's here with me. Her therapist is coming here today. We're going to stay here for a few days at least. She needs to get away for a while."

"Away? But this is her home; she's safe here."

"She was abducted from that house," Rafe said. "She doesn't feel safe."

"I—I don't—" Her face seemed to melt into grief. "I couldn't stop them . . . my little Penny."

"She'll be fine here, Mother," Rafe said. "I'll take care of her. There's a lovely apartment . . . and now, I'm sorry, I must go."

Emil had set up a call with System Defense, whose civilian chief had known his father well. "I was sorry to hear about his condition," Humphrey Isaacs said. "But he is expected to recover fully, isn't he? And return to work?"

"We certainly hope so," Rafe said. "But the damage was severe. The doctors can't tell us how long it will be, or whether any of the problems will remain. In the meantime, I have data vital to our systems security." Isaacs said nothing, and Rafe gave him a brief summary of the situation.

"ISC's fleet isn't more than a match for them?"

"No. It will take the combined forces of several systems to eradicate this threat. They have already overwhelmed several systems. Most of them weak and underpopulated, but one at least—Bissonet—mounted what we all thought was a sizable and effective space defense. Now they have Bissonet's ships as well as their own."

"Well . . . this is not what I wanted to start my workday with," Isaacs said, scowling. "You know—or at least your father knew—what our system defenses are. We depended heavily on ISC to round out our numbers."

Rafe knew more about Nexus's defense establishment than his father, but it would not be prudent to say so. Officially, here on Nexus, he had never had an identity who was supposed to know anything like that. "I will forward you the data gathered from the recent engagement," he said. "It is clear that the enemy have a variety of advanced technologies that give them an edge, ship for ship. We at ISC will be upgrading our fleet as quickly as possible; I would suggest you do the same."

"You don't think they'd attack Nexus, do you?" Isaacs asked. "We're one of the biggest, most powerful systems—"

"We're the richest target around," Rafe said. "And now that they've found ISC vulnerable, I expect they'll try to amass enough force to do just that. That may have been their aim all along. Capture Nexus and you have a central location already equipped as a communications center for all—or most—human-occupied space. Every system they capture gives them more resources—more ships, more weapons, more wealth. And every capture hurts the legitimate governments and organizations—economically as well as militarily, with the decline of trade. Even if the population resists, there will always be some who see personal profit in joining up."

"That's a frightening prospect." Isaacs looked more thoughtful than frightened, however.

"Yes. I believe it's going to require immediate consultation and cooperation with other systems to prevent serious consequences not just for us but for all civilized and peaceful systems."

"Can't ISC release some of its experimental technology to give us back that edge?"

"I haven't had time yet to look into our research program and see what would be suitable," Rafe said. "I do know there's a technology newly patented over in the Moscoe Confederation that would be of immense benefit. When I'm through talking to you, I'll be talking to the patent holder to find out how fast it can be produced."

"Get a license to make it here," Isaacs said.

"I tried," Rafe said. "The patent holder has a preexisting deal with the Moscoe government for local manufacture. But I'm hoping we can reserve the first production run."

"What is it?" Isaacs asked.

"I'd rather not say until I've locked in an order," Rafe said. "But if you can come by my office tomorrow—"

"I'll be there."

"Good. Talk to you then."

Rafe took a few minutes to check on Penelope. She was ensconced behind a desk, staring into a screen.

"How's it going?" he asked.

"I'm not sure what you want me to look for, Rafe. Emil gave me a stack of financial records . . . am I looking for embezzlement or . . . or what?"

"We have several problems, Penny, and I don't know which you'd be best suited to detect." Rafe hitched a hip onto her desk. "Embezzlement is one of them. I started by looking for Parmina's accomplices at the higher levels, the easiest way first: comparing their lifestyles with their known legal income. I figured he had to be paying them, or they had to be stealing from the company. Found one that way. But there are other problems with the company right now, and they're not necessarily the result of illegal actions. What I'd like you to do is analyze the relative amounts we've spent in the main divisions over the past thirty years. I think Research and Enforcement may have been consistently underfunded, but I don't know where the cream has gone."

"You want me to concentrate only on the main divisions?"

"Not if you find something that looks strange. Follow your nose. I need a better idea of where the money went—in all ways—and I need to know if it's fraud or stupidity or just inertia."

"Is ISC really in trouble?" she asked, as she had the night before. "And . . . is it Father's fault?"

"It's in trouble," Rafe said. "That much is certain; it's

what I told the Board. There's new technology loose that has broken our monopoly, though not everyone realizes it yet. We could have had that technology and marketed it ourselves. Instead, we didn't even patent it, and now someone else has the rights to it and has improved it. We're so far behind the curve, it's . . . it's as if we weren't on the same track. About Father—I don't know. One of the things I need to find out is if he made bad decisions, or if he didn't get the right data to make good decisions, or if his orders weren't followed."

"So this is one giant fishing expedition," Penelope said.

"Yup. And a lot of work. Work that needs to be done by someone I can trust. Right now there's no one in our financial divisions I can be sure of."

"I see," she said. "Well . . . I'll do my best."

"I'm sure you will," he said. "I've got to get back to the other stuff—we can talk about that later."

"What did Mother say?"

"What you'd expect. Don't worry about it. You're here and she's there. Later on, when I take a break, I'll take you over to the apartment and let you get your things settled. Or I can have someone take them now."

"No. I'd rather do it myself. If you're busy, where can I get something for lunch?"

"Ask Emil. He can order something up, or you can eat in the executive dining room. If you do that, one of my bodyguards will go with you."

She nodded. "It's . . . it is better here. I'm not seeing . . . that . . ."

"Good. Get yourself back to work, then. Your therapist will be here in about two hours; I'll want to talk to him as well."

As he went back to his office, Rafe was aware that one problem was—if not solved—maybe moving toward solution. At least Penny wasn't crying, and she looked more alive than she had at home.

He looked up the temporal conversions. It was evening on Cascadia Station. Stella might be having dinner with someone; she would not want to be interrupted. But he had to talk to her. He placed the call.

"It's Rafe," he said when she answered.

"I didn't think anyone else from Nexus would be calling," she said crisply. "We will announce the successful licensee tomorrow at noon, as previously stated."

"That's not what I called about," he said. "Are you in a secure location?"

Her face paled. "What—is Ky all right?"

"As far as I know, yes. But what I have to say concerns her."

"I believe this facility is secure, yes," Stella said. "Go on."

"The pirates ran into an ISC fleet. Ky was there. Actually, Ky was the reason the ISC fleet was there—not by my orders, by the way. Against them. But anyway—the pirates chewed up our fleet with ridiculous ease."

"And Ky got away?"

"Ky and a small number of Mackensee ships managed to drive the pirates away."

"That idiot!" Stella said. "She should have run for it."

"That's what I told her," Rafe said. "When I was told an ISC fleet was headed her way, I . . ." He stopped. Stella didn't know about their shared cranial implant. How could he cover that? "Ky's people had repaired a system ansible, a relay. That's what alerted our enforcement division; they sent the fleet, standard procedure, to capture whoever had done the repair. When I found out it was too late to stop the fleet, I contacted her and warned her. It's complicated—she'd already been in one battle, helping some mercenary ships fight off a pirate attack. She wouldn't leave the system because the remaining mercenary ship wouldn't leave. She said a merc relief convoy was on the way to bring supplies and change out trainees, but if the pirates returned in the meantime, the one ship would be helpless."

"So she didn't listen to you," Stella said. "That sounds like Ky."

"A very stubborn woman," Rafe said. "I think it runs in the family."

"You may think that," Stella said. "I prefer to call it perseverance."

"Apparently, everyone showed up in the system within a few hours: the ISC fleet, the merc convoy, and the pirates, who were calling themselves the Blueridge Defense Alliance. And using, according to an after-battle report I got from Ky, captured Bissonet military vessels."

"That's not good."

"No. But the real reason I'm calling you now is to ask if it's possible to preorder onboard ansibles in quantity. I know you haven't awarded any contracts, but how fast do you think you could scale up production, if you had the cash in hand?"

"ISC wants them?"

"Everyone's going to want them, but yes: ISC and also Nexus Defense. I'm sure Moscoe's defense will also want some, but I see Nexus as a prime target. It's clear from the post-battle data that ships without them are nearly helpless against ships that have them."

Stella frowned. "Until we have a test run, I don't know what the real production rate will be. If there's enough demand, we could expand to another factory, I suppose . . ."

"I spoke to someone high in our System Defense this morning; I believe by tomorrow I can get you a firm commitment. And I'm going to be in contact with a respectable mercenary company as soon as we can get their ansible up and running—"

"Mackensee?"

"Well . . . yes. They were involved in the incident with Ky, and their commander on the scene says they'll definitely want some."

"Rafe, this is going to shred ISC's monopoly."

"I know that. I've already informed our Board. We've got to find another way to survive—but letting the pirates take over isn't it."

"What does your father say?"

"I . . . he's still not . . . capable . . ."

"So it's up to you?"

"Yeah. That's a joke, isn't it? The exile returns and is supposed to take over and perform a rescue."

"You will," Stella said. "How's the rest of your family?"

Rafe shrugged. "About like you'd expect. My mother's determined to get things back to normal—which is impossible—and my sister's deep in depression." He stopped. "Which reminds me, I need to talk to her therapist and change her appointment for her. I'll call you later."

That was abrupt, but the best he could do, he felt.

"I suppose it's all right for her to move here for a short while," the therapist said, pursing his lips. "But she'll need careful supervision; she's certainly not ready to be on her own. Really, I felt that the nurturing home environment was the best thing for her."

"Nurturing home environment?" Rafe raised his brows. "You've been to our house?"

"I understand that you were removed from the house at an early age," the therapist said. "Perhaps your resentment has blinded you to the qualities such a home has to offer."

Rafe glared. "That house is the same house in which she was snatched up by a kidnapper and saved only because I shot him. That house is the same one in which she saw her husband murdered, as he tried to protect her, and from which she and my parents were abducted, to be held in captivity and tortured. She hates that house; she doesn't feel safe in that house."

"It is important for people like your sister to confront their fears—whatever *you* think. It's a lovely house—comfortable, beautifully furnished—"

"Did you notice the pale patch in the living room where her husband's blood had stained the floor and the intruders poured bleach on it to clean it up?"

"Er . . . no. If I may say so, you sound quite hostile and angry. It will not help your sister to be around a hostile person in her present state."

"You're evading the issue," Rafe said. "Penny's suffered severe trauma, physical and emotional. She associates that house with danger; she's told me that she can't sleep, that she relives both abductions over and over in that space where they happened. She needs to be where she feels safe . . ."

"You, sir, are not a therapist." The man's face had contracted to a knot of distaste. "You are disturbed; you have always been disturbed—"

"Excuse me?"

"Your therapist was my partner until his untimely death. I have seen your records. A born sociopath, a child killing without remorse; your subsequent course in the best possible therapeutic environment was proof of your deepseated disturbance—"

"Poppycock," Rafe said. He felt the dangerous edge of a magnificent and well-deserved rage, into which all the frustrations and angers of the past two days merged. And yet . . . this was Penny's therapist. He had to be sure she was taken care of. He took a breath. "I was a child who killed an adult intent on killing or harming him, and intent on killing or harming his sister. The fact you can't get around is that Penny and I would not be alive if I had not acted."

"But you should have felt—"

"Feelings are what they are. It's what you do with them that matters. I should have saved my sister and myself— and I did. I was scared; I was terrified; I used that fear to do what needed to be done. But that's decades in the past. Now it's my sister who needs help. And once again, I'm going to get her the help she needs—which is not being told to 'confront her fears' by staying in the location where the trauma happened. I'll be seeking another therapist for her—"

"You! You aren't qualified!"

"To do the therapy, of course not. To find her a competent therapist, yes. You will of course be reimbursed for today's session and this conference."

"You can't do this!"

"Penny is an adult. She is free to choose whomever she wants for her therapist. She does not want you."

"I'll have to hear that from her."

"Penny?" Rafe turned to the door.

Penelope came in.

"You don't really mean—" her therapist began.

"I don't want to keep seeing you," she said. "I know I need more therapy; Rafe will help me arrange it."

"My dear, you don't know what you're saying . . . your brother is . . . is not a safe companion for you."

"My brother rescued me twice," Penny said. "I think I'll take that over your notions of safety."

"Emil, see that this gentleman gets safely to his transportation," Rafe said. When the door had closed behind him, he cocked his head. "Penny . . . I'm sorry. I didn't realize the family had chosen someone like that for you."

"It's not your fault," Penny said. Her eyes were red and glittered with unshed tears; she blinked them back. "I think Mother just went automatically to the same clinic . . . it's what she knew, and she wasn't really thinking clearly. Neither was I. I didn't realize he'd been your therapist's partner. How will we find another?"

"By doing what I should've done in the first place," Rafe said. "The team I hired to get you out: they work with victims all the time. I'm sure they know the best in the business. I'll call Gary." He looked at the clock. "After lunch, I'll call Gary. Let's have lunch together. We can have it in the apartment; we can get you settled in there."

The apartment, meant for visiting VIPs, had a curved window overlooking the river and its park in the dining area. "This window . . ." Penelope said. She didn't look at the trays on the table with their insulated covers.

"One-way glass," Rafe said. "And armored. As well as a full alarm system—look at this strip here, and this. You will set the combination of your bedroom door to whatever you wish—it's unlocked now—but it has a pushbar emergency exit, so you can always get out. And I hope you don't mind—" He opened the bedroom door. "I saw how you seemed cold at home. And you brought only one small case. I ordered in some additional covers . . ."

Her eyes filled with tears again. "Rafe . . . thank you."

"I think we need lunch," he said. "Leave your case in there, freshen up."

"Yes . . ."

She actually ate some of the thick soup and warm bread he'd ordered. "I need to get back to work," Rafe said. "Do you need a nap, or are you good for another round of digging through figures?"

"I'll come," she said. "Unless I'm being too . . . clingy."

She was, but it wasn't her fault. Nothing was her fault, including his feeling of being trapped. "Not at all," he said. "And you'll want to be there when I talk to Gary about therapists—we need to find you the right one."

Gary had a list, as Rafe had expected. Penny's former therapist wasn't on it; when Rafe mentioned the man's name, Gary snorted. "If you're a socialite having anxiety attacks because your cook got sick two days before a dinner party, he might be of use. But not for anything serious. I've had clients before who went to him because he's the big name that social class knows about. Your sister needs one of the others. Consider the woman; all her trauma's been from men, right?"

"Good point," Rafe said. He glanced at Penny. "How do you feel about a woman therapist, Penny?"

"I . . . think I'd like that."

"Frieda's solid, sensible . . . her background's a little unusual, but she's helped all my clients who have gone to her. Want me to give her a heads-up?"

"I was going to call her right away, but—yes." Gary, Rafe knew, had data collected from the site that he had not shared with Rafe, data from the abductors' own files. Penny's therapist should have that.

"Go ahead; tell her we were the extrication team, and that I'll forward the usual background data."

Rafe called the woman's office. When he explained who he was, that his sister had been held hostage, and gave Gary's name, the therapist came online at once. She was a middle-aged woman, with streaks of white in her hair. "Let me speak to her, please," she said to Rafe. "It is her therapy. And if you could give her some privacy . . . ?"

Rafe called Penny over to the console and walked out

to Emil's desk, bemused that someone he hadn't actually hired yet was giving him orders.

"How's she doing?" Emil asked in a tone that made Rafe give him a longer look.

"As well as can be expected . . . Emil, are you falling for her?"

Emil looked startled. "No, sir. I just . . . she seems like such a nice girl—woman—and she's had such an awful experience."

"You're right, and that's exactly why she shouldn't have even such a paragon as you trying to get too close to her too soon."

"I wouldn't think of it, sir. I just hope . . . things go well for her from now on."

Rafe looked at Emil's earnest face and thought about saying more, but Emil was so young. And probably had a girl already, or a string of them. "Just be kind to her," he said.

"All right, Rafe, come on back," Penny called. The monitor was blank; she had ended the call. "I don't know if I like her, exactly, but . . . I feel good about her. I told her that I'd moved out of the house and she said that was a healthy decision." She paused. "I—I hope you don't mind my talking to her without you."

"Not at all," Rafe said. "She's your therapist; there's no reason for me to know everything you say to each other."

The rest of that day passed in a blur; the conference with the sector commanders on readiness, a call to Mackensee's local representative, another conference with the nearest sector commander on tactical analysis of the battle, plus the new Control supervisor wanting authorization for all the overtime doubling shifts would require, and queries from news media about the change in CEO.

He was just wondering whether to have a late supper sent up or go somewhere when his mother called. She looked haggard, and her voice shook. "Rafe! How could you! Firing Doctor Bradon like that—he's one of the most prominent therapists in the city. He called me—he was so upset. He says you're not fit to take charge of Penelope, that your separating her from her family means you want to control her. Rafe, I know you're not as bad as he says, but—"

"Mother, please." Rafe took a deep breath. "Listen— Doctor Bradon was affiliated with the same therapist who caused me so much grief. More important than that, Penny didn't feel comfortable with him. She has a new therapist, someone Gary recommended—"

"Gary—?"

"The man who commanded the team that got you out. He is the system expert on hostage extrication; he has a list of therapists he knows who are particularly skilled in helping people recover from that experience. Penny's already talked to one, and decided to try her for a time."

"Doctor Bradon said you might say something like that, and he said if she got a new therapist it must not be a woman . . . that she has issues which require a male therapist . . ."

"I looked this woman up," Rafe said. He didn't need to tell her it was after Penny had already decided. "She has multiple publications in reputable journals on issues relating to the care of survivors of serious trauma. She has taught in two medical schools, and is still on the adjunct faculty of one of them."

"Oh."

"Mother, I am not interested in controlling Penny. I do want her to heal from all this as quickly and as thoroughly as possible . . . and that wasn't going to happen in the same house where she saw her husband killed."

"I just wanted things to be like they were . . ." His mother was crying now. "I thought if . . . and Doctor Bradon says she needed to confront her fear . . ."

"I'll give you the names of the therapists Gary recommends," Rafe said. "You can see for yourself that they have solid credentials."

"I just want . . ." Her voice choked off. Rafe squeezed his own eyes shut and waited. What she wanted was impossible, as impossible as his child's wish for that awful night to have been a dream. Or his wish now that the abduction had never happened, that he could have come home to have a cool but nonhostile conversation with his father, perhaps visit the house to have a meal . . . and then gone back to his own life, far away from Nexus.

"You must think I'm crazy," his mother said finally. "Crying like this. It's over. I should be over it."

"No," Rafe said. "I don't think you're crazy." His stomach growled, reminding him that dinner was long overdue. He had been hungrier before, he told himself.

"The house is so . . . so empty. So . . . big. And your father . . ."

Rafe had a moment's terror that she was thinking of moving into headquarters with his father . . . the thought of all of them here . . .

"But we have to stay; we have to show we aren't afraid."

"Mother, all you and Father have to do is recover. You don't have to prove anything to me or anyone else. If you need to go to . . ." He racked his brain. They had had a summer cabin in the mountains, but it was too much like the resort where they'd been held, logs and all. "Why not that place in the islands? The warm water would be good for Father; you know the house is cold and relatively isolated in winter. Some of your friends are probably down there already."

She said nothing for a long moment; he was afraid she'd start crying again. "Rafe, I . . . you may be right. I'll talk to the doctors . . . I don't know what Doctor Bradon will say . . ."

"I'll check with Gary and see if one of the therapists he recommends is in the area. I'm sure we can find someone, and Father's medical team can travel with him. If this is what you decide."

"I—I'll think about it. I really will. I'm just so . . . so tired all the time these days."

"Of course you are," Rafe said. "But some time in the warmth and sun might help you more than this gloomy cold." She had always loved the tropics.

"My houseplants—"

"We can get a plant service in to take care of them."

She sighed. "Maybe you're right. Maybe . . . and it's only going to get colder. I'll look up some of the places, see if anything's open."

For the wife of ISC's former CEO, someplace would be open, if he had to bribe someone to cut their own vacation short. "That's what I have a personal assistant for," Rafe said. "Let me take care of it."

"Would you?"

"Yes, but not without checking with you to be sure it's what you want. I'm not trying to force you into anything—" *Not much,* he told himself. He wanted his parents out of the city, into someplace safe, and out of his hair. Yes, he believed it would be good for them to be out of that house, with all its toxic memories, and into a warmer climate . . . but he was still manipulating them with all the skill he had used on unsuspecting marks before. And he knew it.

"Thank you, dear," his mother said. "I'll just let you take care of it, then. I know it's the high season, but if you could, something with a view—"

"I'm sure we can find something you like," Rafe said. After his mother clicked off, he put a note in Emil's file. Perhaps he could get through supper without another crisis. A night's sleep was probably too much to hope for.

TWENTY-THREE

That depressing prediction came true in the middle of the night, when he was woken with the news that the Mackensee home system ansible was now functional.

"I knew you'd want to know right away," the communications tech said.

"What's the time conversion?" Rafe asked, yawning.

"For Mackensee headquarters? It's about midafternoon there . . ." Rafe heard someone in the background tell the tech to be accurate. "Um . . . it should be 1430 there, sir, but I don't know if they have seasonal time changes."

"Thank you," Rafe said. It was 0213 here, and his eyes felt gritty. He lay back and closed them, but his mind raced. He was awake. He was far too awake to go back to sleep. Sighing, he sat up. He was in one of the small guest rooms for lower-ranking overnight guests: comfortable enough but dull, all tans and browns with a single landscape print on the wall. The adjoining bath unit was compact; he showered and dressed, adjusting his suit carefully. A CEO should look like a CEO, his father had always said.

In his office, he set up the secure ansible relay and took a moment to review what ISC knew about Mackensee's current chief. A senior executive in Enforcement had been sent as a personal representative, and had completed a detailed assessment of Arlen Becker, the current CEO. He was still listed: Mackensee's CEOs usually served for five local years in that position. Rafe scanned the file. Becker's profile fit what he'd expected; the man looked like the retired general he was. He had kept himself fit; his implant bulges were almost concealed by silvering hair. And Mackensee, proven innocent in the Sabine affair, had retrieved their bond in its entirety.

No more delay. Rafe activated the link. The first face on the screen wasn't Becker's, of course, but the assistant quickly put Rafe through.

"You're not Garston Dunbarger," Becker said.

"No. I'm his son, Rafe. My father is . . . not competent at present."

"Oh? I'm not sure I like the sound of that." Becker's eyes narrowed. "Family problems?"

"He was abducted and severely injured," Rafe said. "His implant was destroyed, and he's undergoing intensive rehabilitation after neuro-implant surgery. Lew Parmina, whom you may have talked to—my father's chief assistant and intended to be his successor as CEO—was responsible."

"I see. And where were you?"

"Offplanet when it happened," Rafe said. "You may have heard that I was a renegade, a remittance man; unofficially, I was on assignment for ISC, my father's clandestine eyes and ears. When he didn't contact me at the usual interval, I made my way back to Nexus—delayed by such things as that little incident Ky Vatta got us into with Osman Vatta."

"Ah. That. Yes . . . though my commander didn't report you as being involved . . ."

"I was using an alias. If you check that report, you'll find mention of a young man named Rafe who was able to fix ansibles and claimed to be an ISC agent."

"You're the one? Yes, I do recall that. And you're Garston's son?"

"Yes. I am acting CEO while he is incapacitated."

"I see. I presume this is about your . . . encounter with the Blueridge Defense Alliance pirates and some of our ships?"

"Related to that, yes. I presume your commanders on the scene have told you what they've learned about those pirates?"

"Yes. Not all the data have been analyzed yet, but I am aware that pirates invaded and defeated Bissonet System as well as several other less populous systems, and that at least some of the ships in this recent encounter were originally Bissonet ships."

"And I'm sure your commanders told you about the abysmal performance of the ISC fleet," Rafe said. Becker merely grunted his assent, and Rafe went on. "One of the things I did when first taking over here was assess the response capability of our fleet. It wouldn't do any good to try to conceal from you what I found—and what your commanders saw."

"One of your ships blew because its munitions exploded just outside the ship," Becker said. "Did you know that?"

"Yes. Old stuff that had degraded in storage."

"How long have you been in charge?"

"Only a few tendays," Rafe said.

"So . . . you know that I know what you know . . . what is it you want?" *And what are you willing to pay?* said his expression.

"Did your commander tell you about the new technology that the Space Defense Force ships have? Onboard ansibles that can provide real-time communications between ships?"

"He said something like that; I'm dubious. You people have always said it was impossible."

"It's not. I've seen it myself; I know it works—"

"It's ISC tech?"

"No, unfortunately. The patent holder is Vatta Enterprises, associated with the new Vatta Transport headquarters on Cascadia, over in the Moscoe Confederation. We're trying to get a license to manufacture it."

"I see. So you just want to chat about it?"

"No. I assume you're interested in obtaining some of these units . . ."

"I would be, once I'm convinced they exist and work as described."

"And I assume you'd like to take care of the pirates who mauled your ships—"

"Not as badly as they mauled *your* ships." Pride stiffened Becker's tone.

"No argument on that. But I see these pirates as a danger to more than your company, or my company, or any one system—I believe they are indeed intent on dominating as much of human space as possible, and that the widespread ansible failure is at least in part their doing. It's allowed them to strike without warning, to gain ships and other matériel, and grow ever more dangerous."

"I'd agree," Becker said. "I believe I can anticipate your next suggestion. You think we should all join together to wipe them out . . . is that it?"

"Yes. I know that Ky Vatta had a similar idea—which, frankly, I thought was outrageous at the time—"

"A very gifted young commander, my people tell me," Becker said, pursing his lips. "Too young and inexperienced for what she's trying to do, but she did save some of our people in this most recent engagement. You were on her ship—what do you think of her?"

Rafe opened his mouth, then paused. What came into his head was nothing Becker needed to know. "She's . . . young in years," he said slowly. "But she's been through a lot, and she's not immature. Intelligent, of course. Can be impulsive, but less so than when I first joined her ship . . . more decisive than impulsive now, I'd say. Ethically—pretty much a straight arrow. I'd say perfectly willing to use deception in combat, but not to lie in ordinary situations."

"One of my commanders, back in the Sabine mess, was concerned that she had a weakness common to many young female commanders . . . going soft on boys with problems."

"Ky? Well, that's changed, if she ever had it. I'd say she's nearly immune to that kind of thing. Her cousin told me she'd had a bad experience with a first love."

"So you'd trust her in a command setting?"

"I already have," Rafe said. "Remember, I was on her ship when Osman Vatta tried to take it over."

"Do you think she's got a chance with this Space Defense Force she's started?"

Rafe shrugged. "I don't know. To most people, she'll appear just as you said: too young, too inexperienced. But results count more than appearances, in the long run. The last time I saw her, she had one ship but had already found one ally. Now she has—what, five?—and she's survived more than one space battle. If she can convince systems to work with her, and get funding, I'd bet on her."

"But you're talking to me," Becker said with a sly smile.

Rafe grinned. "You're quite right. Ky may have a powerful force in the future, but you have one right now and my concern is immediate. Nexus is a rich, populous system and the communications hub for most of human-occupied space. If that doesn't define target—"

"That's true," Becker said, nodding. "And you've just learned that ISC's famous fleet is a bunch of bright shiny obsolescent window decorations . . . so you want to hire us, is that it?"

"Nexus government has an interest," Rafe said. "So, I'm sure, does the Moscoe Confederation. Do you have the resources to take another major contract?"

"That is a question," Becker said. "I'll need to check on some things. We can't cheat current contract partners. I'm sure we could contribute something, but right off the top of my head I don't know how much."

Rafe was sure he did, but understood the reluctance to make that commitment too soon.

"It won't come cheap," Becker added.

"Of course not," Rafe said. "You're one of the top mercenary companies, if not the best. I might just suggest that payment in kind—say, some of those onboard ansibles—could be arranged as part of your fee."

"I'll get back to you," Becker said. "Let's see, it's—good heavens, man, it's the middle of the night for you."

"It's been one of those days," Rafe said, shrugging. "I'll catch some sleep later."

Slotter Key

"The news from Cascadia is not good," Grace Lane Vatta said. The new President raised his eyebrows.

"What's wrong with Cascadia?"

"Nothing yet. But the following systems are known to have fallen to pirate hordes—" She handed over a list. "And there is evidence that they are led by the same person who attacked Slotter Key civilians from space."

"You mean, who attacked your family."

"It was my family, yes, but the important point to me

as Rector of Defense, and you, as President, is that they attacked Slotter Key. Attacked the planet itself, killing and injuring thousands of Slotter Key citizens. Including many Vatta employees who were not members of my family."

Erran Kostanyan sighed. "I suspect you're about to suggest an official action that you want me to approve."

"Slotter Key maintains a privateer system," Grace said. "A system that has been reasonably successful in keeping the general level of piracy—the one or two ships attacking our trade—to a minimum. As the data show piracy was increasing in several sectors prior to the attack on Vatta interests; concern had been expressed, and the previous administration had even authorized an increase in the number of letters of marque some months before the attack. That was later rescinded, only about forty-five days before."

"Yes, yes, I know that. There's evidence the former president was complicit in the attack . . . cases are in court now."

"My point is, if the purpose of having privateers is to attack pirates, and the pirates are now coalescing into larger groups that no privateer alone can possibly handle, isn't it time to have our privateers join forces with others? With Slotter Key Spaceforce, after we authorize their activity outside this system, or with the space forces of governments we know and trust?"

"You mean, make privateers into a regular military force?" His brows went up again.

"We already have military advisers on nearly all our privateers. This is a natural next step."

"It doesn't seem natural to me. You're talking about having them operate outside the system . . . we certainly can't release Spaceforce ships for that. We have barely enough to guard our own system. If anything, we should call our privateers in—"

"You have heard of forward scouts," Grace said. "Early warning . . . that sort of thing? Let our privateers take on that role, only now operating in groups large enough to be effective against this new enemy. And if we call them in, we not only lose that, we gain the expense. The privateers have always been self-sufficient, though we gave them a cut rate on munitions if they resupplied here."

"You never cease to surprise me," Kostanyan said. "You're new in government and already you know what levers to lean on . . ."

"When it comes to accounting, an interstellar business isn't that far from a government," Grace said. "Except that our bottom line always has to come out on the profit side of the ledger."

"So what, precisely, do you propose?"

"Assuming you're sure we can't send Spaceforce along—"

He shook his head. She could tell he meant it.

"—then consider only the privateers," Grace said. "Contact them. Tell them to assemble . . . I would suggest at Cascadia Station, since that's where they can be fitted with onboard ansibles—"

"We'll need to find a commander for them. And staff, and support services—"

"You already have a commander," Grace said. "Ky Vatta's already engaged this enemy, more than once, and she's familiar with the tactical differences arising from the new communications technology."

"But she's not even an Academy graduate," Kostanyan said. "Even if she were, she'd be only an ensign, maybe a junior lieutenant."

"She has the experience," Grace said. "And she holds a letter of marque from Slotter Key."

"And she's a Vatta and you're a Vatta and you're telling

me that Vatta is the only source of this new technology, which I've never heard of before. Without intending insult, I have to say that this smacks of . . . of . . ." He searched for a word.

"Favoritism?" Grace suggested. "Nepotism, even? I agree. It could be interpreted that way, or it could be interpreted as the inverse of the hostility that led to most of my family being killed and our livelihood destroyed." She smiled at him, letting her teeth show.

"Your appointment was supposed to do that," Kostanyan said.

"My appointment was supposed to give me the access to do what needed to be done," Grace said. "If that turns out to be good for both Slotter Key and Vatta . . . so be it." She stared him in the face; he looked away first.

"I have to be convinced it is good for everyone," he said.

"I have no wish to harm Slotter Key," Grace said. "Nor does the Vatta family, the surviving remnants. This is my home. I want this system to survive; I want the people here to survive. No one should be targeted as we were; I take my duties as Rector very seriously. But the fact is that Vatta family members have done more than anyone else, up to this point." She smiled, showing her teeth. He knew exactly what she meant, and she knew that he knew.

"Well . . . I suppose Spaceforce is in agreement?"

"I have not spoken with Spaceforce," Grace said, raising her eyebrows. "It's an executive decision; it would be inappropriate without your approval, and actually you should be the one to initiate the discussion."

"I'll do that today," he said. "At least this proposal doesn't take our ships out of the system . . ."

*   *   *

"You're pushing very hard," MacRobert said that night over dinner when she told him what she'd done. "You're making some people nervous."

"Some people," Grace said, with emphasis. "Some people would get nervous if you said *boo* above a whisper. You and I both know that there's serious trouble out there, and the best way to keep it away from us is to go meet it."

"It's all the Vatta connections," MacRobert said. "Someone's been snooping around the old stuff, looking for dirt."

Grace shrugged. "Big family, big money, big business. There's dirt, if they know where to look, but no more dirt than anybody else."

"This Osman fellow . . ."

"He's dead now," Grace said. "And a Vatta killed him."

"To silence him, some would say."

"Some would say anything," Grace said. "So they've uncovered the family skeleton, have they?"

"Not all of it, but some. Maybe enough to cause us trouble. I don't suppose you could persuade your niece to allow the new tech to be sold under another name . . . ?"

Grace finished her fish. "I don't know," she said. "I'd think Slotter Key would like to have the credit. It's Vatta family, yes, but Vatta has always been based on Slotter Key, so it's a system thing as well."

"But your niece isn't here, and another system's getting the profits."

"She'd probably license manufacture here," Grace said. "I hadn't thought of that. Would it butter the right side of the bread if units were manufactured here as well?"

"It would lessen the concern I'm hearing that Vatta is abandoning Slotter Key for Moscoe Confederation."

"I'll talk to Stella," Grace said. "And I'll have to see what I can scare up in manufacturing."

* * *

Stella agreed to license manufacture on Slotter Key, but insisted on safeguards so any pirate agents could not get the tech. "You'll need to find a facility able to tool up quickly and still maintain quality control," she said. Grace thought of grandmothers and eggs and sucking, but forbore to say so. "And security," Stella went on. "These new units will give us an edge, but only if the pirates don't get them."

"I've done that," Grace said, practicing patience.

"I'll send you the specs," Stella said. "But not the full package yet. I'll want information on the facility and their estimate, after they've seen the specs, on time to production. And I control pricing."

That stung. "Stella, this is your home world—"

"It's the world that let outsiders kill my family and destroy our lives," Stella said. "I know, the old government's out and there's a new government and you're part of it. But that doesn't bring my father, brothers, and sister back, or Ky's parents, or any of our employees. It doesn't change my responsibility as CEO of Vatta Enterprises and Vatta Transport, Ltd. Slotter Key is getting a special deal— I'm going to license manufacture there. That's it."

Grace looked at that beautiful face, still breathtaking in its perfection. Of course Stella had changed; she had expected Stella to change. But this Stella had changed in a direction Grace had not anticipated. Was it Osman's side of her, or something else?

"Send me the information," Grace said. "I'll forward it, and we'll get back to you very quickly. Has production started there?"

"Not quite," Stella said. "They're retooling from another job."

"What would you sell units to Slotter Key privateers for?"

"Same as anyone else, but for now we're limiting initial sales to established military organizations. The first production run here is completely committed."

"Our privateers are being activated as an arm of Spaceforce," Grace said. "The idea is to have them get together and act as one or two fleets. That should make them military enough for you."

"Have you talked to Ky about this?" Stella asked. "If you want her to command—"

"No . . . I suppose I should. How can I get in touch with her?"

"You'll have to relay through me for now, and even I can't contact her at the moment; she's in FTL as far as I know, and I'm not sure when she'll be back down, or if her destination has a working ansible. Once she's out of FTL, I can contact her onboard ansible. If she lets me know she's available, that is."

"Won't she contact you right away?"

Stella laughed. "Ky? In a way, she's like you—she doesn't call just to chat. She'll call when she has something to say—or ask. She likes being off the leash."

Mackensee Military
Assistance Corporation HQ

The headquarters of MMAC looked much like any corporate headquarters: a typical office building, its lobby all shiny surfaces. Somewhat to Ky's surprise, the young man who met her at the security gate was not in uniform, though from his bearing he could have been.

"So glad you could come, Captain Vatta," he said. "Chairman Becker is looking forward to meeting you." He ushered her past the guards and into the express elevator. "I just wanted to express my own thanks for your actions at Boxtop. My brother was there; one of your ships took him in and gave him medical attention."

"Thank you," Ky said. "Do you know which of our ships?"

"*Sharra's Gift,* ma'am. I know that's not your flagship, but you're the one in charge and . . . and you're here."

"You're more than welcome," Ky said. "I wish we'd been able to save them all."

The elevator slowed, the display showing 31.

Becker's office, as well as the rest of the building, could have been any civilian executive's, even her father's. For an instant a wave of grief and nostalgia swept over her. She knew how offices like this worked; she could almost predict where to find the inevitable person in Admin who knew how to find anything at all, the person who kept the pipes operating, the whiz in Accounting who could fix any glitch.

Her father had only limited information on MMAC in the implant she wore, all recent gleanings from that short period when she'd been in Mackensee hands. She knew—because they had briefed her—that MMAC's CEO was one Arlen Becker, formerly a general. She had seen his image, so when the door to his private office opened and he came out, she knew at once who it was.

What surprised her was how little she felt intimidated by him. He reminded her of the Commandant of Spaceforce Academy, but she was no longer the cadet who had feared the twitch of an eyelid.

"You've done us an immense service, Captain Vatta," he said, leading her into his office. "And a great courtesy in leaving your ship to come meet me here. We have much to discuss." He waved her to a seat in the cluster of chairs around a small table.

"I'm glad we could help," Ky said.

"Would you like something to drink? We have hot and cold—" The service module on the table lit with a selection.

"Tea, please. Hot."

He tapped the module and then handed her a cup and saucer in porcelain that bore no signs of a corporate logo: small blue flowers alternated with red-and-gold butterflies. A plate in the same pattern held thin gold-edged rounds that looked like cookies.

"One of my indulgences," he said, nodding at her cup. "My wife inherited four generations of fine china, and this is a pattern she's never liked and I always did, so I brought it here."

Ky wondered how long this would go on, but sipped her tea. It was his office, and his initiative for now.

"We owe you a lot," he said, setting his cup down. "We would certainly have lost both of the ships in the training exercise, and quite possibly those of the relief convoy as well, if you had not shown up and helped us out. I've read the detailed reports of our people on the scene. And of course I'm familiar with our earlier encounters with you, from that unfortunate business at Sabine to the contract at Lastway."

Ky nodded.

"My people tell me that you have some novel technology for sale, and some proposition you'd like to lay before us. But first, if you don't mind—our ansible has been out for almost a planetary cycle, until a few days ago, and we're still behind on events. You've been out and around: I'd like to have your assessment of what's going on, as far as you're willing to give it."

Ky took another swallow of tea, looked at the cookies, and decided not to risk choking on crumbs while talking. "There's a lot I don't know," she said. "But this is what we've put together." She laid out all she knew of the attacks on systems, citing the three she knew for sure.

"That's a very organized report," Becker said, pursing his lips. "I can see you learned something in the Academy. So—do you think the ansible system's breakup is the result of the same people?"

"I don't know for sure," Ky said, "but it must have made their plan easier to execute. They have communications and others don't—"

"Ah . . . these shipboard ansibles or whatever they are?"

"Yes. That's what they are: small ansibles that give the pirates real-time communications with one another."

"Even between systems?"

"Yes. They don't work in FTL flight, of course, but in real space they're the same as system ansibles. Better, in a way, because there's no lightlag from ship to ship due to the distance from a ship to the system ansible."

"And you have some? You're selling them?"

"They were on the ship I—we—captured. The one Osman stole from the Vatta family. He must have been working with the pirates."

"Colonel Bandes described the way you used that capability in this recent battle—I can certainly see that ships not so equipped would be easy meat for those that are." He took another sip of his tea. "We would be interested in purchasing such units from you, subject to approval by our Technology Assessment group. In fact, if you wanted to sell all your remaining units, we'd be delighted. But let me, for the moment, go back to your own actions. The last direct report we had of you, you had an older, small ship—the tradeship with which you started—and the ship you had taken from Osman, a larger ship originally built as a tradeship, is that right?"

"Yes," Ky said. She explained how she and *Gary Tobai*

had separated and how they finally came back together. He didn't need to know about her problems with Stella or the trial of identity, but he did need to know about her first experience with a multisystem force. He listened intently, not interrupting, until she finished.

"Why do you call yourself part of a third fleet when there's nothing but you?" he asked then.

"Misdirection," Ky said.

"I see. But you really have only three ships of any size, two of them originally trading vessels, only one purpose-built for combat. What can you possibly hope to achieve with such a unit?"

"With all due respect, sir, Ransome's Rangers have considerably more value when fitted with onboard ansibles than conventional tables of organization would suggest. As you know, we were able to take on four of the pirate ships and sustain no damage. If we had not been short of munitions, we could have been much more help in the larger battle."

"Your communications ability was invaluable there, I agree. But I cannot see that your Space Defense Force is any more than—forgive me—a forlorn hope. You have no contract for financial support from any government, no resources for resupply of ships, munitions, or basic supplies."

"I believe we can get such support," Ky said.

"Perhaps . . . though allow me to say that my experience in dealing with governments is greater than yours, and I think it highly unlikely. Effective as your small force may be—out of proportion to its size—it will still look puny to those used to thinking in terms of dozens of ships purpose-built for war." He cleared his throat. "Now . . . as you know . . . we are grateful for your assistance; it is due to you that we lost only one ship, that casualties were less than they might have been, and that the relief convoy didn't run straight into disaster. We have authorized replacement of munitions and a small amount of financial bonus beyond that."

"Thank you, sir."

"We are not prepared, however, to release any of our ships to join you, which I believe is what you hoped for, and part of the proposition you wanted to lay before me."

"I did, yes, sir."

"If we saw support from governments, commitment of sufficient resources, we might indeed cooperate and join such an effort. We would be amenable to a contract with such governments. If your assessment of the enemy strength is accurate—and I have no reason to doubt it—then this is what must happen in future. But it will be done by governments reaching agreement with one another, not by an individual, however courageous and talented."

Ky had to admit that made sense—it was the argument others had made—but she didn't like it.

"There's another problem," he said. "Your ships are all converted merchanters, aren't they?"

"More or less," Ky said. She wondered what Teddy Ransome would think of his decorative little vessels being called merchanters.

"I don't know how far you got into engineering, at your military academy," Becker said. "But there are problems involved in converting ships built to haul cargo into fighting ships."

Ky scowled. "Privateers have been doing it for a long time—"

"Right," Becker said. "But they're lightly armed, and they don't fight very often. Most of the time, privateers fire off a few missiles or scorch someone with a beam, the pirate surrenders or runs off, and the whole thing lasts maybe a half hour. Even so, ships used as privateers have a shorter life span—and less time between refits—than ships purpose-built for combat. Two things go wrong with conversions—one involving the more powerful engines you put in, and the other involving the way the ship is used."

Ky wanted to argue, but she didn't have any data.

"I gather you weren't aware of this," Becker said.

"No, sir," Ky said.

"And you're probably wondering if it's true. Here's how we know: Old John started out with converted cargo ships, just like the ones you have. The shorter interval for refit and the shorter overall life span comes straight out of our files. Sooner or later—and with jury-rigged repairs like those you have on the air locks the Gretnans damaged, it will be much sooner—you're going to start having structural failures."

"Structural . . . ?"

"Yes. Most conversions overpower the original structure—the increased g-forces in rapid maneuver and in repeated, frequent microjumps put more strain on the frame than it was designed for. Repeated rapid missile launches during combat do the same thing. And the waste heat from a beam on full power eventually causes problems with the mount." His look was sympathetic, but Ky felt as if she'd been hit with a length of pipe. She had worried about money, endlessly, daily, but she had never worried about the structural integrity of the ships, as long as they weren't damaged in combat. "I can have our engineers check over your ships—no charge—and give you an estimate of the damage so far," he said. "We'd be glad to do that for you."

"I suppose—" Before she killed someone with ignorance? No, she had to agree. "Thank you," she said. "That's very kind of you."

"Not entirely," he said. "We'd hate to see a gifted and honorable commander killed by a preventable failure. In addition, we'd like to offer you and your other captains commissions in Mackensee Military Assistance Corporation. We understand that you have not had the benefit of our training programs, and the war we both see coming may give no time for that. So it's our idea to use you together as a unit within our existing command structure. I believe our government will be negotiating with others soon, now that our ansible is back up." Becker sat back. Obviously he thought this was an attractive offer.

Ky could think of nothing to say. She had clung to the hope that Mackensee would assign ships to the effort, though she didn't expect they'd let her command their people. From their point of view, they were being generous; she had talked to enough of their officers in the past few days to know this offer was unprecedented.

"Thank you," she said finally. "I do appreciate your offer, but . . . I need to think about it, and talk it over with my people."

"The offer is open," Becker said, with a slight shrug. "I'm not trying to rush you. You're an unusual young officer; I understand your ambition and your desire for independent command. But you're still inexperienced in many areas that senior commanders need; you could gain that experience with us."

"Thank you," Ky said again.

"And on another topic . . . our founder, John Mackensee—we call him Old John behind his back, but I wouldn't advise it to his face—would like to meet you. Would you be free for dinner, say day after tomorrow? I would be present, along with several of our more senior commanders. Your captains are invited as well, though I expect you'll want to leave someone on duty topside. Civilian dress, casual."

Ky grinned. "I'd be delighted, and I'm sure my captains will be, too. Only—what is casual here? On my home planet, casual means recreational clothes—anything from a swimsuit with a towel over one shoulder to hunting camouflage."

Becker laughed. "We'd call that undress. Our casual might be what you'd call business attire, I suppose. Not uniforms, not evening dress . . . daytime professional?"

"The good gray suit," Ky said, nodding. "We can certainly manage that. Day after tomorrow? What time, local?"

"1930 for drinks. We'll send transport for you at the shuttleport, 1900."

TWENTY-FOUR

Ky rode the shuttle up to Mac Station One in deepening gloom. Everything Becker said made sense, sense she didn't want to see. She would ask her own engineering techs about structural stresses, but she was sure Becker had told the truth; she could only hope that the engineers' examination would not show any flaws likely to kill them in the next few months.

Back on the station, she met the other captains at the Captains' Guild, where they usually met for a quiet meal.

"So what's next?" asked Teddy Ransome. He had been asking that every day.

"Mackensee wants to give us all commissions and take us into their organization as a separate unit," Ky said.

"I gather you didn't agree," Pettygrew said.

"I wouldn't, unless you all wanted to," Ky said. "But they think of it as a generous offer. They don't think we'll get funding from any governments because we're so small." She wasn't going to say anything about the structural problems until the engineers had inspected *Vanguard*. If it had symptoms of excessive strain, she would have to warn them.

"Small, but effective," Ransome said. "They can't deny that!"

"They didn't," Ky said. "They said we were far more effective than our size suggested—but I can see the difficulty of saying that to governments. How would they know?"

"So . . . what kind of commissions?" Pettygrew asked.

"We didn't get into specifics; I wasn't ready to sign on the line. But they did say they thought of using us as a single unit within the organization."

"Doesn't appeal to me," Ransome said, leaning back in his seat. "I like working with you, not some mercenary. And it's not like I need the money."

"I'm still technically a Slotter Key privateer," Argelos said. "I don't think it would be appropriate."

"Well, I'd do it," Pettygrew said. "No offense or disrespect to you—" He turned to Ky. "You're as good a commander as any I've served with. But an experienced military organization has a lot to offer . . . a ready-made staff, supply lines and depots already set up. If you do it, I would, too."

"I haven't made up my mind," Ky said. "I want to strike back at the people who attacked my home world . . . and I want to do it effectively. Becker's sure that means joining a larger organization. Think about it, all of you. If one or more decide to sign on with Mackensee, that changes the whole situation."

"You started with one ship," Ransome said, with a toss of his head. "I have two."

Ky was glad to change topics. "By the way, we're all invited to have dinner with their founder day after tomorrow. That one, I did accept. Civilian business attire."

"All of us off our ships at once," Argelos said. "Are you sure that's wise?"

"Actually, you'll have to draw straws—someone's definitely staying up here, just in case," Ky said. "I don't think

Mackensee's up to anything, and the system defenses here are on high alert. But it's just good practice."

"I'll volunteer," Argelos said. "If that's all right with you."

"Fine," Ky said. "Otherwise—the rest of you want to come?"

They all nodded.

The next morning, two Mackensee engineers showed up with a half-dozen assistants and stacks of equipment, only some of which Ky recognized.

"I'm Asil Maturny, and this is Bas Fornit," one of them said. "We're from the main repair yard for Mackensee vessels, and I understand you wanted your ship checked for structural problems, is that right?"

"Yes," Ky said.

"It would be easier if you were in our repair dock, but we brought some equipment with us. I understand you've had air-lock damage?"

"Yes, twice." Ky explained, and handed them the data cube she'd prepared. "I didn't find the usual repair log when we took over this ship, so the repairs are those I had made."

"And you've fought how many engagements?"

"And have you done any weapons practice outside those engagements?" asked Fornit.

"It's all in there," Ky said, nodding at the cube. "Four engagements, but no missiles fired in the second. And yes, weapons practice."

For most of that day, the assessment team roamed the ship, escorted by Ky's own crewmembers. They ran tests on everything, it seemed, with special attention to the damaged areas around the emergency air lock and the old cargo bay entry hatch, the mounts for the drives, and the mounts for the beam weapon. By 1700 local time, they had a preliminary report for Ky; she invited Hugh and her own engineering staff to sit in on the presentation.

"You were lucky," Maturny said. "Or the person who retrofitted the advanced drives and munitions knew what to look out for. As you know, this was built as a standard cargo-hauler—" The schematic for its framing came up on the screen. "Someone did a pretty good job of reinforcing here—and here—" He highlighted the areas. "Just using the more powerful drives and controllers wouldn't over-stress the longitudinal framing. Mounting the beam weapon in the midline reduces problems, but we did find evidence of early deterioration in the beam mounts from insufficient heat reduction. To save space, the refitters tried to combine the heat management with the mounts proper, instead of using more appropriate structures. That's an older design, and suggests the refit was done more than twenty-five years ago. You might find an outlaw repair yard still using it, but no one reputable."

"Another problem is all these hidden passages someone put in," Fornit said. "We didn't explore them, except to note voids that might be problematic. Some of these are." Another schematic. "This reduces your lateral stability, which counts in maneuvering and firing missiles."

"Bottom line?" Ky said.

"Bottom line is that your ship is spaceworthy right now, but needs major work in a good yard if she's to stay that way. I understand you're interested in buying into Mackensee using ships as capital. I have to say that this ship's value is reduced at least twenty-three percent because of what it'll cost to bring it up to our standard."

"And how long will she be spaceworthy?" Ky asked. "Can you give me an estimate?"

"Well . . ." Fornit glanced at her engineering team. "That emergency repair you did . . . um . . . back at

Gretna? That's not going to be good for many more FTL transitions. But fixing that won't address the more serious structural problems. I'd say you've got . . . oh, perhaps two hours total of beam use before one of the mounts fractures, and that could be extremely serious. The lateral members showing stress should be good for several engagements, but if we did take this ship in, we'd put it straight into the yard for a complete refit."

Another blow to her idea of starting her own military force: if her own ship was likely to fall apart, what about the others? And she could not possibly afford a true warship when she couldn't manage even a minor repair like the air locks.

"We'll leave the report with you, Captain Vatta," Fornit said. "If you decide to have this work done yourself—if you don't join Mackensee—we've been instructed to say that our repair yard will do the work at a discount. But it will still be expensive, and your ship will be out of commission for somewhere between one hundred seventy and two hundred days, best estimate."

"Thank you," Ky said. "I'll let you know."

"Contact information is with the report," Fornit said.

After they left, and her engineering staff had gone back to their duties, Ky stared at the bulkhead. Now what? She had no funds; her Space Defense Force was mostly smoke and mirrors, and the part that wasn't, was falling apart. Even if Mackensee bought her remaining shipboard ansibles at Stella's price, even if that was enough to pay for repairs, it would not be enough, in the long run, to finance a war.

Should she give in and sign up with Mackensee? It was the sensible thing to do, considering all the circumstances. She'd have the advantage of their experience, their staffwork. She could almost imagine herself in a Mackensee uniform, commanding a Mackensee ship.

But . . . a mercenary? For hire to anyone with the price? That initial vision of herself on the bridge of a Mackensee cruiser shivered and blew away at the thought. Mackensee might be honorable, within the definition of *mercenary,* but that would not keep them from taking a contract from anyone with enough funds, against anyone—including, for instance, Slotter Key.

For the rest of the day, Ky went about her work and ignored the impulse to call Stella—or even Aunt Grace— and discuss it with them. She didn't want lectures or arguments; it was her decision to make. She asked Argelos and Pettygrew if they'd heard anything about structural failures due to retrofitting merchant craft with military-grade drives and weapons. Argelos said yes, but on the last yearly inspection, *Sharra's Gift* had passed clean. Pettygrew said *Bassoon,* like all the Bissonet privateers, had been built for military use from the start.

So it was her own ship, apparently the largest and best armed, that had the problem. But that wasn't the real dilemma. It was not only her ship, but her people . . . her crew, her family, her planetary government. She was not about to force anyone to join anything they didn't want to . . . and decency required that she help them get back to a place where they could find employment they wanted.

She pushed those thoughts aside as she dressed for dinner in her good gray suit, and tried to put herself in the right frame of mind, but the question kept coming back. By the time she met the other captains at the shuttle to go downside to dinner, Ky had still not decided what to do.

Mackensee's founder had chosen to live within an hour's ground transport of corporate headquarters, on an estate of rolling hills. His residence, built of local stone and timber, nestled into one of the hills and looked out across a valley patchworked with fields and pastures.

He came out to the terrace to greet them, dressed in a suit that Ky recognized as custom-tailored. Ky knew his nickname was Old John but he looked too young for that, despite his gray hair and UV damage to his skin.

"I'm delighted to meet you, Captain Vatta," he said. "I've been hearing about you the past several years."

"This is Captain Pettygrew, of *Bassoon*," Ky said. "And Captain Ransome of *Glorious* commanding Ransome's Rangers, and Captain Baskerville of *Courageous*."

"I understand your home world was overrun," John Mackensee said to Pettygrew. "My deepest sympathies. Did you have family . . . ?"

"Yes," Pettygrew said. "I don't want to talk about it."

"Of course." Mackensee turned to Teddy Ransome, whose idea of civilian business attire included a shirt with ruffles at the neck and wrists. Ky would not have been surprised if he'd had a sword at his hip. "And you—are you aware of the history of your ships' names? I understand that you lost one, the *Furious*."

"Back in the days of Old Earth," Ransome said. "The days of wind and sail . . ."

Ky saw a telltale twinkle in Mackensee's eye, a twitch of his lip.

"You are a student of history, Captain Ransome?"

"Call me Teddy," Ransome said. "And not so much a student of history . . . serious history. Too many years— eons even—pass with nothing to stir the blood. But some are rich with pageantry, with glory—"

"Indeed," Mackensee said; the corner of his mouth twitched. Please . . . do come inside," Mackensee said. "Meet the others."

Dark wood, tiled floors, comfortable furniture in rich

colors, a fire crackling in a huge fireplace. Men and women who, despite being in civilian dress, were obviously Mackensee officers. Everyone was cordial, but Ky felt that she and her captains were under a social microscope. That could cut both ways—they could examine Mackensee as well as be examined.

Mackensee moved them expertly from pre-dinner drinks and light conversation to a dining room whose proportions reminded Ky painfully of her lost home. Here the tabletop was a slab of polished stone veined in pale shades of gray with a few streaks of white, instead of wood. One difference in culture showed up immediately: no sooner had the first course been served than the man on Ky's left, who had introduced himself earlier as Colonel Vitanji, said, "So, you had formal military training—I've never met anyone from Slotter Key before. Did they include Gauschmann's *Tactical Exercises*?"

"Let her eat, Terry," Mackensee said. "At least three bites before business."

"Sorry, sir." He turned to Ky. "Sorry, Captain."

"Terry's an instructor these past three years in our command course," Becker said.

"And he's convinced that Gauschmann's is the best source on tactical maneuvers in the past two decades," said a woman across the table. "I'm Ari Wistrom—didn't get to meet you before dinner. Anyway, Terry will talk your ear off about tactical theory if you let him."

"Not theory," Vitanji said. "Proven, practical—"

"Enough," Becker said, with a quick glance at Mackensee.

Ky tried a spoonful of the soup in front of her: pale green, translucent, and delicious. While she ate, she listened to conversation among the officers . . . business, nearly all of it, in short snatches. She liked the tone she was hearing—brisk, good-natured, touches of wit here and there, competent . . . Mackensee would have picked the best to lure her, she was sure, but these were people she could work with.

After the soup came a delicious main course, medallions of beef, potatoes sliced to make a decorative swirl. Pettygrew, Ransome, and Baskerville were chatting happily with the officers near them; Becker and Mackensee seemed to be discussing gardening. At a nearby lull, Ky spoke to Vitanji.

"Actually, we didn't have Gauschmann's *Tactical Exercises* in our classes. We used Simjuk and Baiye."

"Not bad at all," Vitanji said. "But you should take a look at Gauschmann."

"What I found, once we obtained the shipboard ansibles, is that having instantaneous ship-to-ship communication at significant light-distances both allowed and forced changes."

"I'd expect so." Vitanji grinned. "In the last few days, since we heard of the possibility, I've been trying to develop some ideas, but since you've actually done it—"

"No need for close formations," Ky said. She took another bite of potato, and noticed that the table had quieted. "There's still scan lag, of course, but ships can share position information via ansible, so you know exactly where your ships are. If you have small, fast ships—or stealthed ships—you can shadow an enemy and transmit *that* information to the rest of your group. We lost one of our people that way, Captain St. Cyrien, but the data he provided before they found and destroyed his ship was most valuable."

Now they were all quiet, listening.

"I'm sure we'd all like to hear what you've learned," John Mackensee said, "if you don't mind sharing."

"Not at all," Ky said. "As long as I don't have to miss the rest of this excellent dinner. This beef—!"

He smiled at her. "My own herd. Long ago and far away, I believe my ancestors must have been cattle ranchers, because for someone brought up on spaceships, I take entirely too much pleasure in watching my cows eat grass. These are genetically modified to produce meat with specific nutritional components, which, in the origins of the species, weren't present. For instance—" He stopped himself and chuckled. "Sorry. If you get me started on cattle, no one will hear about your tactical discoveries, and most of these people aren't anywhere close to retirement. They'd much rather listen to you."

Through the rest of the meal, Ky and her other captains answered questions and explained what they'd learned, using tableware and dishes to represent ships. It was the kind of intelligent, challenging discussion that Ky had always enjoyed at the Academy, and by the time they adjourned to the living room with its fireplace, to take dessert pastries from a tiered server on a sideboard, she was even more persuaded that she would fit in here.

So might Pettygrew, she thought; he seemed happy and relaxed. Ransome and Baskerville, predictably, stood out like parrots in a flock of doves. She could not imagine them taking to the discipline Mackensee would insist on. She couldn't tell if they were slightly drunk or just their usual flamboyant selves, but theirs were the loudest voices and most extravagant gestures. Argelos . . . Argelos would try to get back to Slotter Key, she was sure. He had already said he felt bound by his letter of marque.

Her mood darkened; the conversation had become general again, and she let it pass her by. She would love to have had this, from the house itself to the easy camaraderie of the Mackensee officers. This was the life she had hoped for when she argued her family into letting her enter the Academy. And her father . . . what would he want? His daughter running around the universe in a ship that might come apart, trying to fight a war on her own, or in a large, experienced organization of competent mercenaries?

She glanced across the room and saw the clock . . . time to go, but she didn't want to leave, not really. She felt safe here.

With an effort, she turned to smile at John Mackensee. "Thank you, sir, for a lovely evening, but we must go if we're going to catch that last evening shuttle."

"You could stay downside tonight," he said. "Guest rooms here, or accommodations in town if you prefer."

Ky shook her head. "No, thank you. I appreciate the offer, and this has been delightful, but my ship's expecting me."

He nodded, unsurprised. "Duty and all that, eh? Well, I'm glad you were able to take an evening off. It's been my pleasure, and I hope to see you again soon."

When Ky got back to the shuttleport, she had a message from *Vanguard*. "Stella wants to hear from you as soon as possible," Hugh said. "She's really excited about something."

"Excited? Not alarmed? System ansible, or . . . the other?"

"System ansible," Hugh said. "She didn't sound alarmed to me, just a bit miffed that you hadn't called in and weren't on the ship. *Gallivanting around the galaxy,* is how she put it."

"Give her a call back and tell her I'm on my way up from the planet," Ky said. "The shuttle's leaving in about fifteen minutes . . . I should be back in a couple of hours."

"Yes, Captain."

Ky hoped it was good news about money; she had to admit that Becker was right about the cost of supplying so many ships. So far Teddy Ransome's purse had seemed bottomless, but she knew all purses did have bottoms eventually. In that musing about money, she realized she had made her decision. Much as she respected Mackensee, much as she respected and admired the officers she'd met, and recognized that they respected her, much as she had enjoyed the evening and wanted that sort of life for herself . . . she could not join them. She still cared too much about Slotter Key—and she still wanted to make her own decisions. If that meant worrying about money and supplies and repairs . . . so be it.

When she came onto the bridge, it was nearly local midnight; she felt some change in mood. "What do you know that I don't?" she said to Hugh.

He was not quite grinning, but he looked very happy. "I don't know anything . . . but I suspect from your cousin's expression that there's good news. You may not need to take Mackensee's offer—"

"What do you know about that?" Ky asked, annoyed. "I haven't said anything to anyone on the ship."

"Slip of the tongue by someone in a bar," he said. "I think deliberate slip, but I'm not sure. Anyway, it makes sense they'd want us to join them. We're the spice; they're the cake."

Ky snorted. "I think we're rather more than that. But let's see what Stella really has to say." Under the circumstances, it probably had to do with more progress making or selling onboard ansibles—not a topic she wanted to discuss over ISC's network. She sat down at the onboard ansible's console. Stella must have been waiting by her own, because she answered at once.

"Ky, have you sold those other onboard ansibles yet?" Stella asked without preamble.

"No," Ky said. "I've talked to Mackensee about them, and they want them, but it's not a done deal. I don't have enough to supply all their ships, anyway. Why? Isn't their money good?"

"Don't. And whatever else you do, don't sign up with them."

"Stella . . . what's going on?"

"It's Aunt Grace." Stella's tense look widened to a grin. "You will not believe—well, you will, because it's true, but—"

"If you don't tell me, I'm going to reach right through this ansible and strangle you," Ky said. "Just say it."

"Slotter Key's government has agreed to contact all the outlying privateers and order them to put themselves under your command, as an arm of Slotter Key Spaceforce." Stella's grin was even wider now.

Ky's mind went blank for a moment. "It . . . *what*?"

"They've already started arriving here, at Cascadia. You need to get back here with those ansibles so they can be mounted in the privateers . . . we don't have the advanced versions ready yet, but that should at least give you parity with the pirates, yes?"

"Er . . . yes. Yes, it will." Her mind seemed to expand like a balloon with something she realized was joy. "How many privateers?"

"They've made contact with thirty-seven so far. All have contacted me to say they're on the way. The first four have arrived insystem here. How many of those ansibles are left?"

"Thirty-two."

"I'll see how fast Toby can hand-build another five or six or whatever."

"What does the local government think about a lot of privateers showing up? Have you asked them?" Ky could imagine serious problems from that.

"Slotter Key contacted them directly; they've worked some kind of deal. I think there may be a few ships from here joining up, too, but not until they're supplied with the ansibles. In the meantime, though, they've committed some funds for supply, via Slotter Key. How soon can you leave there? What's your travel time to here?"

Ky turned to Hugh. "What would be our ETA for Cascadia Station, fastest safe route?"

"For all our ships?" he asked. Ky nodded. "I'll get to work on it. And if you're contemplating an early departure, I'd say more like sixty hours—we still have munitions coming up for all ships."

"Stella, it's going to be days before we can leave here," Ky said. "We're loading munitions coming up from the surface. I'll have the figures for you as soon as I can."

"Good. Call me any time; I'll be in skullphone contact with Toby if I have to be out of range of this ansible, or use the system." Stella closed the connection.

Ky looked at her bridge crew, who were trying to pretend they had no interest in the messages. "Life's about to get even more interesting," she said. "Slotter Key's sending reinforcements, and they want me to command them."

"Here?"

"No, at Cascadia, where Stella is."

"So . . . you're not thinking about joining Mackensee?"

"Not now," Ky said. She realized she was grinning and tried to smother it, but then she saw the expressions of her bridge crew. "You all knew about the offer?" There were nods and murmurs.

"We thought you'd probably do it," Lee said. "But I said,

No, she's a Slotter Key girl at heart, and they don't take orders from anybody."

"I did for four years," Ky said, but she was too happy to remind him that he was supposed to be more formal. "I don't suppose you had a pool on it . . ." At his guilty look, she laughed. "Of course you did. I hope you won, Lee; your faith is touching." She turned to Hugh. "I'll want you and Martin to start planning how to bring the mostly civilian crews of the other privateers up to military standards. Resupply is being arranged between Slotter Key and the Moscoe Confederation. Now I need to talk to the other captains, and then let Mackensee know the ansibles aren't for sale—"

"And neither are you," Martin said. He and Hugh exchanged glances; Ky could feel their approval.

Ky used the shipboard ansibles to call the other captains.

"What is it?" Ransome asked. He was still flushed from the party. "Have you decided whether or not to take a commission with them? Nice fellows, all, but I think they're too straitlaced for me."

"We're leaving here as soon as we can," Ky said. "If we didn't have to make intermediate jumps that put us at risk if the pirates happen to be there, I'd leave tomorrow, but we will complete loading the munitions Mackensee is giving us."

"So . . . you know where we're going next?" Ransome asked.

"Yes. But the destination will not be given to you until we're near the jump point, and even then in a unique code on a channel we hope is still secure."

"We've found the enemy?" Pettygrew asked.

"No. But we've found allies."

"Really?" Argelos raised his brows. "That's welcome news."

"Our allies need to be provided with the onboard ansibles I'm carrying. The concentration of ships necessary for that to happen would be a very attractive target. That's why secrecy is so important."

"How many ships are we getting?" Argelos asked. "Ten? Even . . . fifteen?"

"At least thirty-seven," Ky said. "Assuming they all get to us safely."

"Thirty-seven!" Argelos and Pettygrew glanced at each other. "That has to be a government—no one else could mount that many ships unless it's a big merc company like this one. And I can't see them giving us that many."

"It is government," Ky said. "But I'm not prepared to say which ones."

"*Ones* plural? So we really are going to be a multisystem force?"

"Looks that way. My source is reliable for . . . some of them, and there's speculation about others. I should've ordered more seals." Ky grinned at them. "So . . . last chance to bail out. I'll understand if you'd rather stay with Mackensee—" She looked at Pettygrew. "—or go off on your own." That look for Ransome and Baskerville.

"I wouldn't miss this for anything," Ransome said. "Of course I'm coming with you." Baskerville nodded enthusiastically, his hair flopping down on his forehead.

"And I," Pettygrew said. "Mackensee seems to be a decent enough organization, but I want to stay with you."

"Slotter Key sticks together," Argelos said. "And my former adviser says you promoted him, so he's yours."

Ky felt a wave of emotion—joy and excitement and affection all mixed—washing away the depression and exhaustion of the past few days. She wanted to think of something stirring to say, but nothing came to her. Teddy Ransome, not surprisingly, spoke up.

"I could almost feel sorry for them," he said. "The pirates, I mean. They won't know what hit them."

Ky laughed, the last tension gone for now. "Tomorrow," she said. "We'll start on that tomorrow."